I0574237

THE CHRONICLE OF TIME SERIES

DALEN PAX AND THE HEART OF STONE

DEDICATED TO MY MOTHER

ONCE YOU READ THIS, YOU WILL KNOW

I HEARD YOU

YOU HAVE BEEN AN AMAZING MOM AND I LOVE YOU

Dalen Pax and the Heart of Stone Dyslexic Edition

Text©2023 Will Grey (Simon)

The Way of Grey Publishing

First Edition

ISBN
Hardcover: 978-1-64372-968-8
Softcover: 978-1-64372-969-5

Dalen Pax and the Heart of Stone

By Will Grey

The Timeline so far.

A.   The opening fight with Dalen and Ben. (The fight that never happened)

B.   Dalen meets Mathias after he is nearly beaten to death.

C.   Dalen wakes up uninjured and David has no memory of losing his wallet.

D.   Ben and Dalen find Mathias. Ben is released from his loop and Dalen is asked to get the Beads of Fire.

E.   Dalen agrees to help steal the Beads of Fire and sneaks out of his house to mee Mathias.

F.   Dalen finds the Beads of Fire and loses six hours.

G.   After refusing to give up the Beads of Fire Dalen plans with his friends to meet up that evening after he is taught magic from the Fire Jinn and leaves this world.

H.   1,000 days at the Brotherhood of Light

I.   20 years at the Temple of All-Faith

J.   Dalen returns to his friends and defeats both Mathias and DeSalvo, during which he drops the Beads of Fire in the infinite frames of time.

K.   Dalen Returns to the Temple of Light with his friends in hopes to find a cure for David who was attacked during the fight with Mathias.

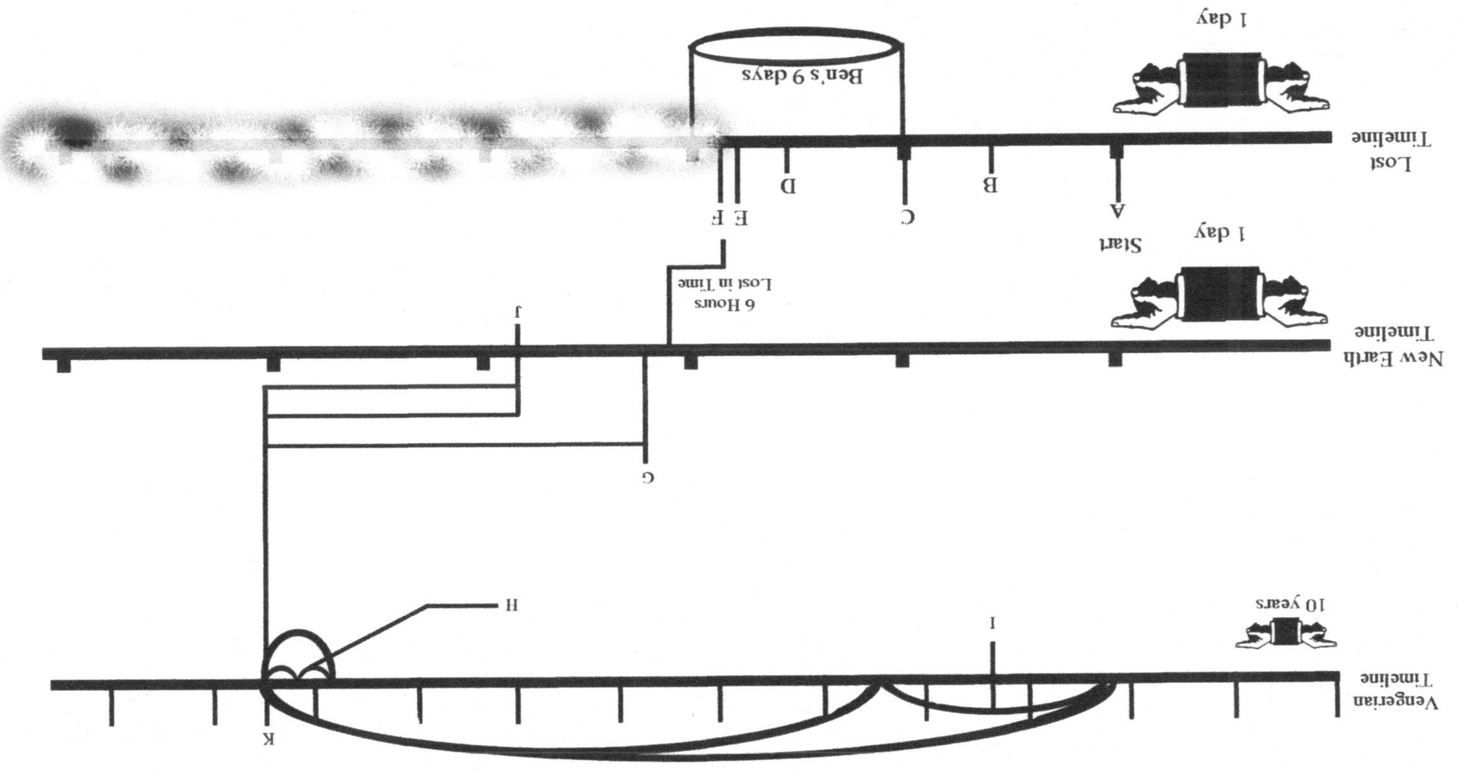

Vengerian Timeline
10 years
K
H
I
New Earth Timeline
Start
1 day
A
B
C
D
E
F
G
J
6 Hours Lost in Time
Lost Timeline
1 day
Ben's 9 days

TABLE OF CONTENTS

Chapter 0: Returning To The Story 9

Chapter 1: Leaping Together 11

Chapter 2: Finding Venger 36

Chapter 3: The Saviors Of Venger 56

Chapter 4: The Garden 84

Chapter 5: Old Friends 125

Chapter 6: A Mindful Carriage Ride 147

Chapter 7: The Royal Vengerians 165

Chapter 8: The Gnomish Curse 198

Chapter 9: Xoxann's New Friend 222

Chapter 10: A Wish Fit For A King 237

Chapter 11: Fulcrum And Gnomon 259

Chapter 12: The Folly Of Xoxann 277

Chapter 13: The Heart Of Stone 289

Chapter 14: He Who Carries The Honor 312

Chapter 15: Running With The Trees 336

Chapter 16: The Time Stone 355

Chapter 17: Leaping From The Falls 376

Chapter 18: The Goblins 397

Chapter 19: The Oracles 424

Chapter 20: The Truth About Dalen 450

Chapter 21: Trying To Not Be Real 475

Chapter 22: The Tree Of Sadness 487

Chapter 23: The Cave Of Fear 496

O

RETURNING TO THE STORY

There are truths about truth. Such as there is more than one. That truth can destroy you as easily as it can save you, especially if it is a truth about you. Truth is malleable and can be molded like clay with emotion and time. It is fragile. It can even be forgotten or lost. If the truth is to survive, it must be protected and sometimes hidden — hidden in stories so that one day they can be told and the truth can be remembered, for there are some truths that should never be forgotten.

I am Sir Will of Grey. My trade is telling the stories and truths of the Kingdom of Venger and the people who make it the most magical kingdom in this entire world. I can sing to you the Ballads of the Dragon Wars, and I can recite the old tales of the City of Dreams, but my favorite stories are of the people of Venger, who found their way to Dorn's.

When last we spoke, I told the tale of Dalen Pax and the Beads of Fire. I spoke of his awakening to magic — not tricks done with cards or coins, but true power. The kind that bends reality and can grant great power to those who know how to wield it. The distinction between the two became very real to Dalen when he met Mathias, a street magician who knew real magic. Because of this meeting, Dalen became connected with not only the Beads of Fire but also with the Jinn connected to them. Dalen was taken to a world that was still thriving with the mystical arts and was trained in the Elements of Reality. Once he found his power, he returned to have a showdown with Mathias and his master, the Genie DeSalvo, leaving one of Dalen's friends, David, injured and close to death. After his victory over Mathias and DeSalvo, Dalen and his friends took David to the place where Dalen had learned about the Body Sphere of Magic at the Temple of Light, hoping the Brotherhood would know how to save him. Little did they know they were at the beginning of a journey that would bring many truths to light, and some of those truths would change them forever.

So, this is where my story continues: at the Temple of Light, where the Grand Master of the Order opens his eyes to the beginning of this new day.

1

LEAPING TOGETHER

It was early morning at the Temple of Light. The sun had not yet risen, and the air was still cold. Master Truth sat in the Courtyard of Faith and smiled as the sun rose, casting light into the world once again. He sipped from his cup, the light passing through him. Master Truth knew this day would bring more than light; it would bring old friends together and, like the dawn of the new day, so too it was the dawn of new beginnings. There would be much to do, and he had to prepare.

Master Truth finished his tea as he watched the sunrise, but then he turned to his work. He reached out with his mind, telepathically calling to the monks that he required. He asked one to transport some expected guests. When the others gathered, Master Truth bowed to each of them.

"Good morning," the Jinn gave a deep bow, and everyone said their good mornings or bowed. "In a very short time, Brother Truth will arrive, and when he does, there will be three things that will be happening." The four of them smiled, commenting excitedly to themselves about Brother Truth's return. They had been there when he left, and many of them still talked about that day. "Yes," Master Truth continued. "It will be good to see Brother Truth again, but right now, there are things that need our attention." The Jinn directed the conversation toward the first of the brethren. "Brother Truth will arrive shortly with five others. Four of them will require quarters. Brother Home, will you please prepare that for them?"

Brother Home's passion was making everyone at the temple feel loved and welcomed, which he'd been doing for over fifty years. Indeed, others revered him for his hospitality, which is how he earned his name. The old monk now smiled and closed his eyes, bowing in reverence at the task set before him. "Of course, Master Truth," he affirmed, bustling off to prepare the four rooms.

"The fifth is injured and cursed." Master Truth focused on Master Love, the head of the healer's order. "How soon can your team be ready?"

Master Love had trained her team to be ready at a moment's notice. "My team will prepare for the patient's arrival immediately and will be ready to respond the moment they arrive."

"Master Tome, the reason I have asked for you to be with us today is because the healers can, no doubt, heal the boy, but the curse is immensely powerful. There is truly little known about how to break it. Because of this, I have a specific task for you.”

“Yes, Master Truth?” answered the thin Moon Elf. He was quiet, with the look and feel of a man who had trained at the Temple of Light for over a thousand years. Master Tome’s long silver hair was tied back to keep it out of his face, revealing that the sides and back were shaved. His thin, enchanted spectacles perched on his nose allowed him to read any language. He was a master but wore the simplest of garb and the lightest of armor on his left side. “How can I be of service?”

“Master Tome.” The Jinn smiled as he nodded to the old monk. “I need you to delve into the knowledge of the temple and bring Master Love all the information you have on a knife called Soul Freezer. It is a cursed blade that freezes the soul of the victim in the body. We need to know how to restore its victim.”

Master Tome cleared his throat, adjusting his glasses. “I believe that is a Genie blade. There hasn’t been an account of one in fourteen hundred years.” Master Tome had a true aptitude for being a librarian, and on the day he became a master, he and the library bonded magically. Since then, Master Tome could access any piece of information held in the library, as if he were remembering from first-hand knowledge and memory.

“Is there a record of how to reverse it?” asked Master Truth.

"Yes," responded Master Tome, nudging his glasses up further on his nose. "The Genie who created the knife can reverse it on command."

Master Truth nodded. "That option is not available at this time. I hoped for another."

Master Tome pondered the request. "I do not recall any others, but I will set my mind to it by asking myself the standard questions." He gave a brief bow. "I will be in the library gathering everything I can, and I will give all the information to Master Love as quickly as possible." Readjusting his spectacles, Master Tome headed toward the library. With a bow, Master Love left to prepare her team.

Master Truth then turned his focus to the remaining monk. "Brother Peace, you have been here for three years, and I believe that your time with us has come to an end. I suspect you will want to travel with Brother Truth and his friends after they arrive."

"Yes, Master Truth." Although still young and scarcely out of his apprenticeship, Brother Peace had looked forward to the day Brother Truth and his friends would arrive, and he was excited that this day had come. "I believe I've achieved what I came here to do, and I have learned so much more than I initially requested. It has been an honor and a blessing to have been given the gift of my time here."

"Only one test remains in front of you at the temple, and it will be harder than anything put before you during your time here," Master Truth mused.

"Yes, Master?" responded Brother Peace.

"You will need to be patient," Master Truth answered with a joyous grin. "Today is the day you've been waiting for, and the temple is only the first stop on a long journey ahead. You will go with them on that adventure, but you must wait for the proper moment to join them."

Brother Peace nodded. "I remember." He drew up his hood and bowed before he left to pack, leaving Master Truth alone in the courtyard.

Master Truth floated to the Elemental Circle in the center of the courtyard. A spell that affected the mind protected the Temple of Light. As a protective measure, the enchantment created a mist, obscuring the temple from those who'd not been granted access. Dalen would be fine, but his friends would not be able to perceive much of their surroundings, and they would need help at first. Master Truth began to weave a spell around the circle to allow anyone standing inside it to see past the enchantment's protection. He completed it as his guests arrived.

The temple itself was built on a spire in the center of a vast canyon, and the closest point to the outer edge was next to the Tree of Travel, the closest anyone could directly teleport to the Temple of Light. The only way to reach the temple was with a Leap of Faith from the tree to the courtyard. On rare occasions, such as this, a person or group not prepared to make the Leap of Faith themselves would have to come to the temple directly. Often, dignitaries visited for political reasons, such as having a master settle a dispute between two kingdoms. For such occasions, the Brotherhood of Light had recently had a ferry made that could float them across the gap between the Tree of Travel and the temple.

The ferry itself is a silver coach without rigging for wheels, and its captain was a master from the temple. Master Faith had known Brother Truth during his time with the Brotherhood and was pleased when he received the request from Master Truth to ferry Brother Truth and his companions to the Temple of Light.

. . .

Although Dalen could teleport his friends across worlds, the closest he could get them to the Temple of Light was the Tree of Travel, located across the canyon from it. Like the City of Venger, there were many protective spells and enchantments to guarantee that individuals could not teleport directly into the temple. When they arrived at the tree, none but Dalen could view it clearly, the surroundings obscured as if by a dense fog.

"Okay, guys?" Ben swung his arm out to find people and bumped into Adam. "This is some next-level fog. This is like scary movie fog."

"Don't say things like that." Becky had never liked not being able to see. She swore on more than one occasion that she was sure people were watching her just beyond her sight. "Dalen? Is there something in the fog?"

Dalen reached out and took her by the hand. She flinched and then laughed at herself. "Get a grip on yourself, Becky." She whispered to herself and held out her hand to see if she was shaking.

Dalen took her hand and placed it in Travis's and then had Ben put his hand on Travis's other shoulder. "Stay together. David is at your feet, so don't go tromping around." The three of them lowered themselves, taking a knee and patting about until they found the body of their friend.

"Where's Adam?" Travis was fewer than three feet from his twin brother, but he might as well be invisible.

Turning, Dalen noticed that Adam was close to the edge. "Careful, Adam. You can't see it, but you are right next to the cliff."

Adam froze in place, not wanting to find the cliff's edge with his next step. He tried in vain to see the danger he was in, but the thick nothingness of the fog obscured his view. "How deep is it?"

Grabbing Adam by his belt, Dalen gently pulled him back. "Way deeper than you'd like it to be when standing so close to the edge."

Adam listened to his friend, backing away from the ledge by groping along Dalen's arm until he found his shoulder. "Good looking out for me."

"Am I understanding this right, Dalen?" Travis's eyes reflected the same intensity as when he was trying to solve a puzzle in their tabletop game. "You can see through this damn fog?"

"The fog is an enchantment to keep out those who'd do the temple harm. I lived here for almost three years, and I don't see the fog. Don't worry — I got you guys. Keep together, and I promise I will not let you fall."

"Oh, good," Travis teased. "Because, my friend, you dropped us into zero visibility fog."

Dalen guided Adam to the rest of the group as he replied. "It would seem so." Dalen looked across the canyon to the Temple of Light. It was a beautiful day, and Dalen was a little sad that he wasn't able to share the view with his friends. "Stay here for a moment, and don't go anywhere."

"Where are we going to go?" Ben's voice cracked as he fought against old habits to be sarcastic. Dalen heard the strain in his voice and sensed the wound in his heart left by all he'd experienced in the last nine days. When Dalen didn't laugh, he added, "Sorry. Just trying to lighten the mood. We'll be right here."

"I'm going to get help. I'll be right back." Dalen had turned toward the temple to make the 'Leap' when he saw the ferry on its way to greet them. It took him a moment to place where he'd seen it before, but he put the thought on hold as he recognized the pilot. "Brother Faith? Is that you?" Dalen leaped aboard the boat and hugged his old friend. "Or should I say Master Faith? The last time I saw you, you were never going to land. What happened?"

"I never did." They both smiled and hugged again.

"It seems you landed on a boat. I haven't seen this thing

since the museum where I got the Beads of Fire."

Faith turned the wheel and brought the ferry up to the edge of the cliff. "Well, this is the only one of its kind, but I don't doubt you. Perhaps this world's future is the other world's past." They looked at each other and shrugged in unison. This made Faith laugh and throw his arms around Dalen once more.

"So, you never landed? Then how are you here?" It had been decades since he was here, and already, the temple had left him in wonder.

"By choice." Faith gave Dalen the same smile that Dalen had seen a thousand times when Faith was trying to convince him it was possible to make his first leap like he knew more than he was letting on. "I wouldn't have missed your return for anything. Not to mention that, while on this boat, I have not officially landed."

Dalen pondered this for a moment before asking: "Your faith keeps this afloat?"

Even as he nodded with humility, Master Faith beamed with pride at his accomplishment.

"So, as long as you are operating this ferry, you are still holding a Leap of Faith?"

"Exactly."

"Outstanding!" Dalen pretended that his mind exploded and then swatted his old teacher on the shoulder.

"I am glad you approve." It was then that Faith turned his attention to Dalen's friends. He drew the ferry as close to them as he could without running aground. "Alright," Master Faith clapped his hands together. He walked toward the edge of the ferry, and with his friendliest greeting, he called out to Dalen's friends. "Hello? Can you hear me?"

Instinctively, Travis waved his hands in wide strokes into the fog. "Yes! We can hear you! We're over here," he called, continuing to wave his arm in the air.

"I can see you. No need to wave." Faith understood that none of them could see him yet and that they were likely disoriented, so he worked to reassure them. "My name is Master Faith, and I am a friend of Brother Truth."

"Who is Brother Truth?" asked Becky.

"Dalen." Master Faith let out an amused giggle. "I am friends with Dalen. When he was here last, he went by Brother Truth," Faith explained.

Dalen got off the ferry and walked over to his friends. "This is Master Faith of the Temple of Light. He was and always will be my friend and teacher. The best part is that he brought us a ride. There is a ... boat." As Dalen took Ben's hand, he flinched, not expecting to be touched. "Just me." Dalen kept his voice calm and centered. "Sorry, bro. I should have said something."

"It's all good." Ben's tone was clear and strong, but Dalen could see his apprehension.

"Connect hands to make a chain and follow me, and we will get you all seated," directed Dalen.

"What about David?" asked Becky.

"Don't worry," Dalen reassured her. Once everyone was on the ferry, Dalen reached out and shifted David between the frames of reality and placed him on the ferry.

Dalen brought his attention back to his friends. They huddled together, afraid of what they could not see. For a moment, he imagined that this was how the Fire Jinn must have seen him once or twice. New. Very new and blind to what was right in front of him, though protected and safe.

It had only been a couple of hours since he'd lost the Beads of Fire in the infinite frames of time, but he missed his friend and wondered if he would ever see her again. She'd told him they would see each other again at the Fountain of Truth, and that gave Dalen hope. She had never lied to him, and Dalen believed there was no reason to believe she would have then. He sent out his thoughts to her, hoping that even if he could not hear her, she could somehow hear him. As he did, he looked out over the canyon. He had missed this place. In a way, he was home, and Dalen drew in a deep breath, soaking in the view as Master Faith navigated the ferry toward the Temple of Light.

As they drew closer to the temple, Master Faith steered toward the large open courtyard at the edge of the cliff face. Standing in the center of the courtyard was Master Truth, who waved as they approached. Dalen grasped Faith's forearm and, with the other arm, hugged him, promising to chat with him soon.

Dalen got his friends to their feet before he greeted his old friend from the edge of the silver ferry. "Hello, Grand Master Truth. It is good to see you again." Dalen gave a proper bow that was reciprocated. "I request permission to enter the grounds of the Temple of Light."

A welcoming glow came from Master Truth. "You are welcome here, Brother Truth. This is your home. You also have the trust of the temple, and your friends are welcome here as well. Please guide them to the Elemental Circle in the middle of the courtyard."

"We are going to move now. As we step off the ferry, there will be a gap. Make sure you step over it." Dalen guided them to the edge of the ferry and helped each of them step correctly onto the stone courtyard.

Master Faith chuckled to himself. As Dalen continued helping his friends, he asked Master Faith to share the joy, to which he replied: "They can't see where they are stepping. Their Faith is with you, but they still are making a Leap of Faith."

Master Faith was not only his friend but had been his teacher in the ability to make the leap. As Dalen helped Ben cross the gap, he saw the wisdom in Master Faith's words. So did Adam.

Adam was the last one to get off the ferry and had heard Master Faith. When Dalen put his hand out to help him across, Adam stepped back. "If it's all the same, I want to do this on my own."

"The gap is a drop-off. Are you sure you don't want my help?" Dalen offered his hand again.

Adam shook his head. "Let me do this. I need to try." Dalen knew Adam enough to know that Adam meant it. He was, by far, the most adventurous of them and often challenged himself to do things he didn't think he could.

Dalen backed away from the ferry but added, "Don't think you can do it. Know you can do it." Dalen thought about the hundreds of times he'd jumped off this very edge and had failed, all because he'd left himself the option to fail.

Adam closed his eyes and inhaled deeply. Under his breath, he declared to himself, "These are the moments that we live for." He opened his eyes and, with conviction, threw himself off the ferry, landing gracefully on the other side.

Master Faith made a little hop and a whoop. "I like this one! He reminds me of Mordecai."

Stunned, Adam ran his fingers through his hair as he peered about, ending with both of his hands resting on his head as he took in everything.

Dalen nodded knowingly, a smile on his lips. "What do you see, my friend?"

"The fog's gone." He dropped his hands from his head, then raised one to cover his mouth in astonishment. "We are at some sort of monastery? A bunch of monks are gathered and..." Adam's attention was finally pulled to the canyon itself. "And what a view!"

The others started asking questions, too many to answer. "Hang on, guys. Follow me, and we will get this fog lifted for everyone." That sounded like a good plan to everyone else, and so they once again formed their line, and Dalen led them to the circle.

"Adam?" Dalen was walking next to Adam. He kept his tone low so that only Adam would hear him. "Can you see the monk made of smoke next to the circle?"

Adam squinted and even created a visor with his hands but shook his head. "No. But I can see this temple, and it is amazing!"

Dalen was proud of Adam for having cleared the fog in his mind on his own, and he knew that Adam would be honored to assist him. "Alright, man! Can you please help everyone else stand in that circle?" Dalen then crossed to Master Truth, bowing with warmth and respect.

Once they were all in the circle, Master Truth activated his spell with a wave of his hand. From Dalen's friends' point of view, the fog dissipated, and they found themselves in the middle of the courtyard of the Temple of Light, surrounded by the brethren who lived there. Standing in front of them was Dalen, who was now wearing robes of black and white. Next to him was a monk made of smoke. Running down his center were seven stones that flashed like trapped lighting storms and matching stones nestled in the palms of each of his hands.

"How did we get here?" Becky gasped.

Master Truth replied, "With a Leap of Faith."

Becky's eyes met Master Truth's, and a moment of surprise shook her as she struggled to process what she was looking at. She sheepishly squeaked out, "What are you?"

"I think he's a jinn," Travis ventured. He hadn't released her hand, and he squeezed it with reassurance.

Master Truth affirmed Travis's speculation, and Travis's squeeze had jumpstarted Becky's brain. "Are you the jinn we met before?"

Master Truth smiled, but it was Dalen who answered: "That Jinn was connected to the Beads of Fire. This is Master Truth and the Grand Master here at the Temple of Light. I was honored to be taught by many of the Brothers and Sisters of Light, but some of my most cherished memories are conversations with Master Truth in this courtyard."

"You echo my mind and heart, Brother Truth." Dalen bowed to him, smiling, and his friends followed suit. "Yes, this has been a beautiful greeting, and I can feel your intent. Thank you for your respect; it is received and noted. Now I ask you to set aside the pageantry and speak to me as yourselves and not as someone desperately trying not to offend a jinn."

Master Truths' candor allowed them to relax a bit, and it was Travis who first spoke. "Our friend, Sir. We need your help." He let go of Becky's hand and stepped forward. "He was attacked, and now his life hangs in the balance. Dalen brought us here to save him."

"Travis, I know why you are here." Master Truth gestured toward where David's body had been placed on the ferry and where three monks were now shifting him onto a stretcher. "While we've been talking, a group of our best healers were readying David to be moved to our healers' wing."

Everybody sighed in relief. Becky turned back around first and asked, "How did you know why we're here, and how did you know his name?"

Master Truth glanced over at Dalen. "You were right about her. Sharp as a blade, this one." He then returned to Becky. "What would make the most truth in your mind?" Master Truth empowered himself, his presence swelling, surging through them. "I am a powerful jinn who can see past your concept of time to a moment where we are friends. I have spent centuries as one of the chief enlightened beings of this world, and simple things like who Brother Truth's closest friends are and the reasons they would come to this temple are well within my ability to divine." At that moment, all of them were saturated with his presence and the raw power emanating from him. He was too much to comprehend, too big to imagine. The pressure of this built within their minds. In the next moment, his entire tone changed and softened to one of camaraderie and friendship as he shrugged puckishly. "Or maybe Brother Truth spent a while here and often spoke of his friends with such spirit that I feel as if I already know you."

Once he shifted, the stress filling them released. Becky nodded in agreement. "Fair enough," she offered. The reasons Master Truth had provided made her feel silly for even asking. Embarrassed, she looked down at her dress, brushing it smooth with both hands. She glanced up and found that Master Truth was still looking at her with an eyebrow raised. "Oh! You wanted me to actually answer that." The Jinn smiled at her, clasping his other hand behind his back. She considered the question a moment in silence before suggesting, "I guess the answer that would have the most truth in it would be all of them intertwined?"

"Sharp as a blade." Master Truth made no attempt to hide that he was proud of her. He looked at the rest and said, "I look forward to getting to know each of you better. For now, there is work to be done."

"What is required?" asked Dalen.

"We can't have them just stand in the circle the entire time they are here." Master Truth smirked at Dalen. "If only we knew someone who could imbue rings with the exact same spell that has been put on the circle." He shook his head. "A pity, really."

Dalen rolled his eyes at the Jinn. He knew that Master Truth was testing him. When he was here last, he had no knowledge of imbuing, but after he left, he spent many years at the Temple of All Faith, where he had learned how. They hadn't spoken since he left, yet the Jinn somehow already knew. Dalen reminded himself that his own future and past were interchangeable from Master Truth's point of view. "Of course, Master. Do you have rings for me to imbue?"

Master Truth cocked his head to one side and, leaning in close, commented mischievously, "If only we knew someone who could magically manifest rings into existence."

"Okay, okay," Dalen laughed. "I'll manifest the rings to

be imbued."

The Jinn smiled.

Dalen smiled back.

Then Master Truth allowed his gaze to wander, drifting in no particular direction. As Dalen focused his Spheres of Reality to begin his spell, the Jinn — not yet done with his challenge — interrupted him. Still pretending to look off into nowhere, Master Truth shook his head with exaggerated woe. "If only we knew someone who could manifest the rings into existence already imbued with the spell required."

Dalen's entire focus broke. "Already imbued?"

"You can do that?" asked Adam. Every face turned to Dalen for the answer, including Master Truth's.

Suddenly, Dalen felt intense pressure to answer the question with a yes. He didn't want to let down his friends, nor did he want to disappoint Master Truth. Dalen closed his eyes and thought about it. He considered whether he believed he could. Then he thought about Master Truth and how the first rule of magic was that he was only as powerful as he believed that he could be. Master Truth led him here on purpose, and he had never asked Dalen to do something that wasn't in the realm of possibility.

He started with that as his launching point. It was possible. Dalen was sure of it. He had learned how to imbue objects during his time at the Temple of All Faith: he'd moved a candle between the frames, and he'd even dropped the Beads of Fire between the frames of reality into time itself. However, he'd never tried to manifest something that wasn't there before. To manifest the rings already imbued with a spell was at the very edge of his perception and was a leap itself, but it was possible. He held onto that one thought until it resonated like a bell in his mind. As it rang out with a clear tone, his mind harmonized with it, and he allowed himself to accept it as a truth. "Yes, I can, Adam."

The question was how he was going to achieve it. It is one thing to tell yourself that you can make the leap; it is another thing completely to step off the edge. He knew he could do it, but he needed to learn what he was required to do.

Dalen focused his mind and allowed himself to flow with the moment. In his mind, he sensed the connection he had with each of his friends. As he breathed, he began to slow down time until it moved so slowly that he could perceive the spaces between the frames of reality. His mind reached out and searched for a place in all of this world where rings like that might exist. The only place he could think of was Dorn's Tavern.

Memories of moments that he experienced there and memories of Dorn himself filled the blank places between the frames. He tried to look at one directly, and he found that the memory was looking back.

"How can I help you?" asked Dorn.

"Is this real?" Dalen questioned.

"Yes, in a very unreal way. You are not physically in my

tavern, but that doesn't mean I am not talking to you."

"Am I changing the memory?" Dalen asked. He'd been warned of the dangers of changing time.

"No," reassured Dorn, "You are fine. You've connected to me in your present. How can I help you?"

"I need to know how to manifest something the same way your bar manifests what you wish to drink."

Dorn smiled at him, folding his arms across his chest. "I will not manifest them for you. Master Truth gave you that test, and he already knows that I can do it."

"So, you know?" asked Dalen. His question was two-fold. He was partly asking if Dorn knew how to make the rings but also questioning if Dorn knew what was taking place at the Temple of Light.

"Of course I do." Dorn laid out a coaster for him on the bar. "Have a drink. I promise it will help."

"Alright, I'll have my usual." Dalen sat down and had three fingers of a bubbly brown liquid.

"The problem is that you are looking at it like two different actions that you're trying to turn into one." Dorn used his finger and drew glyphs made of light in the air. "This is a circle of glyphs you should recognize."

Dalen nodded as he studied them. "Yes. It is the circle and glyphs used to imbue an object with the specific spell that I need."

Dorn continued drawing with his fingers in the air. "The one I am drawing next to it is the spell required to manifest four celestium rings." Celestium was a magical metal that looked much like silver or platinum but was often perceived as white because it naturally produced divine light. It was considered a holy metal, purportedly used in the armor and weapons of the angels.

Dalen looked at it carefully. "I can read what you are doing, and I know I can make them." In the next moment, though, doubt filled him. "Yet, as we can both see, they are two different spells, and I cannot see how to make it a single action. Can you help me see more?"

"Finish your drink," Dorn directed. As Dalen did, the paper coaster stuck to his glass, and as the last drop was drained, Dalen realized he was looking at the spell needed to combine the two seemingly different spells into one, like a composer recognizing how two notes can be played together to create a single harmony. "This is it!" he shouted with surprise. He looked up at Dorn and blurted a grateful "Thank you!" but before Dorn could say, "You're welcome," Dalen was back with his friends at the Temple of Light.

"Oh, and Adam," Dalen said with a bow of respect, "These are the moments we live for."

Dalen pictured the spell, envisioning it on the floor within the circle. Stepping into the circle with his friends, he connected to each of them and then reached out into the divine field to join with its infinite energy. As he focused, he imagined the glyphs in the floor lighting up, and he moved his own Ki, aligning it with the power of the universe and channeling it through himself in harmony with the glyphs. Four beams of light engulfed his friends. He felt their exhilaration mixed with fear. The spell was complete, and Dalen allowed the world to return to normal. The light that had engulfed each of them faded, but as it did, each of them realized they were now wearing a ring made from pure celestium that gave off its own faint glow and was warm to the touch. Their eyes tingled and grew blurry for a moment as the enchantment took effect, but their sight returned quickly to normal.

Master Truth clapped his hands together and then gestured to everyone. "Well done, Dalen! I believe that you each can leave the circle."

As they did so, Becky observed her surroundings for a moment and then took off the ring. She blinked a few times and put it back on. "Fascinating."

Adam ran over and hugged his brother. "Travis! Travis, do you know what this is?"

Together, they squealed like children:
"First! Magic! Item!"

None but Dalen noticed Master Truth approach Ben with a question while everyone else was celebrating their first magic item. Ben responded with tears welling in his eyes. Master Truth nodded and affirmed that it could be done.

Dalen approached cautiously. "Everything alright?"

"Everything is going to be fine." The storms in each of the stones in Master Truth calmed, and as they did, so did

Dalen and Ben.

Dalen asked Ben what was going on, and Ben replied,
"Master Truth asked to help me with something. You have
to understand, Dalen: Twenty-four hours ago, I was stuck in
a time loop where I believed I had violently killed you. I was
manipulated and then tortured by Mathias, and I am not okay.
Master Truth asked if he could help me find the one thing I
need more than anything else right now."

Dalen's heart felt Ben's pain. It was the same anguish
Dalen had sensed radiating from him when they first arrived.
"What do you need, Ben?"

"I need to find peace."

Dalen understood. "Ben, you could not be in a better
place to achieve that goal."

"Wait," Becky interrupted. "You are staying here?
You're leaving us?!"

Ben turned to all of them, and the pain in his eyes was
echoed in his words. "I'm not okay. I hoped that seeing Dalen
at the dance would end this for me — that knowing he was safe
and happy would somehow ease my heart over what happened."
Tears streamed down his cheeks as he spoke, and Becky
remembered how emotional he had become when he'd finally
reached his 'tomorrow.' "I was hoping it would fix all of it. *Any*
of it, but it hasn't. Nothing has changed." They moved toward
him, but he put up his hand and stopped them. "I am so glad to
know that you forgive me, but I have not forgiven myself, and I
need to find that peace."

Travis said, "I can respect that. I don't like it, but
I understand."

"Hurry back to us," added Adam.

A hooded monk stepped forward from the others and led
Ben by the shoulders. He spoke in hushed tones, but they heard
the monk tell Ben that it was going to be okay as they reached
the center of the Elemental Circle. The slightly taller man came
around to stand in front of Ben. Although the monk's hood
cast his face into shadow and his back was to the group, Ben
could now see who he was. He began to weep openly. "Do I find
peace?" The monk nodded, and Ben blew out all of his air in a
jagged exhalation. He took a moment to regather his composure
and looked up into the face of the hooded monk once more.
"Okay, I'm ready."

To the side, Master Truth bowed to Ben. "As you
wish." A gust of wind blew from the Jinn toward Ben. Ben
closed his eyes and faded from sight, leaving the hooded monk
standing alone.

"Where did he go?" demanded Travis.

"Not where, but when," Master Truth answered.

"Okay, then, when did you send him?" Adam's question
mirrored his twin brother's tone.

"Three years ago," replied the Jinn with a wry smirk as
he raised an eyebrow.

"Did he find peace?" Becky had moved past the obvious

questions and asked the one that mattered.

The monk pulled back his hood to reveal his face. "I did." It was Ben. He was clearly older than he had been, taller and stronger, but the most significant was the change in his demeanor. Ben had carried a great weight on his shoulders that this version did not. His smile was not forced and came from somewhere deep inside him. His eyes no longer spoke of pain; instead, they reflected his contentment and joy. "You have no idea how patient I have been since you arrived." It had been three years for him, and he had missed them while he trained, but he was glad to have gone through that training without distraction. He'd needed to focus solely on his training and healing with the dedication he'd had, but now it was time to be with his friends once more. "It is so good to see you all. I have missed you so much." He gave Dalen a proper bow of the Brotherhood and then addressed him directly: "Brother Truth." Then he looked at the Jinn. "You were right. That was the hardest thing I have ever done during my time here." He bowed with warmth to Master Truth. "Thank you for everything."

Master Truth bowed to him and then addressed the group. "May I present to you, Brother Peace?"

2

FINDING VENGER

Hours passed before they got any information from the healers about David. Although the masters had shown them quarters to rest in, none of them could, so they sat together in the dining hall and ate in silence, waiting for news. Early on, Master Love and her team had hoped the issues would be remedied and that David would be on the mend by now, but they had not yet figured out how to resolve his afflictions.

At last, Master Love and Master Tome joined them with an update. Love's smile was well-practiced, but her eyes told a different tale. "First, I am happy to tell you that David is alive, and he is stable, and we are certain that we can keep him that way." Master Love waited a moment while Dalen and his friends thanked the universe. They connected with looks and touches as they rejoiced. "We have healed his wounds, and his body is healthy." Master Love set her gaze on Dalen, and when they made eye contact, she continued. "However, this weapon—the Soul Freezer—attacks all three Spheres of Magic. His body has healed, but his mind is asleep. The blade also wounded his soul, and it is this wound that is our obstacle."

Dalen understood and knew where she was going with her explanation, so he asked the question that he knew would lead her to explain it to them. "The blade wounded his soul?"

"Yes." Concern flashed across Master Love's face. The hours that she had spent trying to heal his wound welled up and spilled from her eyes. "I cannot heal it. You must believe me, I tried."

Brother Peace joined his teacher and held her hand as she allowed herself a moment to feel her frustration and sadness but didn't allow her to marinate in it. "No one here doubts that you have tried everything you know and probably even made something up trying to help him." She nodded, releasing the last of her stress. "Do you remember what you taught me when I first got here?"

Master Love wiped her eyes and nodded as she sniffed, trying to recenter her focus. "If you have tried everything you can think of, don't lose faith. There are many more things to try." Her emotions swung from feeling defeated to appreciation. "You have come a long way, Brother Peace."

Peace patted her hand with his as he explained, "I had a really good teacher."

"You are correct, Brother Peace." Master Love sniffed once more and then cleared her throat as she dried her eyes with her sleeve and began to believe in the impossible once more. "Just because I have tried everything I know does not mean I have tried everything that there is to try. It is just a matter of finding someone who knows more than me about healing the soul."

"Who would be the best choice for that?" Becky inquired. "I thought you were the greatest healer here."

"Here, perhaps, but that doesn't mean that there isn't someone else out there, a person who would know how to heal this wound." Master Love gestured to the Moon Elf beside her. "Master Tome is the head librarian here. Although I know a lot about healing, his knowledge of how to counter curses is far superior to mine. He has been instrumental in identifying and isolating the obstacle."

"What *is* the obstacle?" Travis had his notebook open and was taking notes as he asked his question. His question sparked the others, and, one by one, they all put up their fingers for initiative.

Master Love sighed. "The obstacle is this." She took a cleansing breath as she figured out how to explain what was happening without being too vague, nor did she want to be so technical that those without proper training in the healing arts would fail to understand. "With this kind of blade, there is only one known way to reawaken the victim, and that is to have the genie or jinn who made the blade remove it."

"That is the only known way?" The others had seen
the look on Becky's face before. She was determined to solve
this puzzle, but to do that, she needed as much information
as possible.

"As far as we know. We have exhausted our knowledge
on how to break the curse, and that is speaking for myself and
Master Tome, who has knowledge that covers every word on
every scrap of paper in our library."

"So, who do you turn to when Master Tome does not
know?" Becky was building momentum as she followed the path
their answers provided.

"Master Truth, he is a seer," Master Love explained.
"Every prophecy that he has ever muttered has come to pass.
His knowledge surpasses anything that we corporeal beings have
accumulated. He knew that there was something special about
your friend, much like Brother Truth."

Everyone turned to look at Dalen. "Like me? What do
you mean?"

Master Love seemed uncertain about how to answer
the question. She began to utter an explanation but restarted
after stuttering to a stop. She tried again but failed. Dalen
and Becky looked at each other and, in silence, concurred that
more was happening than they were aware of. Just before they
had time to fully question her silence, Master Truth breezed
into the room as wafts of smoke, his form materializing between
them and Master Love. "Both you and David are directly tied
to magic." His form faded as the smoke moved directly in front
of Dalen, reshaping into the visage of Master Truth. "It's why

you both have one blue eye and one eye that is violet."

Old habits have the advantage of muscle memory. Dalen had spent almost three years with the Brotherhood of Light, and he still saw Master Truth as a respected teacher. Dalen knelt, clearing his mind before he spoke. "I do not understand, Master." Dalen looked up into his teacher's eyes, which resembled lightning trapped within glass orbs; despite their storminess, the eyes of his old friend brimmed with warmth. "Help me see the truth in it."

The jinn gestured for him to rise from his knees and then asked everyone to sit at the large dining table near the fire. When everyone had taken a seat, he addressed Dalen's question. "It was no accident that you ended up living in the same house as each other," stated Master Truth. "Magic will often gravitate toward magic. As infants, both of you were torn from your home, a world filled with magic, and brought to the world in which you were raised. You were lost, not abandoned. There were people who were looking for you, and when they could not find you in this world, they began to search for you in others. Once you were located, you were to be harbored and protected until you came of age, at which point the person who was protecting you would help the magic within you awaken." Master Truth glanced at everyone, gauging how they were handling this revelation. "When you took the Beads of Fire, you connected to magic, but it hadn't awoken within you fully. This means you were able to retrieve the beads and make a verbal contract with Mathias, yet you weren't awake enough to magic to trigger its defenses."

"Mathias mentioned the beads were protected to ensure that they couldn't be retrieved by anyone who had a true connection to magic." Although it had been years since that night, Dalen remembered every moment like it was yesterday.

"Yes, that is correct. Mathias had chosen the precise moment he would meet you with purpose and intent because you weren't quite mature. Yet, the other side of the coin suggests that he really had no choice in the matter at all. He knew the right time when you could retrieve the Beads of Fire. He knew when he would have to make his move or risk being unable to reclaim the beads." Master Truth shrugged like he saw both possibilities as equally valid. "Mathias remembered that day just the same as you do now. Mathias was you, and he had firsthand knowledge of what was supposed to happen. That is why that version of you showed up. He already knew the exact moment you would give him the Beads of Fire, and all he would have to do is partially awaken you to magic." Master Truth created a smoke ring from his being. Within the smoke, a light appeared. He traced the circle repeatedly with his finger, explaining, "You and Mathias are locked in a never-ending time loop: you give the beads to Mathias, something happens, and you spend the rest of your life trying to get the Beads of Fire back, until you one day become Mathias, and go back in time to get the beads from yourself, and then the younger version repeats the circuit forever and ever." With a wave of the old jinn's wispy hand, the ring and the light dissipated. "So, this creates new questions that you will have to one day answer. How does Mathias's master, the genie DeSalvo, get involved with all of this? It happens during your time transitioning from Dalen to Mathias, during which the genie DeSalvo becomes your teacher. Perhaps a wish from Mathias is how they returned to his past, your present. The question you have to ask yourself is, how did the genie DeSal..." Master Truth paused for a moment and looked outward toward the open hall they were in. In truth, he was looking at me, Will of Grey. Like the Fire Jinn, he was aware of me as the narrator as I watched over everything. "Let's just refer to the genie as DeSalvo from now on — it saves time." He took a deep breath in and again addressed those at the table. "How did DeSalvo get involved in the beginning?"

Mathias had only mentioned DeSalvo in passing and had talked little about his training. Dalen shook his head with regret. "I don't know. I have thought about this a few times, and I get stuck in that endless circle of thinking. Yet, at no time do I know how it begins or when I meet DeSalvo."

"I can tell you that DeSalvo picked you for decidedly specific reasons. One reason was that you have a magical nature, but you had been living in a world where, with few exceptions, magic is overall dormant, and you had not awoken your magical potential. He wanted the Beads of Fire for himself, and Mathias had grown too powerful to acquire them alone, but Mathias and his history with you is why DeSalvo knew you could retrieve them."

"Master Truth," asked Dalen nervously. "Can you define what you mean when you say that I have a magical nature?"

Master Truth looked at him for a moment or two, noticeably puzzled by Dalen's question. "Have you not figured it out yet?"

Dalen hated not having the answer, but he understood that it was a requirement for learning. "Help me understand."

"You are from this world, and so is David." The air jinn rested his hand on Dalen's shoulder. "You are a magical being from a world where magic is very much alive. Unfortunately, you were raised in a world where magic is all but dead. There were some who knew of magic, but overall, the world no longer believed in it, and thus, it had grown stagnant and diminished to almost nothing."

Everyone looked to Dalen, who was processing this latest information. "How did I get there?" Dalen had always wondered how he had been found, abandoned as an infant with no records.

"Now and then events happen, and the entire world aligns in a way that produces outcomes that are so random, they would be impossible to predict." Master Truth's words were heartfelt and powerful. "One such alignment took the form of an attack on this world when both you and David had only been alive a short time. Because of this, you were still incredibly young, but being magical left its mark on you both and stayed with you as you grew up in a faraway world without magic. The blue and violet eyes have been a sign of who you were all along."

"So, David and I are magical beings who were born here but were pulled into another world when we were babies?" Dalen breathed deeply to control his emotions.

"They searched for you immediately. As I said, they scoured this world looking for you, and when they determined that you were not in this world, you were searched for in others. Ms. Warren was the primary individual who had been looking for you since you both vanished, and it was your eyes that helped us find you. David was located first and put into Warren's care until you could be located. When that happened, she chose to be there to watch after both of you and was going to prepare for your return to your real home once the summer had begun. Sometime after graduation, when no one would have paid attention to either of you moving away."

"So, where is my home? Who are my people?" Dalen's heart throbbed with emotion and excitement. After everything he had been through, he had learned to let go of his past and see himself for who he had become, but now the possibility of learning the truth was almost overwhelming as all of his wishes to know and understand his past came flooding back.

The jinn gave him a playful grin and cocked his head to the side. "I see a moment in time. It is a beautiful moment when everything comes full circle, and you come to know who you truly are." Master Truth gripped Dalen's shoulder with such intent that Dalen could feel his hand corporeally. "That moment will help define you for the rest of your days forward." The storms in the air jinn's eyes crackled with electricity, and as they did, the sky filled with lightning, and a cracking boom shook the room. It was loud, and it was powerful as the echo reverberated within the confines of the room, and then, as quickly as it came, it was gone, and silence took its place. Master Truth's eyes calmed with it, and his features became soft and sincere. "That moment is not this one, and I would never rob you of that beautiful moment, and I look forward to the day it arrives for you."

Dalen just looked up at him, blinking blankly. That wasn't even close to the answer he had been hoping for, but it was exceptionally delivered by someone whom he respected greatly. There was no choice. He had to accept this as a truth and move forward. He was going to need a minute to overcome his disappointment.

"I will add this," continued Master Truth. "The answers you seek will also provide the reason why it is you who must go to the Fountain of Truth to learn how to save your friend. While there, you might want to ask the fountain other questions. Unfortunately, you will only get one. So, make it count."

"Thank you, Master Truth. I shall need some time to think about this new truth." Before his friends could take the conversation further, Dalen slipped between the frames of reality and reappeared at the stone courtyard of the temple.

Dalen was frustrated. He had more questions than answers, and each answer only created more questions. He wanted to yell, but instead, he remembered where he was and his training. Dalen took a deep breath and allowed himself to drop into a meditative state. He remembered the last day he had been at the Temple of Light. It was the day he learned to find balance within himself and was finally ready to make his Leap of Faith. It was that focus that he was trying to find once more. His thoughts began to clear, and he felt the presence of other beings entering the courtyard, so Dalen reached out with his connections to the body sphere to see who it was.

There were two of them. One far off to the side, watching from what they thought was a hidden location, and another approaching directly. Through his connection, he knew it was Ben, and Dalen noticed how much different he felt. He had changed during his time here, and for the better, Dalen thought. This version was calm, and like all of the Brothers of Light who take a name, he lived the truth of his name and was at peace.

"I was thinking about the day I left here." Dalen was talking to Brother Peace, but he didn't look up from his meditation. "Why did I never see you here?"

"I arrived the day you left." Brother Peace pointed to a high window that was on the other side of the temple. "I waved from there, but I don't know if you saw me. I watched from that window as you, Joy, and Faith leaped together. It is still, to this day, one of my favorite memories at this place. They celebrated for three days and nights after you left."

"I would have loved to see Master Truth or Master Ki celebrate for three days," Dalen was still meditating, but he could not help but give a mischievous smile at the thought of it.

"Master Ki left the same day as you." Brother Peace came around and stood in front of Dalen. "I didn't get a chance to study with him."

Dalen opened his eyes. "He has been gone since I left?" asked Dalen.

"From what I understand, Master Ki was here specifically to train you. Once you left, his time here was over." Brother Peace paused long enough to take in the beauty of the canyon. "After you left, Master Truth said that our best hope for us to find a cure was getting to the Fountain of Truth. He mentioned that Master Ki would be returning with your arrival and that he would be joining us as far as Venger."

"Wonderful!" The news of seeing Master Ki again was enough to get Dalen back in good spirits. "I believe you will like Master Ki when he arrives."

"I look forward to it." It was getting into dusk, and Peace was looking up at the stars that were just beginning to emerge. "With everything that has been going on, I haven't had a chance to catch up with you." Brother Peace pulled his gaze from the stars and gave Dalen his full attention. "It's good to see you, Brother Truth."

Dalen took the time to really look at the young man in front of him. Three years at the temple suited him well. There was a strength within him that came from the core of his being. It wasn't a strength created by aggression as it had been before, but a strength that came from his heart and soul and resonated with the peace that he had come here to find. "It is good to see you, Brother Peace."

They bowed to each other in the tradition of the temple, and then Peace suggested that he was going to check on everyone else and left Dalen to speak with his other visitor. Dalen waited for Peace to leave before he began talking to them. "Ben has changed a lot, don't you think?" Dalen looked over to the side of the courtyard where his friend thought they had been well hidden and waved.

"You both have, Dalen." Becky's words were almost accusatory. "I am glad that Ben has found his peace, and

I think it was for the better. You, on the other hand, have changed in ways I don't understand." There was fear in her words, and Dalen could feel it from across the courtyard.

He walked over and sat on a stone bench along the wall where she stood, approaching cautiously so as not to alarm her. After a few moments, he patted the bench beside him to invite her to join him. "I have absolutely changed, but you have not. Haven't had time, really. This is only my opinion, and if I am wrong, please let me know, but the Becky that I have known would see this as an opportunity to start a new friendship with an old friend."

Becky acknowledged his point with a sheepish smile, yet at the same time, her eyes welled up, and she began to cry. She ran over and threw her arms around Dalen and cried until her fears and sadness were no longer a part of her. While she wept, Dalen sensed that Brother Peace had found Travis and Adam, and all three of them were on their way over. Dalen guessed that his other friends would have the same questions and worries as Becky, and so he felt this would be as good of time as any to try to explain everything.

Travis noticed that Becky was still drying her eyes as they arrived and was concerned. "Is everything okay?"

Becky nodded as she got up and walked over to him, resting her forehead on his chest. "Yeah, it's okay," she said as she nuzzled him. "It's just a lot."

Travis let her as he stroked her hair. "Fair enough."

So much had happened. Just hours before, Dalen had returned to his friends to find Mathias ready to kill them all. After the fight, they came here, and everyone's mind had been on David. For Dalen, it had been almost twenty-five years since he had been with them, and there had been so many nights where all he wished was to see them once more, and now his wish had come true. "I want to tell you what happened to me while I was away." His friends gathered around and took a seat on the floor in front of his bench. "I know that you have a lot of questions, but first, let me tell you more about this place. I spent a thousand days here, learning one aspect of my magical training."

"That's like two and a half years," Travis noted with more than a hint of surprise. "It took you that long?"

"It sure did," replied Dalen. "As Brother Peace will tell you, training here every day will teach you many things — things like patience, respect, and the ability to use your mind and body together as a whole."

"That is what I'm talking about!" blurted Adam, who was too giddy not to interject. "So, you can do all that 'Move with the Wind' stuff?"

Dalen smiled mischievously as he raised an eyebrow. "Oh, yes. Yes, indeed I can, Adam." Dalen jumped about eight feet into the air and fell back to the ground slightly slower than gravity would suggest, giving him time to spin three times around before landing in a seated position in the same place he leaped from.

"This. Yes!" Adam cried. "So, this!"

Everyone fed off his enthusiasm, and their excitement
blossomed. They all started asking for a demonstration, and
Dalen promised them one after the conversation, but there
was more to explain. He explained how he had to learn to
see between the frames of reality and his twenty years in the
Temple of All-Faith, where he learned the secrets of Divine and
Arcane Magic.

He explained that each step that he took changed him
and forged him into a much different version of himself. Then
Dalen slipped off the bench and joined his friends on the floor.
"But the thing that matters is that I am still me. I may be
more mature and see things differently, but who I am in my very
core has not changed. I am still Dalen Pax, and I still love you
all like family." He leaned in and, with both arms outstretched,
he grabbed and hugged all four of them, who hugged him
back. They sat there huddled for a moment, just letting the
moment exist.

"That is so good to hear," Becky acknowledged as
she squeezed the group hug. "I was scared that we lost
you anyway.

"Don't get me wrong," started Dalen, "I am different,
and I feel like more changes are coming. Like you caught me
halfway through whatever transformation is happening." He
let them go and stood up. He helped them all to their feet
and then added, "Whatever changes are still in front of me,
remember it will always still be me."

"Yeah?" asked Travis with a hint of being unsure. "Then what happened to Mathias? Because that was not you."

"From what I have gathered, it was the loss of you guys that turned him that way. As long as we stick together, I believe that things will be much different than his current reality."

"So." Becky didn't want to linger on talking about Mathias. Just thinking of Dalen becoming that awful man bothered her to her core. "What is the next step?"

"We follow Master Truth's plan." Dalen asserted with determination. "We are going to seek out and find the Fountain of Truth, and when we get there, we will ask the question of how to save David." They all responded with cheers and whoops.

Travis was writing in his notebook. He scribbled out the last of his notes and asked, "Do we know how to get to the Fountain of Truth? If not, what is the plan to ascertain its location?"

"Good question. I have no idea where it is, but tomorrow morning, we will set out for Venger. It's the capital city of a kingdom that I spent some time in as well." Dalen assured them. "It's a magical city, and I know of a place within its walls that I believe will hold all the answers that we will require about the fountain's location."

"Okay." Adam's grin was wider than usual. "You had me at magical city." Adam was practically bursting with excitement. "Thank you, Dalen. Thank you so much for taking us on this journey." Adam stood up and took a daring pose. "They headed out on an adventure to a magical city to find the legendary Fountain of Truth." Adam broke character for a moment and added, "Great name, by the way." Then he struck his pose once more. "To seek out the legendary Fountain of Truth." He changed poses by placing his hands on his hips and puffing out his chest. "To save the cursed soul of their friend. Will they be victorious?"

Becky stopped Adam there. "That's a good question. Dalen? Do you think that we can be victorious?"

"If there is another way to save David, we will find it." Dalen put his arm around Adam. "Now that you guys are here, I truly believe that anything is possible."

"Hey, Brother Truth." Brother Peace joined in and put his arm around Dalen on his other side. "You want to show them what's possible?"

Dalen knew exactly what Peace was suggesting. Dalen's grin suggested he was up to no good. "You all want to get your minds blown?" The group unanimously agreed that they did.

Both Dalen and Brother Peace gave demonstrations. Dalen did an impressive display of elemental control, with spouts of fire and water. For his finale, he walked to the edge of the courtyard and glanced over the edge of the cliff. His friends begged him to be careful, but he only shrugged, asked them why, and tipped himself backward off the edge. They all rushed to the precipice, and while they were looking over the edge in disbelief, Dalen floated down on a gust of wind and landed quietly behind them.

He snuck right up behind them and then loudly asked, "What are you guys looking for?" It caught them all off guard. Travis turned and stepped back, but his foot found nothing to step on. Before Travis had a complete understanding of the peril he was in, Brother Peace had him by his belt and pulled him back from the edge. Brother Peace's reflexes were so fast that no one but he and Travis were aware of what happened. They locked into each other for a moment, and in Travis's eyes, he said thank you. Brother Peace gave him the slightest of nods.

Becky hit Dalen three or four times playfully. "Don't do that!" she cried. "You scared us half to death!"

Dalen laughed and ducked the incoming blows. "I think that ends my show. Hey, Peace, why don't you show us what you got?

Brother Peace asked them to wait for a moment and went to get his practice weapon. When he got back, he was especially excited. "I have been waiting to show you all this for some time. Are any of you familiar with the Kusari-Fundo?" They either said no or just stared at him with blank faces. "Okay, it's a weapon that I have thought was really cool since I was a kid. Then I saw someone use much the same weapon here, but in a new way that I thought was amazing. Also known as the Whip-Dart, it is one of the weapons that the Brotherhood of Light trains in. As soon as I saw that some of the members of Light trained in it, I asked to be taught. It became a part of my daily workout when I wasn't training in healing."

It was a chain with a weight on one end, but he held it with tremendous reverence and honor as he moved with it. He

began to spin it vertically beside him, but then, with a flick
of his wrist, the chain used all of its momentum and shot out
straight forward. Brother Peace quickly pulled the chain back
in and began to spin it once more. As he did, he began to do
rope tricks with the chain. He danced with it as it spun through
the air.

From his perspective, Dalen watched as Brother Peace
found his balance with his movement and activated the body
sphere within himself; all of a sudden, he was not just moving
with the weapon. He and the weapon flowed together as if they
were one.

Ben pulled on the chain and changed its direction, and he
began to wrap himself in it. He curled into all but a foot of the
chain, just enough to keep the weight spinning. It seemed as if
he were tied up in the chain, but then he took a step forward
and leaped in the air. As he spun in mid-air, he let go of the
chain in his left hand and all but the handle from his right. As
he did, the weight shot out from underneath him and, in almost
blinding speed, shot straight out and hit the ground, directly in
the center of the circle in the center of the courtyard. Trick
after trick, move after move, he landed his shot again and again
in the same spot. As he finished, the weapon ended up wrapped
around him like a belt, and the weight plopped easily into
his hand.

Together, they cheered and clapped when he finished
and then watched the moon rise into the night's sky, and Dalen
told them of the first rule of magic and of life. He explained
that they had to believe that they could be victorious if they
ever wanted to be. They said their goodnights and each of them

went to their quarters that Master Home had prepared for them. The next day, they would leave on their quest, with their first stop on their journey being Venger to get supplies. Dalen was excited to have his friends meet some new people who would be able to help them find the fountain. They went to bed, not knowing what they were getting into. They only knew that tomorrow they would be in the capital city of the most powerful kingdom in all of the world.

3

THE SAVIORS
OF VENGER

The next morning, they awoke at dawn and got themselves ready. Each of them had brought with them what they could pack in their school backpacks. It had been Becky's idea. She had no intention of going on their adventure wearing the dress she had worn to the dance the night before. Each of them had packed two sets of clothes and whatever items they wanted to bring with them on their journey. It was still rather dark, and the chill from the night before still hung in the early morning hours, so they dressed quickly in sweatpants or denim jeans and a shirt with a jacket or another light layer over it. When they got to the courtyard to prepare to leave, they found Dalen sitting with Master Truth on a bench that was at the edge of the courtyard. They were sharing a conversation over tea while watching the sunrise. When Dalen saw them, he offered them tea as well. It was hot, and it warmed them while they waited for Master Faith to arrive with the ferry.

" I see why you stayed for so long." Becky looked out over the canyon and watched as the sun came up over the waterfall to the east of the temple. Rainbows appeared in the mists as eagles hunted for fish that fell from the waterfall. They were swooping in and out of the falls and catching the fish in mid-air. "I wish every morning for the rest of my life could be this beautiful."

The ferry arrived shortly after Master Truth made his leave of them. He wished them all a safe journey and, as his earthly form began to dissipate, was carried off by a gust of wind. The ferry arriving pulled their attention away from watching the smoke as it danced in the wind. The ferry crested over the edge of the temple from somewhere within the canyon below. Master Faith waved to them as he appeared and brought it around to where they would embark. There waiting for him was a distinguished-looking Asian man dressed in much the same style as the Brotherhood of Light, except his clothes were a mix of blue and white instead of the traditional black and white. He wore his robes open, revealing that along his body were stones much like the ones that Master Truth had, but his looked like rippling orbs of water.

As Dalen and his friends gathered at the ferry, the man gave a graceful bow and offered them a good morning, which they kindly returned. "For those of you who do not know me, I am Master Ki. I have been honored with the task of serving as your guide on the first part of your journey until you

procure supplies in Venger." He then paused long enough to
have it be intentional and, with respect, acknowledged Dalen.
"Brother Truth."

Dalen responded with a proper bow, which is customary
in the brotherhood from a student to a teacher. "Master Ki."

Then, Master Ki repeated the ritual directed at Ben.
"Brother Peace. I hear you have become quite good at your
chosen form. Master Love holds you in high regard and believes
you have the heart of a healer. It is a good thing that you are
coming along on this trip. Your services may be required before
it's done."

Brother Peace bowed and then responded with, "Master
Ki. Thank you. I am honored that she would think so."

One by one, they boarded the ferry and set off with the
highest of expectations and the hope that they would find a
cure to save David. Thanks to the rings that Dalen had given
them, there was no longer a fog that blocked their view, and
they looked out over the canyon in awe as they took in its
beauty. While everyone was gawking at the view, Master Faith
asked Adam if he would be willing to do him a favor.

"Of course," responded Adam without hesitation. "I
would be more than happy to help. What can I do for you?"

"I have a friend in Venger City," explained Faith
casually. "I would like you to deliver him this message." Master
Faith handed Adam an envelope with the white wax seal of his
order on it. "It's for his hands only."

"I will absolutely see it done," promised Adam with enthusiasm. Then he looked over at his friends and mouthed the words 'side quest.'

Faith smiled, "Just deliver it and wait for his answer. His name is Mordecai, and he lives in Castle Venger."

Adam smiled. "The castle? That means I will have to go to the castle to deliver it." Adam closed his eyes and whispered, "These are the moments that we live for."

By the time they reached the other side of the canyon, they were all feeling a little braver, and as the ferry pulled up to the edge of the cliff, they all jumped from the ferry to the grass and then waved goodbye to Master Faith, who waved back and set off for the temple.

Travis looked to his left and then to his right. Except for the drop-off behind them, any direction from where they stood could be the direction they needed to go. "Which way?"

Master Ki took them over to the tree that was growing near the ledge. "This is known as The Tree of Travel. It is one tree that is located in many places. This is why it is also known as the Portal Tree. You can instantly travel to any other location that the Tree of Travel is at, as long as you know where it is."

"I have been to the Tree of Travel outside of Venger," noted Dalen.

"Good. Then, I want you to attempt to use it. Once you touch the tree, you will be pulled into superposition. In this space, you will be everywhere this one tree is at. Once you're there, focus directly on observing the view from the tree that you know. Hold the vision and let go, and when reality collapses in on itself, you will be at the location you desire. Couldn't be easier than jumping off a cliff." responded Master Ki in an encouraging voice. "Everyone, take hold of Brother Truth. You will want to go through with him, or you will be left behind."

All of them put a hand on Dalen, and then Dalen put his hand on the Tree of Travel. He closed his eyes and pictured the view from the Tree of Venger in all of its splendor. Then he opened his eyes. It was hard at first. Hundreds of locations overlaid with one another. He focused on the image in his mind, and the view began to appear in front of him. Dalen locked on to that vision and focused his mind on it to make it more real than any of the others. When he was sure that he had it, he let go. As Dalen let go of the tree, they were standing someplace new. The tree had not changed, but everything else had. Dalen and his friends found themselves taking in the sight of Venger City nestled in the distance.

Only the kingdom of the Moon Elves could arguably claim to be as powerful as the Kingdom of Venger. Ruled by King Gavin the Wise and Queen Hope the Just, Venger had maintained peace and harmony within their own kingdom and had offered it to all who would accept it throughout the world. Whether allies or not, the King and Queen of Venger were respected as powerful leaders and were treated as such by friend and foe alike.

Just like the Temple of Light, the City of Venger was protected by many enchantments and barriers. One of these enchantments made it impossible for most to teleport directly into the city. Only those with special privileges were able to do that. The travel tree was a marker, and the closest anyone could teleport to Venger without permission from the royal family or the city herself, for Venger City was sentient. From time to time, she would grant exclusive access to the city in the form of a mark on the visitor's body made of magic and light.

From the base of the tree began a sloping hill that reminded everyone of an amphitheater, with the city being the center stage. They stood there and marveled at its beauty as it glistened against the ocean and the setting sun. They had traveled a great distance using the tree, and it was already late in the day in Venger. It would be almost dusk by the time they reached the city.

Becky whispered under her breath, "I feel I have been here in a dream." She closed her eyes and tried to remember where she had seen it. When she couldn't produce a solid memory of it, she spoke aloud. "Have you ever had that feeling that you could just stand someplace and stare at it forever?"

"I know. Right?" Travis squeezed her hand. "This is unbelievable."

"When I left you guys before, this was the first view I had when I arrived." Dalen put his arm around Brother Peace. You have no idea how happy it makes me to finally share it with you." Dalen pointed out the road that would lead them to the city, and they began to follow his lead, making their way to the castle.

"Hey, Dalen?" Adam was often described as bold, but as he spoke, his voice cracked and was far more quiet than usual. Dalen looked over and hummed an acknowledgment. "Do we get to do some kind of leveling-up time thingy, too?"

Dalen moved closer to Adam and queried, "Level-up time-thingy?" Adam seemed excited but nervous at the same time, and for a couple of moments, he was silent as he turned red and fumbled for his words. Dalen saw that he was in distress and gave Adam a friendly nudge with his shoulder. "Hey, man. It's me. Just talk to me."

"Well," Adam's excitement began to stir, and his voice began to grow in strength. "I have been dreaming of something like this for most of my life. Now we are on a real quest to save David and heading toward a magic city, and that is awesome, and please don't think I'm not just beside myself with excitement."

"Yeah, brother," Dalen assured him as he patted Adam on the back. "It's all good. What's up?"

Adam shrugged. "I understand that Ben went through some stuff, and he needed to get his heart straight, but he got three years of training and experience. Now he is all leveled up and got a cool name..." He trailed off, not knowing how to finish the sentence without sounding childish.

"When is it your turn?" Dalen finished his question for him, but he said it with empathy and friendship so Adam wouldn't feel so silly for asking.

"Well, yeah." Adam swallowed hard and looked to his
brother for moral support. Travis waved him to go on. "I'm not
trying to sound selfish or anything, but yeah."

Dalen looked over to Master Ki. "Can you do the 'level-
up time-thingy' that was granted to Brother Peace?"

Master Ki looked at him with an expression that Dalen
had seen many times before. Master Ki tended to speak in a
way that sounded like he was very stern, but it was his way of
creating humor, and if asked, he would say he was very funny.
If he had been truly annoyed at the question, he would have
simply said no. In this case, Ki saw this as an opportunity to
continue his tutelage of Dalen Pax.

"I am here to help you through this specific part of your
journey, where you will all have to make certain adjustments
that will require an understanding of the nature of water,"
explained Master Ki dryly. "I am not here to grant wishes to
your friends. I am afraid if you want to start granting wishes,
you will have to do it yourself." Master Ki paused for a
moment while his expression slowly changed to that of great
amusement. "Besides, Adam's wish has already been granted.
It manifested a long time ago by the actions that each of you
have not yet taken."

"Do all jinn talk like that?" Travis's question had no
hint of being impolite. It was a real question that came from
the desire to understand Jinn better. "I have met three, and
all of them, including you, speak in ways that say a lot but tell
very little."

Master Ki was connected to the group in ways that they
had not yet begun to fathom and was able to read Travis and
his question with clarity, so he felt no disrespect from Travis
or his thoughts. "It is interesting that you say that." Master Ki
rubbed his chin while he pondered Travis's assessment. "I would
argue that the flipside of that coin is also true. "What if I say
little, but what I say tells volumes, but only to those who are
willing to hear it."

"Alright, Master Ki." Travis pulled out his notebook and
wrote down what the Jinn had said. "You're right. I have been
taking my perception for granted."

"Then you do understand?" Master Ki was impressed. A
feat that Dalen knew to not be an easy task.

"I don't." Adam had been keeping up with the
conversation, but Travis's revelation left him wondering. "What
do you mean, Bro?"

"Two men are dead in a cabin in the woods. How
did they die?" Travis waited for his brother to answer and
then added, "Here's a hint. I have already given you enough
information to answer the question."

"No, you didn't." Adams' confusion was palpable. "All
you said was that there were two men that were dead in a
cabin in the woods. That's not enough information. They could
have been shot, stabbed, eaten by a bear, or eaten by each
other. That is not enough information to answer anything."

"Or so it seems." Travis shrugged. "Just like I was
saying about Master Ki, well, to be fair, all the Jinn we have

met up until now aren't really saying anything. Now, let's go back to that cabin in the woods. The reason you can't answer it is because your perception has forced you to not see what's really going on."

Adam looked more confused than ever. "So, you're saying that the image I have in my mind is wrong, and that's why I don't understand that you have already told me the answer?"

Travis looked to Master Ki, who only offered up, "Change his perspective."

Travis didn't hesitate or keep his brother in suspense. "Instead of a log cabin, what if it was the cabin of an airplane.?"

"They crashed." Adam placed his palm against his forehead and slowly dragged it down his face. "Two men are dead in a cabin in the woods. How did they die? Adam scoffed. "They crashed."

Travis playfully slapped his brother on the back. "What Master Ki is saying is that we can't see the airplane."

Adam nodded in understanding, "We need to be able to see more than our own perception of the cabin and be careful what we assume is true."

"By the way, Adam, to answer your question more clearly, there is something I want to show you before we get to the city." Master Ki let go of his physical form and became a being of water and light. The Jinn flowed over the ground like a wave and ended up next to Adam. When he reformed into a physical being, he looked like a different person. He was a middle-aged man with a fair complexion. His hair had begun to speckle with silver along the sides of his head and was trimmed short in a way that suggested military service. He wore a tunic of red and blue that bore the Great Seal of Venger upon it: three silver concentric circles embossed with a gold dragon on the left and a unicorn on the right, each reared up on their hind legs. He looked at Adam and said in a voice that they didn't recognize, "When you find me, part of your wish will already be granted, and then I will grant you something greater."

"Okay, that's amazing!" Adam could have almost leaped out of his skin; he was so excited. "Wait, are you still Master Ki, or are you someone else that I have to find?"

"Yes, to both." Master Ki released the form and reverted to the image that they had known thus far. "No matter what form I take, my essence stays the same. It is the very nature of the element of water, my element. That said, you are not looking for me; you are looking for the individual whose form I took."

"How do I find him?" asked Adam.

Master Ki smiled at him and took the form of Master Faith. "You have already been asked to find him." Then, he reverted to his standard form.

Adam clapped his hands. "These are the moments we live for!" and his pace picked up speed. "Last question. What about Becky and Travis? Do they level up, too?"

Master Ki smiled at Adam. "It is commendable that you do not think of only yourself."

"Rule Number Four: You are only as powerful as your team," recited Travis.

"Rule Four?" asked Brother Peace inquisitively. "I don't think I know this set of rules."

"It is a set of rules that Travis has come up with over the years of gaming," explained Becky as she squeezed Travis's hand. "It's a set of rules that will often keep you and your team alive."

Brother Peace nodded his head slowly as Becky spoke. He was chuffed at the idea and truly amused. "Considering what we are doing and that this is the first real adventure for most of us, it might be a good idea for you to teach us your list."

"Thanks, Peace." Travis walked another twenty paces before he continued, "I really should write them all down on a single list. I initially gave them numbers arbitrarily whenever I spoke a new rule. I really should make a definitive list." He gave a little squeeze to Becky, who'd been pushing him to write them down for a long time.

Becky smiled when she recognized her own words being spoken by Travis. Her heart fluttered for a moment, and she realized in that moment that she really did love Travis. She looked down at her hand being held by his, and she felt proud of the guy who was holding it. "You're awesome," She whispered, loud enough only Travis could hear.

"I agree with both of you," Master Ki said. "Your rule has merit, but I believe that Adam was acting in a different mindset. He was thinking of you, for your sake, not his own."

"I didn't mean to say that Adam was being selfish," Travis quickly responded with more than a hint of defensiveness. "It's true that the rule itself is a variant of 'a chain is only as strong as its weakest link,' thus it is wise to make the entire chain strong. I came up with it during a game to keep people from being selfish. Instead of just trying to power up themselves, they should want to power up their team as well."

"You mistake my meaning, Travis," Master Ki soothed. "I was suggesting the nobility of Adam's wish. His intent was not to make himself stronger by strengthening you, but his thoughts were to raise you up with no thought of how it would benefit himself. To specifically strengthen you because he wishes for you to be powerful for your own sake. I think that your rule has merit and is not specifically a selfish concept. It can also be taken empathically. From that point of view, it can be set as a reminder to look out for one another and to preserve the idea that no one is in this alone." The Jinn's grin slowly evolved into a smile and finally into laughter. "I like Rule Four."

They walked down the sloping hill until they reached the cobbled road that led to the city. They talked of adventure and all of the things that made them filled with excitement and joy. They marveled at the beauty of the landscape. Right where the sea kissed the land, there was a group of folk who were camping out on the beach. As Dalen and his friends approached, the beach dwellers waved and offered them a place to rest if they wished. Dalen and his friends thanked them but declined the invitation to stay as they were too excited to stop. But as the city's walls drew closer and closer, it started to sink in that this was more real than they were expecting, and their excitement began to turn to nervousness.

The gate guards were friendly to Dalen and spoke to him as if they knew him, but as the rest of the team approached, they stood and stared at them dumbfounded for a moment. Dalen began to introduce them, but the guards barely noticed him speaking, to the point of almost ignoring him, as they looked at each of his friends. Each guard nodded and smiled as Dalen gave their names, and then they gave informal bows that were more centered on their heads than their waist, gesturing to the team that they were welcome here. Excitedly, the guards asked what their plans for the day were. Dalen explained they were going to go to Dorn's for lodging and asked them if they knew of any good shops for gear and supplies.

"If you require supplies, we suggest the middle ring. It is where the best craftsmen and artisans can be found." offered up the first guard.

"Especially The Forge." the second one mentioned with delight. Dalen thanked them both, but before they could move on, the guards stopped them and added, "We also suggest you stop off at the Saviors Garden before you head to The Forge or Dorn's."

"Saviors Garden. Thank you. How do I find it?" asked Dalen.

"Once you and your friends pass the Great Seal of Venger, you will be in the Southern Bazaar. It's filled with performers of all kinds, from magicians to mages, acrobats, and trinket makers. Once you are there, look for a man who is dressed in the same tunic as I am wearing." It was knee-length in front and back and cinched together with his belt, the cloth split into four quadrants, alternating red and black. "Except, the person that you will be looking for will be dressed in blue and black instead of red." He reached into a small pouch and retrieved a copper token. "Give him this, and he will give you a map of Venger. You can also ask him how to find the Garden."

Dalen took the token and thanked him again. Encumbered by their armor, they bowed again, deeper, more formal this time with their heads to everyone, and ushered them onward. The road went directly through the Southern Gate that led directly into the city, but before you could make it past the thick wall and into the city's outer ring, you had to first pass through a tunnel, which started at the Southern Gate and ended with an identical passage on the other side. These gates were complete with portcullis, which were only lowered in times of emergency. Looking up, Dalen and his friends could see the huge iron structures peeking out from their nest in the heavy, solid wall. Inlaid onto the road below, between the two gates, was the Great Seal of Venger. The Great Seal of Venger was the same symbol that was embroidered onto Mordecai's tunic. Three concentric circles with a Dragon and a Unicorn reared up on each side, but this one was a much larger version.

Dalen closed his eyes and tried to bring his mind to the day he first walked into Venger. At the beginning of his tumble down the magical rabbit hole, Dalen had arrived here with The Fire Jinn. He cleared his mind and did his best to remember what she told him about the Great Seal.

Dalen stopped them just in front of it, and in a bold voice filled with intrigue, Dalen laid it out much like David would have described the scene in one of their games. "Before you is the Great Seal of Venger. The three circles are a connection to the three Spheres of Reality. Body, Mind, and Soul, and it is how the city was designed. The outer ring is where most people live. There are neighborhoods and simple stores. The middle ring is where the higher-end shops and schools of learning are, and in the center is the castle and the very soul of the city. The dragon and the unicorn are symbols of the king and queen who are not seen as owners of the kingdom but rather its guardians." Dalen smiled. "Or so I have been told."

"That's beautiful," sighed Becky.

"Deep," added Travis as he transcribed Dalen's explanation of the seal.

It was Adam who could not curb his enthusiasm. "I love this place!" Adam gave a slow couple of fist pumps. "I dig the idea that they don't own the kingdom. They just protect it."

"Which would include governing and ruling to some extent," suggested Becky as if it were obvious to her.

Travis continued as if he were just continuing her thought. "Much like a parent. They set the rules, govern, and even punish as need be, but all with the intent of protection. Guardianship, but no suggestion of ownership."

Adam looked at the seal again and, this time, examined it closely. "Why a dragon and a unicorn?"

"The dragon is a representation of pure power," Dalen explained. "The unicorn is a symbol of being your greatest self."

Still staring at the Great Seal, Adam asked with a newfound respect for what he was looking at. "And that's the king and queen?"

Dalen watched as something surged within Adam that was powerful and yet serene. "Yeah."

Adam nodded as he held back tears. "Is it... "

Dalen knew that Adam would have broken if he tried to finish the sentence, but Dalen heard his heart and answered it anyway. "They live it. This whole city breathes it. It is their way of life and the code they live by." Dalen placed his hand on Adam's shoulder and gave it a squeeze. "It's real, this place is real, a place of honor and respect."

Everyone knew what it would mean to Adam. He had spent his whole life trying to live it by a code. One that he made up for himself, driven by honor and respect. A code that demanded that he refused to just exist but to live, even in the ordinary. His phrase, 'These are the moments we live for,' was his mantra, his mission statement, and creating those moments was his passion. He had searched his whole life for a place like this. A world that would understand him the way that Dalen and his friends did.

"I guess Master Ki was right," announced Travis after everyone gave Adam his moment. "Our wishes are already coming true." It made everyone laugh, which was needed to get them back on track. "So, let's have a look at this seal."

The Great Seal was so large that you could not pass into the city gates without crossing it, and the road was wide enough to have two carriages pass each other with room to spare. Both the Dragon and the Unicorn were made of gold. The outer ring was copper. The middle ring was made of silver, and the center circle was made of platinum. The outer edge of the circles and, separating each ring, was an inlay of the divine white metal celestium, which glowed like moonlight as dusk was setting in.

The team began to walk toward it, but Dalen asked them to wait for a moment. "I should tell you something before you cross it. The city is alive."

Brother Peace, who found his ability to speak again first, asked, "What do you mean?" Except for Master Ki, all were surprised or confused.

"What he means," answered Master Ki, "is that like any of you, the city is a being, and like you, she has feelings, thoughts, and opinions."

"What?!" exclaimed Adam. "No way! That is so cool! Can we meet her?" The team nodded in agreement with Adam's request.

Master Ki gave a small bow. "You most absolutely can. She awaits you on the Great Seal."

"Talking to her is... Big," Dalen had wished that someone had warned him. "Thought you might want to know."

Adam could not hold his excitement any further, so he was the first person who made it to the Great Seal. He ran his last few steps in a hurry to walk over it, but as soon as he made it to the seal, he slowed down and stopped in the center. His arms dropped to his sides, and he stood there motionless.

"Hey, Adam, you okay?" asked Travis, but Adam didn't reply. "Adam?"

The team stepped onto the Great Seal, moving toward Adam. Once they set foot on the Great Seal, they immediately knew why Adam hadn't responded.

All at once, each of them felt their minds separate from their bodies and move through the city streets at blinding speeds. It was exhilarating yet frightful. They stopped in front of a silver gate with an ornate inlay of celestium. In front of the gate stood a woman wearing a multi-layered gown of red and blue. Her smile gave her a look of contentment, and she raised her hand in greeting as she addressed Dalen and Master Ki. "It's good to see you again."

Dalen and Master Ki bowed with respect in unison.

She slowly moved her gaze to the rest, and she swelled with joy. "Greetings. I am Venger." Her beauty and strength came from the center of her being and radiated in all directions. Her dark skin seemed to glow, and the power she wielded saturated everything around her and left no question in their minds that she was more than human. She was the ground they stood on and the clouds in the sky. "The first time I met you, you had time on your side; now, time is on mine." As she spoke, Dalen felt something unlike anything he had ever felt before.

There was something about what she had said. At that point, Dalen could not understand what it was, but he knew that it somehow mattered.

The statement itself was unique and had caught their attention. "What do you mean?" questioned Becky casually. Her friends knew that she was being tactical. "This is the first time we have met you."

"Yes," said Venger, "but this is not the first time I have met you." She smiled at their confusion. "In my past, you appear from the future. You knew both my husband Dorn and me."

"We haven't met him yet either," Travis noted. "I believe we were en route to meet him."

Ever mindful of his manners and code, Adam took a knee. "We are honored to meet you, Lady Venger. Madam, I'm Adam."

"The honor is mine, Sir Adam. You said the same to me the day I met you. It is good to see you again." She offered him her hand, and when he took it, she pulled at him to stand him up. Once he was on his feet, she embraced him as if they were old friends. She turned to Brother Peace and acknowledged him with a formal bow from the brotherhood. "One day, you will share with me the secret of finding inner peace. You were right," she smiled. "You have always been right."

Becky gave a small wave of her hand. "I guess I do not need to introduce myself."

"No, dear one," Venger replied as she moved closer and placed one hand over Becky's heart. She took Becky in her arms and held her close. "Your true heart, who you really are, is known to me. Centuries have passed, yet I remember you well." Venger let her go and set her gaze on Travis. "And Travis. Your strength and sacrifice will not, cannot, be forgotten. Once a year, on the anniversary of your deeds, thousands of lanterns are lit in your honor." With both hands, she raised the hem of her gown so she could move better and knelt before him. "We owe you everything."

"What did I do?" asked Travis in shock. No one had ever treated him with as much respect as Lady Venger was in that moment.

Venger stood up and gave him a playful grin. "When we first met, you said that we had met before. You refused to give us much information about our own futures. In the time that has passed, I have come to understand the wisdom in such things, so with great respect, I will not say, but I will pass this on to you. By the time you had reached that moment, you already knew what had to be done. Time is funny that way." She gave Travis a wink as she made a popping noise with her tongue and then addressed everyone as a whole. Pointing to the silver gate behind her, she instructed, "Seek out this gate. On the other side of it will be the second of the gifts that I have for you. The first I will give you now." She raised her hands in the air, directing them toward the group, making magical gestures, moving her fingers as if drawing in the air. As she did, each of them felt warmth from their right arm, just below the shoulder, the warmth growing hotter. At first, it was bearable, but it grew and swelled until the heat was blistering. The heat intensified further, and each of them braced against the pain that they expected to accompany such heat, but it never came. A mark appeared on each of their arms: three concentric circles made of pure light. The light and heat blossomed and burned, and then, all at once, it stopped.

They found themselves standing on the Great Seal, still holding their arms. Back in their bodies and physically okay, and as each of them looked, they found that the mark was still with them, like a tattoo made of light. They carefully examined it and found that there was no wound or burn, and their skin felt completely normal.

"You have all been given the blessing of Venger. Think of it as a supernatural version of keys to the city. It grants you clearance even into the castle." explained Master Ki. "Huge honor."

"These are the moments we live for!" Adam howled and danced around. Becky and Travis were still stunned and stood in silence as Adam dropped to the ground and kissed the Great Seal.

Dalen went to check on Brother Peace. He was standing in a meditative stance that Dalen recognized well. His lips were curved in a gentle smile, so Dalen waited until he opened his eyes voluntarily.

"How are you, Brother Peace?" Dalen asked with a matching expression.

Peace opened his eyes and breathed in deep before he focused on Dalen's face. "Now that was some shit."

"Like I said, talking to her is big," agreed Dalen. He slapped Brother Peace on the shoulder and looked over to Travis and Becky. "You two alright?"

"What the hell was that?" Travis was still in shock. He was only responding with his instincts, and logic had not yet kicked back in. With a mix of excitement from the adrenaline rush that his body was producing, a mind reeling with no point of reference to compare what he had just experienced, and a hint of instinctive fight or flight, Travis was buzzing. "I just want to know what actually happened. I don't think we astral projected because we didn't leave this plane of existence — we just moved through the streets. Did we etheric project? I mean..." He was thinking again, but his mind was still not stable. "What was that?"

Master Ki explained. "Willingly crossing the seal creates a telepathic connection to the sentient mind of the city. Lady Venger. Once you chose to step onto the seal, you also made the connection with her, and it was her mind that traveled to that location. Your mind moved with hers because you were connected."

Travis nodded and took a breath as he pulled out his notebook. "Okay." He took a deeper breath and held it for a moment. "Would you say that was closer to etheric projection or remote viewing?"

"It was more like remote viewing but controlled by a being that can ethereally travel." Master Ki confirmed for him.

As Travis wrote everything down in his notebook, Dalen checked on Becky. "Are you okay?"

She looked up at Dalen and blinked. Tears fell from her eyes and rolled down her cheeks. "That was the most beautiful thing I have ever been a part of. Thank you so much for this moment."

"I know what you mean. When I first met her, it knocked me to the ground." Dalen turned his right arm toward Becky and moved a portion of his robe, revealing his bicep and showing her that he had the light symbol, too.

Adam got up from the ground with excitement. "You met her before, right? Did you find the gate?" he asked.

"I had a completely different experience at that time." Dalen rubbed the back of his neck casually. "She took me to the heart of the city where there were four Elemental Blades surrounded by a special sword known as the Horn of the Unicorn, which held the Eye of the Dragon."

Adam grinned with excitement. "That may be the coolest name for a sword I have ever heard." Adam looked past the gate that led into the city, where he could see glimpses of the Southern Bazaar. "I now really want to go find that gate. Besides, it's getting dark, and everything is going to close soon. So, let's go."

It was enough to convince them, so they moved past the Great Seal and entered the Southern Bazaar. It was a large open courtyard built like a half circle. The main gate was the center point, and patrons could walk seventy yards in either direction to enjoy the many shops and street vendors. There was a road stretching forward from the main gate to the outer edge of the bazaar. The bazaar itself was like an outside circus blended with a street market. There were acrobats and jugglers, along with individuals selling trinkets and scarves. One entertainer was using simple illusion magic to create a children's show with light and smoke. There was even a man walking around with a monkey on a leash for sale. The crowded courtyard bustled with beings from many races. There were Elves and Dwarves, and even a few Orc-kin. Orc-kin were only half-bloods but still easy to spot as they towered over most in the bazaar by a foot or two. In comparison, they also saw a few folks who were half the size of a human. Master Ki explained that they were often called Halflings because of it, but they refer to themselves as being a part of the Star Tribe or Star-Kin. There were so many races and groups that it would be possible to spend hours there and continuously see something or someone new, and all of them were shopping and bartering their goods. It was nearly dark, but there was a sense of celebration in the air, and no one showed any hint of closing down.

"Keep an eye on your valuables. More people get pick-pocketed at the Southern Bazaar than in all of the city combined," Master Ki warned with an obvious sense of amusement as he looked over the bazaar.

The team moved quickly through the courtyard, but each of them made notes to themselves of shops that they wished to return to. On the far side, Dalen spotted the man in black and blue that the gate guard had mentioned and made his way to him.

"Pardon me," Dalen called out as he drew close. "The guard at the gate said that I can use this token to get a map from you."

The man in black and blue turned to Dalen and started to answer him, but he stopped, looked at all of them, and froze, disbelief etched on his face.

"You do sell maps, yes?" asked Dalen.

The question snapped the man's attention back to the moment at hand. "Yes. Forgive me, yes." He reached into a satchel that was slung over his shoulder and produced a rolled-up scroll. "You caught me off guard. I was not expecting to see you all here." He accepted the token and gave Dalen the map. "Please allow me to make it up to you."

"There is no need," reassured Dalen.

"It would be my pleasure." He gestured to his black and blue tunic. "Whereas the guards are in red, I am an Information Liaison for the visitor center, and we wear black and blue. You require a map, and that means that you are looking for something. Allow me the opportunity to help you find the location you seek."

Dalen glanced at the team. Peace shrugged and said that he couldn't think of a good reason not to let him help. Adam thought it was a good idea, and Travis and Becky agreed. Master Ki gave Dalen a nod, and with that, Dalen shrugged and said, "As you wish."

"Wonderful!" chimed the information officer. "Where is it that I can lead you to?"

"The Saviors Garden," replied Dalen.

The information officer laughed and shook his head, "I should have known." He turned and began to walk away from the commotion of the Southern Bazaar. "Come with me. I will show you the way."

Everyone followed him except for Travis, who caught up with him to strike up a conversation. Travis had always been obsessed with the details. He felt that the little details made the difference between victory and defeat, but this time, the questions Travis was asking were on everyone's lips.

"So," Travis stated, "I would bet you are the guy to ask about the Saviors Garden."

The information officer took the compliment with pride and said, "You would win that bet. I am 'the guy' to ask."

"Fantastic!" Travis said and put his arm around him. "So, tell me everything about the Garden, and tell me why you knew that's where we wanted to go."

The Information officer stopped and looked at Travis and then let his gaze move to the others. "You don't know?"

Travis shrugged and then slung his arm over the information officers' shoulders. "Not a bit of it, but as you said, You are the guy to ask."

Tonight, the whole city is celebrating the events that happened there. For the last two days, hundreds of people have come to visit the Saviors Garden, and on the eve of the main celebration, you show up looking for it, and you have no idea what it is?"

"Nope." Travis chirped happily. "Not a clue. The guard at the entrance suggested it."

The information officer was beside himself with joy, and his excitement was at a rolling boil. "Then have I got a story for you."

4

THE GARDEN

The information officer took them through the city, and while they traveled, he told the tale of the Saviors Garden and how it came to be. "Thousands of years ago," he mused. "Venger was born from the legendary City of Dreams. The City of Dreams had stood since there were myths to be told, and many of the original myths speak of the original creator of this world and his time in the City of Dreams. Venger knew from an early age that one day, it would be her time, and she would become the new City of Dreams. The City of Dreams, also known as Dreamer, was located at a nexus where multiple ley lines intersected, but the acts of evil men had set in motion a fissure in the Nexus, which eventually allowed a dark being from another realm to cross over into our world.

"The legends say that it took the form of the Chaos Dragon, and it laid waste to the city. This is also the first mention of Time, Dimension, and Chance, who stopped the Chaos Dragon and saved our world, but the fissure was closed at a terrible price. The City of Dreams had sacrificed herself to save her daughter Venger and Dorn, the only being that Dreamer trusted, from certain death as the fissure was closed."

"How did they close the fissure?" inquired Travis as he wrote in his notebook while walking alongside the information officer.

"It was closed by the gods I mentioned." The information officer was pleased with himself that he knew the answer. "Time, Chance, and Dimension are connected to each other much the same way as mind, body, and soul."

"They are connected?" Dalen's ears perked up. "Like the three Spheres of Reality?"

"Indeed." replied the information officer. "Time, Chance, and Dimension are considered the three fields of the Elements of Existence."

Dalen had never heard of the Elements of Existence, and his interest and curiosity peaked. "I may require your services another time to go into this more in-depth."

"Call on me anytime you like. It would be an honor to share with you all I know on the subject, but for now, I have another tale to tell."

Dalen gestured for him to continue, and the information officer turned his attention back to the group as he continued with his telling of the early days of Venger and Dorn. "They found a new location where ley lines crossed and settled down, but in time, the fissure began to reappear. No one knows when it happened, but Dorn and Venger had fallen in love, and once they were on their own and had found a new place to settle down, they had four children. With their children, four elemental blades were created that could keep such fissures closed for all time. Each of the children of Venger connected to the enchanted blades, and on every solstice, they would use the elemental powers the blades possessed to reseal the fissure.

This went on for centuries, and during this time, the world was safe, but then evil found a foothold back into the world.

It came in the form of a girl who'd been given unique abilities to affect time. Time is nothing to mess with, let me tell you. One wrong move and you can wipe out your entire existence, and her abilities, even at her young age, were terrifyingly strong. She began to manipulate, making changes to time to suit her wants and needs, and the fissure that had been so well protected began to unravel. When she refused to stop using her powers to change time, it was decided that the only way to protect the world from the darkness clawing to get in was to neutralize her powers.

She had the assistance of a genie skilled in magic, who was able to show her how to use her powers. But what he was actually doing was seeping into her mind and heart and slowly making her his slave. At his request, she altered the timeline drastically, and Venger's children were no longer able to wield the blades that had been a part of them since they were born.

The girl was afraid, so she turned to a power she didn't understand. She made a deal with a being that was beyond time. This led to events that broke time and allowed darkness to touch this world.

Knowing that Venger would try to stop her, the girl, otherwise known as the Time Mage, shielded herself in a protective field of compressed time. Anyone who touched it would age thousands of years all at once. She had with her an artifact that now is known as the Stone of Time, and it was the source of her powers. If it could be destroyed, there was a chance that the timeline would restore itself, and the fissure could once again be closed. There were two obstacles standing in the way. The first being the protective field itself. To get close enough to destroy the Stone of Time, you would have to be unaffected by the aging effects of the spell. The second obstacle was worse. It was known that anyone who destroyed the Stone of Time, whether connected to time or not, as the stone shattered, they too would shatter through the temporal field and be lost."

"So, destroying the stone would also destroy the person who destroyed it, right?" asked Travis as he wrote out the details.

"In a way." The information officer admitted. "It doesn't mean you would die. It was more like you stopped existing altogether as if you had never existed at all. Lost in time." He paused for effect as they passed through the barrier into the middle ring. "All seemed lost."

"Why was she attacking Venger?" This time, it was Dalen who was asking the question.

"It was the Genie who was pulling the strings. Some say that he was after revenge. Some say that he had gone completely mad and was just trying to bring back the Chaos Dragon just to watch everything burn. No matter his reasoning, before the fissure erupted and the Chaos Dragon that destroyed the City of Dreams emerged from the darkness, five heroes appeared. They claimed to be from the future, and they said they believed they could save Venger from the horrific fate that killed her mother.

"Only someone of royal blood could defeat the Dragon, but Venger had no King. Dorn had been affected the same as his children, so a new line had to be created. A pact was made with two of the citizens. They would carry the Elemental Blades, and their bloodline would continue as the Royal line. They were declared King and Queen of Venger, and their first official act was to face the Chaos Dragon.

"Through the use of a wish, each of the heroes magically transferred much of their power to the King and Queen so that they would be formidable enough to defeat the Dragon of Darkness. It weakened the heroes greatly but empowered The King and Queen with great strength. It was only then they were powerful enough to pull from the Ether a fifth Elemental Blade, the Horn of the Unicorn, which had been fused with the Eye of the Dragon, and with it, they defeated the Dragon and resealed the fissure.

"The heroes who had traveled through time to empower our first king and queen no longer had their awesome powers, but their travels through time had disjointed them from it, and they were no longer affected by it. Granting them the ability

to pass through the field of compressed time unaffected, able
to get close to the Stone of Time. They faced the Time Mage
practically powerless, with only their wits and their weapons in
hand, and in the end, the Time Mage was defeated.

"The Heroes of Time had saved Venger twice and given
all of their power to do so. When they left, a shrine was built
for them in the exact spot where they had made their choice to
fight. Not as gods. Not as legendary warriors but as ordinary
men and women trying to save the world. Eventually, a garden
was built on those grounds, and statues were erected in
their honor.

"Another wish was made, creating an enchantment in the
Garden. Because the Saviors of the City gave their own power
and ability to the king and queen that day, the statues held
objects that rested in their hands. Each of these objects was
imbued with a spell designed to capture and hold the experience
and abilities offered as tribute by those paying homage to the
saviors. It has become a tradition for anyone who is born into
the royal family or married into it to come to the garden and
return the gift that was given. It became not just a tradition of
the royal family but to any and all who wished to give back to
these legendary people. They didn't just save Venger that day.
They saved the world. Pilgrims from all over the world travel
to the Saviors Garden on each anniversary and pray to the
statues. Offering their own experience and abilities, the way
someone might offer a prayer to the Saviors of Venger. For two
thousand years, the Saviors of the City, the Heroes of Time,
have been given this gift... Waiting for their return."

• • •

The team stood outside of the gate that led to the Saviors Garden. The information officer's retelling of the Saviors' actions had been informative, and now they understood who these people were and why this place was so important, but something was not yet said, and they felt that there was still another shoe to drop. They could all feel Travis's next question. They knew the answer before it was even asked. They felt it in their core, but the question still needed to be asked.

Travis took a deep breath and braced himself for what he knew was coming. "Why should you have known that we wanted to go to the Garden?"

The information officer looked bewildered. He stood there blinking at Travis and the rest of them for a moment and then turned to the gate and opened it. "Why don't you see for yourself," He smiled politely and ushered them inside. Travis hesitated. "I'm not sure I want to see what's in there."

Becky squeezed his hand. "Hey, I know it's weird, but this whole thing has been. I think I know what's wrong. You think that it's us, don't you?"

"Yep, that would be the concern."

"How could that possibly be? It was two thousand years ago." Becky nudged him with her shoulder. "Delusions of grandeur."

Travis looked at her, almost hurt. "No. It's not that." He nudged her back. "I just feel it in my bones, and as long as I don't go and look, I am neither right nor wrong."

"So, what you are saying is that it's like Schrödinger's statues?" Dalen added to the conversation, and those who got the reference chuckled. "Too many people have seen them at this point to be anything other than what they have been for a couple of thousand years. I think it's a little too late."

"Well, yeah," Travis responded. "I get that, but let's think about this for a moment. If we leave right now and just go home..."

"Then we never save David." Adam's tone was like stone. "I have no intention of retreating, especially from my own destiny." Adam looked around at everyone. "Look, I am all for being safe, but if Travis is right, and we walk away from this, and we are the saviors, then we walk away from this city that trusts us, and that has counted on us for centuries. I'm not going to do that."

"You can change your fate, but you cannot escape your destiny. It will find you, even on the path that you take to avoid it," added Brother Peace.

Travis realized that they were right, and there was no running from destiny, so he might as well go. Still, as Travis and Becky walked in, they stared at the stone path in front of them, both too nervous to look up. Brother Peace, on the other hand, looked up right away. He said nothing, closed his eyes, and smiled.

Adam threw both fists in the air and exulted, "These are the moments we live for!"

As Dalen walked in, he saw them immediately. The Garden was beautiful. It was littered with cherry trees that were in bloom, and white cherry blossoms were scattered everywhere along the way. The stone path led to a circle, and in the center of it were marble benches.

I had 'happened to be there' enjoying my afternoon tea. I had taken it under advisement that I should visit the garden that day. I was told that the trees were in blossom and if I went that evening, I would see something I would soon not forget.

On the edge of the circle facing inward were five statues. They were made of marble and inlaid with gold and celestium. Even from the distance that Dalen was at, there was no mistaking who the statues were of. Somehow, in their future, Dalen and his friends were going to go back in time and become the Saviors of Venger.

"You might as well look. They are damn good likenesses of us." Dalen teased, and Travis and Becky took a deep breath together and looked up. They were amazing, really. The statues looked almost lifelike and impossibly accurate.

On the outside edge of the circle, just before reaching the benches, a notice was posted. It explained that for anyone who wished to give an offering to one of the Saviors of Venger, all one needed to do was stand in the offering circle directly in front of the statue and proclaim what it was that they wished to give them.

Adam's and Peace's statues were the closest to the gate, with Adam's statue on the left and Peace's on the right. Past that were Dalen's on the left and Becky's on the right. At the far end of the circle, directly in the middle, was Travis's. Each statue stood on a disc of polished onyx, which was inlaid around the outer edge of the circle with celestium. In front of each statue was another circle made exactly the same; collectively, they guessed that these must be the offering circles the notice had mentioned.

"I have an idea," Travis offered. "I know we all want to run over and check out our statues, but we are a team. Let's do this together as a team."

Dalen could feel from his friend that he was stalling. Dalen felt concern and a little bit of fear from Travis. "Yeah, Travis is right." He gave a little nod to Travis. "This is big. Let's savor it together."

Everyone agreed. Adam was chosen to go first because his statue was closest to where they stood. They were so focused; they didn't even notice me.

Adam stood in front of his statue. A golden plaque was embedded in the disc upon which his statue was standing. It read, "Sir Adam the Pure Heart." He placed his hand over his heart and openly wept. When his friends asked if he was okay, he knelt down, touched the plaque, and then nodded.

Becky knelt beside him and read the plaque. "Oh, Adam. You are one of the strongest guys I know, and all of it comes from your heart." Adam knew that if he spoke at that moment, he would break down, so he chose to say nothing and nodded again.

Travis took a knee on the other side of his brother and put his arm around his shoulders. "I know you have dreamt of something like this. I know this is how you have always seen yourself. I have always been proud to call you my brother, and you have always had the heart of a hero." Travis touched the plaque and smiled at his brother with a heartfelt tear in his eye. "You earn this."

Brother Peace put his hand on Adam's other shoulder. "I thought I was brave the day we faced Mathias, but it was you who made the difference in that fight. I am lucky to be your friend, Sir Adam."

Dalen watched as each of them gave Adam their respect, and then, to his surprise, he watched as their respect moved through them and was harvested by the offering circle they were gathered in. *Are you seeing this?* Dalen thought to Master Ki telepathically.

Yes, and I can feel it, as well. This is one of my favorite moments in time, Ki responded.

Mine too, replied Dalen.

Both of them moved to the circle and placed a foot within it. "Hey, Adam," Dalen said. As Adam looked up, Dalen extended his magic to amplify his field of intent and said, "We all believe in you, and I am sure that everyone here would agree... Come on, guys, say it with me."

Together, they spoke as one: "These are the moments you live for."

As he suspected, the circle harvested all that they gave, and as it did, Dalen pointed it out to them. All of them looked down as small spectral lights were pulled from their bodies and were collected in the celestium. The light seeped from the circle and poured into the statue, moving up its body. Everyone's eyes followed the lights until they stopped on a longsword that rested in the outstretched hands of Adam's statue.

"Shut... Up." The words came from Adam's lips in a whisper, but it was heard by all. The mood switched gears quickly, and excitement hung damp in the air.

"Adam," Travis whispered dramatically.

"Yeah, Travis?" Adam rose slowly, unable to take his eyes off the sword in his statue's hand.

"Second Magic item, bro."

Adam giggled with delight, and more tears escaped his eyes. He edged closer to the statue until he was inches in front of it but stopped hesitantly just before he touched the sword. "Hey, guys?" He took a deep breath. "Can everyone take a couple of steps back? I have no idea what this is going to do."

"That's a good one," Travis noted as he backed up about fifteen feet. "Rule Number Twelve: Never test a new Magic item in a group."

Everyone nervously laughed but got up and moved out of range as Adam slowly reached up and gently took the longsword from the hands of the statue. Everyone held their breath, but nothing happened.

"Perhaps you have to draw it from its scabbard," suggested Master Ki.

Adam nodded, shrugged, and gripped the handle. "You guys ready?" he asked with excitement in his voice.

"Do it!" they cried.

Adam drew the sword from the scabbard to reveal a blade made of pure celestium. Drawing it from its scabbard created a resonating tone that was sustained long past expectation.

Everyone cheered for a moment, but then they all fell silent as light shot upward into the sky, engulfing Adam. They stared in awe at him as the gifts that had been left at his statue for two millennia found their target at long last.

Adam could see it all. For the last couple of thousand years, his statue has been visited by countless people, ranging from young girls who wished to find a man with a heart like his, to young men who would give homage to him when they wished to go forth in their lives and find adventure and excitement. An unknown number of kings and queens gave unto his statue the strength they found in truly being the best versions of themselves. Knights and nobles from all over the world had made pilgrimages to the Statue of the Pure Heart. Through the words that had been spoken over the years, Adam learned that the effigy of the Pure Heart had become a symbol to all Holy Knights for staying true to the cause, especially when times were hard, and they offered their time and experience in gratitude. Some made the pilgrimage every year. One knight who had faced incredible odds on an impossible task swore that Sir Adam appeared to him and saved the lives of him and his men. Over the years, a few had claimed the same, but this one gave quiet thanks to the Statue of Sir Adam and offered up a year of his experience as tribute.

Aside from the gift of the sword itself, upon drawing the blade, Adam's body became adorned with a shining set of steel armor, complete with celestium chainmail. The suit of armor bore the Great Seal of Venger on the right arm.

Adam's body burned as his muscles and nerves were taught skills he had never possessed. His body hardened and strengthened. When it was over, and the lights all faded, Adam was standing there in his full plate armor. He was out of breath, and his thoughts were wild as he felt his newfound strength.

"That. Was. Amazing!" Adam screamed as he began to maneuver his sword arm. It knew exactly what to do as if he had had a sword in his hand his whole life. He finished his flourish with the blade directly in front of him, pointing upright. He stared at it for only a moment and then looked past the blade to his friends, who were still in shock. "Oh yeah," Adam grinned mischievously. "I can sword fight."

The team exploded with cheers and applause as they rushed him. Adam barely had time to dismiss his armor and sheath his sword before they enveloped him in a jumping group hug.

"That was amazing, Bro!" Travis got everyone to stop jumping long enough to check Adam over. "Are you okay?"

"I'm good." Adam looked Travis in his eyes. "I swear." Adam tested out his arms like they were new. "I feel a lot stronger, but I'm still me."

"You are the same person you have always been," added Master Ki. "The only difference is that you were magically granted skills and abilities, as well as the knowledge of how to use them." This is why Grandmaster Truth sent me. As a water jinn, I am here to help you understand the ways water can change yet stay the same. When poured into a vessel, the shape will change to fit the container or even physically change due to temperature, but no matter the form it takes, it is still water. In this case, physical strength, dexterity, and even your fortitude have been enhanced, but who you are as a person will not be affected by these gifts. Except, of course, the part of you that now understands how much you really matter to your friends. When each of you shared your connection with Adam, he could feel the depth and breadth of those emotions. In that way, he will be forever changed." They all glanced at Adam, who confirmed what Master Ki was saying with a smile and a nod. "It was added to the statues as part of the gift to ensure that the saviors would always be able to strengthen their bond."

"Master Ki, what are the possible side effects?" asked Travis.

"Powers, abilities, skills, the knowledge to use them, greater chance of survival, and it's really cool?" Ki gave him a smirk and a nod and took a victory sip from a small teacup he had produced from thin air.

"Travis," Adam called out. "I am okay. Really." He smiled and looked at his brother. "I know you want to understand it before you try it, but you are forgetting Rule Sixteen."

Travis chuckled and said, "Yeah? What's that?"

"You're on an adventure." Then Adam slapped his brother on the arm. "Act like it." They both laughed, and Travis agreed to relax a little. He even agreed to the rule and added it to his notebook.

"I'll go next," offered Brother Peace. The statues were in a circle, and, moving from Adam's in a counterclockwise direction, he was next. He walked over to his statue. He stepped into the circle and aloud read the golden plaque that was there. "Master Peace."

Adam was directly behind him, and he put a foot into the circle. "You know what? I didn't really like Ben all that much. Until the end, and then he really stepped up. You almost died the other night. We haven't talked about it, but we all know how close that really was. Brother Peace, you seem like someone that I am proud to call my friend." A white ball of light was pulled from Adam and harvested by the ring around the circle in front of Peace's statue.

Becky put a foot in the circle and looked directly into Brother Peace's eyes. "Yesterday morning, I met the real Ben. It was the first day of his tomorrow. At that moment, I hoped and prayed that the next day would be even better." She took

Brother Peace's hand. "I had no idea that the next day for me would be three years for you." They both laughed. "I am so happy to see that my wish came true. I am so happy to see you as Brother Peace. I am tremendously proud of you." She took a deep breath and closed her eyes. "May our connection help you find your way to an even better tomorrow." Her gift was harvested from her and absorbed into the ring of celestium. She stepped back with a smile and a scrunch of her nose.

Travis stepped in and said, "Brother Peace, the very point that I can call you that is a demonstration of how far I can see you have come. I like who you are as a person, and I am glad you are here."

As the circle harvested the connection and respect from Travis, Dalen stepped into the circle. "Brother Peace, it is a shame we could not have trained together."

"It would have been an amazing experience. Even though we were trained by different masters for different goals, if we had gone in together as friends, we could have shared our teachings with each other. It would have been an amazing bonding experience," Peace said and gave Dalen a bow.

Dalen bowed back and then asked, "You learned different lessons?"

"I did," Peace replied. "You were there to learn the ways of magic. I went there to learn about healing. I mentioned the fact that Master Ki had left the day your training was over. My master was Master Love."

Dalen smiled and took a deep breath in. "You became a Healer of Light? That is phenomenal."

Brother Peace laughed, "Right? The boy who spends his days bringing torment to others finds his path when he dedicates himself to healing."

"It suits you," Dalen noted, and as he took Peace's forearm with his other arm, he embraced not only his old enemy but his new friend and brother. "I see no reason not to do it now. Teach me your ways, and I will teach you mine, and maybe together we will find something greater than both."

The gift moved from Dalen, and he and Peace watched as the light that had been harvested moved up the statue to its outstretched hands and into a rod made of celestium. At one end of the rod was another piece of celestium that formed a three-fingered dragon claw. The three points that extended out from the center were curved, bent up, and inward slightly as if they were meant to hold a sphere at the end of the rod.

"I know what this is," Peace's hushed whisper was filled with reverent shock. "Brother Truth, do you know this weapon? It is one of the rarest weapons from the Brotherhood of Light."

Dalen shook his head. "No, Brother, what is it?"

"It was mentioned to me on my second day at the Brotherhood. I chose to learn the weapon I chose, partly because of this legendary thing, and now it's staring at me."

"Right?" Dalen chuckled to himself. "I swear they can see the future because they always tell you the exact thing you need to know."

Peace nodded. "Right?"

"So, teach me, brother. What does it do?"

"It creates a ball of light at the end, where the claw
is, that is directly powered by the wielder's strength of faith.
The handle has a chain that can extend and retract, controlled
by a toggle on the hilt. It's like having a small sun of Divine
Light on a chain, a sun as powerful as your faith can make it."
Brother Peace said with deep respect.

"Rule One of Magic," Dalen commented with a smile like
he just got the joke. Dalen and Brother Peace said in unison,
"It's only as powerful as you believe it to be." Dalen swatted
Peace on the shoulder and then stepped back out of the circle.

With a slow but steady hand, Brother Peace reached
up and took the rod. He inspected it for a moment before he
chose to ignite it. As he did, a ball of light three times the
size of his fist burst from the rod. The celestium around the
circle glowed more brightly as a pillar of light erupted from
the entire perimeter. When it diminished a moment later, Peace
stood before them in robes much like Dalen's. Brothers Peace
and Truth each recognized them as the uniform and robes of
a full member of the Brotherhood of Light. The chest, back,
and left arm and leg were clad in white armor in recognition
of the guardian warrior that they are. The right side was
unarmored, reflecting their position as monks and philosophers.
His right arm was bare save for a set of three braids, each one
representing the connection to the mind, the body, and the soul
spheres. And the mark made of light that Venger had given him

shone brightly.

"This is going to take a second," Peace said as he stood there trembling.

"You feel it, too, right?" Adam's words were quiet but strong as he walked over to where Peace was standing. "Your system will adapt quickly. I got you," and Adam supported him by his shoulders.

"You do," Peace acknowledged. "I can feel it."

"Right?" replied Adam with a grin.

There was concern from the team, and Becky asked him if he was alright. He nodded, and then they both faced the rest of the team.

"The gifts you gave can be felt. I can..." Peace looked over to Adam and smiled. "We can both literally feel your love, respect, and trust." Adam nodded. "I freaking love you guys." Adam and Peace hugged it out for a moment and then were invigorated with a new luster. In unison, they asked, "Who's next?"

Following the counterclockwise position meant that Becky was next. She was excited to take her turn, but at the same time, she was a little apprehensive. Not of the magic or the new skills, but of finding out what her friends really thought of her. She knew it was silly, but she was nervous anyway. Especially about Travis, but she took a deep breath and walked up to her statue.

The armor she was wearing was light and form-fitting. It showed more of her figure than she was used to, but she was relieved to see that the statue was fully covered from the neck down. She saw two handles in the statue's hands, and she was tempted to touch them but decided to wait for everyone else first. When she looked down at the circle that she was standing in, she noticed the golden plaque that read, "Oubliette: The Shadow that Walks." She read it aloud to everyone else. Even Master Ki thought that the name was awesome.

Adam was first to stand in the circle with Becky. He smiled at her and took both her hands. "You are the smartest of all of us. You are the kindest. Yet, when you stood up to Mathias, it showed amazing power and courage. You are the total package." The gift was harvested, and, as it was, he squeezed her hands and gave her a wink. It made her smile, and with that, he nodded and stepped back.

Brother Peace offered the next go to Travis, but Travis shook his head. He looked at Becky and said he was going to go last, so Brother Peace shrugged and stepped into the circle.

"I will never forget that day, all those years ago." Peace smiled and gave her a bow of respect. "You could see my pain or joy and named it. I have only known one other who can do what you can do. She is the Master who trained me. I have thought of that moment many times in the last three years, and I know this as a truth: You have always been my first teacher on the path to my understanding. Thank you." She teared up and thanked him. Peace started to back up after the statue collected his gift and then added, "In a moment, you are going to actually 'know' what I mean."

Then Dalen stepped up to take his place next to Becky. They turned and faced each other. There was a small awkward moment because Dalen was trying to think of the exact words that he was going to say, and it left the both of them staring at each other longer than he intended. He knew how much power words had. Because of his training, he knew that this was an opportunity to honestly share a part of himself, and since Becky had been unsure and confused about how to know him now that he had changed, he felt that this was his opportunity to let her know that he was still the Dalen that she had always known.

"I want this to go right," Dalen shared nervously. "I know that I am different than I was, but this is a chance for you to know where I stand, and if what Adam and Peace say is true, and you will know the truth of what I share, then let me say this. From the day I went to the museum to get the Beads of Fire to this very day, part of how I think is because of you, I use you as the line from which I judge my actions. I am always wondering, 'Would Becky be proud of me for this?' or 'Dumb move — Becky would be so disappointed.' Your voice is often the voice of reason I hear when I don't know what to do, and even to this moment, it matters what you think of me."

Becky stood there dumbfounded. She stared at Dalen for a moment and then finally got her eyes to blink, and around the time she felt able to move her head, words began to come out, but they weren't yet complete sentences.

"I am what, now?" She gathered her thoughts together. "Why me?"

"Because I respect you and what you think matters to me." Dalen gave her a hug, and as he did, the statue took in his gift.

Travis waited for Dalen to move before stepping into the offering circle. He didn't have a drawn-out speech or long-winded words. He simply walked over to Becky and took her in his arms. She looked surprised for a moment, but then she smiled and nodded and held him in return.

"Becky," Travis said as he looked into her eyes, "I love you." And then he kissed her. A large light glowed as it moved from Travis into the circle as they finished their kiss. They both smiled at each other and then slowly remembered everyone was watching them. They both laughed nervously, but then Travis said, "Screw it! These are the moments we live for!" and kissed her again. Adam howled in agreement. Everyone joined in.

Dalen agreed. These were the moments they lived for. Sharing this with each other. This was worth fighting for, and Dalen felt in his heart how much he genuinely cared for these people. He began to nurture that feeling in his mind and heart and intended to really give it a go on the next one, which was Travis's, but first, it was time for Becky to receive her gifts.

Once Travis was a safe distance away, she reached up and took both handles in her hands. "They fit my hands perfectly." She looked them over carefully and then held them by the grips. She noticed a small toggle on the top of each. "Okay, I wonder what these do..." She flipped the toggles on both grips and as she did, black blades extended downward from the handles. Again, light filled the sky as all the years of skill and training were instilled in her. When it was over, she was standing in the circle wearing the same armor as the statue. It had no color, not even black. If it were black, it would be a color. No, this was more than that. The material absorbed all light, and her form was a hollow silhouette. They were called Midnight Blacks or, more simply, a shadow, a magical armor worn most often by skill masters and thieves. Once she pulled up the hood, her face darkened, and she became a walking shadow.

"Travis," she whispered, and then her knees gave out, and she dropped to the floor. Travis caught her before she hit the ground. He pulled back her hood to reveal her face. She was looking up at him, smiling. "You really do love me."

Travis helped her to her feet. "Well, duh." He gave her a hug. "You just downloaded two thousand years of skill and ability, and the only thing you want to talk about is that I love you?"

"It's the only thing that matters." She smiled. "All of this came from thousands of faceless people who died hundreds of years ago. That came from you."

As Travis helped Becky back to her feet, Adam reached out and gently placed his hand on hers. "That was twelve flavors of epic. I am so glad my brother chose you."

Travis and Becky walked together arm-in-arm. When they got to his circle, she spun him around and kissed him once more. A light just as bright as his was harvested by the celestium. She never said a word. She didn't have to. Travis felt it in her kiss, and now Becky knew that in a moment, Travis would have no question of her feelings for him.

Travis looked down and read the golden plaque. It read:

Lord Travis of Venger.

We will never forget your name.

He looked up at his statue. It stood straight with its head down in reverence. Its arms extended out far enough that its hands came together. It was wearing some sort of light armor and had a quiver on its back.

"I know what you did for me the night we faced Mathias," Peace began. "You saved my life and then protected me while I was unconscious. You are my hero, Travis. Do you hear me? You. Are. A. Hero. I can never repay you, but it is an honor to share with you how much I respect you." And with that, the celestium ring harvested Brother Peace's gift.

Adam stepped into the circle, grabbed Travis by the shoulders, and put his forehead and Travis's together. "You are my brother, and I love you. You are my counterpoint. You and your fantastic ability to understand the outcome of a situation is honestly the reason I am still alive. When I wanted to throw rocks at the beehive to knock it down and get the honey, it was you who cautioned me about getting them mad. It wasn't until three years later that we would find out I am deathly allergic to those little guys. You have always looked out for me, and I want you to know that I think I have a pretty amazing brother, and I would march into hell with you, Bro."

Dalen went last after the celestium had taken Travis's gift from Adam. He had been building up his intent, thinking about all of the things he wanted to say, and then formed them into a single thought. "I don't consider you the friend of my friend. You have always been my friend on your own merit, and I sincerely want to thank you for always being an amazing one." Dalen used the trick he had learned from me and pushed his words with Grey Speak when he spoke. The light was bright that left his body, and once Dalen stepped away from Travis, the harvested ball of energy moved upward to a bow that was resting in the hands of the statue.

"Travis gets to be a bow boy!" cried Adam and hooted loudly. "You always loved archery when you were in the scouts! This is going to be so much better than amazing!"

Travis took the bow from the statue, and it immediately instilled in him the gifts that had been granted.

Master Ki moved faster than Dalen had expected, moving toward Travis while the light was still engulfing him. Dalen opened the mind sphere and slowed time down to a crawl, slowed it to the point that the frames of reality barely flickered. That's where he found the jinn and Travis. "He has taken a hard truth," said Master Ki. "I brought him here so he could have time to process it before everyone saw him.

Dalen had been paying attention, and the jinn didn't have to say anything else. Dalen knew it. Travis knew it before they walked into the garden, and it was the exact reason he didn't want to look up at the statues. The words that Venger had said to Travis and how she said his sacrifice would be remembered. "He's the one who destroys the Time Stone. That means..."

"That means I am wiped from time completely, as if I never existed," Travis's words were acidic with anger, but

Dalen could tell it was just the brave face of fear. "I am going to cease to exist."

"No," Dalen said, trying to comfort his friend. "Not cease to exist. Removed from time. If you ceased to exist, how would anyone know to make a statue of you? Hmm?" Dalen literally grabbed Travis's face and made him return his gaze. "Master Ki here is a jinn who is removed from time."

Travis rose from his despair for a moment and looked at Master Ki, who smiled and waved hi. "What do you mean?"

"Every jinn I've met is no longer directly affected by time. He isn't actually here. He is a projection my mind is making so that we can understand the jinn in some way because he is incorporeal. The rings you are wearing give you the ability to perceive what I am perceiving because during my training I learned to see him, but he is just a shared vision." Dalen's words were strong and confident, and he was getting through to him. "The Jinn that was connected to the Beads of Fire could only be seen by the person who used the Beads. Those Beads were in the treasure room for centuries before they were found, but I did find her, and we will find you."

"Find me? What are you talking about?" Travis was no longer asking questions because of fear, but now he was asking because of hope.

"If I can find a jinn who was locked away for thousands of years in our little town, I don't care what this does to you. I will find you."

"Do you mean it?"

"I do."

"Promise?"

"Promise," Dalen assured him. "And this time, I know a jinn that can see all of time, and by then, we will have learned time travel, too. I promise we will do everything in our power to find you and look," Dalen pointed to Travis's statue. "It works."

Then Travis did something that neither Ki nor Dalen was expecting. He said, "Okay." He paused for a moment, trying to settle things in his mind. "Okay. I can do this. It saves all of Venger, right? And it saves Becky and all of them?" Travis looked to Master Ki for his answer.

Ki nodded, and with great respect, he added, "You save the whole world."

"You do a lot more than that." I had been witnessing the entire event. Jinn don't have a market on slowing and stepping into time; we, Grey, are also full of tricks. "You save Venger and this whole world. The world you came from and countless more. Millions. Billions of lives saved, and everything you see here in the present is due in part to your choice."

"Travis, may I introduce Will of Grey? He is a friend," Dalen said with a nod.

Travis nodded hello but asked, "How do you know this?"

"I'm the one who wrote down the original myth. Don't let this baby face fool you — I'm a lot older than I seem."

"The myth says that whoever destroys the Time Stone shatters themselves through time and ceases to exist in it. That no one would remember him." Dalen remarked. "How is it that there is a statue of him, and people know who he is?"

I looked Dalen right in the eyes and said, "Because you keep your promise."

Dude? Dalen asked. He was talking in Grey Speak and was asking me if things turned out alright.

Dude, I responded in kind. I let him know that if we stayed on the timeline that existed presently, he would prevail, but then I took him by the arm and said, *Careful.* Dalen understood at that moment that time was in jeopardy, and before this was over, Dalen would have to make some difficult choices. Then I turned my attention back to Travis. "Every man will face death. It is one of the things that binds them and gives them common ground. You face something greater. This is greater than you can imagine, and the lives of millions and the fate of worlds will come down to a single choice. But know this, Lord Travis of Venger: there is no one in this world I would rather have made that choice than you. You are the only one who could have made that choice, and it's the reason you do. You save everyone at the cost of everything."

Travis nodded, and a tear fell from his eyes, but he got up. "Truly small price to pay."

"Well said," I added encouragingly. "Someday, I will tell your story," I promised him, and before I went to sit back down, I remarked, "I also have it on good authority that you will be watched over and protected by the God of Time." And then

I faded out of their time and moved back to my place on the bench.

He wiped away the tears and said he was good. Both Ki and Dalen telepathically mentioned to each other how impressive his resolve was. Then, just before they reentered time, Travis added, "Do me a favor."

Dalen bowed to Travis. "Anything."

"Don't tell them," He requested. "It will only bring them sadness, and it will ruin this entire adventure for Adam, and I want to enjoy what time I have with Becky. She loves me, Dalen. Don't fill our last days with the pain of a loss that hasn't yet happened."

"I promise." Dalen understood and knew he was right.

Master Ki shrugged and added, "At least you don't have to worry about the odds on everything else." Travis looked at Master Ki with a hint of confusion on his face. "You know you will survive until then."

Travis smiled, "That's a very good point."

Master Ki gave him a pat on the shoulder, "Thought that would get you smiling. Alright, I am going to let go and let time move again. Dalen, you should do the same."

Dalen moved back to where he had been before and let go of time, and it began to move at its normal speed. Travis was now wearing beautifully crafted white leather armor, the details in all of the buckles shining with the brilliant glow of celestium. On his back, he had a matching quiver that was filled with a multitude of arrows, each with a different fletching. He still looked shaken, but so had everyone else, so it wasn't questioned by anyone other than Becky, who had been the first to reach him.

"You, okay?" she asked.

"It's just big." Travis hugged her and gave her a kiss. And to his credit, when he looked her in the eyes, she could only see joy. "I felt it. I know. You don't have to say it. I know." She hugged him again, but before she could say anything else, Adam and Peace joined the huddle with Dalen shortly following.

Master Ki watched from a distance. He glanced over at me and telepathically said, *That was a nice thing you did. Most of the time, your kind stays out of it. I love that you don't.*

Some stories are worth telling, I said, and then both Ki and I turned our attention to Dalen.

It was Dalen's turn, and, for the first time in a long while, he felt nervous. He took a deep breath and cleared his mind. He knew that he wanted to step into this without expectation.

This time, it was Becky who stepped in first. "I was right. You are no longer that seventeen-year-old kid I once knew. You have years of training and understanding, and for all of those reasons, you have changed, but there are things that will never change about you, Dalen Pax. I don't care what shape you take, whether it's a boy who was bullied, or a sorcerer, or even..." She looked down and read the golden plaque at their feet. It gave her pause. "Fair enough," she added with a smile.

It read:

Dalen Pax

The Reality Bender

Master of Time

"Or even that." She looked past his eyes and into his soul. She smiled when she found what she was looking for. "You will always be Dalen in your core, and that is the part of you that is amazing."

"Thank you. That means a lot." Dalen squeezed both her hands, and as the ring harvested her gift, he let her go and allowed her to step back.

Adam landed in the circle with both feet. "You have given me the greatest gift I could have imagined. You are truly the Fulfiller of Wishes, Dalen Pax. I thank you." His light moved from him and was collected by the celestium before making its way to the statue.

Brother Peace stepped into the circle. He smiled at Dalen. "Brother Truth," he gave Dalen the formal bow of their Brotherhood. He did it with intent and used the skills that he had been taught to saturate his actions with thought and feeling. As he did, his gift was harvested. It was all that was required for the statue to accept his gift. In moments, Dalen would understand completely the meaning behind his bow.

When Peace stepped out, Travis stepped in. "Dalen, I want you to know that I chose my own path, and none of this is on you." He looked around at the garden for a moment, but his gaze landed on Becky. They shared something for a moment, and he brought his attention back to Dalen. "If it weren't for you, I would have never had this adventure with my brother, and I may never have told Becky how I feel about her. You have brought so much amazing, fantastic gloriousness to our lives, and there is no way that we can ever thank you." Everyone gave a hoot or a cheer. "We all know it's dangerous and this world is not safe, but we are in this together, and together, nothing can stop us." Again, they cheered, but while the others continued to cheer, he grabbed Dalen by the arms and brought him in close so that he could hear Travis's whisper, "And if one of us should fall, it is not on your shoulders. My gift to you is that truth. We know what we signed up for." It wasn't until then that the gift was taken by the statue. Dalen nodded and thanked him, then gave him a hug. After a moment, he slapped him on the back a couple of times and let him go.

"Alright..." Dalen said to his team, "Let's see what's in store for me."

He reached up and felt something in the palm of one of the statue's hands. It felt like a small pebble. He grabbed it and then opened his hand to see what it was. It was a small white marble, and Dalen was sure that he had seen it at the museum the night he had stolen the Beads of Fire.

A flash of thousands of people coming to this spot for thousands of years happened all at once. Dalen only had a moment to take a breath before it flashed again. But this one was too much. He activated the mind sphere, slowing down time until it seemed to stand still. Within the quantum space between the frames, he could breathe. As the flash hit him again, the frames of reality splintered and fragmented, creating infinite possibilities in time. The garden seemed to fracture and break apart the way that glass shatters, hitting a stone floor. Dalen focused himself: mind, body, and soul. He had the feeling that if he took a step, he could move through time the way that one would traverse a room. But in this case, the room itself was time, static and unmoving. He, on the other hand, was fluid and could move backward and forward in it as one would move forward or back in a room. He began to wonder what would happen if he moved in other ways, such as left or right. He attempted it, allowing his mind to wander into one of the shattered fragments of garden, and the world began to change. Subtle things were noticeably different, like the stage of growth on the cherry blossom trees, and he was no longer sure if he was looking at the savior's garden that he knew or the same sacred location but in a different reality.

"Don't fry your brain on the left and right, or you'll have nothing left for the up and down." Dalen recognized the Fire Jinn's voice instantly. "Or an inverted arcing loop with a twist, for that matter."

That is as far as she got before Dalen wrapped her in a hug. "I thought I wasn't going to see you again until the Fountain of Truth."

"This is a vision state. I am only kind of here." She looked around for a moment. They were in the garden, but frozen within the very frames of reality that made it up. Dalen's hold on this frame was strong, so time continued to seem as if it were standing still.

"It's good to see you. I wasn't sure how I was going to see you without the Beads of Fire when I got to the Fountain of Truth. I was hoping that the fountain itself, or maybe something like the Omni Stone I had at the Brotherhood of Light, would allow it?"

"The truth of the matter is, ever since you collected the Omni Stone and added it to your silver figure, you have been able to connect to any of the elements."

"Then why haven't I seen you?"

The Fire Jinn lovingly patted Dalen's cheek. "When we met, you were about to go through a massive change, one that would destroy who you were before to make room for who was to be. Because of this, your window of perception required the Element of Fire to help you through it."

Dalen felt like this was old times. Her way of speaking seemed so fitting to the way his mind worked. "I follow. What am I missing?"

"You are now going through a change. Your form is changing, and your shape is changing, but like you explained to Becky, even if your form changes, who you are, in essence, is still you."

Dalen followed her line of thought. "The Element of Water."

"Exactly." Her fire flared up, and it burned brightly. "That is why Master Ki is with you now."

Dalen gave himself a very well-deserved face-palm. He laughed as he remembered that Master Truth had once said that a face-palm is the true stance of the enlightened. Then he quickly looked up with concern as a new thought entered his mind. "Then why are you here now?"

She gave him the same nonchalant look she gave him the day that she explained that she would possess him just to have some of Jax's cooking. She seemed to enjoy saying jarring things as if they were commonplace. "You know how you're at the edge of a change in form, and you are going to have to remember that you are still you? You have Ki for that."

"Yes," Dalen said. "But why are 'you' here?"

The Fire Jinn leaned in at Dalen close enough that he could feel the heat from her flames. Her tone changed as she stated it with certainty. "Because this one is going to be a big change that will alter you and how you see yourself forever. There is no point in arguing that. Master Ki is here to help you understand that the real change you are having has to do with you being able to accept truths about you that have always been there, whether you knew it or not. They have always been true, and that never changes. That is important, but more importantly, you are about to alter your truth about everything you think you know about yourself. The old version will be burned away, and a new perception and understanding will be left in its place."

It gave Dalen a moment of terror. "That bad, huh?"

"You'll be alright."

"Will I see you again?"

She mused at Dalen and gave him a nod. "You will see me again at the Fountain of Truth."

Dalen now understood why. When he got to the Fountain of Truth, he was going to go through another great transformation, and that is why he was going to see her again. "Anything else I should look out for?" he asked, almost afraid to hear the answer.

"You will be presented with an almost impossible challenge."

"Can you give me any advice on the challenge before me?"

"Mathias grasped power because he believed it made him strong. Sometimes, it is a greater act of strength to let power go."

"Will Ki be with me for this challenge?"

"No. He will no longer travel with you once you leave Venger, but there is another who seeks to help you and wants nothing more than for you to break the patterns that Mathias could not. She will help you become what you were meant to be."

"I am sure she is amazing, but I want you to know that I miss you, and I hope that you can see how hard I am trying."

"I see everything you do. I am with you as a part of your very soul, and I will never really leave you. Now, I have a favor to ask of you. I want you to ask yourself a question when the time comes."

"What's the question?"

"Just ask yourself, why is it that you have always been trained by jinn? Specifically, in Jinn Magic?"

Before he could answer, she was gone, and Dalen found himself alone in the frames of time. All he could see were the stars, and his friends faces encircling him. It took him a minute to realize that he was lying on the ground and was looking up at them. He felt an odd sensation all over his body that was akin to being submerged in pudding. He wiped his face with his hands, and as he did, he noticed that embedded in each of his palms was a stone made of celestium that gave off a soft white glow.

"I have stones in my hands like a jinn," Dalen observed in bewilderment.

"Yeah..." commented Becky wryly. "They match the ones in your face."

Without thinking about the spell, Dalen manifested a mirror into his hands and held it in front of him. Becky was right. In the mirror, Dalen could see three stones made of white celestium: one on the top of his head, one over his third eye, and another over his throat. As he let go of the mirror, he dismissed it as fast as he had created it. He ran his hand over his heart and then his solar plexus, feeling that there were stones there as well. He didn't bother to check the last two places he suspected that stones would be. He knew what he would find.

"I am going to need some space, guys." Everyone nodded and backed up, but Dalen hung on to Master Ki and began to talk to him with telepathy. *I was supposed to ask myself something.*

What was your answer? Ki asked, smiling.

Did you know this thing was going to turn me into a jinn?

Master Ki helped him to his feet. *No, Brother Truth. The simple truth has always been directly in front of you. You were trained by us because you have always been one of us.*

I have?

All of a sudden, everything fell into place.

David and I, that's where we came from before we were pulled to Earth. We are lost, jinn.

Yes. Master Ki gave Dalen a bow.

Are you family?

We are connected.

Is that why you trained me? Because we are connected?

Absolutely. Ki bowed again and then asked one more question. *Do you know what this changes?*

Dalen suddenly got the point of why Ki was there. *Absolutely nothing. Because no matter what form I take, I am still me.*

Correct. Now that you understand that truth, a new question emerges.

Dalen thought about it for a moment. *What is that, Master Ki?*

What does it mean to be a jinn?

It was a good question, and Dalen knew he would have to learn the answer to that question the same way he learned everything else: with time and effort.

I get the idea that I have been a jinn since my earliest memories, so the core of who I am hasn't changed, but who I am... That has changed forever. Dalen took Master Ki's hand in his as a sign of respect. *Thank you for being there for me and helping me see that truth, but this coin has two sides, and I have a lot of thinking to do before I am going to be okay with all of this.*

He rejoined his friends and, after a few moments and a bunch of questions that he didn't completely have answers to, Adam saw Dalen's discomfort and chose to help change the subject. "You know what? I think it's awesome! Right?" Everyone couldn't help but agree. "All of us. We got magic gear." Once again, the team agreed with him as he raised their spirits. "Four words... Saviors of the City." He put in his hand. "Who's with me?"

One by one, they put their hands in. With each one, their excitement grew. Dalen was the last to put his hand in as their excitement level reached that of warriors on the field of battle, ready to do combat.

Adam's smile was genuine and true. He looked around at each of them. "I love you guys. Now let's go get 'em!"

They all cheered and threw their hands in the air. They were ready for their adventure, so they decided to go to a place where Dalen felt they might be able to get some answers. I overheard where they were going and barely had enough time to beat them there, but I was sitting at the bar and enjoying my first drink as the Saviors of Venger walked into Dorn's.

5

OLD FRIENDS

Becky stepped into Dorn's, which was much larger inside than it seemed to be from the outside. She stopped immediately and laughed, "No." Without another word, she promptly walked right back out the door and closed it.

A moment later, Adam burst through the door excited. He looked around and then very loudly exclaimed, "No way!" He then poked his head outside, turned his head left and right, checking the size of the building, and then brought it back in very slowly. "Okay, yeah. That is weird." He alternated his view from just inside the door to just outside and back again a couple more times before he went all the way in, followed by Becky and Travis together.

They were holding hands, and as Travis walked in, he looked at her. They held a small conversation with just facial expressions and smiles. Finally, Becky remembered that there was someone else in the world and blurted aloud to Adam, "Right?"

They were followed by Brother Peace, Master Ki, and Dalen, who was himself a member of the Brotherhood of Light known by the name Brother Truth. It was amusing to me to watch them all come in. I knew there was a joke in there somewhere. "Three monks from the Brotherhood of Light walk into Dorn's with an archer who has a noble knight on one side of him and a Shadow Thief on the other..." I worked out a quick joke with a strong punchline and turned to tell it to Dorn, who had been right next to me at the bar, but I found myself telling one of my better jokes to nothing but an empty space. Dorn had moved and was well on his way to meet up with Dalen and his team.

"Welcome back, Dalen. I see you brought your friends this time." Dorn's tone was that of excitement. "We've been expecting you."

"You have?" asked Dalen.

"Five beams of light emanate from the Saviors Garden on the eve of the festival honoring the Saviors of Venger? Yeah. We had a fairly good guess it was you. The whole city does. No doubt you will be expected at the castle in the morning, but that is something for tomorrow. Instead, let's be here." He looked around at all of them. "It's been a long time since I have seen you. I have missed you, my friends."

"This is the guy I was telling you about. Owner and operator of all you see. May I introduce you to Dorn?" Dalen said with a courteous gesture towards their host.

Dorn was closest to Adam and took him by the forearm and looked him in the eye. "Sir Adam, my tavern is now a brighter place because your spirit is in it." Dorn gave him a strong, manly hug and then said, "And you are right — these are the moments that we live for."

"This may be the coolest moment of my life." Adam was sincere in his compliment. It wasn't just something to say. He meant it, and he could see that Dorn took it as such.

"When I first met you two," Dorn walked up to Travis and Becky, "You two had already gone through a lot. You had seen some stuff, and together, your bond had really grown." Dorn paused for a moment, intently looking at them. "Do you understand what I am saying?" They both nodded. "I don't just ask if you comprehend, but do you glean from my words all that I am trying to share with you?"

Both gave it thought, but it was Travis who remembered his conversation with Master Ki earlier and then began to grasp the gravity of what Dorn was saying. "The good thing is that up until the first time you meet us, neither of us has to worry about dying. Both Becky and I live at least that long." It was at that moment Dorn knew that Travis knew his fate. Dorn gave him a sympathetic grin and nodded.

Becky followed suit with, "And that when you meet us, even though it may be hard, Travis and I will have grown more connected." She squeezed Travis's hand as she spoke. "What an amazing gift. Thank you. That makes me very happy." She let go of Travis and gave Dorn a big hug. Dorn looked up at Travis, who shook his head. It was at that moment that Dorn knew that Becky hadn't been told.

Dorn let Becky step back and then gave Travis a hug. He whispered something in his ear, and Travis nodded, but what was said is unknown. Even to me. No one except those two knew what was said, and neither of them ever mentioned it again.

Dorn addressed the monks of the Brotherhood one by one. "Master Peace."

"I am not a master yet. Please, call me Brother Peace."

"Your wisdom has saved our world more than once. I know you don't know yet what I speak. You didn't know then either; anyone can recite what they have been taught; it is expected of children, but when someone can speak from their soul, in a moment of crisis, when all seems lost — that is a Master." Dorn then shook Peace's forearm, much as he had with Adam. "You may not see it in yourself yet, but I have witnessed it firsthand, and I know what lies within you."

"Thank you." Peace slid his hand back slowly, and Dorn matched his movements. As their palms crossed, they bent their fingers so that they would catch one another. As they did, they both closed their fists, creating a spiral. Bending their wrists, they brought their grip in tighter and, with their free hands, placed their open palms, fingers pointing upwards, up against their joined fists, and bowed.

Both channeled their energies into their hands, and it created an effect that was felt by the room. For a moment,

Dalen and his friends stopped and felt their connection as a wave of peace and respect washed over everyone.

"Dalen. My man." Dorn said affably as he moved to Dalen and shook his forearm.

"Not so much these days," Dalen stated with an awkward grin.

Dorn smiled and looked at Dalen's stones. "Ah, yes. The whole 'you're a jinn' business. Well, being human doesn't make the man, now does it? I mean, look at me. I'm not human, and I consider myself a decent enough fellow."

"Thank you, Dorn. I needed a perspective tilt." Dalen laughed for the first time since the Garden. Dalen used Grey Speak so he could send multiple fields of intent at once. *It's good to be home.*

Dorn was used to Grey Speak and was able to glean all of Dalen's intent. "I absolutely have rooms for all of you, and the kitchen never closes. I'll get you some tea." He snapped his fingers, and one of the waiters made his way over to them. "My son Jed will get you to a table." Dorn was still looking at Dalen's stones with some interest. Dalen asked if there was anything wrong, and it pulled Dorn from whatever thought he had been lost in. "I don't mean to stare, but it is quite rare to see jinn stones in this state. They are quite beautiful."

"The stones themselves will change to reveal the nature of the jinn," explained Master Ki. "When a jinn first gets them, they are pure and without intent. It is rare for a jinn to have them for long at all before the stones change, seeing them in this pure form is practically unheard of."

"Wait, so my stones will change to reflect who I am?" asked Dalen, showing no sign of trying to hide his amusement.

"Like bear bellies and pony butts," Dorn chuffed as he went to get Dalen some tea, leaving Dalen in a slight state of confusion.

It was confusing for me, too, at first. Luckily for me, as a Grey Bard, I have the ability to magically obtain the details of a story that I have only heard a part of. So, from my spot at the bar, I cast the spell that allowed me to get the reference. It was a myth from the world that Dalen had lived in, which involved animals that produced symbols on their bodies once they found their purpose.

Jed was leading them to one of the larger booths that had enough room to fit their whole team twice. The booth was circular, with three-quarters of the circle's circumference as seating. The seat was a circular bench; the walls were upholstered as back cushions made of purple velvet that went up to the ceiling. The other quarter of the circle was open to the tavern and allowed for a server to get close to the table to take and serve their order. Once everyone was seated, a small round port opened up in the center of the floor, and a post rose from it that was topped with a crystal cone. When it had risen to about the height of a table, Jed reached over and touched it. As he did, it came to a halt. Then, with a simple gesture, Jed twisted the cone a quarter turn to the right, and a table expanded from the post, creating a large round surface in the center of the booth with a crystal cone centerpiece.

"If you turn it one more place to the right, it will create a field of silence so that you can talk freely," Jed added. "Would any of you like anything to drink?"

Travis shrugged with no reason to argue. "Why not? What is the legal drinking age?"

Dorn had arrived with Dalen's tea, and he mused at the question. "Trying to base whether or not you can drink with only age as the deciding factor is careless. I know elves that are well into their second hundred years who are too childish to drink. You have fought a magic wielder using just your bare hands and survived. You have jumped worlds and been given the truth of your destiny; you are the people who saved the world, this city, my wife, and children. I think you have earned the right. Order what you wish. I can get you anything you want."

"He's not kidding." Dalen grew ever more excited. "Magic bar. They can do anything here."

Dorn was pouring some tea for Peace, chuckled to himself, and threw out, "Also, lunch is on the house today. Order anything you can imagine."

"I'll have an ale," piped up Adam. "And whatever the Traveler Special is. I'll have one of those."

"I'll take an ale as well," said Travis reflexively. Then he read the blackboard that had the specials. "Grilled vegetables, roasted potatoes, whole chicken? Yeah. Make that a 'traveler special' for me too."

"I want a double cheeseburger with seasoned fries." Peace thought for a moment. "And some deep-fried chicken strips."

Dalen laughed. "After spending nearly as much time at the temple as you, that's almost exactly what I ordered, except I got onion rings." Dalen's mouth began to water as he thought about them. "I want to get a plate of onion rings for the table, please."

"What do you want to get for yourself?" asked Jed.

Dalen looked over to Master Ki. "Do I still eat?"

"You can if you choose to," Ki explained. "If you choose not to, you don't, but you are still corporeal and should stay connected to it. I think it would be a good idea to live as much of your life as Dalen as you can until a time comes when you no longer wish to connect to the corporeal world. I found that certain objects that meant something to me helped keep my connection strong."

"Like all those objects in the museum that belonged to the Fire Jinn?" Dalen asked as he looked over the menu.

Master Ki chuckled to himself and then nodded. "Exactly like those."

Dalen looked up from the menu. He could feel the mirth coming off of Master Ki. "What? Did I say something funny?"

"Yes, and a resounding no." Master Ki took a sip of the tea that Dorn had poured for him. "It's not what you said —

it's what you catch onto. You are amazingly fast at learning
some things, yet sometimes the truth is staring at you, and you
have no idea that it's even there." He rolled his eyes and took
another sip of his tea. "You remind me of me when I first found
out I was a jinn."

"I do? What were you like?" Dalen asked.

"A lot like you..." He couldn't go on because he fell into
a giggle fit. When he caught his breath, he gave his attention
back to Dorn and offered him the compliment, "This is really
good tea," and continued to laugh.

Dorn just laid his face in one hand and shook his
head. "I think he's done. Dalen, what would you like to
have tonight?"

Dalen was baffled by the entire sequence that had just
taken place, and at the same time, he was hit with a strong
sense of 'déjà vu,' so he had to refocus and get his mind back
on food before he could answer the question. He read the
specials and decided that he would choose the one that the
brothers had not, which was lamb skewers with rice.

"I would like to have a traditional elven meal. I have no
idea what that is, but I want to try something elven." Becky
was always the one to think outside the box.

"Excellent choice. I have a few questions," Jed was
writing down notes on a small pad of paper he pulled from his
apron. "First, I should mention that there are many different
kinds of elves, and each has their own unique cuisine. My
guess is that you are referring to the local clans of elves, the

wood elves, which, for many humans, are the most commonly recognized breed of elf."

"You know, you're right. I guess that would be like asking if I wanted human food." Jed gave her a kind smile and a sympathetic nod. "So, yes, when I picture the kind of elves I meant, I can see them living in an enchanted woods with nature and that kind of thing. Yeah, let's do the style of the wood elves."

Jed made a quick note on his pad. "Question one: Are you aware that elven cuisine is primarily vegetarian with a few exceptions?"

"No, I didn't, but that matters little. I just wish to try an elven dish." She was excited in a way that most of them had never seen before.

Jed continued with his questions. "Question two: Being that wood elf cuisine is highly toxic to humans, have you taken the supplements that will allow you to eat your meal and not trip your ever-living mind out?"

Everybody gasped or laughed.

"I'm sorry. What now?" Becky asked.

"I'll take that as a no," Jed replied and wrote down a couple of things on his order form. "I know what to bring you. I will also bring you the supplements with your drink. I suggest you take them right away." Becky stared at him blankly. "Or not. That's fun, too."

Dorn finished getting Master Ki a new cup of tea and helped him refocus before he faced and addressed the entire team, "I will give you a bit of time to eat and rest. I am sure you have already had a full day, and even though the night is just settling in when you are finished, I would like a chance to talk with you, if you don't mind."

"Thank you, Dorn." Dalen's words were filled with relief. "We came here to talk to you anyway. I feel there is a lot to talk about."

"There is. You want to know how to get to the Fountain of Truth. I know where and when you find it." Everyone looked back and forth at each other. "I'll be back in a while, and we will talk about the whole thing. And then we have to talk about tomorrow." He gave a small bow and let them be.

To most of the team's surprise, by the time Dorn had finished, Jed was magically back with their food and drinks. Becky also received an Elven wine and a small plate that had two small tablets that were bluish-green. She popped them in her mouth and then took a sip of her wine. The wine was unlike anything she had ever tasted, and she literally moaned with enjoyment. It was the most wonderful beverage she had ever consumed. It was light but sophisticated, with a taste of honey.

"Oh my god, this may be the most delicate, refined sip of anything I have ever had." She teared up a little. "Elven wine is everything I imagined it could be."

The meal continued in that style. One of the glorious things about Dorn's is his daughter, Jax. She is the chef in the kitchen, and her ability to cook is legendary. Today was no exception. Each bite they took forced groans of delicious joy and moans of bliss from their mouths, leaving them wondering how they could ever eat anywhere else, ever again.

After their meal, Dorn joined them at the table. He turned the crystal cone as he sat, and it began to produce a light that filled and extended past the booth and into the rest of the tavern, completing the last quarter of the circle as well. The white noise of the tavern fell silent, and the real conversation began.

"How can I be of service?" Dorn asked with sincerity. "I know that most of you have just met me but know that I am in great debt to all of you, so I am here to help in any way that I can. If you're still having doubts about trusting me, just look to your friend Dalen and your guide, Master Ki. They know me well."

His words were heartfelt, and the team could tell that he meant what he said. They quickly glanced at each other to see if any of them had an objection, and then all eyes fell on Dalen and Ki.

Dalen knew their questions. He could hear their thoughts like whispers in his mind. He had grown accustomed to how the jinn had been speaking into his own mind, and he had even learned basic telepathy as a skill. He often spoke to Master Ki using this skill, but this was different and new. Somehow, when the saviors shared their connection with one another, they created pathways to each other. Dalen opened his mind and saw past the physical and corporeal world. Wisps of light now tethered them together, and their thoughts danced along those connective wisps of light like a spider on its web.

Dalen focused his thoughts and was careful to be gentle with their minds. The web was not strong, and this was going to be new to his friends, so with a whisper, he telepathically spoke to them directly.

I trust him. Their eyes widened, and they leaned away slightly. Dalen felt their fear rise. He gave a small wave. *It's ok. It's me.* Their fear subsided, and Dalen could feel them begin to understand but didn't want to push them, so instead, he spoke: "Yeah. That was me. We can play with that later. Right now, I want you to understand that Dorn is one of the people I know I can trust, and I am asking you to trust me."

"I was already on board," Adam chimed in. "I have complete faith in you, Dalen. If you say he's family, he's family."

Travis nodded along with Brother Peace.

"Dorn?" Becky asked. "Why are you in debt to us?"

Dorn leaned back in his chair, and his demeanor softened. "Because, my dear friend, you saved what was most precious to me."

"We did?" she petitioned.

Dorn reached out and gave Becky's hand a small squeeze. "Yes, both my wife and I are forever in your debt because of your deeds."

Becky blushed. She placed her other hand over Dorn's. "Will we get a chance to meet her as well?"

"You met her earlier today. She is the woman you saw at the Great Seal." Dorn gave her hand a final squeeze, then sat back and gave her a wink. "You will get a chance to talk with her again tomorrow. She'll be at the ceremony."

Adam was holding up a finger. "Will Mordecai be there? I have a message for him."

"The Royal Family will be there. That means that Princess Joanna will be there." Dorn gave Adam a thumbs up. "That's good news for you. Joanna has not been seen in public without her guardian since before she could walk."

"Sweet!" Adam cried as he gave a small fist pump.

Each of them had a question, so they began to hold up their fingers. They referred to it as taking initiative. They had been using this method for some time and found it more productive than talking over each other.

Dalen was number one, so he went first. "We need to find the Fountain of Truth. We have a friend who is ill, and our hope is that a cure can be found by divining it from the Fountain. I brought them here because I believe that if there is anyone who knows how to get to the Fountain of Truth, it is you. If not you, then one of the bards or storytellers that you hire would."

Dorn looked at Adam, who was number two, but all he said was, "Dalen just covered it," and he put his hand down.

Travis had his hand up next, and Dorn directed his attention to him.

"Is there anything you can tell us about what is to come that would benefit us yet not mess up the timeline?"

Dorn considered Travis's question for a moment. He mumbled something to himself and then nodded in agreement. Then he took a deep breath and let it out slowly. "Travis, to get to where the Fountain is, you will first go through another adventure or two. While on those adventures, remember this...." He took a moment and chose his words carefully. "Look for the stone that breathes. An immovable object can only be affected by an unstoppable force, so relent and let the tears of your defeat be the thing that helps you find victory. Sometimes, you just have to step into the fire. Set down the ego, be humble, and remember whose home you are in." Dorn paused for a moment while a grin began to creep onto his face from the corners of his mouth. "Don't listen to the lies; you can have them both."

Travis had pulled out his notebook and was transcribing everything that Dorn said. "Thank you. Thank you very much."

"You understood all that?" asked Brother Peace, impressed that someone could get much understanding from such riddles.

"No, not a bit of it, but I know that he just saved our lives. Not once, but five times." Everyone understood what Travis meant, and they all pictured possibilities where the difference between failure and victory would be found in the clues of Dorn's words.

"You're welcome," Dorn said with an impish smile and a small bow.

"Dalen, I know the location and exact moments in time
when you find and use the Fountain of Truth. I was there for
one of them, and you divulged to me that it was the second
time you had been there. The first had been quick, and you were
not in the position to ask the question you had intended, thus
the second trip." Everyone smiled, and Travis and Adam high-
fived. Dorn shrugged his shoulders and added, "Where is simple?
The tricky part is when."

Dalen knew the answer. He felt it in his core. He could
feel the stones that now resided along each of his Chakras
resonating with the truth of it. It was as real to him as
his name.

Dalen smiled and shook his head. "Exactly two thousand
years ago tomorrow. The day we save Venger is the day we
find the Fountain of Truth." It began to fall into place, and
he saw it laid out in front of him. "That's why we go back in
time in the first place. The fountain was our initial goal, but
in the end, we show up exactly at the moment Venger needs
us." It was coming faster now — too fast to explain. He saw
flashes of moments in time, of a girl in a red dress. He didn't
know who she was, but she smiled at him and said it was a
pleasure to meet him. Then the image changed, and he saw a
dead tree that was filled with sadness and a cave that was
filled with fear. Inside that cave, there was a place where time
had solidified into a large pillar of stone that stretched from
the ceiling to the floor. He saw Lady Venger and Dorn. They
were standing with their backs to Dalen; they turned to look
at him, but before they could make the full turn, the image was
gone. Instead, he now stood on a large open plane. He only
had a moment to look around. It was a large grass field near

some cliffs, and beyond that was the sea. Then Dalen watched as something large and black began to dig its way out of the ground.

In the next moment, the world faded away, and Master Ki appeared in front of him as a being of pure water. His stones created light that rippled through his body as he moved.

Focus. Seeing the future can help, but don't let it cost you the present. Remember where you are. Ki's words helped Dalen and allowed him to refocus his mind. His vision realigned, and he could see everyone at the table again. Master Ki removed his hand from Dalen's shoulder and said, "Much better."

"We... uh, lost you there for a moment, buddy." Adam was waving his hand in front of Dalen. "Your eyes turned all white and metallic like your other stones, and they all lit up. It was pretty neat."

Dalen could sense they were worried about him. "Woo! Gave it a little too much gas." Adam laughed a little. "What number was it about not testing new magic in a group?"

This time, they all laughed.

"Twelve," answered Travis.

They had all watched Dalen drop into a trance and saw his eyes light up. It had been a little unnerving, but Dorn and Ki assured them that Dalen was fine. They were feeling nervous until Dalen began to crack jokes; it was all they needed to feel at ease again. They took a minute and really laughed. It was

cathartic for them. Too much had happened too quickly, and
they needed a good release.

"So," said Becky. The thinking portion of her brain had
kicked back in, and she was trying to solve the puzzle. "To get
to the fountain, we need to travel back in time. How do we
do that?"

"The Pillar of Time." As Dorn said it, the flash of
the stone pillar in the cave went through Dalen's mind again.
"There is a secret way to get to it safely, but to learn that
secret, you will have to obtain that knowledge from two
Oracles who live deep within the forests of the Woodland
Elves. You will have to earn the Elves' permission to travel in
their lands to reach the Oracles."

"I understand that this might be a silly question." Becky
had remarked this often in the past but rarely was the question
silly. "If what Dalen has suggested is true about you, do you
not know where the secret path to the Pillar of Time is?"

There was no pause in Dorn's answer as if he had
planned for her to ask all along. "I assure you if all you
required was that one piece of information, I would go out
of my way to tell it to you. It's on the Eastern side of
the mountain. But there is more that is required in your
journey, and there are some things that cannot be told, only
experienced. I am sure the rational part of your mind will simply
say that there is no cause to go through all of this if I can
just tell you the same things that the Oracles can. But..."
Dorn paused and let the anticipation come to a simmer. He
looked into Becky's eyes until he could see that she was truly
listening. "...will the people you'll have become by the time

that you get there ask the same questions you would today?"
and everyone leaned back like the question was slowly filling
the room.

"Okay," Brother Peace said finally, breaking the stunned
silence. "That was deep."

Travis nodded, "I am starting to understand how you
guys operate." Travis giggled to himself as he looked over his
notes. "No. We won't be the same people, nor will we ask the
exact same questions. So, what you're saying is that the people
who we will become once we complete the adventure to get
to the oracles will ask the right questions. That's why you're
sending us on the quest in the first place?"

"It's not just a matter of you asking the right question.
It is about how you perceive and receive the answer." Master
Ki stretched like a cat. "It goes both ways, and that doesn't
even begin to cover the Cave of Fears, which you will
have to figure out how to negotiate." Ki took a sip of tea.
"Just saying."

"Can you make us who we need to be?" Adam's question
created a stillness in the room. The question almost seemed
reasonable after everything they had just gone through.

"Sorry, my man. Magic is an immensely powerful thing,
and there is a reason that the only way that Ben could find
peace was through time. It's the same reason the statues
imbued skill and ability and the physical strength and dexterity
to use them, but they didn't make you brave or wise." Dorn
could see them putting the pieces together in their minds as he
was handing them to them. "When this world was created, there

was a single law that was created with it, even before the Rules of Magic.”

“Free will,” Dalen's voice came as a surprise. They were so focused on Dorn that when he spoke, it broke their concentration.

“What do you mean?” asked Travis.

“Dalen is correct.” Master Ki took a sip from his tea and then continued, “Magic can make you powerful, but it can't change who you are. You have to do that on your own by examining your perception of events, choosing how to manage things, and by the actions you do... or don't take. All of those choices will mold you, and, in the end, it is your free will that will dictate and govern your reality.”

Dalen face-palmed himself and slowly dragged his hand down his face. “I now understand why the first rule of magic is that your magic is only as powerful as you believe it is.”

“And it's why Adam could see the temple once he chose to make the Leap of Faith on his own,” added Master Ki.

“Okay,” Travis said. He had been writing in his book for the last few questions. “Let me get this straight. Tomorrow, there will be a big ceremony in our honor, during which we will meet the Royal Family of Venger and Venger herself. After that, we are going to take a journey to the Woodland realm to ask the Elves permission to travel through their lands so that we can find a couple of oracles and ask them the correct questions to give us the right knowledge to survive the secret passage to the Pillar of Time so that we can go back a couple of thousand years and save Venger — which is why there is a ceremony. Oh, and defeat a Time Mage after we grant all of the power that we just absorbed to the king and queen so that they can defeat a dragon and become the original bloodline of Venger. The bloodline responsible for maintaining the elemental balance with magical blades and protecting the world for all time?"

Dorn nodded. "Yup."

"Sounds like a plan." Travis held up his mug, and those at the table followed suit. "Here's to my friends, old and new." They all took a sip, but Travis was not done. "Today has been the greatest day of my life." Adam gave a woot. "May tomorrow be even better." This time, everyone cheered. "If we are to define our own destinies, then I say, may we be brave, may we find courage in the face of fear, and when the darkness surrounds us and the time comes to choose, may we remember that we are heroes. The Saviors of Venger. May we push back the darkness and always remember we are the light that we seek!"

They erupted into cheers. At that moment, they were ready for anything. They celebrated a while longer before Dorn gave each of them their own room for the evening. It was still early in the night, but they were exhausted. Becky gave Travis a small kiss goodnight before she went into her room and closed the door behind her. Adam had waited for them to say goodnight before grabbing his brother. They stayed up and talked, making guesses about what was to come. They talked for a few more hours before they finally fell asleep. Brother Peace and Master Ki joined Dalen for a meditation session before Peace went to his room. Master Ki did not require rest and said that he would stand guard for the evening.

Their final thought before they drifted off to sleep was of their friend David, who was still cursed, and they wished that he could be with them. They slept deeply and dreamt of adventure, but even in their wildest dreams, nothing could prepare them for all that was to come.

6

A MINDFUL CARRIAGE RIDE

Dalen only slept for a short time. It was closer to a deep meditation or trance, and it was an effort to maintain it. When he opened his eyes, Master Ki was standing near his bed watching him.

"Did you need something, Master Ki?" Dalen's question was in earnest, but he also wanted to know what Ki was doing, watching him sleep.

"You still struggle with that incorporeal thing from time to time." They both smirked. It had been an ongoing joke with them. "I wasn't here until you opened your eyes. I am only here while you perceive me, remember? It's your image of me that you see, not a physical body."

"Then I have a question for you." Dalen had pondered this previously and now seemed like as good a time as any. "How is it that you take a physical form that others can see? I completely comprehend my mind making you real, and thus it thinks it can see you and even touch you, but how is it that the others can see you, too?"

"The rings." Master Ki's hand liquefied and changed form, and as it resolidified, he was now holding a small teacup. He seemed pleased with his cup and smiled at it kindly before he took a sip from it. "As for your friends, look at the spell you cast upon them. Examine it closer in your mind."

Dalen closed his eyes and tried to remember the moment that he cast it. When the two circles had become one. As he found that exact moment in time, his mind relented to it. He was no longer in his room at Dorn's. He was in the moment that he cast the spell to create the rings. Dalen was amazed to see how clear of a picture he could bring up of the moment he had created the rings. Master Ki stood beside him and placed his hand on Dalen's shoulder. "Well done."

Dalen walked around the frozen image of himself casting the spell for the rings. "What am I looking at? I can see myself, so this can't be a memory."

"Jinn magic." You are looking at that moment from the eyes of the universe. From here, you can look at any moment. At first, you will only be able to see your own, but once you progress a bit further, you will be able to see any moment. For now, let us focus on this achievement. As you can see, you can look at this memory from an outside point of view but remember that you cannot change it."

"Is it forbidden?" Dalen wondered.

"Think more like you can't drink nine." Master Ki took a sip from his cup while Dalen tried to imagine it anyway. "You are looking at a static memory. A picture of a moment in time. Changing the image only changes the image and would have no real effect on the actual moment."

"I follow." Dalen focused on the spell itself. "What am I looking for?"

"What is the spell actually doing?" Inquired Master Ki, sounding like the teacher that Dalen had learned to listen to.

Dalen examined each piece of the spell craft as it floated in front of him. "The wearer of the ring is imbued with the sight." Dalen looked at the waves of energy that created the markings of the spell. "Not sight. Perception."

"Who's perception? Not the universe's. It's too big, and their minds would dribble out of their ears."

Dalen couldn't see the answer and thought he could stall with, "It was Dorn's spell. How am I supposed to know?"

"Master Ki swatted the back of Dalen's head for such an amateur answer. "How dare you cast a spell without knowing what it does. I thought you were a Reality Bender. You are making this too hard on yourself. Relax. Follow the line back to the source."

Dalen did as instructed and let go of his stress, and reminded himself of the first lesson that Master Ki had ever taught him. That it was okay to not know an answer, if he knew everything, then how would he learn anything? He found the glowing glyph that represented the perception and followed it along the line back to the source. "That's why I couldn't see it. I was confused because the source of the perception is entangled with the source of the spell. "They are not seeing you. I am projecting my perception of you to the rings; their minds translate it and cast my image of you into their minds."

"Exactly." Master Ki gave Dalen a satisfied grin and a nod. When Dalen trained with Master Ki, he would wait for a moment like this, and it meant everything to make his old teacher proud once more. "Your understanding of magic is becoming exceptional. Keep up the good work, but for now, we have to return to the present. It is time for the rest of your team to awaken and begin this day."

Dalen opened his eyes and found himself back in his room. The moment he had just been in still felt very real to him, and his mind had to take a second to readjust to the actual reality he was in now. Much as if he had woken from a dream and couldn't tell the difference between the dream state and reality.

He took a deep breath and got up from his meditative position to wake the others. Becky was already awake when Dalen knocked on her door and was the first to leave her room. Brother Peace finished his morning meditations and was ready before Adam and Travis, who had stayed up much of the night and had fallen asleep planning. They were the last to emerge from Travis's room, sleepy and not well-rested. They yawned and stretched, and once they were all awake and ready for the day, they went downstairs together.

As they made it to the bottom of the stairs, the smell of food took over any other thought they may have had. They followed the smell and found that on a banquet table near the back, Dorn's had set out a breakfast spread. There was bacon, sausages, and eggs cooked a few different ways. There were nine different kinds of toast. Pancakes, hash browns, muffins, and different pastries covered the table.

They all began to fill their plates until Adam noticed something odd. "Hey, Dalen." Dalen came alongside him and asked Adam what he needed. "I took a pancake, and it's here on my plate, but it is also still on the stack. What's going on?"

"Oh, this is fantastic!" Dalen clapped his hands. He was hoping that he would be able to share this with his friends.

"Those are ever-fill platters and bowls. They will never run out." Dalen watched as understanding washed over Adams's face.

"Are you saying what I think you are saying?" asked Adam with excitement and glee.

"I am," Dalen smiled impishly and leaned in close to whisper, "Unlimited bacon."

Adam threw his free hand into the air in a fist. "Unlimited Bacon!" and began to fill his plate with meaty goodness.

"This is amazing!" Becky took a cinnamon roll from the table and a couple of sausages. "This is like a dream come true."

"Wait until you get to try Dorn's Dinner Dash Delirium. It's like this, but there is a tent, and when you walk inside, the table is filled with whatever you desire. Then, when you go back a second time, it's like you never ate the first time. I went back like five times. I also met an Orc-Kin, and we had a chicken-nugget-eating contest. He won. By a lot. I did my best to stay in, but when I tapped out, I was hurting. I was so full I waddled back into line. Then, I just walked into the tent, and it was like I hadn't eaten a single nugget. It was epic. And, every time you walk in, the food changes based on what you want!"

With big pleading eyes, Becky turned to Travis and said, "Can we just live here?" She jokingly grabbed him by the front of his leather armor and shook him lightly with each of her words. "I want to eat all the things and then have it never happen." She let Travis go and turned back to Dalen. "Do they have ice cream?"

"Yes! I had some ice cream with a faerie the first time I was ever here," said Dalen as he grabbed some eggs and toast for his plate.

You could hear the disappointment in her words as she playfully sulked, "You had ice cream with a faerie, and you never mentioned it? Dalen, you failed me."

"I'm sorry," Dalen winced in shame as he spoke.

"Don't be sorry -- fix it." She gestured with her head at the seat next to her with a smile. "Come sit down and tell me all about it." She waved down Jed, the waiter, and asked for a small cup of chocolate ice cream.

Dalen felt a sense of relief to see her back to her old self. Yesterday had been tough, but so was she, and she was ready to enjoy the adventure. Adam sat down with two plates. The first had a nutritiously complete breakfast, and the other was stacked with bacon. Both Dalen and Becky glanced over at his plate and then at him. "What? You want some bacon? I have enough to share." They both continued to stare at him. "Rule Twenty-Three? Never pass up magic bacon?"

Both Dalen and Becky burst into laughter. Travis wrote down the rule as he sat down and said that it was going on the list. The morning was just beginning. A few people began to trickle into Dorn's for breakfast. It was the day of celebration, and a few folks were getting an early start on the festivities. They listened in on the conversations and had breakfast together. Everyone was talking about the saviors or the parties that they were going to attend in their honor. As they were finishing their meal, a message came from the castle.

It was time. The team was being summoned by the Wise King of Venger, His Royal Majesty King Gavin, and suddenly, things became very real.

While everyone was getting ready to go, Travis went to find the person running the breakfast shift, which happened to be Christophe. "I love the ever-fill plates. I have a question."

"Absolutely, Travis. What can I do for you?" Christophe
was friendly and made Travis feel like they had been
friends forever.

"By any chance, do you have something like that in a
glass?" Travis asked.

"Well, you are in luck; I believe that we can do
something like that for you. Since today is the two-thousandth
anniversary of you saving the world, I think I can say with
certainty that whatever you require is on the house. What kind
of glass? A mug? A champagne flute?"

"Well, my father used to travel a lot for work," Travis
explained, "and every time he went somewhere new, he would
get a shot glass. He wasn't a big drinker — he said he gave
it up in his youth. He always used to drink cran-grape juice
from them. Called it nectar." Travis got lost in the memory
for a moment and then shook it off. "Anyway, I would love to
get one to take with me as a reminder of home and maybe the
coolest souvenir of all time."

Christophe let his eyes slide all the way down the bar
and fall on a shot glass that was sitting in a chalk circle
at the end of the bar. "Coolest souvenir of all time, eh?"
Christophe brought his attention back to Travis. "It would
be an honor for you to take a shot glass with Dorn's logo on
it." He reached under the bar without looking and pulled out
a shot glass that had 'Dorn's' written on it. He filled it with
water and took a shot. Even as he lowered the glass, it was
full again. He grabbed a large empty pitcher and began to pour
from the shot glass. When the pitcher was about half full, he
stopped pouring. Travis was impressed, but Christoph explained

that there was more. He put his hand over the top of the glass
and spoke directly to it. "Thank you." When he removed his
hand, the glass was empty. "You follow me so far?"

"I follow you so far," Travis echoed while he watched
with amazement.

Then Christophe held the shot glass out and said, "I
could use a drink," and as he spoke, the glass filled back up
with water. "Yes?"

"'Thank you' turns it off, and 'I need a drink' refills it.
Yeah, I'm with you." Travis began to slowly reach for it.

Christophe held up his hand as though to tell Travis to
wait. He said "thank you" to empty it again and then poured
a shot of whiskey into it. He grabbed a mug often used for
ale and began to pour the whiskey into the mug. When it was
about full, he stopped pouring and thanked the glass again.
He repeated the process with cranberry and grape juice before
turning the glass over and thanking it for the last time as he
handed it to Travis.

"Hang on to that," said Christophe. "You never know —
it may someday save your life."

"Thank you. It's perfect." Travis was about to walk away
but then turned back. "Dalen has been an amazing friend in all
of this. Can I also get one that's a teacup for him? Or is that
too much to ask?"

"You really are a good friend." He reached under the
bar again, but this time, he procured a small porcelain teacup

done in an Eastern style with no handle. He then asked whoever was in the kitchen to prepare some herbal mint tea from the brotherhood. "Dalen loves this tea. It's the only kind I have ever served him."

The tea was sent once it was properly steeped. Christophe poured some into the cup and then placed his hand over it and thanked it. He handed Travis the now-empty cup and wished him luck, sending him off to meet with his friends, who were gathering at the front door. The message informed them that they were going to be picked up by carriage and taken directly to the castle.

They were nervous yet excited. They waited until there was a knock at the door; the sound caused them to look at each other with nervousness. They took a deep breath and left for the next part of their journey.

The coach itself was beautiful and made of cherry wood with deep, rich hues and gilded with gold. On the door, the Seal of Venger was inlaid with gold as well. Instead of getting in right away, they walked all the way around it, marveling at its beauty. The thing that was so amazing about the coach was that there were no horses. The coachman was sitting where he was supposed to be and was even holding reins, but oddly, the reins swept down and under the coach. After a few minutes of marveling at the carriage, they finally got in and closed the door behind them. As the coach moved through the city streets, they had time to enjoy their ride and get a feel for the city. There were multiple streets that had been blocked off, and there was dancing and celebration in the streets everywhere they went. They crossed through a large wall that had huge open archways built into it, and as they passed through them, they felt a small wave of energy pass over them.

"What was that?" Travis looked to his friends for verification that they felt it, too.

"We have moved into the middle ring; what you felt was the city acknowledging your presence," announced Master Ki. "The middle ring is where you will find the schools of skill and trade. There is an amazing school for magic and, of course, the Divine Forge."

"That sounds special," Brother Peace said with exuberance.

"It is, Brother Peace," replied Master Ki. "That forge is one of the most magical places in the city. It's run by a Dwarf named Spider and was originally created to forge your weapons."

Adam looked at the group with an expression that reminded Dalen of a heartbroken puppy. "I want to see the magic forge."

Travis patted his brother on the shoulder. "No doubt. If time allows us to, in any way, I promise to stop back at the forge." Adam's response was like a child who was just told he could have another cookie.

After a short while, they came across another wall. This time, as they passed through the arch, the air went thick somehow, like they were moving through water. It let up quickly, and it left a high-pitched tone in everyone's ears for a moment.

"What is that?" asked Becky as she put her finger in her ear and moved it back and forth to get the tone to stop.

"Venger has many defenses. Some of them are magic barriers called Veils. You just passed through two of them. There is almost no way to get to the castle without passing through the Veils, and once you have, the Royal family and the city herself know of your presence. Once you make it through the first Veil, you are marked and can be tracked through the middle ring. If it is decided that you are not to enter the castle, the second Veil becomes impregnable, and you will not be able to pass through it.

"That, of course, is only if you make it past the Great Seal of Venger," Dalen added with a smirk.

"What do you mean?" asked Becky. Dalen could tell that the question was on everyone's mind; she was just the one who vocalized it.

"Everyone can agree our experience at the Great Seal was intense, yes?" Dalen looked around at his friends, and his gaze was met with nods of agreement. "Now imagine what that would have been like if Venger decided that she didn't want you in the city and, instead of being kind, decided to..." Dalen raised an eyebrow. "Aggressively detain you, or if you were a threat, even harm you."

Dalen was connected to each of them. He could feel it as they recalled how intense and vibrant the whole experience was and imagined the same experience from the perspective of Venger being an enemy. What they came up with was terrifying and probably extremely accurate. Each of them shuddered or flinched from the idea.

Dalen. Master Ki's voice spoke into Dalen's mind as if it were his own thoughts. *Your presence at the edges of their minds has not yet been noticed, but I feel that it would be rude to linger or push further without permission.*

Dalen pulled back from their thoughts right away. It had become a habit for Dalen to trust Ki's suggestions and opinions.

Did I do something wrong? Dalen asked in his mind.

With most forms of magic and in most actions, for that matter, it is best to have the permission of the individual with whom you are interacting.

Is that a rule?

It's common decency. And yes, it is also a rule of magic. You can use magic on those who did not give you permission, but the universe has a way of reflecting your own ripples back to you. If you extend aggression, aggression will find you. If you create pain and suffering, those two will be returned to you. This was one of the great follies of DeSalvo. He brought great suffering to this world and the one that you and your friends come from. Years and years of it. It explains why he suffers so.

DeSalvo is suffering?

It may have been you who made the wish, but it was DeSalvo who was in control. He brought about the end of his world in a desperate attempt to save it. You don't do things like that because you're happy.

Fair enough.

The good news is that the reverse is true as well. If you sew joy and peace into the world, that is what you will reap. So, with that in mind, I suggest you create for yourself a code of conduct that brings forth the greatest outcome for all, grounded in respect and honor.

One of Dalen's favorite things about Master Ki was that he never demanded that you follow his teaching, but his advice was always sound. He would say something like, "Do you see that hungry lion over there? I feel strongly that you should not walk over to it and slap it in the face." Then, he would step back and let you make your own choices. After Dalen figuratively slapped the lion a couple of times, he learned it was best to listen to the master and not question the teaching.

Dalen's thoughts were interrupted by Brother Peace. "Dalen, are you aware that the stone on your forehead is glowing slightly?" There was concern in his voice but not fear.

"Forgive me, my friends," Dalen said, slightly embarrassed. "I have been trying to get used to the new state that I am in."

"What's up?" Travis's voice echoed friendship and brotherhood, and Dalen could tell that he was dedicated to Dalen's wellbeing. "We will do our best to understand." Travis had always been the one to want to acknowledge and embrace the differences in others. It was one of the things that drew Becky to him in the first place. He never treated her differently because she was a girl; he just always treated her like a person.

"During my training, I learned how to open myself up to the truth that, in the end, we are all one. Because of this, I can connect to your thoughts and feelings and even send my own to you. Remember in Dorn's when I conveyed to you that I trust him? Like that."

"So, you have the ability to read minds and speak into them? Is that what you are saying?" Travis was now in it and really trying to grasp the idea.

"Yeah, but before, it was an ability I had to think about before actively doing it; since last night, everything has changed," Dalen blushed a little.

"It's different for all of us, but I imagine that this is extremely difficult for you," Brother Peace's words were soothing.

"You see, the thing is this..." Dalen looked to his friends and hoped they would understand. "Now it's the other way around. I don't have to concentrate as hard anymore. Now that we have shared a connection, it's hard for me to ignore, and I keep slipping into a state where I can feel your feelings and hear your thoughts. I also have to be careful not to startle you by randomly starting conversations telepathically. I did that at Dorn's, and it took you all a little off guard."

It was Adam who now responded, but his words were not of surprise or anger — he was excited and a small bit confused. "So, now you're telepathic. Is that why your stone was glowing over your third eye?" Everyone looked at each other and made vocalizations suggesting a 'eureka' moment in their minds. "What's the problem, Brother?"

"The problem is that it's now instinct and that it takes an effort not to do it." Dalen glanced over to Ki, who gave him a nod, coaxing him to continue. "It has been explained to me that it would be considered rude to do this without your knowledge and permission. For the record, I agree. So, I will do my best not to."

Travis gave him a nod of understanding. "I get it. If it's instinct, then you are fighting subconscious reactions. I guess it would be like holding your breath. You can make it stop, but only when you concentrate and not forever. As soon as you let go, instinct kicks back in, and you start breathing. That must be extremely difficult."

"It can be," Dalen agreed.

"Well, I may have an answer," Travis had a look on his face that suggested he thought his answer to the dilemma was ingenious. "You are talking about general surface thoughts and feelings, right? You would have to intentionally go digging to get into our personal thoughts and memories?"

"Right. I can't go digging into your deep stages of thought without having specific intent and concentration. What has become easy to me is picking up the generalized sense of mood, like when you felt fear at the table a moment ago, and if you had a thought directed at me, I would hear it," Dalen explained. It was difficult to put into words, but he wanted to be accurate.

"Well, then, this is a simple fix for me." Travis's smile dripped with amusement. "I trust you, Dalen. I give you my permission. I mean, don't go digging, but I give my consent to allow your connection." Travis looked around the carriage. "All in favor?"

One by one, they put up their hands. A warm rush of connection and trust rolled over Dalen, and in it, he could hear the thoughts of his friends echoing Travis's words. It was overwhelming, and it brought Dalen to tears.

"Thank you, my friends," Dalen said as he regained his composure.

"We aren't friends anymore, Dalen." Everyone looked over at Becky. "After all of this, we are family."

Brother Peace extended his right hand flat with his palm facing to the side. Dalen reached his hand out in the same way until his fingertips touched Peace's. Together, they looked at their team, and Adam reached out the same and touched the tip of his middle finger to theirs. Then Travis and Becky followed. Just as Ben had done with Dorn the night before, he slowly moved his hand, and as he did, he curled his fingers inward. Each of the team mirrored his movements until their hands all came together to form what looked like a galaxy with five spiral arms reaching out to each of them.

Instinctively, they declared together, "Family." An odd sensation came over them. The connections that they had built the night before ignited within them; suddenly, it wasn't just a word; it was a pledge.

The reward of the truth is trust. Ki said into Dalen's mind with pride. *You made a wise choice: to trust them and tell them the truth. They then gave you their trust. Because of this, you are all stronger. Do not forget this moment. This lesson will be needed by the end.*

They were given only a moment or two to enjoy it. They had arrived at their destination. Since the second Veil, they had officially been on the castle grounds, but now they were approaching the castle itself. The castle was surrounded by a circular courtyard. The courtyard was made of stone inlaid with a hypotrochoid shape made of celestium that encompassed the castle. Surrounding the castle and evenly spaced, six locations were marked with obelisks. Each obelisk was designed and erected in recognition of the six Elements of Reality.

In the center of the celestium shape, the castle rose up gleaming white, with six towers placed around the main building. Red and blue flags flew from the point of each tower, and statues of heroes and gods were erected everywhere they looked.

The coach pulled up to a clearing near the main doors of the castle and was met with a roar of cheers and applause. The team glanced back and forth at one another as the excitement rose in each of them.

"Are you ready?" asked Travis, but it was too late. Adam had already opened the door and was well on his way out before he could finish.

7

THE ROYAL VENGERIANS

"These are the moments we live for!" Adam threw both fists in the air and was met with an explosion of applause as a fanfare erupted from silver trumpets. Adam swung his head into the coach. His tone was calm, but everyone could feel the seriousness of his words. "These people are expecting to see their heroes." Adam's eyes danced back and forth as he looked at each of them. "The people they wanted to be as children. The saviors that they have put their faith in since they were born. They have believed in us their entire lives, and it has been that way for thousands of years. Do not..." He paused long enough to choke back his emotions. "Do not mess this up for them." He swung his head back out and waved enthusiastically to the people, who all cheered.

Adam's words hit them like a wet fish in the face — a good wet *thwack* that left them with a lingering impression well past the initial hit. They couldn't step out of this coach as a bunch of seventeen-year-old kids who, two days ago, were only worried about what they were going to wear to the dance. If they stepped out, they had to step out as the Saviors of Venger. For all of Venger ... and themselves.

Brother Peace stepped out of the coach. He reached out with both hands and waved at random people.

Travis sensed the nervousness radiating off of Becky. "Hey, take a breath. You have it easier than any of us. When you pull up your hood, no one can see your face." he said and squeezed her hand reassuringly. She nodded, pulled her hood over her head, and got out of the coach. An eruption of applause. Dalen leaned in close to Travis. "Why don't you go next, my man? I need a second."

"Okay, but I intend to make an entrance." Travis cracked a mischievous grin. "I'll be hard to follow."

"Make Adam proud." Dalen quipped as he began to get himself ready.

Travis stepped out, and in a fluid set of motions, he fired an arrow overhead and attached his bow to his back. So smoothly that they appeared to be simultaneous actions. As he waved to the crowd, the arrow exploded into an array of white fireworks. They boomed and crackled, and the crowd launched into glorious applause.

Dalen opened the Spheres of Magic, and all the stones

on his body lit up. Adam, Travis, Becky, and Brother Peace
had all turned to look back at the carriage; a hush had fallen
over the crowd. A thick cloud of smoke formed at Adam's
side; ghostly white lights flickered inside, flittering about like
a swarm of fireflies in a fog. Half flying randomly different
than the other. It was an illusion spell that Dalen controlled
from the coach, but it made for a fantastic effect. The lights
converged to the center, formed into a vertical line, and began
to grow brighter. As they did, Dalen moved quantumly to the
center of the cloud. His timing and aim were perfect so that
he appeared with his stones ignited exactly where the glowing
orbs had been. The cloud dissipated at his command, revealing
himself as the source of the lights. It had the desired effect on
the crowd; they lost their minds with awe and wonder, exploding
into a roar of screams and applause.

Something was happening with the crowd as they
cheered. Dalen had spent decades as Father Light and had
studied divine nature for a long time, and the thing that he
recognized coming from them was faith. True, unadulterated
faith. The kind that empowers gods.

As the crowd poured their love and faith towards them,
Adam leaned over, still waving, and with heartfelt words said,
"Well done."

"I'm in this adventure," Dalen replied, and then together
they called out, "Act like it."

"There is hope for you yet," Master Ki noted wryly as he
flowed out of the coach and reformed next to Dalen. Most of
the people couldn't see him, so he didn't bother to wave.

The world stood still, with none of them knowing how long they were being given to move along the courtyard and wave to everyone. The saviors were eventually approached by a herald dressed in pants and a tunic that was patterned half blue and half red, with the right arm and left leg being blue and the opposite in red.

"Greetings. It is an honor to have you with us today," he announced with a large enough bow that it could be read by the crowd. "It has been requested by His Majesty King Gavin that you accompany me to the main greeting hall." He gestured toward the front door. "If you please."

The team agreed and followed the herald, and as they walked, they continued to wave at the crowd. Becky, always watching, noticed that in front of the castle, there was an area that was open, free, and clear of any people or objects. She thought it odd since there were so many people here; why would they not use it?

"Why is that place kept open?" Becky whispered to the herald, pointing in the direction of the unused space.

"Your formal meeting with the royal family will be viewed by everyone here. That is the location where the spell will happen." The herald straightened his posture and stuck out his chest. It was obvious to the team that he respected and was proud of the idea. "It will be seen by everyone in the entire courtyard. That way, everyone can be a part of this moment. There will also be an illusionary spell that will allow you to see the crowd. While the spell is in effect, you will not be able to see most of the actual room you are in, nor will you be able to see the other individuals who are also in the room but standing just outside the range of the spell's illusion."

"A king who thinks of his people. A king who takes the time to go out of his way to share such moments," Travis jotted something down in his notebook. "I like him already."

"Both the King and Queen loved the idea as well, and both of them agreed to it, but this gift was given to us by Her Royal Highness Princess Joanna."

The girl in the red dress flashed once more in Dalen's mind. Her fiery red hair adorned with a ruby hairpin, and her kind smile filled Dalen's consciousness. The flash faded, and Dalen shook the image from his mind.

Brother Peace was walking beside Dalen and reached out to take his hand. A sense of calm washed over Dalen as he understood the gift that Brother Peace was sharing with him. Transferring some of his own ki to help Dalen refocus. *Thank you.* Dalen whispered into his friend's mind.

Brother Peace playfully grinned as he raised an eyebrow and thought as clearly as he could. *It's what I do.*

They moved into a large open room with staircases embellished in gold running along each side of it. As they walked toward the stairs, they became smitten with the art in the room. There were paintings of the greatest heroes to have ever protected Venger, complete with small plaques made of gold that gave the names and dates of their service. Large portraits of former queens and kings, including Christophe, who was standing next to a beautiful woman with multiple strands of different colored hair, were prominently displayed.

At their feet, another Great Seal had been masterfully crafted, embedded within the stonework on the floor, taking up most of the space.

They were guided toward the staircase on the right, which opened into a hallway at the top of the stairs. As they reached the top, they were impressed at how beautifully decorated it was, littered with artifacts from the past few hundred years. Between the two landings, where the double staircase led into the upper hallway, was a set of double doors. The doors were carved oak, and each was gilded with the Great Seal of Venger. The celestium in the center made both doors glow in a beautiful dim light. Guarding the doors were two men dressed in black and red. As they approached, the guards opened the doors. To their surprise, it seemed as if they had walked back outside; however, this time, in the empty space in the courtyard, there were now two large thrones flanked by two smaller yet beautiful ones.

On the throne that was left of center sat Gavin. He was old enough for gray to be speckled in his hair but young enough that his face did not yet give his age away. He wore his hair short, and his beard was neat and trimmed. His pants and silk vest were blue; his long coat was a deep royal purple with brilliant blue embroidery that stood out against the richness of the purple.

To his left, Queen Hope was adorned in a gown that was the same deep purple as the king's. Her bodice and matching shoes were deep red, which brought out the natural reds in her chestnut hair, draping elegantly over her shoulders.

Sitting beside the queen was the girl from Dalen's vision. Because of where she sat, Dalen assumed that she must be Princess Joanna. As they entered the room, both the king and queen stayed seated, but Joanna approached them with a practiced demeanor of hospitality. As she greeted everyone, her smile triggered Dalen's realization that his vision was somehow a memory of this moment specifically, as if he'd remembered it before it had occurred. The sense of déjà vu rippled in him, and nausea momentarily flooded his system. Dalen regained his bearing quickly, but it made him uneasy. He felt almost unnerved that experiencing the déjà vu would make him sick. Something didn't sit well with him. He convinced himself it might have been just nerves. After all, everyone was nervous, and they were all doing their best to be respectful. Becky removed her hood so her face could be seen, and Adam gave a long, deep bow.

"Greetings. It is a tremendous honor to have you with us today. As you know by now, we have kept your memory alive throughout the ages. The bloodline of Christophe has not failed you. We stand here today as a testament to your gifts and sacrifice as a beacon of hope to this world. We have championed the weak and stood against the darkness so that one day you could stand in this very spot and look out at the city and her people, this kingdom, and the world and know that everything you have done for us has created this beacon of honor, respect, joy, understanding, wisdom, and love." The king and queen then rose from their thrones to stand by their daughter. Together, they dropped to one knee and, in unison, said, "We thank you."

Everyone in the courtyard fell silent. Like a wave rippling outward, row after row, everyone knelt before them. They stood there stunned. As much as they thought that they were ready, they were not prepared for this.

Finally, it was Adam who broke the stalemate, "Arise."

Gavin, Hope, and Joanna got up, and as they walked back to their thrones, Hope took Joanna by the hand and told her, "You did that so well. I am proud of you." Joanna leaned her head on her mother's shoulder for a moment, and then each of them sat in their separate places.

Adam looked out over the people. "There are no words to describe what we are feeling. There are no words to properly explain how moved we are. Even now, I fight to speak — the magnificence of this moment is overwhelming and more than anyone could ever ask for. From our very beings, we are honored, and we thank you."

The people applauded, and more than a few cried out that this was "a moment they had lived for." Adam raised his fist in the air in response, and they applauded again.

When Gavin raised his hand, the crowd fell silent. Dalen and the team took a moment to watch it happen. In that instance, they understood how much power Gavin had and that it wasn't power based on fear but rather grounded in respect.

"It is fortuitous that you have arrived today," Gavin stated. His voice was warm and inviting, and his smile was genuine. "We are doubly blessed: not only have you arrived on the day that we celebrate your wisdom, bravery, and sacrifice, but you have arrived on a day that the Kingdom of Venger needs you once more. For two thousand years, the royal line has proved their worthiness through the undertaking of four tasks, the claiming of the four Elemental Blades. Protecting the blades that were passed to us has been a birthright and a responsibility.

"When I came of age, the Water Blade vanished. I had to travel to the ancient sunken city of Palaris to reclaim it. When Hope and I became betrothed, the Fire Blade vanished, and she had to retrieve it. Even though the moment her hand touched the Fire Blade, she became immune to heat and fire, and all wounds caused by heat and fire were cured, she still had to prove herself by plunging her hand into a magma pool to claim it." Joanna looked up at her mother, who put a kind hand on her shoulder and told her she would be fine when her time came. "When I became King, the Air Blade vanished, and I had to retrieve it from an altar protected by Sky Giants, and the day that my daughter is betrothed, I shall have to do it once more."

"So, wait, every time someone is in a position to take the crown, the entire line has to prove themselves again?" asked Becky.

"The king and the crown prince, and the queen and the crown princess are tied together, when a new king or queen is able to rise, by birthright or marriage, the ruling monarchs must show worthiness to continue to rule. Or face the consequence of their rule coming to an end," Gavin replied. Most adults would be annoyed if an adolescent interrupted them, but his response was direct and respectful as if he were talking to an equal. "Princess Joanna will answer the call soon."

"How do you know this?" asked Brother Peace.

"For generations, it has been the same. In her thirteenth year, she will be considered a woman, and if the Queen and I both died, she would be old enough to rule without a steward; however, there is one event that precedes Joanna having to claim her blade. The Queen must prove that she is still worthy to rule now that her daughter is coming of age."

"When will the Earth Blade vanish?" asked Becky.

"How did you know that one would be next?" questioned Adam.

"Process of elimination," she retorted lightly, giving him a wink and a half-smile. "And Earth is often connected to mother figures."

"A good example would be the image of Mother Nature," added Travis.

Adam frowned and thought about it for a moment. "Fair enough."

"You are correct. On both points, really," Gavin added. "The Earth Blade, which has always been wielded by the Queen, is also known as the Mother's Blade. Similarly, the Air Blade is also known as the Father's Blade."

Gently returning the conversation to the topic at hand, Hope responded to Becky's question. "It vanished this morning when I reached for it while dressing for this ceremony." Queen

Hope's voice was beautiful and harmonious as if she had learned to sing while speaking.

"And what happens if the queen fails to recover the Earth Blade?" Travis had pulled out his notebook and was feverishly writing down everything he could.

"The Fire Blade would vanish. Princess Joanna would begin her quest to recover it. She will do this to prove that she is worthy of the bloodline, and then once she is able to return it here, she would need to recover the Earth Blade as well, thus earning her the right to rule." As Gavin explained, Joanna took a deep breath and sat up straight in her chair with strength and grace. "If successful, she would become the ruling Queen, and I would stand down as King to take a position as trusted council. Whoever is lucky enough to get her hand would become a successor, and they, too, would have to earn their right to marry her by finding the Water Blade. To earn the right to sit on the throne as king, her betrothed must also recover the Father Blade."

"Not to suggest that you won't be successful or that there would be any real reason to ask this, but strictly from an academic point of view, what happens if she also fails?" asked Travis. He had already worked out that life in the castle would continue as normal if she succeeded.

"The Elemental Blades would be lost. Venger has a volatile vortex far beneath the surface. The energy of the blades harmonizes and works together to keep the vortex calm. A terrible rift would form without their presence, leading to cataclysmic events that threaten to allow the Black Chaos Dragon to reemerge and destroy the world." Joanna's words were unbelievably powerful. This young girl wasn't even quite their age yet but lived with the knowledge that, someday, she would be the difference between prosperity and annihilation. Somehow, she had stared that truth in the eyes and found resolve. Right then and there, this intrepid band of young heroes understood what it meant to be worthy to sit on the Throne of Venger.

"As long as I breathe, she will not fail." Mordecai stepped into sight from somewhere just past the illusion of the crowd. They all cheered and called his name. Silver streaked the sides of his hair, mustache, and goatee, but his very presence was powerful, and he gave no indication of weakness due to age. Even as he took a knee next to the princess, Dalen passed on to his friends telepathically that this was the guy that Adam had a letter for. He was a great war hero from the Dragon Wars who had risked everything, including his life, to protect the innocents in a village that his commanding officer had demanded he destroy because they 'thought' that there may have been Dragon-Kin hiding in the village somewhere.

"Even if it requires my final breath, she will not fail." A huge nine-foot-tall Orc-Kin stepped forward. Dalen telepathically told his friends that he had met him at Dorn's. His name was Snuggle Bunny, and he had an amazing heart. He'd saved Gavin's life at the cost of the last two surviving members of his tribe. Gavin made a blood oath on the field of battle that Snuggle Bunny, because of his loss and sacrifice to save a stranger, was now family and that he and his family would be Snuggle Bunny's tribe. He was considered a brother to the King and uncle to the princess.

Dalen did not recognize the next four people coming into view from somewhere past the illusion spell of the crowd. As they emerged, it seemed as if they were coming from the crowd. Each of them entered the area of visibility uttering the same phrase. "Even if it requires my final breath, she will not fail," and then knelt beside the princess in a line.

Master Ki's voice whispered in their minds.

The Star-Folk dressed in a Shadow like Becky's is known as Blink. His real name is Eldon Nightshade. His father, Elrick, was once the Headmaster of the Venger School of Skills and Stealth. Elrick disappeared with his son for years, only recently returning. Eldon challenged the school and defeated each class challenge required to graduate in a single day.

The Monk from the Brotherhood of Light is Master Redemption. Once a child trafficker and pimp, he was saved by Master Love. She had known him in her youth, and it was his redemption that granted her the title of Master. He is now a master himself and lives every moment in the belief that anything can be overcome.

The Moon Elf in white is Ila Nevelis. She is the Chosen One of the Elven Goddess of the Moon. She often has visions of the Goddess herself and does her bidding. Her gifts of healing are legendary and rival even the skills of Master Love.

The man dressed in brown and green and carrying the bow is Stringer. His parents got lost in an enchanted forest while traveling when he was still very young. The forest claimed their lives but left Stringer alive. It is believed that a spirit of the enchanted woods took pity on him and chose to raise him as their own. With his bow, he can hit a bird in flight against a crosswind at two hundred yards, and his tracking abilities are considered supernatural.

"But, of course," The Queen chimed in, breaking their link, "this is only if I fail."

Each of them blinked and had to refocus as Gavin Spoke. "This is where you come in,"

"How can we be of service?" Adam replied without hesitation.

"From what I understand, part of your journey will involve traveling to the Wood Elves and earning their permission to enter their realm and find the Oracles." King Gavin reached out for his wife, and she took his hand. "The Queen needs to go to the Wood Elves to retrieve the Earth Blade. Helping her helps you achieve your goal. It would indeed earn their respect, and, undoubtedly, if you succeed, they will grant you passage."

"Who gave you this information?" asked Becky. "We only decided this recently."

"I told them." Lady Venger materialized, and instantly, the crowd fell silent and knelt in reverence. "I believe that, just as you arrived the moment we needed you two thousand years ago, you have once again arrived in our time of need. Your path and ours are intertwined, and I believe that you are destined to help our Queen."

"You make it sound so simple. My guess is that it will not be," Travis answered.

"It will be very difficult," Venger responded. "And the hardest part of it happens here and now."

The team glanced at each other. "How so?" asked Brother Peace.

"Because it is here that you have to decide whether or not you are going to help," replied Venger. "We can find other people to accompany the Queen if you say no, but right now, at this moment, the fate of everything is being offered to you."

Joanna's guardians looked up at them with anticipation and expectation, and the princess was watching them intently, waiting to see what they would say. The King and Queen simply sat on their thrones, patiently waiting for them to respond.

Dalen and the team looked out among the hundreds of people who were now staring at them in anticipation. They could see it in their eyes. They believed in them and believed that they would say yes.

Adam took a step forward. He took a knee and whispered to himself, "These are the moments we live for." He took a deep breath and made eye contact with Lady Venger. "Even if it means my final breath..."

The crowd lost their minds with excitement as Adam began to recite the oath. No one except for the people standing in the room with him were able to hear him finish it. Dalen closed his eyes and listened with his heart. Each of them knew what came next, and each of them knew that time had already said that they would. They reminded themselves that they weren't just kids anymore and that their destiny had called. He could sense their fear, but to the surprise of Dalen and even more so themselves, each of them found the strength and the courage and made their choice.

The roar of applause and screams from the crowd swelled louder as each of them took the oath. They looked up to see hundreds of people hugging each other, and some were openly weeping. Joanna's guardians looked at them with reverence and respect. The Saviors of Venger had come to save the world once more and accepted it unflinchingly as the world had always dreamt they would.

Dalen gazed at Adam, who had always been the heart of the team, and wondered if they would have so easily made that choice if it weren't for Adam leading the way. Adam was contently gazing at his team, and as he did, his chest swelled with pride.

These are the moments we live for, Brother. Adam looked at Dalen. He knew immediately where the thought had come from. In an attempt to reciprocate the communication, he nodded and squinted, scrunching his face like he was thinking really hard. Through the web of connection that Dalen had with his friends, he knew that Adam agreed and that he was trying to share how proud he was of everyone. Dalen gave a nod back, letting Adam know he understood.

King Gavin raised his hand, and the crowd fell silent once more. "There are matters of state and events in motion to discuss. We must speak with the Saviors in private for a moment. But fear not, my people, once what must be said is said, we shall return for the rest of the festival. Be patient, and thank you." His words were gentle, but behind them was the presence of great strength. The crowd bowed to the king and the Saviors, and with a wave of Lady Venger's hand, they were gone.

The team found that they were standing in a grand hall. Red banners were hanging to the left and blue on the right, with the Seal of Venger laid in silver in the center of each one. The floor was white marble veined with gold. Behind the thrones and looking out over the courtyard was an immense window of stained glass depicting the Great Seal.

Now that the illusion was dismissed, everyone relaxed a little. Joanna's guardians rose to their feet. Mordecai stayed close to Joanna while the others socialized and chatted with Dalen's friends.

Snuggle Bunny moved to intercept Dalen. "Little Buddy! I wanted to say hi, but I was doing Vengerian stuff. Very important."

"Me too. Savior stuff." Dalen had bonded with Snuggle Bunny over dinner at Dorn's and sharing tales of battle during his first visit to the enchanted tavern. His father was human, but his mother was Orc, which made him Orc-Kin. He was big and strong, but none of his physical attributes were a match for the size and strength of his heart and character.

Snuggle Bunny thought about what Dalen said for a moment, glanced over at the rest of Dalen's friends, then swung his head back to Dalen. "Right!" He slapped Dalen on the shoulder. Dalen had been expecting it and braced himself for the blow. "Why didn't you tell me Little Buddy is the big savior?"

Dalen built up his ki and whopped Snuggle Bunny on the arm with a decent blow. "I didn't know until last night, big guy."

Snuggle Bunny rubbed his arm for a second. "Little Buddy, you are so strong for a little guy. You hit like an Orc."

"I do?" Dalen was kind of proud of himself.

"Yes. A baby orc is still an orc." Snuggle Bunny had a laugh that scared most children: it was one part roaring like a tiger, one part laughter, and one part slobber, much like those big dogs with the jowls.

Although his laugh could be frightening to some, Dalen could feel his heart and the joy radiating from him. It was infectious, and Dalen began to laugh as well.

"Brother. Brother! Come meet Little Buddy." Gavin had started to walk over, and Snuggly Bunny was waving him in.

"This is incredible!" King Gavin threw open his arms and put one around Dalen's shoulders and the other around Snuggle Bunny's waist. "When Snuggle Bunny told me about his night at Dorn's Dinner Dash a few nights ago and how much fun he had with his new 'Little Buddy,' I was so excited. Don't get me wrong. The kingdom has been rather accepting of my brother, but once I heard the tale of his new friend, it did my heart good. Thank you."

"You're welcome, your Majesty," Dalen replied, trying not to trip over himself while meeting the legendary King of Venger. "I hope to see him at the next one. Your brother is an amazing guy."

Gavin leaned back, intently looking at Dalen, "He is... and you saw it." Dalen could tell that Gavin was looking at the stone that lay over his third eye as if he were examining it. "You could see it, the good in him, and this was before the ... um..." Gavin pointed at his own forehead and then to Dalen's. "Stone thing, right?" Dalen agreed. "Shows that you were a decent person before you came into power. I consider that a good sign."

The whole conversation caught Dalen off guard for a moment, and it took him a second to understand what Gavin was saying. "Yes, Your Majesty. I met the Big Guy while I was still in training. Mind you, from my perspective, was twenty years and a deathmatch with a genie ago."

Gavin stepped back with a look of understanding on his face, stopping before his hand left Dalen's shoulder. His free hand moving to rest on the hilt of his sword. "Tell me about it. Try ruling Venger sometime." He patted Dalen on the shoulder briefly and turned his gaze to Dalen's friends. "Speaking of which, when I'm in the big chair, it's 'His Majesty' and whatnot. When I'm not in the chair, it's just Gavin." He turned his head back, and when the two of them locked eyes, Gavin had a slight golden glow; he looked into Dalen's soul, and with certainty, Gavin stated, "It's the man that makes the king, not the title that makes the man."

"Yes, your –" Dalen caught himself. "Sorry. Yes, Gavin. I will keep that in mind."

"Thank you." Gavin gave a heavy sigh, blowing out all of his air as if he had been holding it. At the same time, he removed his hand from the sword, and his eyes returned to normal. "It has been amazing to meet you, and if we get the chance to sit down and talk later, that would be great. For now, there is a lot to get done, and I don't want to be rude, so I should introduce myself to everyone else."

"Yes, please do that. I would love to talk with you." Dalen quickly shook his hand before he turned to leave, "I've had a few people mention you in conversation, and if you are the man they say you are, it should be an amazing discussion." Gavin took that praise to heart, and it showed. "Adam is going to take meeting you extremely seriously. It's just who he is."

"Noted." Gavin gave Dalen a nod and then was off to meet Travis.

Snuggle Bunny left with Gavin. "Snuggle Bunny meets Little Buddy's friends, too."

"They can be your new friends, also," Dalen called out to Snuggle Bunny; he made sure it was loud enough that the team heard it too and were prepared. Snuggle Bunny smiled and gave a thumbs-up but never lost pace with Gavin.

Dalen only had seconds to take in his amazing meeting with the legendary King of Venger before another drew near. As if she had been patiently waiting for her turn, Queen Hope approached Dalen once Gavin stepped away. Her demeanor was one of powerful kindness. This can be taken in one of two ways; one could say that her kindness was very powerful, but the intention here is to illustrate the type of kindness that can come from power. The way that someone might shield a kitten from the rain. A benevolent tenderness that comes from the heart of someone who has the ability to be anything they want and yet chooses great kindness.

"As my Vengerian Guardian, I wish to bestow upon you another gift." Queen Hope handed him a small circular brooch about the size of a silver dollar. The metalwork resembled the Great Seal minus the Dragon and Unicorn. The outer ring was gold, the inner ring was silver, and the center circle was made of celestium.

"It's beautiful," Dalen said. "Thank you."

"You are welcome, Dalen Pax." She admired it for a moment. "It is. Isn't it?" she commented as if she were looking at it for the first time. "It is a badge of your position as a Vengerian Guardian. This will allow you clearance to teleport directly to anywhere within Venger as long as you have that location saved. Except for inside Dorn's, due to the fact that the inside of Dorn's is not technically in the City of Venger."

"Fantastic. Don't get me wrong, you have beautiful countryside, and the walk from the Tree of Travel isn't too long, but I am glad that I can teleport directly to the city now."

"This only works within the city limits. If you tried to teleport to outside the walls, chances are it would just send you to the tree of travel. The only way to teleport directly to Venger is with a teleportation gate that was made here. A few of our most trusted allies have been gifted a Vengerian Gate so that they, too, can access Venger directly, but even then, the sister gate that they step through is in the outer ring. With the pin that you now have, you can teleport to anywhere in the city, including the castle." Queen Hope mused, "Who knows, teleporting directly to the castle may save one of our lives someday."

"How come it won't teleport me to Dorn's?" Before she could answer, Dalen also threw out, "You said Dorn's isn't in the city, but we just came from there."

She raised her finger and gave Dalen an impish grin. "The outside of Dorn's is in Venger City. That, you can get to, but the inside of Dorn's is somewhere completely different."

"Where?" Dalen asked, now enthralled with this new information.

The Queen shrugged. "Your guess is as good as mine."

"Have you asked him?"

"He won't say."

"Could you ask, as a queen who wants to know what's going on in her city?"

"Venger doesn't belong to me."

"You are queen, are you not?"

"That means I am in charge of taking care of Venger. Venger has never belonged to the royal line. We belong to Venger."

"Wow." Her words struck Dalen deeply, and he had to pause to regain his ability to think. "That's really beautiful."

"Yeah. That's what I thought, too, when Dorn said the same thing to me. The day I tried to demand as queen to know. Like I said..." Hope gave a sad little sigh, "He won't say." The mood quickly lightened, and she playfully smiled at Dalen. "I have a few more of these pins to give to my Vengerian Guardians if you will excuse me.

Joanna and Mordecai approached shortly after. Joanna gave a small curtsy and asked, "May we speak?"

"Yes, of course. Dalen Pax. It's nice to meet you." Dalen gave a small bow to each of them.

"I am Princess Joanna, crown princess of Venger." She gave a formal curtsy this time, but as she rose, she crossed her eyes and stuck out her tongue. "Now that we've been all fancy and pretended like neither of us knows who the other one is, we can actually get to know each other better."

"Excuse me, Princess," Mordecai interjected. He pointed at the ground near their feet. "But I think you dropped your diplomacy on the ground over there."

"I am using diplomacy."

Mordecai folded his arms in front of his chest and raised an eyebrow. "How so?"

Joanna smiled at Dalen. "Will you excuse me for a moment?" As she spoke, she turned around and addressed

Mordecai. "This teenage kid just found out that he and his friends are the only things standing between life and the destruction of all of time. He may be one of the only people in the world who understands me as I understand him."

"That is not the definition of diplomacy," Mordecai responded.

Joanna rolled her eyes at him and slowly turned to Dalen. "Do you feel I am against you?"

"Um, no?" Dalen said hesitantly.

"Do you feel I am trying to make friends?"

"Ugh, yes?"

"Do you think we could be friends?"

Dalen started to see where this was going and realized this was more a game between them. "Yes, I do."

"Dalen Pax," she took both of his hands and, with an exaggerated, dramatic tone, said, "Will you be my friend?"

"Absolutely."

Joanna turned back toward Mordecai and shrugged. "Diplomacy."

He held a stern look for a moment, but it then melted away and was replaced with laughter. "You win."

"Mm-hm." Joanna turned around, and although she kept

her light and friendly demeanor, she gestured to Mordecai. "May I present my teacher, my second father, and best friend: Lord Mordecai of Venger."

"Master Faith told me the tale of how the two of you ended up at the Brotherhood of Light. Ever since hearing that story, I have hoped that I might meet you, if for no other reason than to say, "Well done.'" Dalen took Mordecai's forearm and gripped it tight.

Mordecai let go and slid his hand into position to create a galaxy with their hands. As they curled their fingers together, they raised their other hand to rest alongside them, Mordecai said, "I hear you were with him on his final leap. It is an honor to meet you on many levels, Dalen Pax."

Dalen took the compliment in. He could sense from him the spirit of respect and gratitude. When Dalen had been told the story of how Faith and Mordecai had met and how they had saved each other's lives, Faith spoke about him with deep respect and reverence. Mordecai lived up to the legend.

"Even if I didn't know who you were," Joanna said, "you have Mordecai's respect, and that would be all I needed to know." Dalen smiled in response and gave a small bow. "I see Mother has given you your Vengerian Pin. Are you familiar with its workings?"

"I know that it allows me to teleport anywhere in Venger," Dalen responded, looking at his pin more carefully.

"Indeed, but to do so, you must first go to that location and save it with your pin," Joanna explained.

"Really? So, you can save locations and then just bamph to them wherever you want?"

"Bamph?" inquired Joanna.

"Yeah, bamph," Dalen said casually with a shrug and grin. "It's slang for *teleport*."

Joanna thought about it for a moment. "Just give me a few minutes. I'll finish my schoolwork and then bamph right over." Dalen could tell by her expression that she was amused by the word. "He bamphed in, stole the cake, and then bamphed out." She slowly grinned as her eyes widened with glee. "I like it."

"Take it," Dalen offered.

"I shall," she said. "And here's one for you. Bibitz."

"Bibitz?"

"Yeah. Depending on how you use it, it means very good or very bad."

"Example?"

Joanna grinned and thought about it for a moment. "That amazing thing over there. Yeah, it's the bibitz!" She pointed to Dalen. "You're the bibitz." Then she looked up slowly like she had just noticed a twenty-foot monster behind Dalen. "Minotaur? Oh, bibitz!" She then stuck out her tongue and made a sour face. "Ew, that monster smells like bibitz."

"Got it. Thanks." Dalen handed her his pin. "Can you show me how to save a location?"

"Sure." She pinned it on the white banner that went over his left shoulder and then led him over to the side of the room. "Now, with your thumb and middle finger, touch the outer ring on the left and right of it. Then tap your index finger in the center twice." Dalen did as she asked, and as he tapped the center, he heard a small, high-pitched ping. "Did you hear the tone?" Dalen nodded. "Now walk over there," she pointed to a space a few feet away. "And picture this spot. Tap it again, but this time, only press the center once and hold it."

Dalen did as she requested, and sure enough, as he thought of that spot, he heard the high-pitched ping again. The next thing he knew, he had teleported to his original position.

"How many locations can be saved?" Dalen asked.

"Twenty," responded Joanna. "And that's not even the best part. It creates a telepathic link between everyone wearing your set, and it can also do this." She reached up and touched her own pin. As she did, she was now wearing red leather boots and matching vests. Her riding pants and blouse were black. Her hair had changed, and she was no longer wearing any makeup. She tapped it again, and she was wearing the outfit she had been wearing before. "You only get ten of those. I had to let go of my other favorite gown to have this one saved for today. You might also wish to save your attire in private. When it first saves the outfit, it will leave you with only the pin in your hand, so either activate another set of clothes or have another set ready. Just saying." She gave him a mischievous grin. "Anyway, just hold down the center, and that will show you all the combinations that the pin can do."

"Thank you." Dalen held the center of his pin, and an illusion spell cast an image of his pin in the top right corner of his vision. "This thing has a H.U.D.? That's the bibitz! Did I use that right?"

She nodded. "Perfect. Now, while holding it, say *list*."

Dalen did, and underneath the image of the pin, scrolled a list downward. Each time he looked at a specific item on the list, the rings would light up, showing him where his hand needed to be to create each combination.

"Okay. That is, truly, the bibitz."

"Yay! I am glad you like it." It was clear she was genuinely pleased. "Okay. I am going to say hello to everyone else."

Dalen stopped Mordecai. "Have you spoken with Adam yet?"

"He is the only one we have not yet spoken to." Mordecai offered up, tugging at his tunic nervously.

"He doesn't want to admit it, but Mordecai has considered Sir Adam the Pure Heart a hero of his for as long as I have been alive." Joanna nudged Mordecai, who grumbled at her. "I think he was saving him for last on purpose."

"You should really meet him. I know he wants to meet you," Dalen said.

Mordecai openly flushed for a moment. "He does?"

"Yeah, and he has a letter for you from Master Faith."

Mordecai smiled and took a deep breath. "What a wonderful reason to have to go talk to him. Farewell for now, Dalen Pax." And then Mordecai whisked the princess away and made a beeline to Adam.

Dalen saw them as they talked for a minute and watched as Adam gave Mordecai the letter. Mordecai opened and read it. He looked up at Adam and then read it again. He excused the both of them and walked over to the Queen. Dalen looked at Adam, who shook his head in bewilderment and shrugged.

After a moment, the queen gasped, "What?" After the briefest of moments, she added, "Well, that must be remedied." She crossed over to Adam and asked him to follow her. Hope then leaned her head toward Lady Venger and stated, "Turn it back on!"

With a wave of Lady Venger's hand, the audience reappeared. It was clear that they were taken off guard, as they looked at each other with surprise and then gave their attention to see what was happening.

"Kneel," commanded the queen, and as he did, she strode to a wall where crossed swords and a coat of arms were displayed. She drew a blade and crossed the room until she stood in front of Adam. Mordecai took a position behind him, drawing his blade as well.

Adam looked over at Dalen with concern and mouthed,

"What's going on?" Dalen shrugged. He didn't know what was happening.

Have Faith. Dalen projected.

Adam nodded and faced the Queen. Both she and Mordecai had raised their blades high into the air. She lowered her blade to rest on Adams's right shoulder, and from behind, Mordecai set his blade on Adams's left.

"I have just received word that this man has never been officially knighted," Hope said, loud and clean. The audience roared with applause. "As he is one of my Vengerian Guardians, I think we must remedy that."

"Wait!" Adams's words rang out, and the audience gasped. Adam looked up at the Queen with uncertainty in his eyes. "I thank you for such an honor, but you are honoring me for things that I have not yet done."

"What are you saying? Are you saying that you aren't the Savior of Venger?" asked the Queen. She smiled and looked up at Mordecai; he nodded to her.

"I am saying that I have not done it yet. Do I believe that I can? I don't know, and I won't know until I am there, but this is big. I know from your point of view, this is really old news, but to me, this is something that has not yet come to pass. So, I don't know if I deserve this." Adam looked up at her and swallowed. "Your Majesty."

Again, the Queen and Mordecai exchanged looks and smiled.

Mordecai turned to the team. "Who amongst you would stand as a witness to this man's deeds?"

"He was the only one who made the Leap of Faith unassisted at the Brotherhood of Light," pronounced Dalen as he stepped forward.

"With his bare hands, he faced a magician who was threatening to kill all of us and landed many blows," added Brother Peace as he stepped forward to stand beside Dalen.

"He is braver than all of us combined," added Becky. She joined Dalen and Peace.

Travis stood along Adam's side between Queen Hope and Mordecai. "My brother is stronger and braver than any three of us. His heart is powerful, and he knows no fear. My brother is my hero." Travis ruffled Adams's hair, then took his place next to Becky, taking her hand in his.

"Obtaining the Queen's favor is no easy task. Gaining the trust of Master Faith is another great deed," Mordecai's words were strong and proud. "Obtaining a knighthood is an honor that many dream of."

"Including myself," added Adam.

"And yet you pause because the meaning of it is more important to you than obtaining it. You have successfully achieved the first requirement. Any true knight must accomplish three goals. The second is that you must have witnesses to attest to your deeds. The third is the most important of all."

"What is it?" Adam's gaze still rested on the queen.

She smiled and said, "You have to believe you are worthy." Adam slowly let his gaze fall to his friends who were standing beside him. They nodded at him, but the Queen tapped him on the shoulder with her blade, and he gave his attention back to her. "It doesn't matter what they think now. The only person who can answer this question is you. Are you worthy?"

Adam closed his eyes. Dalen could hear his thoughts. He was asking himself real questions about who he believed he was and who he knew he was. He finally decided what his truth was about himself and opened his eyes.

"These are the moments that we live for." He looked up at the queen as one tear rolled down his cheek. "Yes. Yes, I am worthy."

Together, Queen Hope of Venger and Mordecai spoke aloud, "In the name of the Dragon." They switched shoulders in perfect unison. "In the name of the Unicorn." They switched again.

This time, only the Queen spoke. "I dub thee Sir Adam the Pure Heart.

They switched shoulders one last time, and Mordecai added, "Rise, Sir Adam, Knight of Venger." The audience cheered and began to chant Adam's name. They continued long after the illusion was relinquished.

This was the moment that Adam stopped pretending and stepped into being his true self. Dalen could sense it off him.

He had made the leap and would never be the same again.

Dalen remembered that feeling from during his training period. Like a phoenix, one thing is burned away, and from its ashes, something else emerges. Dalen remembered how hard it had been and how the change was difficult and frightening. Like fire, the burn could be traumatic and painful. Now, being able to see this 'Phoenix Burn' from the outside, he could see that it was also beautiful and that it filled the darkness with light. With this recognition, Dalen's heart ached for his old friend and strained to hear her voice, hoping that, in a moment like this, he would be able to hear her once more. He slowed down time and allowed the moments to stretch out before him. He allowed the frames of reality to all but stop. In the deepest recesses of his soul, he could almost hear the Fire Jinn's voice. "One believes. Three to go."

8

THE GNOMISH CURSE

Many hours had passed since Sir Adam had been knighted. Once the Illustrious band of young heroes stepped back out into the courtyard, they spent time meeting the people of Venger. Many townsfolk had stories to tell them and wanted to share that they had given of themselves to the statues and how much of a great honor it was for them to have the opportunity to meet them.

They were Vengerian celebrities at first. It was exciting and fun, but the longer the day went on, and the more people told them of their tales of how they had given a part of themselves to the statues, and more than that, regaled them of stories and traditions, of parents and grandparents bringing their families to the garden, and how important it was to them to be able to do so. The more the weight of it all began to feel heavy upon their shoulders. The parties and cheering were exhilarating, but somewhere in all of it, it also became very real. It was up to them to save the city. It wasn't just that they had to save the people that they had met that day, but the generations upon generations that had come before them were in their hands as well. Powers or not, this was a lot for a seventeen-year-old to take in and accept.

By nightfall, they were exhausted. Their bodies were tired, and their minds and hearts were drained. The celebration was to last throughout the night. The Queen was leaving in the morning, and it was explained that her Vengerian Guardians were needed for planning their departure. Once they were gathered and out of the view of the population of Venger, it was explained to them that it was a ruse to give them a much-needed break. The only thing that was required of them was that they were rested and ready to escort the Queen in the morning.

They were shown to a large room that served as a common room to six different chambers for sleeping. The chambers themselves were decorated with beautiful art and furnishings: a bed, a wardrobe, a desk, and a chair. The rooms were simple as most of the accommodation was found in the common room. They had table games and darts on one side of the room and large couches surrounding a large oak table on the other. Each side of the room had its own sizeable fireplace. They were told that the kitchen would stay open for them throughout the night and that if they needed anything, they could ask Janell, who would be their server until early in the morning when her shift ended. They were served dinner and then given something that they had all secretly wanted.

Peace and quiet.

During the day, Dalen had made the time to explain their pins to them and had taught them how to find the list of combinations. They spent the first hour of their evening going through all of their gear, setting up the different outfits that they thought they might need, and saving them to their pins. Once they were done preparing, most of them gathered back together in the common room. As they all lay there, either on their beds or stretched out on one of the couches recuperating, all at once, they could hear Becky's voice speak directly into their minds.

‹One. Two. One Two. Can anyone hear me?›

"Of course, I can hear you," Travis answered. "You're, like, three feet away from me."

‹Bibitz! You can hear me!›

Travis sat up and looked over at her. "Yes. I can hear you."

Becky responded, but it left Travis stunned because as she spoke, her mouth did not move. ‹But I didn't say anything›. She just sat there wide-eyed as if she were as surprised as Travis, on the verge of tears.

Adam was on the other side of the table and sat up and looked at her. "It sounds like you did. I even heard it from where you're sitting."

Travis spun around and looked at his brother with wild eyes. "Yeah, I thought so too, but watch her mouth." They both looked back over at Becky.

Becky rolled her eyes at them in disappointment. ‹I swear you boys are slow.›

"Ha!" Travis cried, and Adam stood up with a look of surprise on his face.

Brother Peace came out of his room and said, "What are you doing? I can hear you talking out here, but I can hear it as clear as if you were in my room with me."

Dalen bamphed into the room. "It's telepathy."

"It feels completely different from when you do it," mentioned Adam.

"Agreed." Travis nodded. "Take off your pin and say something to us using your telepathy."

Dalen took off his pin and set it on the table. Then he opened up the Spheres of Magic and found his connection to them. *This is the thought I am sending at this moment.*

"Yeah," Travis said. "It's completely different."

"How is it different?" asked Becky. This time, using words.

"When Dalen does it, it feels like the thought is almost my own."

"Yeah." Becky agreed. "How is it different?"

"When you do it, it sounds like a P.A. in my head, and you are talking on a microphone." It was Peace who spoke, but when he did, both Adam and Travis nodded and pointed at him.

Dalen put his pin back on and held the center switch. He checked the list, and the first thing on it was how to establish a telepathic link. He guessed that Becky had activated the list and was just checking it out.

To activate the telepathy, all you had to do was press the center and then, without breaking contact, smoothly move your finger outward in any direction. To deactivate, you did the opposite by pressing on the outside ring and then smoothly moving back to the center. Because of his understanding of the Spheres of Magic and how they connected to the Seal of Venger, the motion sequence made sense. The next step was to think intentionally to send. He activated the pin as directed, and as he did, there was a small sensation of tingles that moved through his body outward from the pin like a wave. Set and ready, he looked at his friends and thought 'at' them with intent.

‹This is telepathy with the pin.›

Becky's eyes widened. "Yeah. That's completely different." She was now standing. I could hear you as if you were speaking. There was directionality, and it was clearly your voice, but not."

"What happens if you do both at the same time?" Adam asked.

Dalen tried it, but the effects were something they weren't ready for. It amplified everything, and while he was doing it, Dalen was in their minds. What he did was a crude, accidental version of Grey Speak. An ability my kind has practiced and perfected over time. It can be very dangerous if not used correctly. Much by accident, Dalen touched their souls.

"Too big!" Becky screamed, pulling her pin from her belt, where she had been wearing it.

Travis grabbed his ears like it was too loud and demanded Dalen stop.

Peace sat down on the floor and began to try to refocus his mind.

Adam stood his ground. He shook his head, trying to get a hold of what was happening to him. He was in obvious distress, but he didn't shy away from it.

Dalen deactivated the pin. *Master Ki. What do I do?*

Do you remember how you were calmed when you first received the beads? Master Ki's voice was soothing and allowed Dalen to focus.

The Fire Jinn had used the stones on her body to enact a spell directly. He activated the spheres once more, embracing the connection to their energies; he reached up and touched the stone that was in his throat. He could feel it activate, and his words became powerful as he spoke.

"You're okay. Everything is alright." Immediately, each of them began to relax and show signs that their stress was diminishing. He telepathically connected to them while speaking at the same time. It was much closer to true Grey Speak, and he had control of it, so it came easier to all of them. *Relax. You are alright now.*

"Thank you." Travis was lying on one of the couches. He was just getting his breathing under control. Once he did, he laughed and jokingly said, "So! That's what happens when you do both."

"I am so sorry, my friends. I had no idea that would happen." Dalen's words were apologetic, and they knew he had meant no harm.

"It's alright, Brother," said Adam. "It was my idea." Adam blinked a couple of times as if he were testing out new eyes. "Woo! You pack a wallop."

"Obviously, you were able to correct it," added Becky. "Well done. I went from overload to chill in two seconds."

"Master Ki reminded me of a Jinn method, plus I added something I learned from a Grey Bard during my training."

"Grey Bard?" asked Travis.

"Empathic telepaths that can magically create illusions directly in your mind. You can't tell that it's not real because it feels real to both the mind and the heart."

"Damn," said Travis. "They sound scary."

"Oh yeah. If they wanted to be, they could be absolutely terrifying. Luckily, the one I met was awesome." Dalen wasn't kidding. My ghost stories keep adults up at night watching the shadows for monsters in their minds.

"It wasn't too much; it was just too much, all at once, on the first run." Brother Peace had found his center and his voice. "I think I would like to train in it."

Dalen wasn't sure how to respond to the idea. "I don't know about that, Peace. That looked painful."

"It wasn't." Brother Peace walked over to Dalen and gave him a reassuring look. "I want you to try again, but first, I suggest everyone who is not up for the challenge to disconnect from the connection altogether."

"Your right." Adam sat down on the couch next to his brother. "It didn't hurt. It was just big. Way bigger than I was expecting, but now that I know what to expect, I think I'll handle it better."

Becky put her pin back on her belt. "Adam's right. You have already explained that your natural telepathic ability is something you have to fight to keep from happening, correct?"

"We already covered this, and everyone agreed that it was okay." Dalen didn't mean to come across as defensive, but his tone suggested it.

"Still do, sweetie." Her words were kind, and Dalen remembered who he was talking to. "If you slip on accident, we should be ready for it." She stopped as her thought had concluded, but then she added, "If you could also use whatever you did just a minute ago, that was really helpful. Could you somehow add that to help ease into it?"

Suddenly and without any warning, the Queen bamphed into the room. She was wearing a traveling outfit. Leather pants, boots, and vest, with a flowing white shirt made of bleached linen. She was about to say hello when a fellow of gnomish descent bamphed into the room as well.

"Nobody do anything!" He looked around the room at them and began to sniff the air. "Playing with telepathy, eh?" Gnomes are smaller folk. They stand about sternum height of their human equivalent. He was dressed in fine clothes and wore a gold ring on one hand and a metal bracer on his forearm that had a large sky-blue gem inlaid in the center of it. He also wore a pair of goggles that had different colored lenses in them. He pulled the goggles over his eyes and then flinched at whatever he was looking at. "Three different kinds of it, too." He looked around the room and then at each one of the team. He stopped at Dalen long enough to add, "A jinn." He smirked. "That explains a lot." Turning back to the group, he flipped his goggles back to their place on his forehead. "Has anyone lost any memory chunks?" He looked at their blank faces for a moment, but everyone was just staring at them, stunned.

"Hello?"

"Pardon our intrusion." The Queen said. "May I introduce you to Flibberbitz. He is one of the heads of our security."

"Raise your hand if you understand me." All of them did. "Great, now, as I said before, have any of you lost chunks of memory?"

"If we forgot it, how would we know if we lost it?" asked Brother Peace.

"What are you?" Flibberbitz pulled down his goggles and took a long look at Brother Peace suspiciously. "So wise you went around the horn, and now you're stupid again?"

"My apologies." Peace said. "I did not mean to offend."

"No, no. I apologize." He gave what looked and felt like a sincere bow to Brother Peace and then said. "I should not have been so rude. It just drives me nuts when wise people say dumb things because they are trying to sound wise." Flibberbitz rolled his eyes and spoke directly to the Queen. "This could also be a sign that we are going to have to get them all checked out. Their minds could be blown." He then looked up at the ceiling and yelled, "Oh, shut up, will you!"

"We didn't say anything," said Travis.

The gnome spun on his heels towards Travis. "I wasn't speaking to you, good sir." He stopped and looked around at everyone for a moment. "Let me guess. No one in the room can hear the voices but me?"

"Voices?" asked Becky.

"Yes." He rested his face in his hands. "Every time I get around you hero types, I can hear them, and oh, how they drone on. It's maddening."

Brother Peace asked Queen Hope, "Is he not stable?"

"None of the gnomes are." She said with an air of mystery in her voice. "No one knows why, but all of the gnomes have been quite mad for some time."

Flibberbitz scoffed, "Some might say believing in a sentient city is mad, but here we are..." He looked around. "Standing in one." He paused again and looked under the table. "And tell me this. If I were mad, why would you hire me as one of your head security agents? Eh?"

He knew the truth. All gnomes did. You would have to be crazy not to notice how mad they were.

"There they go again." Okay. Please, for my sanity, can everyone just stop moving around and don't do anything? Just answer my questions and hold still. Can we do that?" Everyone nodded. He took a deep breath in and tried not to scream. "One-word answers, and everyone, answer together if you can. Can you remember a week ago?"

"Yes."

"Can you remember last year?"

"Yes."

"Can you remember being a little kid?"

"Yes."

"Okay. See. That wasn't hard." Flibberbitz rubbed the back of his neck, "Look, they seem fine. They got lucky, and nobody lost their mind. I'm going to go; you know how to contact me. Explain the rest, but I have to go, and for the record, I love you guys. It's not your fault. You're amazing. Nice to meet you, but I got to go where the voices are not." With that, he bumped out of the room, and as he did, he yelled, "Damn it!"

Everyone took the initiative, and fingers started going up. Becky was kind enough to explain what was going on to the Queen as fingers went up.

"Travis was in first position. "Can you explain to us what just happened and why?" Everyone else put their hands down.

"I, too, have a Vengerian Pin, and I am connected to the pins as much as you are. You all had just figured out how to create the link. I was about to say hello, and then all of you were in peril. I called for one of the best magical security members in all of Venger, and we arrived as fast as possible. We thought that perhaps you were under attack. It's the only reason we would have invaded your private quarters." She sat down on one of the closest of the couches and gestured for everyone to join her.

Hope called for Jenell and asked her for refreshments. When she brought them their order, Travis gave Dalen his cup. He explained that it was already prepared with his favorite tea.

"This is really amazing, Travis. Thank you." Dalen took the time to examine his gift. He activated it, took a sip of his favorite tea, and then gave Travis a hug. "This truly is one of the coolest gifts I have ever gotten, and I mean that."

Travis showed him his, and they both took a sip off each other's before they sat down. Sliding a bookmark between the pages of his journal where he had been writing before, Travis turned to a new page and got himself ready to write. "Can you help me understand why gnomes are the way they are and translate what he was saying?"

So, over tea and sandwiches, the team had their first official meeting with the Queen, starting with her answering the question and telling the tale of how the gnomes were cursed.

"It is said that the gnomes were cursed by an unknown villain for reasons we are unsure of. It happened at least three generations ago because my grandfather remembered them mad as well." Queen Hope's voice had a nonchalance about it as she explained that it had always been that way, and people just came to accept that's how they were. "We never really think about it honestly, which in part has to do with the curse."

"How so?" asked Becky.

"There are six parts to the gnomish curse. Some good, some bad, together they make for an interesting outcome. The first is obscurity."

Travis had been writing but looked up from his notebook. "What do you mean?"

"There are so many examples. Here are just a few. No one but gnomes can create Gnomish Magic. What comes naturally to them baffles our greatest magical scholars. Their form of magic has been studied by the greatest mages of all kinds, and none of them can understand what they are doing.

We have a spell that will identify magic. It will name it and describe what the magic will do. If you cast the spell on a mundane item, the spell fizzles out, and nothing happens. It only functions on enchanted things. If you try to magically identify a gnomish object, the spell goes off, meaning that it worked and the object is magical, but identifies the object as mundane."

"That makes absolutely no sense," Dalen said, trying to picture in his head what he would have to do to try to create an item that would have that effect. "From what you say, the spell would only go off if it is a magic object. The objects identifying as mundane would suggest that every item considered gnomish is imbued with normalcy?"

"That's actually a better answer than what we have come up with so far, but it gets worse," Hope said. "You can replicate a gnomish coin down to the nicks and scratches, and they can still tell the difference between our gold and theirs on sight. We have no idea why, and they can't explain it either. They tried until both sides were frustrated. There are gnomish magic items that we don't even know how to use or what they do, nor do they."

"Why not?" asked Brother Peace.

"The origin of them is unknown. We believe that they do something, but since we have no idea how to activate them, we don't know what they do. When identified, the spell simply says it's a mundane magical item. The problem is that none of us, including the gnomes, know who to ask. No one that is alive today has any memory of the Gnomish Lands. We have no idea where they are. It isn't on any map. It's like they never existed in the first place, and the truly interesting part is that even though we are talking about it right now, shortly after, it will quietly leave our minds as if you aren't meant to think about it."

"Well, I now have it written in my notebook." Travis patted his book. "I'll remember."

"The problem isn't remembering. I remember that we have a wand in our vault that hums and glows with magic power, but we have no idea what it does. Identifying it only lets us know that it is a mundane wand. It's not that you will forget about the curse. It's that you won't think to look at those pages." She took a sip of her tea and grabbed a sandwich. "The second and third parts have to do with their vast intellect and extraordinary skill in all that they do."

"That sounds good, right?" Adam suggested, hopefully.

"In many ways, yes." the Queen replied. "All of your items were Gnome-made. To create a magic object that could do what those weapons can do is beyond our ability to recreate. Even our Vengerian Pins are Gnome-made."

"Help me understand how this is a curse." requested Brother Peace. Dalen watched him clear his mind. It was a Brotherhood of Light technique. The idea was to clear your mind of everything, including your assumptions about what you personally considered truth. Allowing the listener to understand someone else's truth without the interruption of their own biases.

"When someone has a fever, their body is hotter than normal. This causes the world around them to be perceived as cold. The higher your temperature, the colder you feel your environment is." Hope explained.

"Yes. I follow you so far." Peace replied, trying to keep his mind open.

She smiled and shook her head. "From their point of view, everywhere they go, they are surrounded by morons that continuously ask them the most basic of questions. Questions from those who claim to be masters in their field. The gnomes perceive others as intellectually inferior."

Becky snorted. "I know how they feel." She was met with a barrage of "Hey!" as her friends all chimed in, throwing a hailstorm of butter crackers that had been served with the tea at her.

"The next two parts of the curse are bad." The Queen looked at each of them slowly while taking a deep breath and then continued. "The next part of the curse is that they hear voices and see things that just aren't there. They have learned that no one else can hear or see what they do. From what they tell us, sometimes they are horrible visions of the macabre and great violence. The second part is horrific and amplifies the other. They are prone to have instances of abject violence toward their own race. They have been known to randomly kill one another violently for no known reason; they don't even know why. Because of this, you can have three gnomes in a room; one will violently kill another, while the third looks on doing nothing. There's a good chance they will believe it's just a vision and do nothing to stop it. The only thing we do know is that it gets worse the more gnomes you have together."

"Oh my god, that's terrible." Becky was almost in tears.

"It is terrible." Hope's eyes saddened. "Their mind makes them think that it's an illusion even as they are doing it. I have seen them look for loved ones for days, not realizing that they had killed them."

"That is a terrible curse." Peace was only partly in the conversation. His own memory of being forced into a violent rage no longer affected him, but he knew their pain.

"The final part has to do with the amazing ability to withstand the curse." Hope continued, trying to keep focus on the subject. The team could see her struggle to maintain it.

Brother Peace just nodded in understanding, but Sir Adam had questions. "I don't understand. What is it that I am missing?"

"With all of that happening, they still find a way to function. When I went to the brotherhood, I was a mess. The only thing about me that was strong in those first few days was my ability to keep functioning like a person while inside I was in free-fall, so I get what she is saying."

"They know they are cursed." Hope explained, heartbroken now that she was thinking about it. "So, they try to avoid one another when possible, and they accept that no one can hear the voices but them. They answer our questions about magic when they can while bearing the great weight of knowing how much they could teach us but having no way to explain it. They deal with having no place to call home, yet at the same time, they say they are rather happy not knowing where the gnomish homelands are. If any of them were to ever go there, they fear they might destroy everything they find. Now, add the voices and visions. Yet somehow they manage to hold down jobs and maintain something that resembles a life."

"Sounds like someone wanted to build super slaves," Travis said idly.

Hope's demeanor changed as if his words had pulled her away from the sadness. "What do you mean?"

"What?" Travis looked up from his book and saw that everyone was looking at him. "Just a thought?"

"No." The Queen interjected. "Why would you think that?"

"Travis looked around at his friends and then back to the Queen. "It was just a thought." He looked to Becky for help.

"Go ahead." She was sitting by this point; she put her hand on his knee and gave it the smallest of squeezes. "You're brilliant."

Travis smiled. "I'm not brilliant like you or wise like Brother Peace. I don't have amazing powers like Dalen nor the courage of Adam."

"Sir Adam." His brother reminded him.

"Forgive me. Of course... Sir Adam." Travis reached over and gave Sir Adam five. "My thing is puzzles. Tactics. My mind can just see it."

"It's one of the main reasons I started to notice you," added Becky.

Travis smiled and squeezed her hand before he continued. "If I wanted slaves that were beyond powerful but controllable, this is how I would do it. Extremely smart and understands magic well beyond anything we can understand but hobbled. Visions and voices keep them from mentally seeing clearly yet do not affect their understanding of magic. Also, a streak of terrible violence toward their own kind. This keeps them from organizing together and keeps them separate and alone. At the same time, none of this keeps them from their work due to their ability to resist the curse enough to function. Unlimited power except the ability to save themselves."

"You just now came up with that?" Hope was impressed.

"Yeah. Plus, if you also keep in mind that no one can find their origins, and the point that, if you are correct, as soon as we stop talking about it, we are going to forget to think about them again, It's a perfect way to make sure no one ever stops someone from enslaving an entire race of people right under your nose." Travis had been writing this all down again in the back of his book. He tore the page out and handed it to Queen Hope. "Take this. Take this, and do not stop thinking about it. Hold it up and reread it over and over until you are standing in front of someone who can do something with it.

The Queen reached up and touched one of four pins on her vest. "Please come here for a moment."

Flibberbitz bamphed back into the room. "Yes, Your Majesty."

"I just want to say I think you are handling things amazingly well." blurted Becky.

Flibberbitz rolled his eyes. "You told them?"

"The queen said, "Yes, I did, and this is something that Travis came up with." She handed him the piece of paper.

Flibberbitz studied it carefully. His eyes widened with shock. He leaped from where he stood and landed in Travis' lap. He grabbed him by his shirt with both hands. "How are you able to think about it long enough to come up with a plan?"

"It's the only thing that makes sense," Travis answered. Dalen could sense his fear.

"Make sense?" Flibberbitz looked down at his hands gripping Travis. He let him go and hopped off him. "I... I am sorry. Sorry for jumping on you like that." He looked embarrassed. "As you can tell, and by your notes, you understand why we have never been able to understand why we have been cursed." He put his hand over his mouth and just stared at the paper for a moment. "We are slaves, and not by these good people." gesturing to the Queen. Vengerian people are the ones who took us in when everyone else was afraid of us. They treated us with kindness and respect." He began to tear up, but then he started to get mad. "But someone has done this to us." He snapped his gaze upward to the Queen. Permission to leave. Permission to take this to the Knowledge Keeper." He dropped to his knees and hung on the Queen's leg.

"Please! Please let me go before I forget again. Please!"

"Flibberbitz, I relieve you of duty until you decide to return. Go and save your people." The Queen was nearly in tears herself.

The gnome turned back to Travis. "You may have just saved our people. I have nothing worth what you have just handed me, but please take this. "Flibberbitz reached up to his ear and removed what looked to be a celestium stud earring.

"Thank you," Travis said, "but I do not have my ear pierced."

"No problem." Before anyone could act, Flibberbitz teleported back onto Travis's lap and, with a single swift move, pierced Travis's left earlobe with the celestium stud. Travis winced in pain. "There you go. All better." Flibberbitz swatted Travis a couple of times on the shoulder and hopped down to the floor again. "It helps me..." It was obvious that the gnome was struggling with his words. "It helps me think clearly. It should do wonders for you." Flibberbitz began to turn around but then stopped to say. "It should help you think clearly, too." He paused and thought about it for a moment. "Not that you need it." He turned back to the Queen. "What was I doing, Your Majesty?"

"Look at your hands." the Queen said and pointed to Travis's notes.

"What's this?" Flibberbitz looked over the paper in his hands. His eyes widened as he stared at it in shock. "Oh yes. Now I remember." He returned his attention to Hope. "I. I have to go. While I can." And then he bamphed out of the room.

"Travis, I do believe you may now be able to be credited with saving an entire species if that pans out." Queen Hope said with some certainty. "We have never been able to spend time thinking about it because of the curse. I wonder if you weren't affected because you did not come from this world."

"Look at you!" Sir Adam's tone was whimsical, but he meant what he said. "Saving the entire gnomish people and whatnot." He gave his brother a high five.

"Yes." Peace said. "Never underestimate your abilities."

Becky squeezed Travis's hand. "I am proud of you." and then she gave him a kiss.

"Hang on, guys." I haven't done anything. We don't know if that is even what's happening."

"Yeah." Hope responded, "Just as easily, it could be the difference between their slavery and their freedom. You will find, Travis, that often, the actions that change the entire path of a country can be something small and simple. It's a reason that phrases like,' It's the small things that count' exist. We do not know what it will bring, but for now, you brought Flibberbitz hope where he had none, and that in itself was a gift."

"Thank you." Travis looked around the room. "All of you." He took a moment to recompose himself and then asked, "So, what's next?"

"I was hoping you would let me stay." The Queen seemed excited. "I want a chance to bond with you guys before we leave tomorrow if that is alright." She was met with a resounding agreement. "Wonderful. In that case, I agree with Brother Peace, and I think that we should try to acclimate to Dalen using his gifts in tandem with using the pin. It will be imperative to be ready for as many things as we can."

Everyone agreed, and so they began. It was hard at first, but the initial thought was correct. It had been a shock, but now that they were expecting it, they were acclimating toward it quickly. Dalen's use of Grey Speak to help ease their emotions was instrumental to their ability to withstand direct connection of the mind. Once they were in control of it, they began to practice working the Vengerian Pins using methods Hope taught them. They began to learn how to transmit to a single person or the entire group, based on whether or not their intent was aimed at a single individual.

Dalen excelled in this field and spent the next few hours helping his friends get to a place where they were able to connect to the group or a singular individual and then finally being able to switch it back and forth with ease.

Afterward, they talked with the Queen about their home world and what they were like before all of this started, and she shared about her life before she was Queen. By the end of the night, she was a part of the team. Sir Adam said she was like a cool aunt, and Hope hugged him for such a compliment. It had gotten late, and it was time to sleep. She said goodnight and then left the room using the front door, excited to share with Gavin how she had gotten to know everyone.

The team spent the next bit in their own rooms. Travis and Becky turned off their pins and discussed their relationship with each other privately before all of them reconnected once more to say goodnight. Then everyone shut down their links and fell asleep.

Tomorrow was going to be a big day for them, and they knew it, they were as ready as they could be, and sleep was the only thing left to do.

9

XOXANN'S NEW FRIEND

There was something to be said about the day that the Saviors of Venger earned their moniker. There was a lot that needed to be said. The tragedy of it was that the words had never been spoken. Any child older than the age of five knows of the Saviors. Their names are legend. It is known that they traveled through time, which is a feat in itself. The only known way to travel through time was with the Pillar of Time, and it was almost impossible to achieve. Yet the saviors did and traveled in time to save not only Venger from the Chaos Dragon but the entire world. The Chaos Dragon undoubtedly would have continued its rampage, destroying everything. It was known they arrived and chose to give their powers to the first King and Queen, who used that power to become strong enough to stop the Chaos Dragon.

Everyone knows this story. It is taught in schools. Every year, somewhere in the city, young children put on a play about the Saviors. It's adorable. It is even known that once they gave up their powers, they had to face a Time Mage who was threatening the city and had caused the rift that the dragon was using to tear a hole in our reality.

This is what is not known:

How.

It was lost or forgotten or intentionally left out; whatever the cause, it is one of the unsolved mysteries of this world. What is known is that at one point, the saviors had given up all their powers and faced this vial being who was attempting to destroy our whole world, and somehow, these young adults, seemingly powerless, defeated the Time Mage. The greatest moment of their known career. The moment that earned them titles and fame, yet there was nothing. Nothing captures the heroic events that led to the defeat.

As a Grey Bard, I have many abilities and tricks up my sleeve used to extract the truth of a story, even those truths that have been lost. I have tried on more than one occasion but have never been able to glean what transpired, even in my state as the narrator of this world. This means at one point in our history, the details were intentionally hidden. Dorn and Venger know. They will only say that it was forgotten with purpose. Whatever that purpose may be, the causality is that no one else knows what happened that day because it was erased from time.

It is said that the Time Mage they faced had an object of great power: the Time Stone. The Time Stone was considered an artifact of tremendous power that had overwhelming potential. It is also known that there was a warning connected to it: if anyone were to destroy it, they would be removed from time. They would not simply cease to exist, but time would shatter in such a way that any connection to them would also be removed as if they had never existed. Even their parents wouldn't remember that they'd ever had a child.

That is not to say that their time didn't happen, and they weren't in it at all, but they would be lost between the frames, and there would be no memory of them. Time would be wiped clean of their presence.

There was a possibility that someone had done just that, destroyed the Time Stone, and the reason that no one remembers how the Time Mage was stopped is because the person who did it was wiped clean from time. Causing the greatest moment in the Saviors' lives to become unknown, erased from memory.

This is why I found myself on my knees in front of Dalen, asking him to carry with him a special magic item. It was a brooch that he would wear on his person. It was designed by me and engineered with Gnomish Magic. Whatever happened to the Saviors while on their adventure, I would have the ability to see and hear as they experienced it, no matter where they moved in time. Once and for all, I would know what happened, and for the first time in Vengerian history, the whole story of the Saviors of Venger would finally be known. I explained to him why it was so important, and he was kind enough to agree to take it with them the day they left the castle.

It worked, and I was able to learn the entire story. Because of that, I am now proud to present to you the story of the other person who was there that fateful day in the garden.

• • •

Xoxann Velo hated going to school. Most ten-year-olds do, but her mother always told her that it was the law and that she had to go. She had no choice but to, even every time she pretended to be sick to get out of it. Her mother didn't understand how cruel kids could be and had no idea that the kids at school called her Xox the Pox and how it had become a game to avoid her as if she were a plague rat. They were poor, and it was difficult for her mother to make ends meet, so when her daughter told her about how the kids teased her, she was just too stressed to comprehend what her daughter was saying. Her mother scoffed and mused, "School is for learning, honey, not making friends, Xoxy."

Xoxann, wanting to make her mother proud, would go, and every day she was teased and ignored. She was an alright student; she was smart enough to understand the material, but a sadness had been slowly building in her since her father passed away. He was her strength, and without him, her mind was consumed with sadness until her grades began to slip and her desire to be around other people dwindled.

Accustomed to being alone, Xoxann would take walks outside of Venger, following the stairs along the cliffs down to the beach. A lot of the older kids went down to the beach to hang out and have fun, but she'd found a narrow path covered by wild brush that led to a small private beach that no one else seemed to know about. She'd watch the waves for hours there. It was her quiet place, where she didn't feel the weight of her sadness pressing in on her at all times. She would often stay there until dusk before making the climb back up the stairs to Venger.

She often arrived before her mother, who she knew would be exhausted from working in the grain mill all day. So Xoxann would make dinner and have it ready for her when she got home. Her mother loved her and was always grateful when Xoxann helped her out. Each morning, Xoxann would wake to the sound of her mom singing while making breakfast for the both of them. They took care of each other. They had to; it had been three years since they were suddenly left on their own. Xoxann knew her mother was sad, too, though she was careful not to mention it. When she did, it brought her mother pain, and she would begin to sob.

Then, on one random day, in the middle of the week, on her little piece of the beach, things began to change for her. The day had gone like any other. It began by having breakfast with Mom and then plunging into abject humiliation. As usual, when she first arrived at the beach, she began to cry. She cried and sobbed, doing her best to get it all out of her system. She had been out there for a little while and had just begun to regain her composure when the sound of the waves lapping up against something caught her attention. She looked out over the water to see that it was a small, battered boat that had been pushed closer to the bank by the waves. She stood there, just staring at it for a moment or two. Nothing had ever washed up on her little beach before, and she was afraid to go

investigate. The tide was pushing it onto shore, but the tide
was going to change soon. Once it did, it would pull the boat
back into the sea; if she were going to investigate, she would
have to do so quickly.

Xoxann decided to act and waded out cautiously to
where the boat was. When the tide washed in, the water was
waist-deep, which was enough to knock her over if she wasn't
careful. She grabbed the bow of the boat and began to pull it
onto shore completely, looking for a place to secure it. That's
when she found the body.

She screamed as she saw the girl in the boat. Her throat
had been cut. She was pale, and her eyes were still half open.
Even at Xoxann's age, with no sense of medical knowledge, she
could tell the girl was dead. Her dress was made of silk and
satin, and she was beautifully adorned with jewelry. The style
was unfamiliar to Xoxann; she guessed that the girl must have
come from a kingdom across the sea.

Time seemed to lose its meaning as she stood there. She
had never seen a dead body before, and she was entranced by
a mixture of fear and curiosity. Her mind created stories about
how she must have gotten there. Each one was fueled by her
own sadness. In her mind, every version of the story became
worse and worse. She openly wept for the girl and said prayers
to any gods who might be listening. She prayed over her and
asked that she be saved from her pain and finally find peace
now that she was dead. Envy welled in Xoxann as she thought
about how the girl would no longer feel the same great sadness
that was in Xoxann's own heart. She decided that she needed
to remember this moment; she wanted to take something of the

girl to remind her that after it was all over, she, too, would find peace. She was wondering what to take as another wave pushed in, moving the boat enough to bump her, causing Xoxann to have to regain her balance, yet the girl had not been jostled. She had heard that a dead body would stiffen. She figured that this must be the position she died in and thought nothing more of the stillness. That's when she noticed the dead girl was holding something close to her chest.

"This must be the most important thing she owns if she kept it right next to her heart when she died. This is what I'll keep," Xoxann thought to herself as she worked to pry it loose. She finally got the object out and inspected it to see what was so important. It was a small black metal figurine of a man that had been twisted out of shape. She barely had enough time to look at it before the girl's head turned and looked at her.

As her head turned, Xoxann screamed and tried to step back, but as she did, the water flowed in from a wave and knocked her over. She scrambled to get back on her feet just in time to watch the boat strike her across the face. The next thing she knew, she was being dragged out of the water, her face burning from the saltwater in her wounds.

"Hey! Stay with me, alright?" A girl a little older than Xoxann had her by both wrists and was pulling her out of the surf. "You just hang on, and everything's going to be alright."

The girl pulled Xoxann to the beach and then collapsed with exhaustion right next to her. Both of them lay there for a moment, catching their breath, but the shock was beginning to wear off, and the pain from her head began to pound.

Xoxann put her hand to her head to assess the wound.
As she pulled it away, she saw that it was covered in blood,
and fear took over. Xoxann began to scream and cry. "I don't
want to die!" All of her ideas about how lucky the dead girl
was suddenly vanished, and she realized for certain she wanted
to live.

"I can heal you," said the other older girl. "But you
have to wish it. Do you want to live?"

"Yes!" Xoxann screamed with all her heart. Her vision
was going dark, and she was beginning to get sleepy. "I wish
to live."

The girl put her hands over Xoxann's wound, and light
began to pour from them. There was a moment of searing pain,
and then it was over.

Xoxann leaped into the girl's arms. "Thank you," was all
that Xoxann could get out as she cried into the girl's shoulder.

"It's alright. You are okay now." The girl rocked Xoxann
back and forth until she calmed down. It's the least I could do
after you saved me."

Xoxann didn't understand at first. She looked up at the
girl and examined her carefully. The dress and jewelry were the
same as the girl on the boat. It frightened her, and she backed
up a few steps. "Are you a ghost?"

"I don't know what I am at this point." Xoxann began
to back away slowly. "No," the girl said quietly. "Please don't
go." She patted the sand next to where she sat. "Listen. You

saved me from being trapped forever on that boat. You have the figurine to which I am attached. I would have been trapped out there forever if it weren't for you." The girl reached out her hand. "Please. I owe you everything that is left of me, but all I really want is to be your friend. That's why I healed you. Won't you trust me?"

"If you are a ghost, how did you help me?" Xoxann asked slowly, moving back toward the girl.

"I have a magical friend. A genie named DeSalvo," the girl said. "He's the one who healed you with magic."

"A real live genie?" Xoxann's mind was instantly filled with fantasies of wishes and how her life could be different with a genie as a friend. "Can I meet him?"

"Yes." She smiled as Xoxann sat back down next to her on the beach. "But first. Before I introduce you two, I want to get to know you."

"Why?" asked Xoxann.

"Because we are going to be the best of friends, and I want to get to know my new best friend." The girl said and put her arm around Xoxann's shoulders. "Let's start at the beginning. What's your name?"

"Xoxann Velo, but my mom calls me Xoxy."

"Nice to meet you, Xoxy," the girl said. "My name is Kim. Kim Collard."

Xoxy and Kim talked for hours. Xoxy had lost track of

time and didn't realize it until it was getting dark. She didn't want to be rude, but she knew she had to get home.

"Don't worry about it," Kim said.

"How am I not supposed to worry about it?" Xoxy said as she started to head toward home.

"We are friends now, right?"

"Yes. We're friends," Xoxy shrugged. "You are my only friend."

"Well, it doesn't have to be that way." Kim smiled at Xoxann. "I think you should meet my magical friend, the genie. You could wish for a better life. You could have anything you want."

"Is he nice?" asked Xoxy. She had heard tales that genies could be mean and terrible.

"He's nice to nice people," Kim said and winked at her dramatically. "Look. Friends trust each other, right?"

"Yes."

"Then you should trust me when I say that DeSalvo can be your friend and help make your world better. Want me to prove it?" Kim asked.

"No. It's ok. I believe you. Friends trust each other." Xoxy was afraid of losing the only friend she had. "What do I have to do?"

"You know that black figurine you have? It's how you call him. Hold it in your hand and call out his name."

Xoxann retrieved the figure from the pocket of her dress. It was as black as onyx and carved to look like a man who had been twisted as if he were being rung out. She closed her hand around it and said aloud, "DeSalvo." Black smoke filled with little red sparks began to flow from the figure. The smoke began to solidify, taking the shape of an old man. Finally, all of the smoke vanished, and DeSalvo stood in front of Xoxann. He was dressed in black robes, with a banner over his left shoulder that draped down to his knees in both the front and the back, held in place by a thick belt on his waist. The banner was embellished with a magic fire design; like a real fire, the design moved and flickered. He had a black stone on his throat and over the third eye that she could see, and his eyes matched the stones. It was odd and unexpected, but his smile was kind, and he bowed dramatically, which made Xoxann smile in return.

"My goodness, what a beautiful little girl you are. How old are you?" DeSalvo said as he stood back up and smiled sweetly at her again.

"I am ten, Sir."

DeSalvo smiled and gave a dramatic bow again that felt like play to Xoxann. "I am DeSalvo. I am the genie who is connected to the figurine in your hand."

Xoxann giggled and curtsied. "I am Xoxann, but you can call me Xoxy."

"It is a pleasure to meet you, Xoxy. It broke my heart when Kim and I were lost at sea. I can do a lot of stuff, but I can't stop death. When I knew she wasn't going to live, it broke my heart, but you know what I did?" He leaned down so he could be at her height. "A wish was made. I wish that her spirit would find a good, kind person to have my figure. Someone with a good heart and someone worthy of their wishes being granted." He gave her a comical shrug and asked ever so politely, "Is that you?"

Xoxann looked to Kim, who smiled at her and nodded. "Yes, I am," she said with glee.

DeSalvo dropped down to one knee and took Xoxann's hand. "Oh, this makes me so happy. I was so worried that someone would find it who was mean and terrible, but if Kim believes in you, then I do too." DeSalvo turned Xoxann toward Kim.

"Thank you, Xoxann. You have saved me again." She began to wave goodbye. "You will always be my friend, no matter where I go from here. Thank you."

"Don't go, Kim." Xoxann began to cry, "I don't want to be alone again with no friends."

"I will always be with you, sweetie, and I would never leave you alone. From now on, DeSalvo will be your friend. He promised me that if I found him a new friend, I would be free to go to a better place."

"That's right, and I am so glad you got to be Kim's friend before she moved on." DeSalvo began to wave goodbye.

"It was wonderful to know you. Thank you for all your help. I free you." With that, Kim blew Xoxann a kiss and then disappeared.

DeSalvo held her while she cried. Then he dried her tears and reminded her that he was there and that he wouldn't leave her. They were friends now, and he was going to help her because that's what friends do for each other.

"I have to get home. I am going to be late, and I won't have time to make dinner for my mother," Xoxann said.

"That's easy. First, let's get you home, new friend." DeSalvo put his hand to his chin and thought for a moment. "Hey, I have an idea. You could wish for it. Then I could help."

"How many wishes do I get?"

"There is no set number, so don't worry. You won't be wasting a wish." He winked at her comically. "Just make a wish."

Xoxann closed her eyes and said, "Alright. I wish to get home really fast."

"As you wish," DeSalvo smirked. "This is going to feel ... odd." DeSalvo took over Xoxann's body and leaped straight up and over the cliffs. He then relinquished control but did not leave her body.

"That was scary," Xoxann said.

I'm sorry, it was the fastest way to get you home. My magic won't let me teleport you into Venger, so I got you as close as I could. Now I need you to take me into the city.

"Okay, but don't do that again. It was icky." It was the only word that she had for the sensation of being possessed for a moment, but she felt that it got the point across.

Absolutely, DeSalvo was speaking into her mind. *If you don't like it, I won't do it again without your permission.*

He hid in her mind, deep in her thoughts, as she crossed over the three concentric circles at the front gate and made her way home quickly. It was still late; she was going to make it home before her mother, but without enough time to make dinner.

"I wish I didn't have to make dinner tonight," she said aloud.

Somewhere in her mind, DeSalvo chuckled and said, *"As you wish."*

When she got home, her mother was home early and waiting for her. "Where have you been?" she asked.

"I was down at the beach and, Mom, guess what! I have good news. I made two new friends today."

"That's wonderful!" her mother exclaimed. "I have good news as well." She sat her daughter down and tried to wipe some dirt off her face with some spit and her thumb. "I saved a man from being run over by a carriage today. It's like he didn't see it and just walked into the road; I pulled him back to safety just in time. He was so happy that he gave me thirty gold pieces. It's all he had on him, but he said he was looking for a cook and asked me if I wanted the job — and he offered me three times what I make at the mill. I said yes!"

"Oh, my gods, Mother, that is amazing!" Xoxann squealed and leaped into her mother's arms.

"I know! It just happened out of nowhere, like magic!" She danced around the room for a moment with her daughter clinging to her neck. "Don't worry about making dinner tonight. Tonight, we are going out. We are going to buy nice new dresses, and then we are going to go to a real restaurant, and you can order whatever you want!

Her mother went to fetch their coats. Xoxann smiled. She looked into a mirror that was nearby and said, "Thank you, DeSalvo."

That's what friends are for. DeSalvo was quiet for a moment and then added, Can you do me a favor?

"Anything."

Don't tell anybody about me. If you do, they will want to take me away from you, and then we will both be alone again.

"I promise. I won't tell anybody."

10

A WISH FIT FOR A KING

Dalen and his friends had been traveling south for two days when they entered the forest of the Woodland Elves. Master Ki had decided to return to the Temple of Light. Now that they were in the hands of her Royal Highness, who knew what was to come during the next part of their journey. They followed the southern road until it reached the forest. The road cut through the western part of the woods and was the only way through. A treaty made during Gavin's grandfather's reign granted the humans a solitary path going through their lands, making it easier and faster than going around. It was a day-and-a-half journey toward the west to take the perimeter and then another day and a half to get to the Hunters Lodge, which was the closest outpost to the Elven woods on the far side. Cutting through the forest was exactly one day's travel.

The distance was decided by the treaty, and two campsites were created a third of the way in from either side. The treaty stated that there would always be food, water, and firewood at each camp provided by the Elves. In addition, anyone using the road to pass through the forest or using the camps would be protected from anything that might be lurking in the woods. This included the Elves themselves, who undoubtedly were lurking in the woods, watching every step taken while in their lands. The humans agreed that no one would be allowed to step off the road. There would be no hunting, cutting down trees, or picking berries. The road and the camps were the only places they were allowed to set foot and were the boundary of the elves' leniency for being on their land. The elves disliked humans in their home and were more than happy to provide everything at the camps.

Today, they were going to walk the very fine line that allowed for the only exception to the rule. When the Mother Blade vanished, seers were consulted about the location of the blade, which is never found in the same place twice. Some could sense them and a rare few beings could see through time and space and divine the locations of the blades. They foretold that the Earth Blade would be found only if the Queen participated in a ceremony that was to commence in the Woodland Elves territory. They said the Earth Blade had chosen that location because it was time to finish a promise that had been made generations ago. A promise that would eventually touch the generations to come. Gavin and Hope both knew Vengerian history, and they believed they knew what had to be done. The promise made by Gavin's grandfather would be remembered, and the elves would honor it, permitting the royal family to enter their woods. As long as it was specifically for a royal matter and furthered the fragile treaty that the two kingdoms observed.

Once they arrived at the first camp, Queen Hope explained that they would be walking from there and had everyone exit the coach. Each of them activated their pins to enable their telepathic link with one another and checked the connection while the queen had her coachman unload the gift that she had brought before dismissing him. It was only once he and the coach were out of sight that she called out to the elves.

"Good afternoon." She spoke with a loud, clear voice. "I am Queen Hope of Venger, and these are my guardians. We request, with great respect to you and your forest, the opportunity to honor the promise made. Thank you."

‹Did we just ask permission to keep a promise?› asked Travis, amused at the idea.

‹ That's what it sounded like to me,› added Sir Adam playfully.

‹For years, humans used to wander into their forest and take what they wanted. They would hunt mystical animals and cut down sacred trees.› The queen's voice was solemn in their heads. ‹In response, the Elves closed their lands, and anyone foolish enough to go into their forest was never heard from again. Elves live a long time, and those who enforce the old ways still rule this forest.›

‹Are we in danger?› Becky began to scan the trees. ‹Scale from one to ten.›

‹Eight, but only if we step off the road.› answered Hope. ‹Which is the problem, because the Earth Blade is out there somewhere.› as she gestured out into the woods. ‹But for now, I would give it a three. Two maybe?›

They haven't responded, thought Dalen, along the connection of their minds. *Perhaps they didn't hear us.*

‹Oh...› The queen chuckled wryly. ‹No, they heard us. They are just going to make us wait. It's a sign of dominance in their lands to make us wait. Like we don't matter to them. It's expected.›

So, they waited. After a few hours, it started to get dark. Dalen used only the wood that was left for them to make a teepee shape in the fire pit, and with a quick wave of his hand, flames engulfed the pile.

Four large logs that had been carved into benches surrounded the fire pit. They were beautifully carved with adornments of oak leaves and acorns. The team gathered around the fire, each taking a seat on the benches, everyone watching the back of the person who sat across from them. They sat in quiet, each of them listening for approaching footsteps. They listened well into the night. Nothing. Then, early in the morning, just as the light began to push its way through the canopy of the forest, an elven herald walked out from the woods and into their camp.

Dalen, who had stayed awake to watch over them as they slept, was the first to see him. As the herald approached, Dalen used his ability to touch their minds while sleeping to send a message. *It's showtime. Someone's here. Wake up and reactivate your pins for communication.* Each of them began to stir; one by one, they woke up, and as they stood up to greet their visitor, each of them covertly activated the telepathic abilities of the pin.

He spoke in Elven, but Dalen cast a spell on himself that allowed him to understand any language spoken in his presence. He translated telepathically to his friends as the herald spoke. "Hope, Daughter of Galamad. I have come to give you permission to keep Venger's promise."

The Queen spoke in Elven as well as a sign of respect for being in their kingdom. "Thank you. The hospitality of the Elves is kind and generous to allow me to ask."

The herald gave a small tilt at the waist, exhibiting a distant cousin to a bow. "I see you have not forgotten your manners, Your Majesty. Since you are being so respectful, we shall offer you the same in return. You have come at an interesting time, Your Majesty, Queen of Venger. Why is it that you have chosen now to honor the promise made by another king, made when you were only a child?"

"The promise of Venger and the honor it holds belongs to any king or queen who can earn the right to rule. I may have been a child when it was made, but I understand its weight and respect its power." The queen stepped forward, and to the surprise of the herald, she knelt before him as if he were the representative of the entire elven people. "The timing to collect on that promise has to do with the future of my kingdom. The time has come for my daughter to come of age. As you know, I am the first to be tested. We believe that the Mother Blade is within your lands, and even though it could mean the destruction of us all, I would never set foot in your lands without your consent." She lowered her head and pleaded with him. "I beg of the Eleven Kingdom: please allow us safe passage."

He paused for a moment, and then Dalen used the Spheres of Magic to see the world through supernatural methods. Dalen could see that the herald had a telepathic link with someone, but he could not hear what was being said.

From what seemed to be a far-off distance, Dalen began to feel the presence of an old friend and teacher. *Focus your thoughts,* Master Truth said directly into Dalen's consciousness. *Follow the line with your mind.*

Dalen listened closely and followed the magic to someone deep in the woods. They were elven and female. Dalen was sure of that, but when he tried to look closer, she looked away. She laughed at Dalen and said aloud, "No peeking." And Dalen lost contact with whoever she was.

Not bad, but clumsy. She saw you. Master Truths' tone was playful in Dalen's mind.

Who was that? Dalen opened himself to the forest around him, trying to find her physically within the body sphere.

That was Queen Adila White-Tree of the Woodland Realm. Master Truth explained *It is impressive that you were able to track her on your first attempt. Just be careful. If you connect to someone too strongly, as you have seen, they will become aware of your presence.*

The elven herald continued as if nothing had happened. "We suspected as much, and we thank you for your trust." He gave a formal elven bow that reminded Dalen of his old friend, Master Joy. "We are here to assist you in your endeavor. So, if you follow me, Your Majesty, I will take you to your trial. Your guardians may accompany you but know this: You must accomplish your task without their aid."

"Thank you for your hospitality toward me and my guardians. I know this task falls to myself, and I am ready for the challenge."

The herald scoffed, "Yes, but is the challenge ready for you? The world does not revolve around your needs, Hope, Queen of Venger."

"We will do as you command." Hope lowered her head again to the herald and then rose to her feet.

"Good," he smiled. "Very good."

‹This guy seems slightly threatening. What do you want us to do?› asked Sir Adam.

‹Nothing aggressive. We are guests, and we shall treat the elves and their forest with respect.›

‹Understood.› Sir Adam nodded but let a slight grin slowly pull at the corners of his mouth. ‹In that case, can we all just take a moment to realize how absolutely amazing it is that we are about to walk into an enchanted forest ... It is enchanted, right?›

The queen had to fight for a moment not to laugh. She nodded just once. ‹Yes, Sir Adam. This is an enchanted forest.›

‹Yeah.› Sir Adam thought. ‹Enchanted elven forest.›

Dalen saw it coming a moment before it happened. He had just enough time to align his magic with the pins, harmonizing his friends, and all of them spoke together in a single thought. ‹These are the moments we live for.›

You imprinted this moment in their subconscious. Master Truth's voice was clear and strong in Dalen's mind. *They will remember this moment forever, and so will you.* Dalen could feel Master Truth's hand on his shoulder, even though Dalen knew he wasn't actually there. *Always remember. It is not the amount of power you have that defines you. It's the actions you choose to take with your power that do. I'm proud of you.* Dalen felt him let go of his shoulder. *Now, get back to reality and pay attention. You are on the move.*

Dalen blinked and started to pay attention just as Queen Hope and the team were asked to follow the herald, who was instructing them to stay behind him and to stay on the path. As he led them through the woods, the shrubs and trees moved out of the way, creating a small footpath, and as they walked along it, the plants and trees moved themselves back into position behind them. They traveled for close to an hour in silence, only speaking to each other when necessary by using their pins and always staying on the path. They eventually stopped at an encampment of a hundred or so elves. Upon arriving, the group was intentionally taken through the main part of camp and brought to a tent that was made of linen. The fabric had an elaborate design of a tree, complete with branches and roots embroidered on it. The shape was circular, with a radius about twenty feet across. It was easily the largest tent in the camp.

There were two guards, one on each side of the doors, and once the team was in place, they reached out in unison and opened both sides. An elven woman stepped out from the tent. She seemed aged but still had life in her. The silver in her hair had overtaken the strands of chestnut that wove themselves intricately into braids cascading down her back. In her hair, a crown of wood that wreathed her brow was still alive with green leaves and red berries. Her floor-length dress was green with a silver embroidery of a tree and sleeves that flared at the wrists. She stepped out, regal and proud.

"Hope, Queen of Venger," she said with a voice that was practiced at being powerful and strong over hundreds of years. "I have but one thing to say to you." Hope gave a formal curtsy and held it with her head bowed. "I am so proud of you." Her sternness washed away and was replaced with a bright disposition that melted away all concerns that any of them had.

‹Oh. Thank goodness! I thought we were going to have a situation for a moment.› Becky breathed a sigh of relief.

‹Yeah, I thought I was going to have to draw on Grandma here.› Sir Adam meant it as a joke, but Dalen could feel them all take a breath of relief, including Hope.

"Greetings, friends. I am Queen Adila White-Tree. My apologies for how you have been treated, but it was a part of Hope's trial. A lot can be understood about someone in power when their power is removed." Adila gave Hope a proper curtsy. "You could have yelled and demanded that you be treated

in a way you felt you were entitled to. You could have tried
to show strength and take what you wanted, demanding that
everything you did was for the needs of your people. You could
have claimed birthright. Instead, you were respectful, even when
it wasn't returned. You were patient, even though your entire
kingdom is in jeopardy. I find you to be worthy to take the trial
and welcome you here."

"Thank you, Your Majesty." Finally, Hope rose from her
curtsy and lifted her eyes to meet White-Tree's.

"We are both queens," White-Tree said. "More
important than that, we are women. Please, call me Adila. Do
you mind if I call you Hope?"

Hope took Adila's hand in hers. "Our hearts agree with
each other, sister. I would prefer to be here as who I am, not
what I am."

"Oh, dear sister, tomorrow you will have to be both.
There is no way around that." Adila shared a look with
Hope, and Dalen saw something in their eyes that he did not
understand. It was a look that only a queen could give, and
only a queen would understand.

"Then you know what my trial is?" Hope asked, trying to
get an understanding of what lay before her.

Adila's words were filled with respect, like what she
offered was a great honor. "Yes. Tomorrow, you will fulfill
the promise made and help us rebuild part of what was lost.
Tomorrow, you will Run with the Trees."

"I don't understand what that means. What is Running with the Trees?" asked Hope.

"An amazingly good quality for a queen to have. Knowing you don't know everything. I have great hope for you." Adila patted Hope's hand and then pointed off into the encampment. "Another good quality is the ability to seek out knowledge and to discover the truth. So, the next part of the trial tasked to you is this. Walk amongst my people and find the knowledge you seek."

"Very well. In this task, may I bring my guardians?" asked Hope with her namesake in tone.

"Only you can retrieve the Earth Blade from the Father Tree. That task is for you alone, but this trial is different, and your guardians may go with you, though I would like to speak with one of them."

"Which of my guardians do you wish to speak with?"

"The Jinn. I wish to ask his opinion on something." Since Master Ki had not joined them, and Master Truth was just a voice in his mind, Dalen assumed she meant him.

"Dalen Pax, the queen of this realm, wishes to have a moment of your time and council. What say you?" Hope looked over to Dalen, awaiting his answer, but telepathically asked. ‹Help a lady out?›

"I would consider it an honor and a privilege to help in any way I can. If I may, I would also like to add that it would be a personal joy to have the chance to speak with you." Pleasantries. The Fire Jinn once told him that they could take you far, and she was right. Hope took the team into the encampment to meet with Adila's people while the Queen took Dalen's arm and returned to her tent.

"Leave us." Adila didn't look at any of the elves that were in the tent; there was no need to. The few attendants that were in the room picked up their things and left at her command. Adila raised her hand and, with a few gestures paired with a word in elven, created a magical field that encompassed the inside of the tent.

Time slowed to a crawl for Dalen as he watched every gesture in slow motion. Absorbing how to master the nuances of her movements. He looked through his supernatural sight and watched the spell take form, and he understood how to create it. Moreover, with his knowledge of the craft, he saw how it could be improved upon. He slowed time further to where the frames of reality could be seen as separate and independent. He stared at the spell. He touched it. He felt its form and came to understand how it existed in real space, and in doing so, he knew that he could also collapse it, effectively dismissing the spell and escaping if needed. Once he knew what it was and he was sure he could dispel it if needed, he allowed time to catch up again.

"Neat spell." Dalen was now looking at it normally with mundane eyes, and it was beautiful. Waves of light rippled across the interior surface of the tent, much like an indoor Borealis plastered along the walls and ceiling. "I hope you don't mind. I may use it from time to time."

"You learned the spell by watching me cast it just once?" There was a look of surprise in her eyes that was followed by a nod of respect.

"As you cast it," Dalen replied.

"That fast?" Adila's questioning wasn't of disbelief but rather an attempt to understand something.

"It was longer for me than it was for you."

"So, you are affected differently by time?"

"Through training at the Temple of Light. There, I was blessed with the opportunity to learn other lessons in magic that have helped enhance my abilities. Using my combined knowledge creates a skill that allows me to control how I perceive time." Dalen did his best to be modest about his abilities, but he also saw no reason to hide them either.

What do you think, Master Truth? Should I be worried about telling her too much? Dalen asked.

Master Truth was with him instantly, and Dalen could feel his presence in the room.

Use your wisdom and intelligence to choose what to say. Dalen could feel his master's presence in his mind. *She is friendly, and I sense no malice, but knowledge is dangerous. Especially when in the hands of people who have amassed power.*

"That is amazing!" She clapped her hands together and, with her fingers interlaced, brought them up to her chin. "It was you who peeked, right?" Dalen nodded. "How did you do that? How did you find me so quickly?"

"I listened." Dalen did his best to give her a friendly smirk that let her know he was playing. "Once I knew that it was happening, it was like following your voice." Dalen chose to listen to Master Truth and did his best to answer her questions yet did not offer much for answers either.

She laughed aloud with surprise at his answer. "In my many years, I have never encountered one of your kind. The myths and legends only tell one version of a tale, and I may never have this opportunity again. I am sure you understand, and I know that you must be asked this often, and for that, I am truly sorry."

"Forgive me, but before you continue, I must ask you something." Dalen's tone was of respect but also slightly assertive. "If you think that you can force me into something, I have terrible news. I am not sure what you have planned in the next few seconds, but the point that you decided to put us in a magical barrier before you attempted such things creates a level of concern, and no matter how much I respect Hope and wish to save Venger, I am not in a position to bargain, make contracts, or enter into any form of relationship at this time. So, with all that said, Your Majesty, what is it that I am supposed to understand?"

Adila's tone swiftly changed to concern mixed with amusement. "No, no, no. You misunderstand me completely. The barrier spell was so that I could speak to you candidly without the rest of the camp hearing what I had to say. I don't wish to trap you or try to buy you off," she shook her head, "or any other thing like that. I was hoping you would grant me a wish."

Dalen relaxed. He shook off his suspicious thoughts, took a breath, and began to think to himself.

Can I? Can I do this? I know the stone from the statue gave me a lot of power, and I believe that what they gave me is enough to grant a wish, but am I able to pull it off? Am I good enough?

What's the first rule of magic? Master Truth's voice was calm and soothing in Dalen's mind.

Dalen slid the silver figurine from its pocket on his belt into his hand and focused his thoughts on the man he wanted to believe he was. *Your magic is only as powerful as you believe it to be.*

He laughed at himself for a moment; then, he reached into the satchel at his hip. He retrieved his teacup, allowed it to fill, and began sipping on it while he continued his conversation. "Okay, I thought ... It doesn't matter what I thought. What matters is what you actually meant, and I might be able to help. There are some things I will not do."

"Can't or won't?" the Queen asked.

Dalen smiled and took a sip. "Both," replied Dalen.

Adila shrugged. "Fair enough. Where are the boundaries, and what is your price?"

"I will not break the laws of reality, and I will not tamper with free will." Dalen took a sip of his tea. "So, no changing time. If Bob died five years ago, that's how

Bob stays."

Adila laughed. "Nothing like that. Bob can stay dead. Never liked him in the first place. What I require is something more possible."

Dalen took another sip of his tea. "What did you have in mind?" As he spoke, he allowed his mind to focus. He connected to the universe and wiped all thoughts from this mind. He pictured himself standing in the Magic Circle in the Temple of All-Faith. He looked up at the ceiling and allowed the Divine light to pass through him.

"My son. He has no direction, and I am getting old. He will one day be king, but he is still a boy in many ways. I know that I am partly to blame for this. He wanted for nothing and never had to earn anything he'd been given. When he was born, I was embarrassed and ashamed that I had him out of wedlock to a man who wooed me but had no intention to stay. I spent the first half of his life telling him that he would never need to have any responsibilities in this world and that he would never be king. Things between him and I have gotten better, and it is my desire that he take over the kingdom. But I am worried that the caustic words of my past will get the better of him, and he will never believe that he has the potential to rule. I am afraid that I will die before he is ready. He lacks ambition or drive, and without correction, he will be a very weak king. Or worse, a cruel one driven by his selfishness." Her tone was pleading, practically begging, and she dropped anything that looked like pretense. At this moment, she was a mother worried about her son and a queen worried about the future of her kingdom.

"What is your wish?" Dalen said calmly.

"I wish that you could change that."

"You wish for me to change him. That is messing with free will."

"What if he chooses it himself?"

Master Truth, I need your help. Is what she is asking possible? Dalen pleaded with his old master, hoping for insight.

Dalen was not abandoned, and Master Truth's words began to articulate in Dalen's mind: *If he chooses it himself, then yes. You will have to imbue an object with the potential that she asks for but have the object require his free will to activate it. Let me show you the way.*

The world melted away, and all that was left was the circle that Dalen was standing in and the light of the universe pouring down on him from the infinite beyond, with Master Truth standing in front of him. Dalen brought the light into him and channeled it through his ki.

Picture the intent, Master Truth spoke into Dalen's mind as Dalen found his center. *See it play out in your mind and look forward to the future to the moment that her wish comes to fruition.*

Dalen moved through frames of time, searching for the moment that King White-Tree took the throne. He tried to look at it, but the image was different than he expected. Flashes of Princess Joanna appeared in his mind. Then those images warped, and as they came into focus, she was much older. Well into her forties. Dalen saw her next to King White-Tree while they stood side by side. He thought he had somehow done it wrong and tried to move past it.

Don't fight it. The problem with seeing the future is that you put too much expectation on it., trying to will it in a certain direction. See it for what it is and accept the truth.

Dalen cleared his mind and tried to find it again, but when he found the potential where, in reality, her son would become King White-Tree, the image was not of the throne of the elves but the throne of Venger.

This is the future? Dalen was confused and could not accept what he was seeing.

You are looking through time to a potential, corrected Master Truth. *You are looking at the outcome of events if he chooses to step forward and step up. If he chooses to take the object, this will be his destiny.*

And if he doesn't? asked Dalen

Then, his destiny will be something else. Destiny is the destination of your choices and actions.

Where does fate fit into all of this?

Fate? Master Truth laughed. *Fate happens in the choice.*

His fate will change based on his choice?

No. His destiny will change based on his choice. His fate is that he has to make a choice.

Okay. I don't understand completely why that is true, but I accept that it is. Dalen looked at the frame in time hard enough that it began to become real. As he did that, he looked at the moment when the prince would have to leave his childhood behind him and choose to step up and become the king he could be. He saw an argument where friends became brothers, and the prince needed to prove himself. Dalen entangled the two frames together and made the choice a trigger so that the only way one would become real was if the other was completed.

Well done, Master Truth said. *Now, create in your mind a path between the two. A path that will be his responsibility to achieve. Don't look at each frame separately; allow the universe and time to fill in the details. Now, take this spell and imbue it into an object so that accepting the object is accepting the responsibility to achieve that moment in time. Then seal it like a magical contract.*

Dalen did as was suggested, but he had to imbue it to an object. He allowed the wish to guide him, using its power instead of his own. The wish took him to a moment in the future. Coins were being made with the king's face on one side. The other side bore the symbol of the Vengerian Seal. It was only a sample, but Dalen reached into time and grabbed the coin, pulling it into the present. He turned it on its side, and while he traced the edge with his finger, he embedded the spell into the coin, tying it to White-Tree's choice. He held it in his hand and focused all his will on creating that moment. And focused on being in the frame of existence where the choice that triggers the wish is made. He closed his hand around it and allowed time to come crashing back into his reality.

From the queen's point of view, she had barely asked if it could be done when she saw Dalen put out his hand and then close it again, then watched as light shot from between his fingers. When he opened it again, there was a coin in his hand. He handed it to her for inspection. It was a gold piece that had her son's face on it. He was older and wiser than the boy she knew, and it pleased her to see him become a strong man. On the other side, she saw nothing, for the choice that would reveal that side had not yet been made.

"The magic is locked by contract," Dalen explained calmly and clearly so that there was no mistaking that the coin and the wish were dormant. "Make no mistake, there is nothing that will come of this until the moment he decides he is ready to walk the path needed to reach his greatest potential. That way, he has free choice. All he has to do is know what this coin means and what it does, and then with full knowledge of what and why, he has to choose it," Adila flipped the coin over to reveal the side that had his face. "But hear this. Once he chooses it, he will be held responsible for that future, and he must take action to bring it to fruition. Without his effort, the spell will die, and so will the future that could have been."

Adila handed it back to him. "Agreed. This is the wish I have asked for. I didn't want him to be handed his kingdom; I want him to earn it."

Dalen was tired. Creating the wish had taken a lot out of him. "That I can guarantee. If he takes his future into his own hands, he will definitely have to earn it."

"Then, before I accept this, I want to know what your price is." Her tone became serious. "I will not be swindled out of my kingdom or, worse, have my people be enslaved to you over this bobble. I have heard tales of the Genie DeSalvo. I know how he almost destroyed my people generations ago because people were too hungry for his wishes."

"Nothing like that, Your Majesty." Dalen shook his head. "I'm not that guy. As a matter of fact, I am about as far from that guy as you can get." He offered the coin to her. "Take it with my blessings."

Adila reached for the coin and then stopped. "That is very kind of you. Magic always has a price. There must be something you require."

"There is, Your Majesty. After Hope finishes her quest and returns to Venger, my friends and I will require your permission to enter further into your lands. There are two oracles that have the information we need."

"I know of whom you speak. Granted. Once Hope has finished what she must do, I will have a guide lead you to the part of the forest where they live, but then you must traverse the rest yourselves. If I do this, you will consider us even?" asked the queen.

"Indeed, I will. Take the coin, and may your son choose his own path."

The queen took the coin and then gave Dalen a hug. "You are more than anything I could have hoped for, and I wish you luck on your journey. I will arrange everything tomorrow. For now, thank you. Please, return to your friends and your queen." She paused for a moment and then added, "You have given this old woman hope again, and for that alone, I will always be in your debt. Call on me if you ever need my assistance." With a wave of her hand, she dispelled the barrier and allowed him to leave.

I hope in the end he chooses wisely, Dalen thought to Master Truth.

That is all you can do sometimes. You saw a possible future, but it doesn't mean it will come to pass. It only means that if he chooses to act, the door will be open.

What if he doesn't?

Then the world will be lesser for it, but it is not on you. It is his free will that will cut the path of his destiny.

I think I am glad for that.

I know that I am. Now go and find your team. Tomorrow promises to be an interesting day.

11

FULCRUM AND GNOMON

Dalen got about ten feet away from the tent when his body began to tingle. He was sure that granting the wish did something to him as a jinn and somehow affected him physically; he felt as if something inside him was terribly wrong. He became feverish and clammy and began to feel his organs quiver, which made him nauseous. It lasted only a few moments, his system returning to normal quickly, but deep in his being, Dalen knew that something was wrong.

When Dalen located his friends, they were speaking with a small group of elves. As he drew near, he called out, letting them know he had returned.

"Everyone," Hope quickly got everyone's attention. "This is the other member of our team. I know he may look a little different, but I assure you he's a good guy." Then, through her pin, she asked, ‹Are you okay?›

Dalen reached up and activated his pin as well. ‹I feel fine. Why do you ask?›

‹You have physically changed.› The queen's words were still ringing in his head as he looked around and saw concern in his friend's eyes.

The elves walked toward Dalen to greet him properly. Dalen noticed two things as they approached; one was that most of them looked at the stones on his forehead, directly over his third eye, or the one in his throat. And two, that although they were willing to stare at his stones, all of them avoided direct eye contact.

Dalen tried to hide his own rising concern as he manifested a mirror into his hand. Letting the queen take over the conversation, he backed up as calmly as he could and looked at himself in the mirror, hoping to understand why everyone was responding the way that they were. He stared at an almost unrecognizable reflection. His eyes had become like the stones in his body and gave off a white glow. His complexion had turned from a beautiful coffee color to as white as marble, far past the limits of flesh, and his hair had been stripped of all color. It was as white as his skin and had thinned out, looking as though he had recently been ill. He looked more like a living statue than a human. Even his face had taken on new chiseled characteristics as if he were cut from stone.

Dalen reached out to his entire team with his telepathy instead of using the pin. He wanted them to 'feel' his words.

I'm okay. I don't know what has happened to me, but I'm all right.

‹ You're so pale,› thought Becky.

‹And you don't seem completely real.› Travis's thoughts were filled with concern for his health.

Sir Adam took a deep breath and slowly released his hand from the grip of his sword. ‹That was almost awkward.› Everyone laughed slightly nervously.

‹I knew it was you,› Brother Peace added. ‹ You're pale, and you look more like a living statue, but I can still tell it's you. Besides, the stones gave it away.› Peace's words were the voice of reason resonating in their minds.

‹What happened to you?› Even in their minds, the queen's voice still had a hint of melody, but now there were tones of concern. ‹What did Queen Adila want with you?› Dalen could feel a sense of protection coming from her like a mother bear getting ready to beat the living hell out of someone who messed with her cub.

‹Whoa, nothing like that, Your Majesty. She asked me for a wish. She wished for there to be a path forward where her throne would be left to someone who deserved it. By opening potential that her son could strive to reach to be worthy of it. Nothing harmful. Nothing that I felt was more than a mother looking out for her son and a queen looking out for her kingdom.› Dalen had resumed using just the pin. There were a lot of emotions happening at once; the pins helped filter out a lot of that amplified emotional white noise, making it easier on everyone.

‹And did you help her?› asked the queen.

‹I did. I felt it to be a worthy wish, one that, in the end, would benefit many. After all, you don't want your elven neighbors to the south ruled by a weak king who has no interest in being there, right?› Dalen decided not to mention the flashes of her daughter and the vision of Venger and the Elven Kingdom merging into one. It wasn't that he felt it was a bad thing that he should keep from her; it was that somewhere in his mind, he understood that people should never know too much about their future.

‹You made a wise choice to help her. Thank you for doing so,› added Hope with the slightest of nods.

‹I have a possible theory.› Becky held up a finger. ‹Since you are now using your abilities as a Jinn, maybe your body is beginning to take your 'true form,' for lack of a better phrase.›

Master Truth's voice spoke into Dalen's mind. *She is partially right. This change is due to you using the stone's power.*

Dalen agreed. ‹Yeah. That makes sense. Jinn look like their element. I should have expected this. Good call, Becky. For now, let's go with that until we're in a place to sit and take the time to figure all this out.›

‹I am glad that things are explained for the time being. I agree we should move forward and talk more about this later before our hosts get bored watching us stare at each other.›

Hope was right. Everyone looked around and remembered that they were not alone.

Most of the elves they had been talking to had decided to let them have their moment and had gone back to what they were doing. Everyone seemed to be getting ready for some festival and were more than happy to go back to their prattle. All except for one elven maiden who looked to be about the same age as the team.

"Wow!" Dalen said aloud. He looked at the elven girl and then back at himself in the mirror, blinking wildly. He smiled and raised an eyebrow as he slowly turned to gaze at the girl. "I look pretty silly." As he opened his hand, the mirror disappeared. He patted himself down, and then, with a grin, he teased, "Don't worry. It's not contagious." The elven girl laughed. "I am Dalen Pax. What's your name?"

She spun all the way around and ended with a flourish and a curtsy. "I am Gnomon of the Eastern House." Her actions were playful and over-exaggerated. She flourished again and ended with a very formal curtsy. "My father is the head of the Eastern House." She looked up and shrugged her shoulders. "I have two older brothers. One is a master craftsman, and the other is a ranking member of the Queen's personal guard." She stood up and playfully scoffed. "No pressure or anything. After having two male heirs to bring the family name honor and respect, my father thought and thought, asking himself, how could he improve on such greatness? He could only think of one way — one way to enrich the line of the Eastern House, and that was by blessing my mother with a daughter at last."

Dalen shared with the others as she spoke that he could 'feel' immense pride in her words. It was pure, with no worry of judgment or comparison to any other. Her house was not greater than yours. It was simply great, and she was truly proud of who she was. Dalen could also sense a fear deep inside; there was still a scared little girl who felt she was either going to prove her worth and live up to the family name or die trying.

Becky was almost in tears. Dalen's explanation of Gnomon's pride and personal need to prove her worth touched her deeply. "I come from a faraway land, and there, we have a phrase — do you know what it is?" Gnomon smiled but shook her head. "Girl Power. This phrase has gotten me through hard moments in my life. Never forget that you have it, too. Do you think that you must prove yourself because you are a girl? I say that because you are a girl, you will succeed in ways they can't see coming or plan for. You have a secret weapon that they will never understand!" This was Becky's way. She had this fantastic ability to say something that would blow past all of a person's layers and hit them in the core of their being.

All of Gnomon's strength fell away, and she stopped her dance of flourishes. She simply walked over to Becky, rested her head on her shoulder, and began to cry. "You have no idea how badly I needed to hear that. Just once from someone other than myself."

‹Hey, guys?› Hope's voice filled their mind. ‹I think Becky, this girl, and I are going to need some time for girl talk.›

The guys nodded and did their best to act like everything that had just happened was normal as the three women walked away from the encampment.

"Right. Well ... That was unexpected." Travis noticed that one of the elven men had a look of concern on his face as he watched Gnomon get moved away from the camp. "I think they may need a minute."

"I am that girl's father, and you will move out of my way." His tone resonated with absolute clarity.

Travis stepped out of the way. "I had no intention of stopping you." Travis let him walk by before he spoke again. "The two women she is with are the Queen of Venger and my girlfriend, who is, like me, a Vengerian Guardian."

The elven man turned around, strode up to Travis, and stood toe-to-toe with him. "Are you threatening me, boy?"

Seeing the elf walk up on his brother, Sir Adam began to move toward them, ready to defend Travis. ‹I got this;› Travis gave his brother a look that let Sir Adam know that he was all right and then turned his attention to Gnomon's father. "God, no!" Travis replied but didn't back down. "I was just letting you know how safe she was. Also, I figured you deserved fair warning that three women were breaking down, crying, and sharing feelings."

He scoffed. "I have heard that human males hide their emotions and do not share their feelings, even with family."

"Yes, I am sure some do. But that is not what I meant. If what your daughter said was true, then you are the Head of the Eastern House?"

"I am."

"I guess that you are very wise."

"I am."

"How old are you?"

"Fifteen hundred years old," the elf said with pride.

"When three women are having an emotional moment, and a man walks in and disturbs them..." Travis leaned in ever so slightly. "In your fifteen hundred years, have you ever seen that go well?"

The elf thought about it for a moment. He looked over at his daughter and then back at Travis, and a smile began to creep onto his face. "True wisdom comes from being able to recognize it when it's handed to you," and then he laughed a hardy bellow.

"My name is Travis. It's a pleasure to meet you." Travis offered him his arm.

The elf took him by his forearm and gripped it firmly. "I am Fulcrum, Head of the Eastern House. Thank you for helping my daughter. Her mother passed away last winter, and I may be a good father, but I am a poor substitute for her mother."

Travis gestured to Sir Adam. "This is my brother, Sir Adam, the Pure Heart of Venger."

Adam walked over and shook his hand. ‹You just introduced me to elven royalty as Sir Adam. That is so Bibitz!›

Adams's face did not betray him, and he casually shook hands with Fulcrum. "Nice to meet you."

Fulcrum started to say hello but then stopped and said something in Elven that Dalen had to translate. ‹By the stars and the moon.›

"Are you all right?" asked Adam.

"You are that Sir Adam, are you not?" Fulcrum asked hesitantly.

"Yes," Sir Adam nodded humbly. "I am that Sir Adam."

It began to dawn on Fulcrum, and he began to look at each of them with a new perspective. "You're Lord Travis. Master Peace. And Dalen Pax."

They timed it through telepathy, but together in unison, they said, "At your service."

"Is that Oubliette talking to my Gnomon?" Dalen could see it in Fulcrum's eyes, but more so, he could feel it rippling out of him in waves. He was starstruck, and he was doing his best not to let it overtake him completely.

"It is, but when we're not working, she goes by the name Becky." Travis smiled. "Like I said, Gnomon is in good hands."

Fulcrum stepped back respectfully. "Forgive me. I did not recognize you. If I had known..."

"You would still have acted with your daughter's best interest at heart." As Dalen spoke, he generated the intent to relax and commanded it to ride on his words; as the head of the Eastern House heard them, he breathed a sigh of relief.

"Thank you for understanding." It was obvious that Fulcrum was embarrassed. He quickly got himself together and tried to salvage the conversation. "Why are you here?"

"The Queen of Venger has been tasked to Run with the Trees. We are here as her Vengerian Guardians," Sir Adams's words made the whole thing sound very official.

"That is why we are here as well." Fulcrum pointed to Gnomon. "My daughter and I are part of a family of twelve that are directly connected to the Eastern House; our house is part of a larger community of fifty others who are all part of the Eastern Province."

"The event is new to us. Can you help us understand its purpose?" asked Peace.

"Certainly," Fulcrum said. "Please, come join me at my camp, and I will tell you why we Run with the Trees."

Dalen sent a message to the queen telling her that when they were done talking, they could find them at the girl's camp getting answers from her father. Hope simply sent back ‹Understood› and continued talking with the girl.

The rest of the group followed Fulcrum to his tent. It was larger than most of the tents in his camp, and for good reason. Once inside, it was easy to see that it was the shelter for his entire family of twelve. There were several large beds and mats on the floor. In the middle of the room was a large wooden post that held up the center of the tent, with multiple posts that went around the edge to give the tent its height and shape. Next to the center pole, there was a wooden table that had a few large maps laid out on it, with some smaller ones stacked on top of each other as well.

"All right, gather around, and I will give you a basic understanding of what is to take place tomorrow." Fulcrum had everyone form a circle around the maps.

The first was of the entire forest. Along the southern edge, stretching for miles and miles were large regions that had been marked off in chunks.

"This is the Elven Forest after it had been ravaged by the Dragon Wars three decades ago. What was lost during those dark times is almost unbearable to think about. Ancient, enchanted groves were destroyed by the Dragons who were trying to burn us out of our homes because we would not submit to them. King Gavin's father, King Durvelis, was on the throne at the time. He honored the agreement that was made by his father, King Noris, and stood with the elves in our time of need, and together, we ended the Dragon War."

"You were there?" asked Sir Adam.

"I was. It is how I earned the right to be the head of the Eastern House. My father passed it down to me when I came back from the Dragon Wars." Fulcrum rolled the first map to the side. "This is a map of the Elven Forest today." The map suggested that a little more than half of the forest had been returned.

"Are you restoring the original forest?" asked Dalen.

"No. That would be catastrophic to the environment. The price is too high to try to resurrect the original forest. Too much life energy would be drained from the outlying area. We decided as a people that it would be better to replant." Pointing to the map, he added, "This is where we will be tomorrow." He pointed to a section that had been circled, and then he rolled that map into the other. The third map was a larger image of the specific section that Fulcrum had just shown them. The area was a large circular meadow that had roughly a two-hundred-yard radius.

"In the center of this meadow, a Father Tree has been planted. The Father Tree can fertilize the entire area that we have marked out. Tomorrow, in four separate locations representing each of the four directions, a Mother Tree will be planted. We have powerful Nature Mages that can affect growth in plants and, after years of study, have perfected the ritual. This is how it will work."

They all leaned in over the map as Fulcrum laid it out.

The elven people were going to gather at each of the locations where the Mother Trees were to be planted. They then would give their own life force to help it grow. This was considered an honor but also a test.

"The Mother Tree will take from you all that you offer. It will drain you of everything if you let it, and on rare occasions, people have died giving too much. Everyone gives what they can to help the Mother Tree grow, but if you give your all, the Goddess of Nature and the Forest will, from time to time, be pleased and grant you her favor. It's a difficult thing to accomplish, and it has only happened to a handful of people whom the Goddess found worthy. This is why some have died. They gave more and more of themselves trying to earn her favor." Fulcrum explained. "It's not just about how much energy you give; it's about how much of yourself you give. Which is why some fail. It has to do with what you offer. Your heart. Your soul. The Goddess takes into consideration the whole offering. Not just what you give but how and why you do it.

"Once everyone has given to the Mother Tree, it flourishes and grows. The moment that the first of her acorns falls to the ground, the cycle starts: all that the Mother Tree has been given is returned, and a blessing from the Goddess is bestowed. The rare few who gain her favor are temporarily transformed into many different types of magnificent things. Each transformation empowers the runner, helping them during the next part of the challenge.

"As the transformations take place, the acorn will sprout another Mother Tree that will quickly grow and drop an acorn as well, and new trees begin to sprout where each acorn falls. Around the outer circle, this repeats again and again, spreading in both directions, along the perimeter of the clearing until a ring of trees has wreathed the open area. This happens in a very short amount of time; while this is happening, each participant who is running leaves an offering to the forest and the Goddess. Once the circle is complete, the offerings that were placed at the base of the Mother Trees vanish and are transformed into magic objects that have been given the blessing of the goddess. These objects reappear at the base of the Father Tree.

"Once the blessed objects appear at the Father Tree, there is a moment where everything seems to stop as if the world is taking a breath in preparation for what comes next. Then, the peace is broken. Starting from the outside perimeter and moving in like a wave, the entire forest repeats the pattern. Each new tree drops acorns, sprouting another fully grown tree from the ground instantly wherever they land. Within seconds, the whole area regrows until it reaches a ring of toadstools that encircle the Father Tree about ten yards from its base. Once the forest reaches the ring, the growth rate slows down, and for another ten seconds, grass and flowers grow toward the Father Tree.

"Any object that is still at the base of the Father Tree once the grass reaches the Father Tree vanishes, and whoever did not claim their item loses their status within the community until they can run again."

"And the runners?" Travis was writing everything down. "They have to run from the Mother Tree to the Father Tree while all of this is going on? Surely not everyone can make it there in time."

Fulcrum agreed with Travis and pointed to the map of the area where the run was taking place. "Time is short; because of this, the amount of time that you choose to wait dictates the level of prestige a runner will receive." Fulcrum pointed to a couple of beds that had cribs near them. "Parents with young children who wish to have them recognized by the community can run the moment the offerings vanish. Any young adult who wishes to be recognized as a grown adult is allowed to run after fifteen seconds have elapsed. If someone wishes to be considered a hunter, which is a high honor in the tribe, they must wait additional time before they can run with the leaders, who must begin their run at the edge as the forest begins to regrow.

"The reason that the amount of time matters is because of the level of danger and the timing needed to successfully make it to the Father Tree. The danger is very real. If the forest catches you while you're running, you will be caught where trees are exploding from the ground to full height, during which time their limbs are erupting outward. Many elves have died, skewered by trees that grew directly into and through them; others have fallen from great heights as trees grew directly underneath them, launching them into the air."

And there it was, staring them in the face. They understood what Hope would have to do. She was going to have to offer up her life essence to feed the Mother Tree. She would have to do this wholeheartedly enough to please the forest and the Goddess it was connected to. Aside from giving of herself, she would also have to give a physical offering, likely the celestium blade that she had been carrying since the Earth Blade had vanished. Finally, she would have to wait until the last second and run with the trees as they exploded from the ground all around her. If she survived the ordeal and her offering pleased the Goddess, then in the place of her celestium sword, the Earth Blade would be waiting for her at the Father Tree with Nature's blessing. When Hope arrived with Becky and Gnomon, the guys sat down with them and caught them up to speed with the trial.

"There are a few rules that have become doctrine

that cannot be broken," Fulcrum explained. "Once an offer has been taken, no one is allowed to help or interfere with a runner." This rule made it impossible for the team to help her. They asked if they could run, but in the end, two things prevented them from doing so. The first had to do with the power they carried. It was too much, and if they gave all they had, as tradition dictates, it would harm the Mother Tree. And secondly, since this was to be the Queen's challenge, they could not interfere with her claiming it. They knew that was going to be the case, but now that they were there, staring at it, it made them feel helpless.

"There is one thing you can do for me," Hope's words were kind and motherly. "You can believe in me."

"That we can do, in great abundance." Sir Adam meant what he said. They all did. They had talked with her for a few days and watched as she showed great strength and even greater compassion. This was a queen they could follow, and they were ready to watch her succeed the following day as she ran with the trees.

Dalen wanted to help both Hope and Gnomon but was advised by Master Truth not to. They had to do it on their own. So, that night, before everyone retired for the evening, Dalen spoke to them both. "I want to wish you both good luck tomorrow, but I can't. In doing so, I would doom you to fail, so know that instead of wishing for luck, I will give you something better. I will have faith in you both and leave it at that." Hope hugged him and said that was all she could ever ask.

"Thank you for having faith in me. I'm still not sure if I have it in myself, but I know that Hope believes in me, and so does Oubliette." Her words were calm, but Dalen could feel her doubt.

"They do, and so do I, but it means nothing without one very important ingredient." Dalen leaned in close and almost whispered, "I can tell you the secret, but if I do, you have to promise me that you will spend the rest of the night thinking about it, and tomorrow, I want it to be the last thought you think before you run. If you do that, I will tell you the secret you will need to achieve anything you set your mind to."

Her eyes lit up. "Yes. I promise. Please, what is the secret?"

"It means nothing that Hope believes in you, or Oubliette, or me. It doesn't matter that your dad loves you and already believes in you unless..." Dalen paused and allowed his words to hang in the air with anticipation.

"Unless what?" Gnomon begged.

"The first rule of magic is that your magic is only as powerful as you believe it to be. You are only as powerful as you believe you are." Gnomon stared at him as her brain tried to understand what he was saying. "Us believing in you is important because it helps you believe in yourself, but tomorrow, on that field, we cannot help you. It will be you and you alone that will carry you across the line. You must believe in yourself. Without it, you are doomed."

"But that is so difficult," Gnomon argued.

"You were built to do difficult things. Impossible things from impossible dreams. All of them can be yours, but first, you must believe. In you."

"But-"

"Nope. You made a promise to a jinn. You gave your word, Gnomon of the Eastern House, that you would spend the rest of the night and tomorrow thinking about it, and I intend to hold you to that word."

She looked at the jinn and then her father, who only gave her a look suggesting that breaking her promise was not a strong option. Hoping someone would give her an out, she looked at Becky with pleading eyes.

"I think that's checkmate," Becky just shrugged and shooed Gnomon toward her bed. "Goodnight."

Gnomon turned to Hope, who hugged her. "I have no doubt you will have success in your run and achieve recognition as an adult, but I will not keep you a moment longer. Giving your word to a jinn is serious business."

She said goodnight and, as she promised, went to bed thinking about what Dalen had said, but there was another thought that crept into her mind as she fell asleep that night. She had no intention of just waiting to run with the other young adults who were being recognized, she intended to wait longer, to take her place in the Eastern House as the youngest Hunter to ever run with the trees.

12

THE FOLLY OF XOXANN

Xoxann awoke the next morning to the sound of her mother singing, and she had hope, for the first time in a while, that today might be better. She got dressed and had breakfast with her mother, who was then off to give notice that she was leaving her current job and to say goodbye to the few women who had become her friends before she left for her new, well-paying job.

Xoxann kissed her mother and then waved goodbye until she could no longer see her; once she was gone, Xoxann reached into her pocket and grasped the black figurine. DeSalvo appeared the moment she touched it. "Good morning, Miss. I hope you slept well. I did what I could, as you wished, to create the most beautiful of dreams for you."

Excitement welled up in her as she remembered her dreams. "I was on a beautiful beach with white sand, and I was with a herd of horses, and each one was a different color of the rainbow."

"That sounds beautiful!" He smiled and clasped his hands together. "What did you do?"

"The green one was the leader. I named her Lettuce. She let me ride her, and then do you know what happened?" she squealed.

He knew, but he pretended that he didn't so she could tell her story. "What happened next?"

"We flew in the air because they were rainbow horses, and we made a giant rainbow, and then they made me their princess."

"That sounds amazing. I'm glad you liked your dreams so much." He booped her on the nose, which made her giggle. "So, what wishes do you want to make today?"

"Oh, DeSalvo!" She clasped her hands and brought them to her chest. "I get more wishes? But you have done so much for me already."

"Dear, sweet Xoxy. Can I call you Xoxy?" She nodded. "Dear, sweet Xoxy. You are such a special little girl. I think you deserve more wishes. Unless, of course, you don't want them?"

"No, wait! Thank you, and please. I would love more wishes." She hopped up and down with excitement. "I wish there was something I could do for you."

DeSalvo closed his eyes, drew in a deep breath, and smiled. He got down on one knee and said, "There is something you can do for me. I could really use your help."

"I would love to help you, Mr. DeSalvo. What do you need?" Xoxy was elated and could barely maintain her composure. She started to sway back and forth until she was dancing in place.

"There is an object of great power I need you to get for me."

Xoxy squealed and danced around more. DeSalvo just smiled and shook his head at her innocence.

Suddenly, it was as if someone disengaged her body, took all that energy, and directed it to her mouth. She took a deep breath and in one go asked, "What do you want me to get? What's it called? Is it pretty? Why do you need it? Is it far? Do we have to go now? Should I leave Mom a note? Will we be back in time for dinner?"

DeSalvo clapped his hands and laughed. "My dear, sweet Xoxy, you have made this old genie very happy." He stepped outside with her and continued while she put on her shoes. "No need for a note. I will whisk you away magically and have you home in time, not to be missed. I think it would be best if you went to school first. We don't want anyone missing you there. We will go after school. Besides, you never know; there may be a wish or two you want to make before the day is done."

"Like what?" Xoxy asked as she finished the buckle on her boot and started walking to school.

"Your heart's desire." DeSalvo looked at her and shrugged. "I suggest frozen cream and cake for lunch."

They both giggled at the idea and headed toward her school. She normally went around the long way because she always tried to avoid the other kids, but DeSalvo convinced her to take the direct route, telling her not to worry because he was there to protect her. They had only walked a few blocks when they came across a boy in Xoxy's class named Kavlin. He was one of the boys who continuously picked on her and called her Xox the Pox.

He was by himself, but he started running his mouth the moment he saw her.

"Well, look at who it is. Xox the Pox." He put his hand over his mouth. "Watch out! She will give you the pox!" He laughed, and as he did, DeSalvo clenched his fists and ground his teeth.

"Just leave me alone," Xoxann said, trying to go a different direction.

Kavlin cut her off, standing directly in her way. "What's wrong, Xox the Pox? Are you going to cry?"

DeSalvo didn't like Kavlin, but he knew that if he did something to the kid, it would either be seen by the city or the city's security teams. They had ways of watching events that happened within the city, even after the event had taken place. A flash of energy pulsed in the air, and DeSalvo smiled with amusement. A wish had been made to guarantee this instant in time would be blocked from the watchful eye of the authorities. He recognized the magic, for it was his own, and he made a note to convince the little sun drop to make that wish in the future. He drew his attention back to Kavlin with a newly found amusement in his eyes. He calmly knelt right next to Xox and said with anger in his voice, "I hate bullies. I have been bullied most of my life." He caught her eyes and stared deeply into them. "You have the power to stop this, and I promise you, he will never torment you ever again."

"Go away, Kavlin — I'm warning you." She clenched her fists and stood her ground. "I have a magical friend, and he will make you stop, so you better."

Kavlin just laughed at her. "Now you have a magical friend." He wiggled his fingers at her like he was casting a pretend spell. "Oh no! Help!" he cried. "The Pox has her imaginary friend pointed at me." He laughed and laughed.

Xoxann couldn't take his stupid laugh for another second. She closed her eyes and said aloud, "I wish you would just go away and leave me alone forever!"

The laughing stopped abruptly, and Xoxann opened her eyes to find herself standing on the road with DeSalvo alone.

"Where did he go?" she asked.

"I gave you exactly what you wished for. He is away, and

he will never bother you again." DeSalvo said with a grin of satisfaction on his face. "I am glad. You know why?"

"Why?" she asked.

DeSalvo reached over and, with the side of his finger, collected the teardrop that had welled up as Kavlin was laughing at her. "Today is such a pretty day, and you had such a pretty dream. It would be a shame to ruin this wonderful day with dumb boys who are mean and want to make you sad." He hugged her. "Now that I am here, your days should be filled with joy, and you will never have to cry again."

She hugged him back. "Thank you, DeSalvo. You are my best friend."

"I am your friend, and friends help each other." He let her go and gave her the sweetest smile that he could muster. "Just like you want to help me. Right?"

"Right." They both smiled, and then DeSalvo took her by the hand, and together, they skipped to school.

They had a wonderful day together. They snickered in unison at roll call when Kavlin was marked absent, and then DeSalvo helped her with her math test. DeSalvo made the mean girls trip and spill their lunches at the wish of Xoxann. One of the kids at school had a birthday, and their parents had made sure that there was cake and frozen cream for all. Everything was going better than Xoxann could have ever hoped for until an assembly was called halfway through the day.

"This sounds boring. I wish we didn't have to go to it," he said with a sad look on his face. "Don't you?"

"Yeah. I wish we didn't have to go either," she replied without really thinking about what she was saying.

"Perfect," said DeSalvo.

From Xoxann's left, a voice called out, "Xoxann Velo, can you please come here?"

Xoxann looked over and saw that her teacher was calling her over, and her mother was there with her.

"Why is your mother here?" asked DeSalvo. "I wish I knew why she was here."

"Me too," Xoxann said absently.

She walked over to her teacher and mother, and they began to speak to her in hushed tones.

"We weren't going to say anything until everyone was together, but your mother is here to pick you up, so I am going to tell you what's going on." Mrs. Miller, her teacher, had a very concerned look on her face, and so did Xoxy's mother. "One of the students has gone missing." DeSalvo could feel her panic, so unbeknownst to her, he magically helped her stay calm. "He disappeared from Venger, but he didn't leave through the front gate. When his disappearance was investigated, there was a residue of some type of magic that couldn't be identified, and when they tried to divine what happened, it was a blank slate for two minutes in both directions, so whoever took Kavlin knew how to hide their tracks through magic. The city is now on high alert. We have gathered the kids together to tell them that Kavlin is missing and to ask that they keep an eye out for him. We are going to warn them to stay away from anyone they don't know and will keep them here until their parents can pick them up. Your mother works for one of the men who was doing the investigation. He informed her of the disappearance, so she is already here to get you, and you should go directly home with her now."

Xoxann didn't know what to say, so she just nodded and left the school with her mother. The whole way home, her mother asked if Xoxann was alright or if she saw anyone strange on her way to school. She was scared and now very nervous about the whole thing, but she didn't want to be in trouble, so she told her she was fine and that she hadn't seen anyone she didn't know that morning. Once they made it home, her mother let her know that she had to go back to work and told Xoxann that she was to stay in the house and lock the door. She was to let no one in unless they knew the password. It was "roly-poly" — Xoxann had picked it out years ago.

Her mother left, and that's when Xoxann stopped pretending that she wasn't freaking out on the inside, she turned to DeSalvo. "What do I do?"

"What do you mean?" asked DeSalvo casually.

"Kavlin is missing, and they know that it was magic." Fear slowly crept up her spine with icy fingers.

DeSalvo smiled. He could tell that she had no idea that he was actively cultivating her fear, helping it to grow on the inside. "You have nothing to worry about. You are about to wish that only those who were there would know what happened. Do you want them to find out?"

The idea frightened Xoxann. "No."

DeSalvo pushed her fear a little more and then asked, "Do you wish that they would never find out what happened?"

"Yes. I do." The idea of being caught for something this big was beyond terrifying.

"And now they won't." He smiled at her with a kind smile. "As soon as they said that there was a blank slate when they tried to divine what happened, I knew you were going to make that wish."

"But I hadn't made the wish yet. How did it already affect things?" she asked.

"Genie spells work both directions in time. It's really hard to change time. Often, you can tell what's going to happen in the future by how the wish being made in the future is affecting the present. That's how I knew you would eventually make the wish that nobody would discover we were involved.

"But what if they figure it out?"

"You just wished they never will, so they won't."

"But what if I don't want him gone forever?"

"That is specifically what you wished: for him to go away and never bother you again." DeSalvo crossed his arms. "I was only granting you what you wished for, and unfortunately, I can't take it back. It happened, and there are very few ways to change time." DeSalvo directed his gaze out the window. "One of them is the Pillar of Time, but it seems to have unpredictable results." He started to get angry for a moment but took a breath and smiled outside. "I am sorry. I was cheated by a person who wants me to cease to exist, and it still frustrates me."

Xoxann wrapped her arms around his waist and hugged him. "Don't be sad. It will be okay."

DeSalvo patted her on the head and, for a moment, let his heartbeat, but he had no time or need for such things and refocused his thoughts. "The point is that there is only one other way to change time and save Kavlin, but you have to be brave, and you have to be willing to break a couple of rules. If you are brave, maybe we can help each other."

"What do I have to do?" She was lost and scared by this point and was willing to take any answer as long as it got her out of the mess she had made.

"We have to go to a place called the City of Dreams. There, I will help you get what you need to save your friend, and then you will help me get back what was stolen from me." His eyes glinted with hatred.

DeSalvo drained all the fear from the little girl and replaced it with courage. "Of course, I will help you," she exclaimed. Then Xoxann took DeSalvo's hand in hers. "Whatever they stole from you, we'll make them give it back."

He smiled at her and said, "Okay. If you really think we can do it, we will do it together."

"What did they take from you?" she asked sympathetically.

"A long time ago, I used to be a Jinn with free will, but I was tricked — my free will was stolen from me, and I was turned into a genie. As a genie, I am enslaved, which is why I can only grant the wishes of others. We have to use the will of another to empower our magic."

"You are enslaved?" Xoxy asked wide-eyed.

DeSalvo hung his head, and he looked like he might cry. He finally nodded. "For a thousand years. My free will was fashioned into an artifact called the Beads of Fire, which can be used to connect to my kind. I was trying to get them back, but someone stole them from me. He cast the Beads of Fire into the void, and they disappeared from time and space."

"What are you going to do?" Xoxann asked.

"This person's name is Dalen Pax, and he is a Jinn." He wiped his eyes and sniffed. "I am going to make him give me back what he stole, and if he can't, then he will have to give me his free will as retribution."

The little girl's heart ached for her friend. "How are you going to do that?"

He looked back at her and smiled at her innocence. "Together." He knelt so they were eye to eye. "Last time, I wasn't ready, but this time, I am, and I have you." He gave her a big bear hug. "Together, we are going to get what you need to get Kavlin back, and then after that, you will help me by leading that evil-thieving jinn into a trap. He thinks of himself as some sort of hero, but he is an abomination, and everything he has, he stole from me. We are going to get his attention, and when he shows up to pretend to be the hero, we will make him give back what he took. Together, you and I will set right everything that has gone wrong."

"Okay," Xoxann said. "I'm in. I wish to help you in any way I can. What do we have to do?"

DeSalvo breathed in deep as her last wish took effect. She had just wished her free will away, and now he was in control. "I'll tell you when we get there. Take my hand. I know a shortcut."

Xoxann took DeSalvo's hand, and with a blink of an eye, they were gone.

13

THE HEART OF STONE

There are moments that are unknown to all but those who lived them. There are rare, monumental moments in time that even Grey Bards, such as I, are not privy to, where people do impossible things, and any who witness those events are considered truly blessed indeed. This is one of those times. If it weren't for the pin that I gave Dalen, it would have been lost forever. During his training, Dalen made three Leaps of Faith that took him closer to his destiny. As Dalen meditated that night, he had no idea that he was about to attempt his fourth.

Before his change, Dalen had the option to sleep, but since granting the wish to Adila, he had lost touch with the part of him that was human. He hadn't eaten, and he no longer slept. Instead of sleeping, he spent hours in meditation with Master Truth. With his help, Dalen began to understand more and more about what it meant to be a jinn.

You are going to have to remember what this feels like when it matters.

Master Truth's words were confusing to Dalen; he did his best to clear his mind to grasp clearly what Master Truth was trying to explain. *Why must I remember if this is what I am now?*

Because this is what you are now, after the power of thousands of people over thousands of years has been given to you, but you do remember that this power is not something you get to keep, right?

No, it is not. Dalen started to see where Truth was going with this. *We are going to have to give all this power to the King and Queen of Venger so they will have enough strength to stop the Chaos Dragon and seal the gaping wound in reality.*

It's poetic, really. The people gave of themselves for two thousand years so that you could carry it through time, back to the beginning, to ensure their existence.

That's why I will have to remember how this feels. Because this is all going to be taken from us?

Taken? No... Given. But for your friends, this is a glimpse into who they can be, and by the time they relinquish their given power, each of them will have already begun the paths that will lead them back to who they are now.

So, we get the power back?

No. Something far better. They will each create their

power through their lives and experiences, and when their paths have been traveled, the power they will have will be theirs, and that power will stay with them forever.

Why do you keep referring to them separately?

Your path will be different from theirs. Their gifts enhance them, but the gift you received from the statue, the stone, is hindering you.

But I am more powerful than I have ever been.

Dalen, you cannot lie to me. I know you have already felt it and seen how it is changing you, and I know that you know it is not for the better.

I know. I have felt it.

So, what are you going to do about it?

I don't know. If I let go of the stone, I will lose all my power.

All of your power? You had none before you received your stone?

I see your point. I did have power, but with this stone, I became a full Jinn, and I have even granted a wish.

Did you or the stone do that? Truth's question was simple, but Dalen realized he didn't know the answer for sure.

It was me. I made the choice, and I created the coin.

Could you have done it without the stone?

Dalen paused. He wanted to blurt out "Yes!" but he held his words and remembered his training. He cleared his mind and thought about his truth before he answered. *I honestly don't know if I could have done it without the stone.*

That is why it is detrimental to you, and unlike your friends, this is the exact reason you must let go of these given strengths. Being a jinn and wielding jinn magic requires you to know your own potential and believe in it. You have no idea if you can believe in yourself without it.

But what if that power is needed on this journey? What if I give up the stone, and I am not strong enough to save my friends if they need it? Where if I had kept it, I could?

That is fear and doubt of yourself. You were trained by the Brotherhood to let go of fear and doubt, and then Diem taught you how to have true faith. You have had the stone for a very short while, and you have already lost all of yourself and all of the teachings.

But this is the power of so many people over thousands of years. How could I ever be as powerful without it?

Sometimes, the simplest lessons, the very lessons you have passed down, have more to teach you.

I don't understand.

The power you create will always be more powerful than the power you are given. Dalen's mind was silent. Master

Truth let him marinate on that statement until it was almost unbearable. *Now tell me why.*

Dalen opened his mind and allowed the Spheres of Magic to align themselves with universal truth, and they spoke directly into his being. Dalen perceived the voice as his old teacher Diem, and he could hear him speak warmly into his mind as if they were his own thoughts.

The power you are given is only as powerful as the magic that created it. The power you create within yourself is charged by your free will and belief in your own skills and abilities. Thus, the power given will never be as strong as the power created by you because...

Rule one: Your magic is only as powerful as you believe it to be. Therefore, it has no limits. Dalen was no longer just listening but was one with his thoughts, and it shook Dalen to his core, pulling him out of his meditation. He sprang up, alert. "I was supposed to ask myself something ... When I awoke."

Dalen. You are ready. Come and find me in the woods. The voice was oddly familiar, but he couldn't put his finger on it.

Dalen focused and tried to reach out to the voice, to sense where it was coming from.

Seek me in the forest. It came from everywhere. It was as if the Natural Element of Reality was communicating directly into his mind.

He moved quietly through the camp until he reached the tent that Hope had constructed. He stepped in and moved as silently as he could, being careful not to wake up Becky. "Hope," he whispered, shaking her shoulder.

Dalen heard from under the Queen's pillow the sound of a knife being pulled from its sheath as one of her eyes flashed open and then slowly closed. "What can I do for you, Pax?" Her tones were calm, even as she sheathed her blade.

"Thank you for not killing me."

With her eyes still closed, she murmured, "Anytime," as she snuggled back into her pillow. "What can I do for you, Dalen?"

"I am being called into the woods by a voice that is connecting to me telepathically on a much deeper level than the pins."

Hope sat upright, and both eyes were open now. "Be clear, please."

"I have to go, but I gave you an oath. I need to find out what is out there and why they are calling to me." Dalen was still whispering, but his need was pronounced.

Hope glanced over to Becky, who was still asleep, and whispered, "You intend to go alone, or you would have woken us all up." She looked back to Dalen. "Do you have any idea how long you will be away?"

"No, and I mean none, but I hope I will be back before you make your run."

"Dalen, I give you leave. Thank you for honoring what you have already set into motion and for not just running off without coming to me first. I truly respect you for that. You should also ask the Elven Queen, and for the same reasons." Dalen began to leave, but Hope stopped him on his way out with a request. "Please don't make me cover for you long."

"Thank you, my queen," Dalen whispered. He ducked out of the tent and stepped far enough away to avoid disturbing his friends. He bamphed to Queen Adila's tent by stepping outside of the frames of reality and using superposition to place him where he wanted to be. The queen's guards were not amused to be startled, but Dalen said he had urgent requirements and humbly requested to see the queen. One of them went to send the request while the other stayed behind to watch him.

The first of the two guards returned with the message that the queen would see him. She was surprised to see his appearance had changed. When asked about it, he had no complete answer for her and did not want to alarm her by telling her it only happened after he had granted her wish. He simply apologized for his appearance. She was worried because he didn't seem well, but he convinced her using Grey Speak that he was alright.

"I wasn't expecting visitors tonight, but considering the circumstances, I think I will make an exception. What is it that you require?"

"Permission to leave this camp and permission to go alone." Dalen knew the elves' feelings about humans traipsing around in their forest, but he was hoping that they would feel differently about a jinn.

"Why do you require this?" she asked, but as she did, a wind blew open the tent. Dalen heard the voice call again as a leaf carried by the wind fluttered into the room. Adila watched with awestruck eyes as the leaf was pushed through the room, circled three times, and then came to rest on Dalen's head. "Oh. I see the forest has spoken."

Dalen took the leaf off his head and presented it to the Elven Queen. "With my greatest respects, I will leave without your permission if I must. But as a choice, I am asking first."

"Go. You have my leave, and I will make it clear that you are not to be bothered." She took Dalen's hand in hers and said with compassion and excitement, "Good luck."

Dalen ran from her tent and out into the wilderness. Every time he stopped; the voice called out to him again. Dalen, each time sensing the direction the mysterious voice was coming from, would continue to run toward it until it led him further and further into the deep woods. The chase ended as he clumsily stumbled into a clearing. It was small, with a twenty-foot radius between him and the woman who stood in the center. As Dalen approached, she turned to face him.

It had been years from Dalen's perspective since he had seen the woman who was his foster mother, Ms. Warren. This version of her was much younger, yet there was no mistaking her. He had seen her young like this before, during a trial he faced on his last day at the Brotherhood of Light, but that version was just a mirage to illustrate an understanding of the Earth Element. At that time, she at least looked human. This time, she looked like a living statue carved from black marble. The marbled colors were rich hues of earth tones that complimented the vibrant green stones along each of her chakra points on both the front and back of her body. Each one was wreathed in silver veins that then reached out like the roots of a tree within the marble, forming beautiful striations. She was clothed in a thin strip of mossy earthen material that formed a top across her breasts and a sarong-type bottom that allowed her to keep her modesty.

"Ms. Warren?" Dalen asked as he walked toward the center of the clearing.

You see me as Ms. Warren because it is the only image of me, you know.

"So, like the other jinn, you are incorporeal and have no actual body to be here, so my mind is using images from my life so I can perceive you. I understand."

You understand very little. She folded her arms in front of her and gave Dalen a look that was part amusement and part sass. It was a look that he had seen more than a few times from Ms. Warren. *Kids these days.* Dalen felt scolded and became embarrassed. The look that was on her face shot right past all of his defenses, and his eyes began to search the floor for anything else to look at other than her gaze. As he did, a very gentle hand lifted his chin. Her face was kind, her words were caring, and her voice was filled with love. *It's time to set that down, son. You have something to do, and it is going to take everything you are. Ya hear me?*

Dalen nodded. *Yes, Ma'am.*

Do you know why you are here?

Yes, Ma'am.

You know what you have to do?

Yes, Ma'am.

Do you know how absolutely proud of you I am?

Dalen paused. He sat in it and let it permeate him. Tears began to well in his eyes.

She decided that Dalen needed to hear it from a source he would trust, so she spoke his own words back to him. *Our belief in you is important because it helps you believe in yourself, but now, on this field, we cannot help you. It will be you and you alone who will carry you across the line. You have to believe in yourself. Without it, you are doomed.* She stepped back to the edge of the clearing as Dalen stood in the center. *Now answer me this. Do you want the power of thousands of people over thousands of years, or do you just want yours?*

Dalen dropped to his knees. "I am enough. I have always been enough."

She knelt on one knee and bowed her head. It was a beautiful moment between mother and son, but the time for beauty and sentiment was over. She looked up, and her eyes and stones began to glow as she rose to her feet. *Prove it.*

Dalen reached up and touched his Vengerian pin. His clothes changed into his swim shorts. It was the only outfit he had saved where he could easily access the stone on his chest. He closed his eyes and said a little prayer that this would work, and if possible, he would like to survive the whole ordeal.

His mind raced, and for a second, he had thoughts about keeping his gift. This power didn't own him. He could own it. This could be his power if he chose it. He knew that he could walk away from this clearing and keep all that had been given. It was his; it had been given to him. Magically imbued to him. In a way, it was him. Shaking his head, he stopped himself before the thought could run its course. He knew that he was scared and that this was just his mind trying to find a way out of doing what he knew he had to do.

He fought the flow of his thoughts and realigned his mind sphere. It was up to him how he chose to see this challenge. Either he could focus on the fear that was pulsing through his veins, causing him to doubt everything, even though he knew he was strong enough to do what needed to be done, or he could see this as one of the strongest things he had ever done. A moment that could define who he was for the rest of his life. Dalen fumbled for his coin and stared at the silver side as he acknowledged his fears, but then he turned the coin over and stared at the gold dragon on it and reminded himself that there was always more truth to be seen. Was he going to take the safe bet, keeping the power he'd been given, or was he going to double down on the belief and faith that he had in himself?

He remembered how hard it was to let go of the Beads of Fire. He remembered that the loss of them meant the loss of his friend, the Fire Jinn. He knew that this would be even harder, but giving up power always was, especially if there was the option to keep it. This was the choice in front of Dalen Pax, and only he could make it.

Dalen had integrated this borrowed power and was
using it as if it were his own. As he used it, he began to lose
his humanity, and it changed him. It was true that it gave
him unbelievable power, but he recognized that he was losing
himself, and a part of his mind could not help but wonder how
much more he would change and how much more he would lose if
he allowed it.

Master Truth had convinced him there was another path.
Dalen had been brought here to make a decision, one that was
fair. He already had tremendous power. More than he could
have possibly imagined, or that he knew what to do with, but
if he was willing to give it up, he had the possibility to take a
much larger step onto his own path.

The leap of faith at the Brotherhood of Light had taught
him a valuable lesson. He was meant to literally make a leap of
faith hundreds of meters to the other side. He had been given
the option of using a belt that would save him if he fell, and
for a thousand jumps, he wore it. In the end, it was the belt
that kept him from leaping. Using that safety net was an act
of doubt and fear. It let his heart and mind accept failure and
even expect it enough to plan for it. It was only when he let
the power of the belt go and made the leap with complete faith
in himself that he achieved it. This was no different. If he were
going to reach his potential as a jinn, he would have to do it
without the belt, which now was the borrowed power that he
was wielding.

The choice seemed simple from a base point of view, but
questions and doubt still tried to take control. What if he gave
up the power and then wasn't strong enough to ever be that

powerful again? What if he never was that strong? What if giving up this power meant that he wouldn't be powerful enough to help one of his friends when they really needed him? What if he couldn't believe himself powerful enough? Having the ability to have unlimited power didn't mean you had it; it only meant that it was possible. Not even probable.

That's why there was hesitation. That's why he knelt there in the forest and tried to convince himself of the sentence he had just spoken aloud. He was trying to convince himself that he was enough, but was he? Was he enough to be everything that they said he was? Was he good enough to be what he needed to be?

Dalen's fear slowly crept in, creating doubts, and he knew if he tried to do this with doubt in his mind and heart, he would doom himself to fail. Dalen's fear began to weave its tale. It was better to keep it. It was safer. Safer for himself and his friends. The team would be fine. They still had all their powers, and time had already shown that they arrived safely. There was a plan, and his giving up all his power to help his friends was not a part of it. What if giving away his power led them into danger that he couldn't save them from? It was better to keep it. This was silly. He had worked himself up, and now he was fixing to ruin everything. The answer was no.

"NO!" He screamed aloud. He closed his eyes and talked directly to his doubt and fear. "I will not let you diminish me a minute longer. You have no power over me. I am enough. I have always been enough; this power has made me doubt that and myself. I must remove it as if it were a disease!"

The Earth Jinn watched from the side. She made no movements to help or hinder as Dalen reached up to the stone that was directly over his heart and, with both hands, attempted to pull it from his chest.

Immediately, Dalen could tell that the stone was not affixed to his skin but was very much a part of him. The stone itself was embedded in his body, and it felt like he was ripping out his own heart.

Dalen dropped his hands into his lap. "I can't. It's too difficult." Dalen looked up at her and pleaded, "It hurts too much."

Not succeeding is only failure once you give up.

Dalen's frustration at himself turned to anger towards her. "You have no idea how hard this is!"

Dalen Pax. Hear my words and take them to the soul. I am here to be with you during one of the most difficult moments in your life. The moment when you have to decide if you are worthy of being the chosen one. The one who is stronger than all of this. To be the chosen one, the one who chooses it must be you. The Earth Jinn placed her hands over her chest. *Dalen, you were never meant to do this alone.* She reached into her very being and pulled out her stone heart. It was a beautiful emerald, and it shone with the power of a thousand torches. She raised her hand, and in a voice that came from everywhere, she said, *Behold the Heartstone of Power.* It flashed with light that came from within it, and Dalen could feel that it was the life essence of the jinn.

Dalen was entranced. To see it felt like gazing at her soul, and Dalen could feel the connection it longed to create with him. "I can feel your soul."

It is made of the element that resides at the heart of all things. It is the element that is all six as one. She let it drop as she fell to her knees, but it stopped short of the ground and hovered a few inches from the grass. It floated to where Dalen was and hovered a few feet above his head.

The jinn looked up at Dalen; it was obvious that pulling out her heart had caused her great trauma. She was diminished, but she was alive. She closed her eyes and put her hands together as if she were about to pray, but then she separated them, and as she did, the trees around the clearing obeyed her command and pulled away from the center to reveal the moon directly overhead. As the moonlight hit the Heartstone, it flashed a pulse of light that made Dalen blink. Just as he did, it split into seven smaller stones, each one a crystal ball etched with glyphs. As the crystals separated from themselves, they began to project colored moonlight through them. There were seven in total, each one representing one of the Elements of Magic and Reality. Each one fell from the air in an arching motion like falling stars and planted themselves into the ground, save the green one that still floated overhead. As each stone landed and planted itself into the soil, large elemental stones arose from the ground, and Dalen found himself kneeling in his Circle of Magic.

Dalen tried to reach out to Master Truth but found only silence.

It is to you and you alone that this task has been given. No others will help you when the person you need right now is you. Her voice was encouraging, and Dalen knew she was right. This was about the faith he had in himself and his struggle with whether or not he was ready, and, more importantly, he had to decide if he was worthy.

Dalen reached up to his chest with both hands and with all of his strength, he gripped the stone. He closed his eyes and told himself he could do it over and over as he slowly began to pull the stone from his chest.

The pain was formidable, and Dalen almost stopped as the first wave hit him, literally like a heart attack. It ripped at his body, and it tore at his soul. His strength shattered into a thousand pieces as all of the power that had saturated him was drained out of him like a sieve. A guttural roar rippled through him from his core and produced a scream that would tear at the ventricles and make the spirit weep.

Light poured from his body and into the stone. He felt as if it was taking too much, and even though he was afraid that it might take his life, he put everything he had into removing it completely. As the stone cleared his body, there was a large flash of light that filled the clearing as if, for a moment, the sun had replaced the moon. Then all was still.

Dalen lay on his side. In his view, he could see the stone from the statue lying in the grass a few feet away. He tried to get up, but moving in any way caused his whole body to send shockwaves of pain as muscles tried to cramp and release. He whimpered in pain, but that, too, caused suffering.

The jinn was still on her knees, quietly watching him as he tried to catch his breath. Dalen fought through the pain and tried to get up. His second attempt was as fruitless as his first. Yet, he tried again and pulled himself up to his knees. He knelt there dying, trying to understand the images of his life that were flashing before his eyes.

He had lived a mortal, corporeal life in a nonmagical world. For whatever reason, when he was seventeen, magic found him. He learned about the Elements of Magic and how to harmonize with the Spheres of Reality. When at the Temple of Light, he learned to connect to and move with the body sphere. At Dorn's, he learned about the Quantum Field and how to mold it by actively being the observer. On that day, he had accomplished a connection to the mind sphere. At the Temple of All-Faith, he became one with the connection to the Divine and mastered how to work with it to empower the Arcane. After years of work and dedication, he made his third leap of faith and became a part of the soul sphere. It was only when he was able to connect all three that he became the Reality Bender. He had touched on his true potential for a moment the day he had to face the Genie DeSalvo and protect himself, his friends, and the world from DeSalvo's wrath by giving up the Beads of Fire. In those moments, he was one with something profound, something that he was meant to be but was never brave enough to claim.

Until now.

Dalen flashed back to reality. The Earth Jinn was breathing slowly, but it was labored. *This is a juncture in every jinn's life. There is a point when they have to choose to become what they were meant to be or to decide to step away and choose a mortal life.*

"I have the choice?"

You always have the choice. She smirked and spoke aloud, "Angels fall every day."

"Not today." Dalen was determined to proceed. It was still painful to move. Every ounce of his ability and might had been drained by removing the stone. He was glad that his friends weren't there because they would have tried to stop him.

Dalen could still feel his life slipping away from him, but he slowly rose to his feet. He was shaky, but he kept his balance. He slowly staggered over to the position of the Imagination Element, turned to face the center, and then — much like the Earth Jinn — dropped to his knees in exhaustion. He retrieved his silver figurine, and with what little strength he had remaining, he held it out, and it began to glow as if it had turned into celestium. As it did, he gave everything that he had left to ignite the Quantum Element that was across from him. Two new lights began to glow over the Arcane and Kinetic Elements. Dalen looked to the Kinetic; as the light began to grow, he saw Brother Truth standing on the Elemental Stone, and he, too, was holding a silver figure. Dalen's eyes moved to the Arcane position, and he saw Father Light there, also holding a glowing figure.

Father Light said a prayer and the Divine Element lit up. As he did, Brother Truth charged his Ki and pushed it to the Natural Element, which ignited as well.

Dalen's mind expanded, and he could now see from the point of view of all three versions of himself. Each one of him was no longer a 'them' — just three views of a single being.

As Father Light, he looked upon his broken, exhausted self and knelt in reverence. He was empowered with the infinite power of the divine and would certainly succeed, but this kid, in the hardest moment of his life, only had himself, and that was truly impressive.

As Brother Truth, he knelt in respect. He held up his coin from the brotherhood. "Do you remember the lesson we learned that day? It's easy to be happy on a sunny day." It was a reference to the question, 'When is someone at their most powerful?' One truth suggested that someone was at their greatest power when they had reached their highest potential. Another truth suggested that it wasn't at one's time of greatness, but rather the time when in the pit of their despair. When they are the weakest, when they have nothing left to give and don't believe that they can reach up and take hold of their life. In that moment when they do, when the deck is stacked against them, and they have nothing left yet somehow take the impossible step... That is when someone is at their strongest. Because they face all of it alone, with no power, and still take that step. As Dalen looked at the coin, he remembered the lesson, and he knew this was his moment; he had to find a way to take one more step.

All three of them began to push with everything they had toward the center. They pushed with their body, heart, and soul. Father Light began to sustain a low note as he gave his voice in prayer to the act. Brother Truth pushed from his diaphragm, lending his voice with a powerful Om. Dalen let go and screamed with every bit of energy he had left.

The silver figures simultaneously floated up and out of their hands. A new fourth figure, being held by Dalen in the center of the circle, appeared. The three floating figures pulsed a sustained beam of pure energy into the fourth, and all of them moved to converge with the Heartstone, which was still floating just a foot higher than Dalen's head.

He could feel it; he could sense it. This was the being he was the night he faced DeSalvo, the true Reality Bender who was greater than the sum of his parts. He tried to see from another one of his perspectives, but they were gone; only he was left standing in the center of the circle. All four figures touched the Heartstone at the same time, and as they did, they merged into a single stone that looked like it was made of silver celestium. He reached up and took it and instinctively knew what he was supposed to do. He took the new Heartstone and placed it where it belonged. As his chest enveloped the stone, he felt his heart begin to beat once more, and life began to flood his practically empty vessel. He could feel the other stones form in his body; he watched as silver celestium stones formed in his hands. With no effort, he began to float off the ground as he felt the stones emerge in his feet.

While he was floating, the stones in the ground that had formed the magic circle retreated to the center of the clearing and reformed the Heartstone of Power. The Earth Jinn meekly raised her hand, and it flew to her. It was smaller than it was before, but as she put it back in her chest, it glowed brightly.

"You gave a piece of your Heartstone to create mine, didn't you?" Dalen could feel the truth in it but wanted to hear her say it.

"I did. This is the pattern. The circle of life, if you will." She smiled sweetly and got back to her feet.

"Is that why you are here specifically? Because Earth is about birth and rebirth? Phases of life and patterns?" Dalen asked, knowing his time with her was short.

"It is part of why you perceive me the way you do. The other part is because I chose to be here. I wanted to be the one that stood by you through this step, and I wanted to be the one who gave their heart." She touched hers, and he could feel his beginning to warm with a deep love and connection.

"Who are you?"

"I think you know. You may see Ms. Warren, but I am physically... corporeally here." She nestled her feet in the grass and grabbed it with her toes. "All mothers want to see their children succeed." She began to move away from the clearing, and Dalen instinctively knew that she had to go. He also needed to get back, but he felt in his heart that he would see her again.

When Dalen looked down, he noticed that her footprints were still there. This jinn was actually present. "Mother?"

"I must go. The Running of the Trees will be starting soon, and both of us have vows that must be kept. We will see each other again."

Dalen slowed time and stretched it out until the frames of time flickered. He flew to her and embraced her. "Thank you, Mother."

"I love you, Dalen. Now that you have been found, I will always be here for you. I am never far away." Both of their Heartstones brightened, and Dalen was moved to tears by the overwhelming love she had for him.

In her left hand, she still carried a piece of her own Heartstone. It glowed bright, and Dalen could feel it through his own Heartstone. As she held it up, she allowed it to change form into a crystal ball. She shook it like a snow globe, and as she did, etchings appeared on it of six circles, one on top and bottom, one on each side, and one in front and back. They were all the same size, and each circle's edge touched the edge of the one beside it in symmetrical harmony. She shook it again, and etchings of all six elements appeared within each circle.

She handed it to Dalen. "This is for your brother, Deveris. Give it to him the next time you see him."

"My brother?" Dalen asked.

"Yes. The boy that was with you when you were pulled from this world is your brother."

Dalen knew that she meant David. He felt the truth of it in her heart. He looked at the crystal orb. "What is it?"

"It's a **Reality Field Generator**. Think of it as a travel practice circle. Once you have revived him, he will need your understanding and knowledge if he is going to be trained as well, but unlike you, he will have to learn it in a completely different way."

"You really think I am the right one to train him?" Dalen looked up, but she was already gone. It was dawn, and he knew it was going to be pointless to try and find her in the woods, so he just called out, "Thank you!"

Emotion overtook him, and Dalen could do nothing but allow it to flow. He wept alone with no one but the forest to witness it. There were no names for what he felt at that moment, and concepts like joy or pain were too simple. What he felt was larger than his body could endure, and so it wept. It had all been so much, and he just wasn't ready to soldier on.

When he did pull himself together, Dalen opened up a pocket dimension that was not connected to time. One could put a piece of cake in there, and three years later, it would still be fresh. He had learned how to make it when he studied the arcane arts and often kept personal effects that he didn't want to carry in there. He placed the generator inside. He wasn't sure what would happen if he touched the stone from the statue again, so he used telekinesis to lift the stone and placed it in his magical pocket as well before closing it again. He looked back at the clearing. He had met his birth mother. She was nothing like he had imagined, but she was better than he could have ever dreamed.

"Thank you...Mother." It was only after he spoke that he remembered what she had said. The running of the Trees would be happening soon. He still had time. He pictured the Queen in his mind and used his magic to locate her. He only needed to take a single step, and he was standing by her side.

14

HE WHO CARRIES
THE HONOR

Hope awoke just before dawn. This had always been her favorite part of the morning. The air was still cold from the night before, and there was a mist in the air that clung to the last fragments of the night. Her hand fumbled for her Vengerian pin. Her fingers tapped out the sequence as she thought about what she wanted to wear, and her clothes changed to the desired outfit. The leggings under the three layers of her dress and skirts were warm and comfortable. Over that, she wore a light jacket and a shawl to wrap up in. She stepped outside of her tent and bundled herself in her shawl, pulling it tight as she watched the warmth of her breath turn into wisps of fog. Stepping away from the camp, Hope decided to take a short walk to the location where the ceremony would begin.

Years ago, during the Dragon Wars, one of the tactics the Dragons used was to fly over lush places and light them on fire. The Dragons knew that the elves would prioritize saving the forest over fighting them. Overall, their method had been sound. What they did not count on was that Venger had rallied anyone in the city who was prepared to fight in a Dragon battle, and they had all converged with the elves in the forest. The Dragons had not been ready for the sheer numbers they faced the day the elves and humans stood together as one.

The areas that had been burned had been put out, but the forest had more holes than a wedge of cheese. The elves had saved special acorns in case of such a disaster and went right to work planting the new father trees in preparation for the ceremony that was soon to take place.

There were a few guards who had watched the site through the night, making sure no one tampered with the location before the ceremony started. One of them approached her as Hope drew near. He was respectful but forceful and wanted to know who she was and what she was doing there.

"I have just come to take it in. I'm running today, and this will be my first time. I hope that's alright." Queen Hope remembered that she was in the kingdom of the elves. She may not always know their rules, but she was kind and meant no harm; she hoped that he would understand. She was unassuming, casting away any notion of station or rank, and just spoke to him as a person.

Whether it was that her musical voice soothed him or because he could tell she was just nervous, meaning no harm, possibly a combination of the two, he let his demeanor change, dropping the persona of Elite Elven Guardian. "You must be Queen Hope of Venger." He gave her a small nod, and with respect, he added, "Your Majesty."

She gave a small, innocent smile and a shrug with a hand gesture that said, 'You caught me.' followed by a curtsy. "Please, Sir, just Hope."

"Well, just Hope, I am just Kryzon." He was still on duty, so he continued scanning his field of sight for movement in the woods while they spoke. "If you have come to walk the field, I have bad news: I can't let you onto the field."

"I understand. Just trying to prepare. I thought if I saw it, it would help bring the nerves down, or perhaps I could walk it..." His eyes shifted over to her with a look that was unaggressive yet also unbudging. "But no. I guess not." Kryzon's eyes went back to scanning the area. "Now that I understand that it's not permitted, I'm more than happy to look at it from here."

Kryzon broke his scan of the outlying area to focus on Queen Hope; this time, his demeanor was kind and, to some, would be considered friendly. "The wisdom of your husband is legendary. But it seems that wisdom is a trait that both sides of the throne possess."

Hope gave Kryzon a small curtsy in thanks. "May I ask you a question?" She paused for a moment to allow him to answer. And once Kryzon gave her a nod, she continued. "Thank you. I would like to ask you if you have ever made the run, but I do not know if it would be considered rude within your culture to do so."

Kryzon went back to scanning the trees. "There is no harm in your question. Running with the Trees is an intricate part of our culture now. It is both a rite of passage and a holy experience. It is how we know if people are worthy to be hunters or leaders."

Her next question was neither rude nor patronizing but sought deeper understanding. "Because they are fast enough to do the run?"

Kryzon tilted his head down to hide his amusement. To him, her question had the naivety of a child, and where he understood that this was all new to her, to hear such a question asked endeared her in some way to him. He knew she meant well and didn't want to offend her, but she noted his response nonetheless.

Hope thought that she must have said something stupid and that this elven chap thought it funny as he failed slightly at trying not to laugh at her directly. Then she reminded herself that it was probably something far simpler. "I am missing something, aren't I?"

"My apologies, I meant no disrespect."

"Nor did I, but I think I may have made a joke."

"It's not because they are fast enough to do it. If anything, it is that they are brave enough to do it." He looked back to the empty field. "The amount of heart you must have. Not just to step up to the line and run the distance but run it while the forest is literally exploding to life all around you."

Hope looked toward the field as well and clutched the shawl a little closer. "It sounds scary."

"It's terrifying." He chuckled to himself. "Whatever you are imagining, it's worse than that because even if you can imagine it, it's only imagining it. Living it is quite a different thing."

Hope shuttered at her own imagination. "So, it has to do with having the courage to run."

Kryzon went back to his visual patrol. "Partly. There is also the courage to withstand the needs of the Mother Tree."

"I thought that you could choose how much the tree takes." Or at least that was how Hope remembered it.

"Sure, you can, and you will be recognized as a member of your house." He shrugged. "And you can live out your life in mediocrity as a baker or a poet. Or you can give something other than what is required. Only those who are brave enough to give of themselves until the first acorn falls prove themselves worthy."

Hope was now intrigued. "How does this prove you worthy?"

"The Mother Tree will drain you to the point of death if you let her, and many people have given their lives to the Mother Tree trying to receive her gifts. If you are still alive and connected to the Mother Tree when the first acorn falls, not only will you be revived, but you will also gain a blessing from the Goddess of Nature and Life herself. This blessing is two-fold. The power you are given to run with the trees can be different from person to person. The second has to do with the offering: if you only give but a little, your offering will be returned to you with a blessing that lasts until your next run, but if you have proven yourself to the goddess, she will alter your offering permanently."

"Have you ever run it?"

Kryzon looked back at her, his eyes unfocused. "I was there." His eyes glassed over as his memories flooded in. I fought in the last battle of the Dragon Wars. I lost my brother that day and more than a few of my brothers in arms. I ran in the very first one." Kryzon pulled himself from his thoughts. Hope could tell his emotions were being tested as he struggled to be present in the conversation, but he collected himself and found the strength to focus on the good. "It was glorious."

"How many ran in the first?"

"There were a hundred of us."

"There is so much room on the edge of the circle — why so few?"

"Yes. On the outside edge, there would be enough room for a thousand. But where are they all going to go when they get to the middle?"

Hope realized that Kryzon was right. Simple geometry would suggest that if you had people standing even twenty feet apart, they wouldn't make it halfway before they were running into each other as all of them tried to fit into the center.

"Excellent point."

"I asked to run on the second as well, for my brother. He had died honorably, and I wanted him to be remembered." Kryzon's posture straightened, and he returned to watching the trees. "My brother was one of the greatest men I have ever known, second only to our father."

"Who is your father?" Hope asked, knowing this was a point of honor in some way.

"Master Javerus, Head of the Southern House."

Hope quickly put things together in her mind until she felt that she understood who she was talking to. "Did they let you run for him?"

Kryzon nodded. "There was a condition. I would have to run for his honor and his alone. I would gain nothing for a victory, and if I failed, I would still lose all of my honor, just like any other who failed."

"If you fail, you lose your standing?"

Kryzon nodded. "Until you can run again."

"No pressure." She said sarcastically while she laughed nervously.

Her words derailed his mind; he looked over to the queen with a look of utter bewilderment on his face. It took him a moment to understand she was joking, but once he did, he smiled and said, "No pressure at all. It's just a walk in the park." He closed his eyes for a moment and mused at the idea.

"I mean, yeah. The park is exploding out of the ground while full-grown trees grow up and outward with branches shooting in every direction all at once, but when you look back at the..." Opening his eyes, he gestured palms up with both hands at the general elven forest in front of them and said, "Park..." He laughed aloud and braced his hands on his knees. "You want to know what it's like?"

Hope was now just curious to see what he was going to say. "Do tell."

"Have you ever been chased by a forest?" They both broke into laughter. It was very cathartic for each of them.

"Wait. No, wait, stop. I'm going to pee. I mean it! You have to stop." was the only thing that Hope could get out as her nerves gave way to humor instead of embracing the horror that she was facing.

"Very well. I should go back to my patrol, and you should go remedy what ails you." He turned and began to walk toward the field.

"Please wait for a moment." Hope was still holding her side. "While I catch my breath, tell me, how did the run for your brother go?"

"During the Mother Tree, I decided that I was going to bring the highest honor to my brother I could. When it was time, I didn't just let it drain me; I pushed from my end as hard as I could. It wasn't just something I let the Mother Tree take. It was an offering that I gave freely. It was the difference between death and the blessing I was bestowed."

This was the question that was driving Hope at that
moment. She knew she would have to push herself past her
limits to earn the right to be the Queen of Venger, but she was
madly curious about how to survive it. "Why?"

Kryzon smiled and held out his hand as if to shake hers.
When she grabbed his hand, it was limp and relaxed in hers.
It was like holding a sleeping squid in her hand. "I am giving
nothing to this, and therefore, there is little that can be taken
from it before there is nothing left." He then rolled his wrist
and made a fist that was now pushing against her palm. "Now I
am putting something into it, and because of this, it has more
power to give."

Tears rolled down both of her cheeks. "I understand."
She reached past his hand and grasped his forearm, and he did
the same. "Thank you." He nodded and let her go. "How did
she bless you?"

"When I retrieved my sword that I had offered up to
the Goddess, it had been altered. She returned it to me with a
single difference. My brother's name was etched into the blade,
and the etching gave off a greenish glow. I had it looked at by
one of the sacred women of our order. They said the blade now
carries the honor of my brother with it permanently."

"Okay. Never tell my daughter I said this aloud, but that
is the Bibitz." She then spent the next few minutes explaining
the phrase.

"The truly amazing part was that the holy woman said
that my blade could now hold the honor of more people other
than my brother. When I run, I declare that I am running for

one of my brothers and sisters who fell in the Great War. Every time I run, I risk the chance of not making it back to the Father Tree, and if I fail, the sword and the honor it holds will be lost. So, every time I give with all that I am, and every time I get to the Father Tree, my sword awaits me with another name on it."

"How do you choose which name to run for?"

"I don't. The first time, I ran for my brother, but after that, as I chose to run for and honor my people, the name has always been chosen by the Goddess."

Hope was in awe at the idea that someone would risk everything for not just his brother, whom he loved, but for a random elf that fell in the great war. "How many times have you done this?"

"I have run in every ceremony since the beginning." He drew his sword, and all along the blade, elven names were etched in green light. "Eighty-seven in all. Eighty-six on the blade."

Hope stared at the blade. It was forged with elvish craftsmanship and looked more like platinum than steel. It was flawless and polished to a mirror finish, with eighty-six names written in elvish. The names were etched and gave the blade the appearance that it was made of a glowing green core that was then covered in beautiful elvish steel. It was one of the most beautiful things she had ever seen. "You carry the honor of eighty-six elves?"

"Eighty-Seven. I carry my own within me as well." He looked at the blade for a moment and smiled. "I knew many of them, and for the ones I didn't know, I sought out their families and told them of their family member's honor. Who knows? Perhaps one day, after I have passed, someone will run for me, and my name will be added to the sword. "I think that would be a fitting end."

Hope was still wiping tears from her eyes. "Yes. That would be an amazing end."

Kryzon put his sword away with respect. "Now, really. I have to go, and so do you."

"Right." Hope became slightly embarrassed that she told him that she almost peed. "I really should get going. Good luck today, Kryzon, son of the Southern House and honor bearer of the elven dead."

He waved and headed back toward his post. "To you as well, Queen Hope of Venger, and I have no doubt soon-to-be-bearer of the Earth Blade."

As she turned and walked away, the queen spoke to herself under her breath. "Well, Hope ol' girl. You passed the second test. You know what you need to do. Now, all that is left is the impossible." She looked up at the sky and then back to the empty field. "It's going to be a beautiful morning."

She headed back to camp and finished getting ready for her day. The sun had just risen when she came out of her tent for the second time; everyone was just waking up and preparing themselves. Suddenly, Dalen bamphed to her location.

It gave her a start, and she was glad that she had already relieved herself.

"I am sorry, Your Majesty. I believe you requested that I return before too long. I am glad to see that I haven't missed your run." Dalen looked a lot better. The color had returned to his face, and his features had softened; he no longer looked like a moving statue. Rather than solid white, his eyes once more sparkled with color, one a brilliant sapphire blue and the other a deep violet.

"Very well, Mr. Pax. Are you feeling alright?" She broke roles for a moment, and the mom in her came out. She began to look him over and brushed his now silver hair off his face. "It's a good look on you."

He playfully batted her away. "Yeah? Easy for you to say — you are all noble and motherly. Wait until my friends see this."

Almost as if they were on cue, the rest of the team came out of the tent.

"Hey! Look, guys! Dalen's stones have changed," Sir Adam cried.

"Just like bear bellies," responded Travis.

Then Becky added, "And pony butts."

Dalen rolled his eyes. "Yeah. Yeah. Yeah." He looked over to the Queen and said, "See what I mean?"

‹Are you sure you are all right?› Hope sent through the pin to Dalen alone. ‹All things considered, you look as though you have gone through a lot, and I don't mean the obvious.›

Dalen kept the channel closed so that only Hope would hear him. ‹It is more than I can explain right now. You're on it, and I thank you so much for honestly caring. The more time I spend with you, the more I understand why you deserve to be Queen. I am alright, just shook. I took a big step in the right direction — just a lot to take in.›

Dalen turned toward Brother Peace. "How about you, Peace? You're the master of giving me a hard time."

Brother Peace gave Dalen a respectful bow of the Brotherhood. "I swore an oath to never tease you again."

"Well, my guess is that the true intent of that oath had to do with not causing harm?" Dalen asked.

Peace nodded. "I gave up finding joy in hurting others."

Dalen gestured for Peace to stand by him. "Excellent! We are brothers, are we not?"

As Peace walked over, Hope asked ‹What is it that you need right now?›

‹This. I need to play and have a laugh.›

"Alright, my brother." Dalen put his arm around Peace. "I'm not asking you to intentionally attack me. I'm asking you to be a part of the family. I mean, look at me. Are you going to tell me you got nothing?"

Peace looked to the team. Travis and Becky looked like they were coaxing a puppy. They were smiling, and Becky was nodding. Travis quietly encouraged: "You can do it."

Adam just smirked and said, "I say take the offer."

Peace looked to the Queen. She just shook her head and said, "If the turkey walks over, hands you an ax, and then lays its neck on the chopping block. I mean..." and then she just trailed off, shook her head, and walked over to grab her canteen.

Brother Peace rubbed the back of his neck. "You're sure about this?" Dalen nodded. "Okay. For old times' sake, but remember you asked for it." He walked over to Travis, "Let me see your notebook for a moment." Brother Peace wrote down a few notes and handed it back.

Travis, Becky, and Adam read what he wrote.

"Damn," Becky had been caught completely off guard. "And that was quick, too."

"How does he come up with it so fast?" asked Travis.

Adam ran over to Brother Peace and shook his hand. "Well done, Sir. Well done," he praised him and then moved back near Travis, who was obviously having a private telepathic conversation with Becky about the joke.

She rolled her eyes and said, "Boys."

"Alright, Dalen. I am going to have to admit, this new look for you is kind of working." Brother Peace's verbal burns always started friendly enough. "I mean, it's a lot better than the white stones, and now you look like you again. The 'all-white Dalen' was a little odd. You looked pale and a little creepy. Right?" He looked around, and his friends reluctantly nodded.

Ben gestured to the Queen. "It was a bit of a surprise," she said flinchingly, knowing that, somehow, she was only helping him.

Ben nodded in agreement. "See? Even the Queen thinks this is better. Well done. Well done indeed."

Travis, Becky, and Adam jokingly gave a half-hearted cheer, "Yay." Followed by the quietest round of applause they could muster.

"Also, I dig that you have not yet set foot on the ground, and for whatever reason, you are just hovering an inch or so off it. That's a very nice touch." Dalen looked down. He hadn't realized it, but Brother Peace was right: he was hovering off the ground. Dalen had no idea that he had been doing so and wondered if he had been doing so since his arrival. Brother Peace slowly began to walk around Dalen, looking him over. "And the silvery stones. They seem to be placed over each of your chakras, right?"

Dalen knew it was coming but couldn't see where he was going with it. The suspense was killing him. "Yes," he said cautiously.

"All of them?"

"Yes, Peace ... All of them." Dalen began to see where things were going, but he knew that there was no way to eject now.

"That includes the root chakra." Travis tried hard not to laugh as Ben set up the joke. "Tell me, Dalen. Do you have Silver Balls?" As he said it, he gestured with one finger to the team and, in unison, to the tune of the holiday song 'Silver Bells,' they sang:

Silver Balls! Silver Balls!

Dalen Pax has silver testis.

Hear them clang. Dan-a-lang!

I don't know how he sits down.

With... Silver Balls! Silver Balls!

The three of them couldn't make it through another verse as each fell into a heap of laughter.

Dalen was still hovering, but he quickly turned to Brother Peace and hugged him. Peace was surprised at first, but once he realized that Dalen was laughing just as hard as the rest, he hugged him back.

"That was the bibitz!" Dalen let him go but fell into another fit of laughter. He held his stomach and laughed until he ran out of air, yet his body continued to convulse for a moment before it allowed him to breathe. He inhaled deeply. "I do," he replied and began to laugh again. It wasn't exactly true, as the root chakra is slightly higher than that, but the punch line was too good. "I do have silver balls."

They all roared with laughter, and Hope spit out her entire mouthful of water from her canteen.

Dalen was laughing with his friends, but as he did, he split his location with the mind sphere and imagined himself standing next to the Queen. It was as simple as breathing for him. Even he marveled at how his magic had changed. There was no ritual or spell. He simply thought what he wanted, pictured the magic in his mind and reality bent to his will. Hope coughed and tried to catch her breath as a second version of Dalen appeared beside her. She shot a bewildered look at this second Dalen, who glanced over at the original version of himself, nodded, then returned his focus to Hope.

"What can I do for you, Dalen?" asked the Queen.

Dalen spoke through the pin on a private link. ‹It's what I hope to do for you.› He looked at himself with his friends and smiled. ‹ Sir Adam has a phrase. Do you know it?›

‹Everyone in Venger knows it: *These are the moments we live for.* It's taught as part of the curriculum for Vengerian History.›

‹Do you know why he says it?›

‹It empowers him.›

‹It does. It absolutely does, but he doesn't say it to empower himself. He says it to empower others.›

‹Empower others?›

‹It's not 'these are the moments I live for.' Try it and see.›

"These are the moments we live for." She said loudly and with power.

The team matched her energy and repeated it back, then whooped and hollered.

She smiled, and a tear found its way to the edge of her eye. ‹There is absolutely nothing like seeing past a legend and finding a man still worth respecting.›

‹You should tell him that sometime. Coming from you, it will mean a lot.›

‹I will make it a point to do so.› She wiped the tear from her cheek. ‹I noticed they didn't see you. Are you an illusion?›

‹In a way. Think of it more like high-definition telepathy. There is no illusion to see. I am using the pin as a connection point and then adding my natural abilities to do it. I tell you, I am glad I learned how to use jinn telepathy while using pin telepathy, or this would be very difficult.›

‹I would love to have you tell me more about this, but I feel I am taking you from your point.›

Dalen was still watching himself laugh with his friends. ‹Once this starts, I will be unable to help you until you get to the blade. Until then, you are on your own and will have to rely on yourself.›

‹I am aware, Mr. Pax.›

‹Are you aware that there are a lot more powerful things than just knowing that, if you fail, there are consequences?›

‹Yes. I will be bringing my strength and my perseverance, my drive and all my will to this run."›

‹Yes but ask yourself this. For what do you have strength? Why do you persevere? What empowers your drive? In that moment, you will be more alive than at any other moment of your life. But what is it that you live for?›

‹My daughter. If I am honest, I love my husband, and I love my city and kingdom, and I will fight with everything within me to save them, but I will win because of her.›

‹Bring that with you. Have it empower you and others the way that Sir Adam does. Keep it with you. Never forget the things you live for. It will empower you in ways you will be shocked to witness.›

‹How do you know all of this?›

Dalen looked at her; she could still see the mark of whatever had happened to him in the night. ‹Because I have just done it myself. I didn't have exploding trees, but I had to give everything I had, including the sacrifice of an object that I have had since my life began. It was far more precious to me than I have words to explain. To achieve, I had to sacrifice, but I'll tell you what, without question, it's worth it.›

She looked away from the Dalen standing next to her
and looked at the version standing with his friends. ‹They are
what empower you. This moment, just laughing with your friends.
This is a moment you live for. Isn't it?›

‹I will remember this moment for the rest of time.›

Hope was called for, and it broke her concentration. It
was time for her to prepare for her run. She looked back to
where Dalen had been talking to her; he was gone. She reached
up and activated an open channel. ‹Look alive, folks — the time
has come.› Everyone tapped their pins, and then each of them
were in full Vengerian Guardian attire.

They traveled through the woods, speaking to each other
about what was to come. Hope told them of her morning and
what she had learned from Kryzon.

Collectively, the guardians said that Kryzon's words
made sense and, if she was going to do this, she should take
his advice. The question of whether he could be trusted came
up, but Hope said she truly believed in him and what he
had said.

Once she arrived at the edge of the circle, the guardians
were reminded that they could not interfere. They were then
asked if any of them had any training in healing. Both Peace
and Dalen said they could help in that way, and they were
given direct orders. They could heal anyone who obtained their
item, and they could heal everyone who did not make it. They
just had to wait until the grass reached the Father Tree, and
the event was over, not a moment before. They both gave their
word, and they were moved to the Father Tree.

Gnomon and Fulcrum found Hope, and Gnomon asked if Hope would run by her side with her father. Hope agreed, and the three of them walked up to the starting line that was placed near the spot where the Eastern Mother Tree would be planted.

"Once you cross this line, you can't go back," Gnomon's voice filled with determination. "Let's cross over it together."

She took her father's hand in one hand and Hope's in the other, and together they stepped over it.

Hope gave her a look of pretend fear. "Oh no, now it's too late."

"I guess we will have to go forward." Fulcrum gave his daughter a wink, and they moved into position. "Remember, they will give a signal when young adults are supposed to run."

"Don't worry, Father. I know when to run." She kissed him on his cheek and then took her position. Quietly to herself, she said, "I know exactly when I intend to run."

In the Elven tongue, a speaker addressed the crowd. He spoke for over thirty minutes about the Dragon Wars. He reminded them how they were the guardians of the forest, and it was put upon their shoulders to rebuild it. He then continued explaining how they were the chosen ones of nature and how this blessing connected them to the forest. It was an amazing origin story to explain why they ran with the trees and how they derived their honor from it.

Then, it was announced that the Queen of Venger was running with them, and a hush fell over the crowd.

"Many years ago, it was humans that came and ravaged our lands. They disrespected the forest and our way." Whoever was speaking had done something magical to project his voice over the entire field. Voices could be heard calling out from random elves who had gathered to watch the run.

"That's not fair!" demanded an elf from the crowd.

"For humans, it was generations ago."

"There is no wisdom in hating a man for his great-grandfather's deeds."

An elven man who was standing near the father tree raised his hand, and the crowd fell silent. "And then one dark day in our history when our world was burning, and all hope seemed lost, it was Venger who came to our need and saved us all!"

The crowd exploded into cheers. The man who was speaking began to walk away from the Father Tree and headed straight for her.

"The humans came to us when we needed them." The cheers grew louder. "When we needed them, they were there!" His voice punctuated each word, and voices from the crowd were screaming and applauding. "And now, in Venger's time of need, we have been given a chance to return that favor! Who's with me?"

The forest echoed the thunderous applause for miles and
then diminished into silence as he raised his hand once more.
He was finally close enough to see clearly, and Hope recognized
him immediately. "I am Kryzon, the last son of the Southern
House," he smiled at Hope and gave her a nod as he stood
alongside her. "Bearer of the honor of the elven dead, and I
ask you, Queen Hope of Venger: Will you run with us and fulfill
your destiny?"

The crowd was silent. Wind could be heard through the
edge of the trees. Kryzon was holding a stone that he had been
speaking into that allowed his voice to be heard over the entire
field. He handed it to her and stepped back slightly.

Hope brought the stone close to her face and spoke.
"Know what you want to say, my father used to tell me. And
if I didn't know what I wanted to say, it was better to say
nothing at all. I have spent years preparing for diplomatic
moments such as this. I have spent hours practicing all that is
necessary to be a proper queen. After spending time with you
and hearing just a few of your stories, I am aware that the
elven people are truly lucky. Because it would take me hundreds
of years of study to be able to come close to finding the words
to explain how honored and humbled I am to be here with you."

She paused for a moment while the people cheered. She
turned to Kryzon and addressed him directly.

"Kryzon. You are known and respected. You carry the
honor of eighty-seven men and women. I will remember this
morning and the opportunity I was given to speak with you;
it was an amazing moment. Very rarely do you get a chance
to meet a legend and then find out that, beyond the legend,

there is a real person worthy of respect and honor." Again, the people cheered. Once they quieted down, Hope continued, "You are a legend. I would expect no argument about that by any who can hear my voice." Another round of applause came, but then she raised her hand, and the clearing fell silent. "I was recently able to meet a legend from my own culture, and I have been blessed by his accompaniment on my journey. He, too, is someone that, when you look past the fame and the stories, you find a greater man than you expected, and if he were standing here with me, he would know what to say. It is the only thing that he would say, and his words are the only thing that I can find within myself to be worthy of saying now." ‹Sir Adam, this moment is for you.› She raised her fist over her head, and with all her strength and power, she cried out: "These are the moments we live for!"

In one collective voice, the forest cried back, "These are the moments we live for!"

Sir Adam was brought to his knees. The cheering was louder than anything he had ever heard before.

Then, a hush fell over the crowd as the four plant mages took their position on the edge of the field, one for each direction. The ceremony of the Running of the Trees had begun.

15

RUNNING WITH THE TREES

Dalen and Peace were asked to move to the center of the circle, near the Father Tree. As healers, they would be needed there the most. Many of the runners who weren't fast enough to keep up with the trees would still finish before the grass made it to the Father Tree. They would be injured, but once they made it to the Father Tree and claimed their offering, the monks would be allowed to heal them. Often, they would be injured by being hit by a sprouting tree but not disabled. The obvious reason to have the healers in the center was so that they could provide aid immediately once the runner had completed their dash. The other reason had to do with the viewpoint, which was not only beautiful and frightening as the forest closed in around them from all angles, but it granted them a specific advantage. The healers in the center could use their vantage point to see where people were failing as the run occurred so that afterward, they could get to the injured quickly.

Adam, Travis, and Becky were going to have to stay behind with all of the elves who were not running due to the limited amount of space available on the field of play. Hundreds of people could stand on the outside edge, but Kryzon was right: there was just not enough room for everyone in the center. A hundred people were running, but there were five to six times that amount here, consisting of friends and family that had come to cheer them on, wish them well, and care for the wounded if they happened to fail.

They were sad that they wouldn't be able to watch it, but then, all of a sudden, Travis stopped in his tracks and began to laugh. He reached up and tapped his pin. ‹Hey, D? Could you do me a favor? Check out the pin's second-to-last command.›

Dalen opened the menu to his pin's commands and scrolled down to the bottom. The second to last command was called 'Eye of the Beholder' and included the following instructions: Tap center once and then trace the middle ring to create a scry system that allows others to see through the wearer's eyes and hear what they hear. ‹Oh, that's beautiful, Travis. Way to think outside the box.›

‹The only thing the box is good for is to carry the tools.› Sir Adam put his hand up, and Travis gave him a high five.

Travis found a good spot that would be out of the way. While using the Eye of the Beholder, they would be in a partial trance, and he wanted to find a place where they would be safe to allow themselves to lose track of what was happening around them.

Dalen reached up and activated his pin. To everyone else, it was going to be like an intentional daydream. The scry worked through the mind sphere, and thus, the action they wanted to watch was only perceivable when directly observed. If they closed their eyes and chose to look at it, they could see through Dalen's perspective, but they could just as easily open their eyes and dismiss it.

‹I am going to turn on mine as well.› Hope said as she activated it. ‹The same way you can choose to telepathically talk to a single person, you can choose which person you are watching.› She then had to take her focus back to what she was doing. Things were beginning to start, and the time for conversations was over.

The team closed their eyes and chose to see through Hope's perspective. Hope knelt in respect as the priestess took her position to plant the eastern tree. She was beautiful and wild. She wore a pair of worn leather shorts that didn't quite make it to her knees. Her leather top looked just as worn and left her arms bare. Along her arms and legs, there were many marks; some were tattoos, and some looked to be brands, but all of them together created beautiful works of art that ran the length of her body. Although Hope did not know the magical symbols herself, she could tell they were sacred and connected her to her abilities and faith.

Four of them had graced the field that day, one in each direction like a compass, and they stood directly in front of the heads of each house. Fulcrum was the head of the Eastern

House, so she took her place in front of him. Gnomon was next to her father but spaced out far enough that if both extended their arms, they would not be able to touch. Hope was a similar distance away from Gnomon, and over that distance again was Kryzon. Normally, he would be with the Southern House, but today, he was running with the Queen, and no one thought any less of him for it. Together with the other members of the Eastern house, they knelt in a circle around where the Mother Tree would grow.

As she gave her opening prayer, the priestess spoke about remembering the Goddess, how they needed to connect to her, and how the mind would be key. Then she reached into a pouch that hung on her belt, retrieved a sacred Mother Tree acorn, and planted it into the ground. From a pouch on her other side, she took a sprinkling of glowing dust and let it fall over the ground where she had buried the seed.

She began to caress the space above the buried seed, and then she pointed to the ground with two fingers and spoke an incantation that was neither common nor elven. As she raised her hand slowly, the tree broke ground and began to grow upward. She opened her mouth and allowed sound to fall from it, singing to the tree with no specific words. When the tree grew to the height of her shoulders, she began to bring her hands together, but it was obvious that her motions were not just gliding through the air as if she were performing a simple ritualistic dance. She was pushing her hands together with all of her strength as if she were passing through a great force, and she strained her muscles to bring her hands together. As they touched one another, she swiftly split them in two different directions, and the Mother Tree obeyed her commands;

two main limbs exploded from the trunk as it continued to grow. The priestess continued with her song; the tree danced with her movements as each hand motion created branches that began to grow in new directions, and the Mother Tree began to take shape.

It was a young tree now with more growth than a sapling, but still thin and spindly, not yet ready to produce. The priestess finished her song and moved out of the circle. "Ready yourself and steel your mind. There is no going back." The priestess kneeled and called to the goddess to hear their prayers, and the Mother Tree began to pull.

It was stronger than Hope was expecting. It hit like an implosion with the Mother Tree at the center. It pulled them forward like they were trapped in a current, leaving their arms outstretched toward the Mother Tree.

The current began to pick up strength, and Hope could feel her life essence being drawn out of her, which was frightening. Every instinct in her screamed for her to pull back, and she felt her body try to act in reflex, to the point that she had to force herself to maintain the connection. Every moment she held on she fought her own instincts. Her body and mind fought back and told her it hurt, trying to make her let go. When she refused to listen, it only made it hurt more.

Gnomon was fighting her own battles. Hope could see the agony in her eyes, and then the girl began to scream.

"Pull back, Gnomon! You have given enough! You don't have to prove anything to me!" Fulcrum was fighting for every word, and the force of the pull was only getting stronger; it took everything he could muster to speak at all.

Gnomon felt the essence of her life being pulled out of her by the Mother Tree, and she was starting to lose consciousness. "I love you, Father, but no!" The current pulled her harder, but she refused to let go. "I have to. For me!" It was all she could get out. The pull was too strong, and trying to speak had become too much.

They had reached the point where a choice had to be made, and in that moment, Fulcrum looked passed his little girl and saw the woman she was trying to become. This was the moment that he had been trying to postpone since the day Gnomon was born. Today was the day that his little girl was going to grow up, and at that moment, he knew that he was holding her back. He knew that if she was going to succeed, he was going to have to let her go. He lost himself in the moment, and although he was in pain and suffering, he wanted to stretch that moment out until the end of time so that he could have his little girl forever.

Dalen had the ability to slow down time, when it was taught to him, it was explained that it was a natural occurrence and that he would need to learn how to activate and control it. However, it can naturally occur within anyone. There is a place in the mind that slows things down, and when activated, a moment can take a lifetime. In this moment, Fulcrum's title and prestige faded away. He was just a father watching his little girl become a woman. His heart swelled with pride for her and what she had become. Fulcrum sobbed as he said goodbye and then let go of her as his mind sped back up. "Gnomon!" he cried out against the pull of the tree. "Don't just let it take you. Push! Hard!"

Hope's hands began to whither, and she knew that she had to do the same. She could hear whispers of her Vengerians in her mind, giving her encouragement. Then, from the center of her mind, she heard Dalen's voice speak to her as clear as day. *Who are you?*

Her life flashed before her eyes. She saw her childhood, growing up in the kingdom across the sea, in her home city of Lions Crest. She saw momentary flashes of her travels across the sea to meet her betrothed, a young Prince Gavin. Then she remembered her trial to become the new Fire Princess. Flashes of when she married the love of her life and had to retrieve the Earth Blade. That time, it was in the bowels of a cave filled with nightmares. The images came faster now; years flipped by with her daughter and her husband. All of the pieces forged together into an understanding that allowed her to remember. Powerful... Respected... Loved... She was the heart of her kingdom, and she knew who she was. She was the Earth Queen of Venger.

Queen Hope, The Earth Queen of Venger, was never the woman to just sit there and be broken. Her soul was fierce, and her heart was pure. In becoming the Fire Princess, she learned how to set aside fear and risk everything in the moments that mattered. She reached down into the center of her being and pushed with all she was.

Kryzon had been right. As they pushed their essence at the Mother Tree, it created a charge within them. The charge became more powerful the more you put in, giving the Mother Tree more than just their energies to feed on. As the Mother

Tree fed, it began to widen, taking years of growth in a matter of seconds, and as it bloomed to maturity, it dropped an acorn.

Hope watched it in slow motion as it fell from its branch. She felt her life being pulled out of her, leaving her with nothing other than the static charge that she had built. The world began to go dark, and her eyes became heavy, but as the acorn touched the ground, the polarity of the force reversed, and a ring of life-giving energy rippled out from the Mother Tree. They stayed kneeling, but the force pushed them back and held them there with a continuous wave of energy. Hope was too weak to fight against it and relented as it engulfed her, but as it did, it began to rejuvenate her and make her strong. By the time the wave ended, all of her life force had been returned to her, in addition to the charge that she created within herself.

The acorn that had fallen was filled by the current as well and had already completely grown. This was happening in all four locations. Four Mother Trees had then bloomed, dropped an acorn, and its sister tree had grown in full standing next to it. As the first acorn fell from the sister tree and touched the ground, the charge within the queen bloomed.

She didn't see that the sister trees continued around the circular field to the right. One tree after another, around the edge of the clearing, starting at the Mother Tree at the Eastern point, until it reached the Mother Tree at the Northern point of the circle. Nor did she see that trees from the Southern Mother Tree had followed the edge and had met with this Mother Tree. She missed it completely, as together, the four Mother Trees and their offspring had created a circle of new trees. The only thing she noticed was the power of the charge within her, blossoming throughout her body all at once. She looked at her hands and arms and realized that she looked and felt like a living Damascus statue wearing her clothes. She felt a need to remove her boots, and when she did, she could feel the earth underneath her and the life that was about to spring from it.

"Well done," said Kryzon. "You both have been given the blessing of the Goddess." He had grown deer antlers, and he looked to be part elf, part stag, standing then as a quadruped instead of a biped.

She looked to her right at Gnomon, who had grown in size and looked to be a mix between a girl and a fox with nine beautiful tales.

Hope drew her Queen's Blade made of celestium, which she then set at the foot of the Mother Tree. Kryzon set his sword next to hers. On the other side, Gnomon placed her bow beside the Queen's Blade.

Fulcrum looked like he belonged to the same herd as Kryzon. He had taken off his family's crest ring before the beginning of the ceremony. With teeth, because his hands were more like hooves now, he picked it up and sat the ring at the foot of the Mother Tree. "Your mother would be so proud of you; I know that I am. You have gained the Goddess's blessing. You have nothing left to prove. Now that all of that is behind you run, my dear. Run for you.""The Goddess wants you to be free," the Priestess said. "She wants you to take your place among your people, but only you can decide where that is." She smiled at Gnomon and then looked upward to the clouds above.

She raised her hands with closed fists, and the clouds began to drop a fine mist. She turned her gaze to the field and opened her hands; the wind carried the magical dust that was in them, spreading it across the field. Just then, the sun crested over the treetops, creating a rainbow that fell to the earth, the end of its arch directly touching the Father Tree. As the light hit it, all of the offerings at the foot of the Mother Tree vanished.

The moment the light touched the Father Tree, men and women carrying infants and young children began their run. Hope could hear them calling out to their children to stay close and run as fast as they could. She could hear the screams of frightened children echo from all across the field.

The little ones were more than three-quarters of the way there when a horn sounded, and the other members of the Eastern House ran as fast as they could. The only ones that were left were Kryzon, Hope, Fulcrum ... and Gnomon.

"What are you doing?" Fulcrum prodded his hooves on the ground. "Run."

"This is the one moment you can't interfere, Father. Once the ceremony starts, no one may interfere with a runner until it is over." She lowered herself until she could touch the ground with her hands, and then she set her legs to prepare to run.

"My light, I love you," he said, panicked as he watched the other young adults that his daughter was supposed to be with get further away. "Please! Run!"

"It's too late, Fulcrum!" Hope yelled across to him. "You can't stop her! But you can still help her!" Time was moving too fast, and Hope knew she was about to move. She could feel the earth shift beneath her feet like it was begging for a command.

"You see the Father Tree?" Fulcrum asked sternly. Gnomon nodded. "That is the only thing that matters. Keep your focus on it, but keep your surroundings in your peripherals; the obstacles must be respected while never taking your eyes off the prize, or they will catch you by surprise. And daughter ... run!" He took a deep breath, and the horn sounded again. "RUN!"

Hope tilted forward and started to push with her legs. The ground responded to her desires and propelled her forward like a wave. She almost lost her balance immediately, but the forest caught her. Trees began to erupt around her, throwing rocks and dirt in every direction. She took a wider step and leaned into it; the wave obeyed and began to propel her faster than the trees were growing. This was good in some respects because, if she could keep her pace, she would be sure to get the Earth Blade in time, as long as it was there, but she had no time to think about the 'what ifs.' The thing she had to deal with was the destructive carnage of the trees in the front line as she passed them. Both Fulcrum and Kryzon were ahead of the trees, and she could see flashes of them as the forest grew behind them.

There were a lot of people already at the Father Tree. A few of the adults who had already made it were helping the others who had finished to stand out of the way as more runners came in to claim their items. Peace was helping a woman with a sprained ankle, but so far, that had been the only injury.

Dalen looked out from his position to the East. The queen had not yet emerged from the trees. He wondered if she was going to stay behind the line and play it safe. If she stayed just behind the line, she would be clear just after the circle of toadstools emerged and still have time to reach the Earth Blade. He closed his eyes and saw her perspective. He smirked and said aloud, "She has no intention of playing it safe. Where's the fun in that?" He turned around, knelt, and opened his eyes. Before him was the Vengerian Earth Blade. It was a beautiful Damascus longsword, the blade forged of steel and celestium with a pattern folded over a thousand layers. The guards and pommel were done in the same style but had fewer layers, giving them a distinctively different feel. The handle was wrapped in beautiful, rich white leather, and there was a large emerald in its pommel and on either side of the guards. It was the most beautiful sword Dalen had ever seen.

It's here, Hope. I'm staring at the Earth Blade. It was all the motivation that Hope needed, and she made the choice to push through. To get past the line, Hope had to move at amazing speeds through the forest, and because of the trees, it wasn't going to be a straight shot. The gift granted to her allowed her to move at great speeds with phenomenal control as the ground itself propelled her. It also made her resilient, so the few times she did graze trees as she ran by, it left her undamaged. She made her way through, dodging trees as they exploded from the ground with branches that seemed to be reaching out to stop her. It slowed her down a bit, keeping her in the carnage as she moved across the field at the same speed. She was in the one place she didn't want to be: right at the line where the forest was being created, and Kryzon's question echoed in her thoughts.

"Have you ever been chased down by a forest?"

She knew if she stayed there, she would eventually be taken out by something. Much like the Mother Tree, she knew she had to push with all she had if she was going to survive the ordeal. She let out a warrior's scream and pushed through.

As she reached the edge of the growth line, trees were erupting from the ground everywhere around her. She held her course but had to duck and dodge as limbs shot from the ground, trying to catch her. She knew that, like the other trials of her past, this moment would haunt her dreams for years to come, remembering how she was stuck in the maelstrom of the evergreens, but that would be her mind processing the fear that she had no time to explore in this instant. Instead, she focused on the Father Tree and kept her eyes open for the dangers that surrounded her.

Kryzon and Fulcrum were at the tree, retrieving their items with many others who had reached the finish. As they did, they reverted to their elven forms. Dalen and Peace were counting out loud the number of people they saw taken by the forest, keeping track of how many people they had to find. Dalen had just watched a tree spring up in front of an elf who was running at full speed. He heard the dull thump as the elf hit it blindly at full tilt. "Seven."

Then Dalen saw Hope emerge from the carnage of the trees. Right next to her was Gnomon, who was running ahead of them. Magically, he enhanced his sight, and his vision became telescopic as he focused on them. They were beautiful. Gnomon was running like a quadruped, and Hope shimmered in the sunlight as she rode on a wave of earth.

Hope looked to her right and saw Gnomon running just ahead of the trees and keeping pace, sustaining a high-pitched warrior's whoop.

Hope was now in the field, and it was a smooth ride. She pushed forward, and the earth obeyed, and her speed tripled. She brought her arms back with her hands tilted, making wings to help stabilize her. She gave a high-pitched whoop as well until she reached the ring of toadstools, and the wave she was riding came to a rest and set her down directly at the sacred ring. She knew she had made it and with time to spare, so she stopped and turned to see a sight she was sure she would never see again.

What she saw was Gnomon running for her life. Being chased by a forest. It was violent. It was chaotic. It was powerful. It was beautiful.

Then Hope saw something else. Gnomon was no longer whooping. She was screaming. Her leg had cramped, and the muscle had torn. The forest was catching her. "Run!" Hope called out, but it was too late. Gnomon was almost to the ring when the final tree erupted underneath her feet. It sent her flying through the air out of control.

Becky gasped and reached out to take Travis's hand as they watched Gnomon sail through the air through Dalen's eyes. Dalen wanted to catch her but knew he could do nothing but watch.

Gnomon was able to use her acrobatics to leap from the tree as it launched her upward. This allowed her to control herself in the air and get herself right while she fell, but the height was too much, and she was going too fast. Her femur snapped in her right leg, and both bones in her left leg came jutting out of her skin.

"I can heal her," said Peace, and he moved to intercept her. Kryzon pulled his blade, and, with no sign of mercy, he looked Brother Peace in the eyes. "If you touch her before the run is over, I will kill you where you stand."

They both locked eyes with each other, and each of them recognized the warrior in the other. "Not a second before." Brother Peace moved his gaze away from Kryzon and set his gaze on Gnomon. "But not a second after." He ignited his ball of light and moved close but did not approach closer than a few feet.

Fulcrum was screaming incoherently, and three elves were trying to keep him from his daughter. The tree had flung her most of the way, and she was only a few feet, but the grass and flowers had already crept to her toes. She gained consciousness and wished she hadn't. She began to scream, and Hope rushed to her side.

One of the elves that had already finished their run tried to stop her, but she looked him dead in the eyes and screamed in his face. "You cannot interfere with a runner while the run is in progress!" She was right. She had not yet claimed the Earth Blade, and officially, her run was still happening. He raised his hands and moved out of her way.

"Hope! Grab the sword!" Travis called aloud. He was so entrenched in the moment he forgot he wasn't there.

"Get up, Gnomon! Get up!" The queen was lying on the ground right next to her but didn't touch her.

"I can't!" She screamed as her tears fell from the pain.

"You left 'can't' at the Mother Tree when you chose this path. Well, here it is, Gnomon. You don't get to quit!" Hope gaged the distance from where she lay. "You only have three feet, but you are running out of time!"

"It hurts!" she screamed.

"Yes! It hurts! Pain lets you know you haven't lost yet. Now move!" Hope pounded the ground next to her. "This is it. You against the pain. This is the only fight there is. The question is whether you are the little girl your father thought you were or are you the hunter you believe yourself to be. Now! MOVE!"

Gnomon opened her eyes. She was lying on her chest, and the grass was beginning to grow under her neck and chin. Her body wanted to give out, but she reached up with both hands, dug her fingers into the ground, and dragged herself a third of the way. It was brutal on her legs. They pulled and stretched as she dragged them behind her. As she dragged her

body along the ground, she could tell that her ribs were broken,
and moving was jamming the broken pieces into her organs,
causing her to begin to bleed on the inside.

‹Hope. Get the sword,› Travis repeated.

Hope looked up from the ground in defiance. She looked
at Dalen, knowing that the others would hear and see her.
"This young woman is being more of a queen than anyone I
have ever met in my life. How could I ever call myself a queen
if I abandoned her now?" She looked back at Gnomon. The
grass was catching her. "Come on, Gnomon. You can do this.
It will all be over the moment you have your bow in your hand.
Now pull!"

Gnomon reached up with both hands and screamed as she
pulled herself onto her hands, much like a pushup, and, step by
step, walked her broken body to the tree.

Fulcrum had knocked out two of the elves who were
keeping him back, and Kryzon stepped in and grabbed him by his
collar. Looking him in the eye and with a calm and easy voice,
he said, "Have faith, brother. She will not fail."

Hope slid herself along the ground right next to the
girl the whole way. When they were within arm's reach,
Hope reached up and took the Earth Blade from the tree to
everyone's relief but never took her eyes off of Gnomon.

"You made it," Hope said. "All you have to do is reach
out and take it." Her focus moved from the girl to the grass.
It was nearly to the tree, but Gnomon didn't move. "Come on,
Gnomon, you have to — you have to right now. There is no more

time, and you have come all this way. Please! Reach out and take your destiny!"

Gnomon's chest was hardening. Her internal bleeding was filling up her chest cavity. The world darkened, and she began to grow cold, and all she wanted to do was sleep.

"I know you have nothing left." Hope's voice was commanding but still filled with compassion. "This is where your inner strength and power, the very stuff that makes you who you are, matters. This is the real test right here. Right now. When everything is on the line and everything is in your hands. Your goal is directly in front of you. Now reach out with your hand and take it."

Kryzon was watching the grass. "Three. Two ..."

Gnomon reached one hand out. It trembled with the last scrap of strength she had in her and grabbed her bow. An instant later, the few items that were left un-retrieved vanished from the Father Tree.

Brother Peace's ball of light intensified from the dragon claw, and as he drew near, the light merged with Gnomon.

The scene had created a crowd of runners who were standing nearby, watching as Gnomon had fought. They erupted in cheers.

By the time that Fulcrum got to his daughter, she was already healed, and he swept her up in his arms and embraced her tightly. "That was the most impressive run I have ever seen. You were amazing!"

Dalen used his magic, and all of the elves who were unable to make it to the finish were teleported to the center, where they were immediately given treatment. It was a good day, and all of them survived.

They had done it. Their very first mission was a success, and all of them, including the Queen, took a deep breath of victory and let out a sigh of relief.

16

THE TIME STONE

Xoxann looked around in bewilderment. "Where are we, DeSalvo?"

"What lays before you are the ruins of the City of Dreams. It is the place where time was first broken." DeSalvo scanned the ruins. "This is where the creator of this world almost destroyed it."

Xoxann took in the skeletal remains of a long-lost city. They stood at an arch that was once a mighty gate. The wood from the gate littered the landscape as if it were blasted from the inside and blown outward, shattering it into a thousand pieces. The edges of the arch were blackened as if there had been a fire.

Through the arch was what was left of a large city. The stone foundations were there, but the stones seemed to be the only thing left. She could make out streets and where buildings had been, marked by knee-high walls. In the center of the ruins, there was a building, which, other than the arch before her, was the only thing taller than her. It was warped and bent in odd ways. To Xoxann's eyes, it looked like it had been made out of clay, and someone had dropped it, hoping that no one would notice it.

"There was a great price paid by this city. One of the many scars this accursed place carries is that it's frozen in time. The moment that has to stay frozen forever. DeSalvo started to walk into the city, but Xoxann started to back up. "Xoxy? What's wrong, little one?"

"I'm scared." Xoxann was now frightened of the castle. It looked like it had been warped by something terrible. She took another step back as she wondered if there were people in it when it happened.

"What's wrong? Why are you scared?" She had already permitted DeSalvo to be in her mind and already had allowed him to hide in its little corners. As was his way, he never left. He set up camp in her psyche, and now he saw an opportunity; he decided to hold her fear in place.

"What if it's haunted?" Xoxy asked and started to rub one of her hands with the other.

"Oh. It is quite haunted." He pushed her fear and held it again.

She started to cry as her fear began to grip her coldly, and she began to wonder if the city was haunted. were the ghosts looking at her right now? "I don't want to go. DeSalvo, I'm scared, and I don't want to go. Please don't make me go."

DeSalvo moved close but held her fear. "Why are you scared?"

"You said it's haunted." Her fear was getting the best of her, and in her head, she was starting to think about terrible ways this could go.

"It is, but you forgot you have a secret weapon." He sustained her fear but didn't raise it.

"What's that DeSalvo?" She was scared, and her mind was not helping her at all. She wanted to fix her mistake, but she was paralyzed with fear.

"Me." He took her hand, and just as he did, he released her fear.

Xoxann's mind cleared. Just having DeSalvo with her made her feel brave. "Will you protect me?"

It was like taking candy.

"Of course I will." DeSalvo smiled and gave her hand a squeeze, and as he did, he removed all fear and raised her sense of safety. "Stay close to me, and I will keep you safe. We're best friends, right?"

"Best Friends." She loved having a best friend, and she loved that he was a magical old man who could grant her wishes and keep her safe. She began to feel like maybe they could fix her mistake and bring Kavlin back. "What if we see a ghost?"

"Not all ghosts are scary. Remember Kim? She was a ghost." DeSalvo had gotten her moving, and they began the walk into the city and toward the castle.

"I guess, but she wasn't scary. She was nice." She looked up at DeSalvo with the face of an angel and started to swing their hands back and forth. "How did you meet her?"

DeSalvo let her swing her arm with his, but while she playfully skipped down the street, he kept a vigilant eye out for anything that might be there. It was easier to keep her happy if she were distracted and not thinking about the true peril that they could very well be in, so he told her a version of how they met.

"The villain, Dalen Pax, had taken what was mine, and the thing I need to finally be free of my slavery, and threw it into the space between time, losing it forever. I tried to stop him, but he defeated me." He looked down at her and shrugged. "It was very unexpected."

He was being silly, and she could tell. She giggled for a moment and said, "Then what happened?"

"Well, once I was beaten, I returned to the object that binds and enslaves me." The Magician, Mathias, had done his best to help me, but he was killed by Pax. So, I was stranded because Mathias was my only friend."

"That's so sad." Xoxann stopped swinging her arm and started to look at her feet.

"It was sad. I didn't know how long I was going to be trapped in there, and not only was I trapped, but I was trapped alone, mourning my loss." He pushed her sadness.

"Tears began to well up in Xoxann's eyes. "Oh, DeSalvo! I'm sorry you were so sad."

"But then I met Kim, and she was really nice." He released the throat hold on her sadness and allowed the girl's memory of Kim to flow. "She was kind and very nice, and you know what?"

Xoxann smiled. "What?"

All of this happened outside of a ball." DeSalvo watched her eyes glaze over as the dream of going to a real ball played out in her head. "Pax had gone to the ball with Kim, but he had abandoned her there. We decided that right then, it must be fate. Both of us had our hearts broken by Pax, and she agreed to help me try to make right what he had done. What he had done to both of us."

"Pax sounds like a very bad man." She had really liked Kim, and not only did Pax keep DeSalvo enslaved, but now, he also had hurt Kim.

"When Kim was about to die, I told her that I couldn't bear the idea that she would die with unfinished business. It can do horrible things to the soul if it still has things to do. That's how you can get bad ghosts. You wouldn't have wanted her to be like that, right?"

"No. I really liked Kim." The idea of Kim being a bad ghost was a sad thought to Xoxann.

"Me too. Also, she was going to die slowly of starvation on that boat. It's a painful, slow death, so I asked her if she wished me to not only end her suffering quickly but be able to preserve her soul until she felt like she could move on."

Xoxann smiled at DeSalvo. "What did she say?"

"After I explained that it was the only way, she made the wish. When the wish was made, it created this knife." He reached into his coat and produced a sapphire dagger. Xoxann started to reach for it, but DeSalvo pulled it away. "You have to be careful, little one. This is a magic dagger. Anything it cuts dies, but their soul is preserved, and since the dagger is used by me, I can release the soul. Kim agreed that I would set her free once she found a new friend for me that could be trusted and had a good heart."

"So, you cut her neck, but you did it to save her?" Xoxann was doing her best to understand.

"Yes, Xoxy. It was very sad, but because I did, I got to meet you." He smiled and gave her a wink as he put it away. "Don't you remember? Once she knew you could be trusted and were the amazing person you are, I made sure she got to say her goodbyes, and then I set her free. Just like she wanted me to." They walked for a little while before DeSalvo spoke again. He could tell that Xoxann was fixating on Kim's death. "She really liked you." Then, he shut off any sort of worry or fear that she had left. "She really did."

"Yeah? How do you know?" The idea that Kim liked her made her happy.

"She picked you. Remember how she wanted to talk to you first? Well, she was getting to know you. Make sure you were the right person to meet me before she left. If she introduced us, that means she trusted you with finishing her job. She decided she could count on you and believed in you. She looked into your heart and decided that you were strong enough and good enough to be worthy to be my friend."

She began to swing her arm again, and she squeezed DeSalvo's hand a little harder. They walked a few more blocks towards the castle before she began to ask more questions. It seemed that she had accepted DeSalvo's tale, and she was now starting to pay attention to what was around her. "What happened here?"

"Love happened here." DeSalvo seemed to be amused at the idea, but it pained him.

"I don't understand. How could love do this?" Xoxann looked across the ruins of the City of Dreams. It was desolate. Nothing grew here, not even weeds between the bricks of stone that lined the streets. No birds could be seen flying overhead. The sky was hazy as if it were at dusk. Neither night nor day.

"Love can be one of the most powerful things in the whole world. It can be more powerful than pain or sorrow, but it can also bring pain and sorrow, and the stronger the love, the stronger the sorrow. The stronger the pain." DeSalvo talked to her in tones like he was telling her a bedtime story. "At the beginning of this world, there was a Creator Being."

"You mean the being that created All Father? I thought he was just a myth." To be fair, so did most of the world. The myth says that in the beginning, there was one Creator Being that was more powerful than gods. The myth suggests that this being created the world and walked amongst it for a while before growing weary of it and leaving. Before they left, they created the gods to take care of their creation and were never heard from again.

"Far from it, little one." DeSalvo stopped in his tracks and looked around. He had sensed something nearby, and his attention focused on the immediate area around them. He hadn't been lying. Things that once lived still moved about in this place. DeSalvo could see what she could not. There were hundreds of them, perhaps thousands, throughout the city, and all of them were converging on the life force of the little girl. This would not do at all because he was going to need her for a bit longer, so as they moved in, DeSalvo asked Xoxann, "Do you wish to get to the castle, get what we need, and get out undetected and unnoticed by anything, here?"

"Yes. Very much so." Xoxann read his tells and began to look around, too. She felt as if there were eyes on her, but she couldn't tell from where.

"Wonderful. Thank you." DeSalvo took a deep breath in and brought his fist to his chest. As he breathed out, he opened his hand. Dark red splinters of light covered in a thick black smoke poured from his hand. It surrounded them both and then dissipated into the air. As soon as it did, the feeling of being watched stopped. "We should move on."

Holding his hand tightly, Xoxann hurried across a few more streets, turned right down the next street, and then turned left after that so they could continue toward the castle. "DeSalvo?"

"Yes, little one?"

"I wish for you to tell me the story of what happened here. No, I don't; I take it back before you make it real." She looked up to see if he was going to be mad.

DeSalvo wasn't mad, but what he thought odd was that he didn't feel compelled to grant it. DeSalvo guessed this was because, in the near future, Xoxann would wish she hadn't wished it. Something compelled her to rescind the request before he could enact it. That suggested guilt. Guilt was a good tool to keep her in line later. He didn't want her making random wishes and messing everything up. "As you wish, but Xoxy... I thought we were friends." DeSalvo looked hurt.

"We are friends. Best friends." She looked down at her feet. "Are you mad at me for making a wish?"

"No, I'm not mad. I'm just kind of hurt. When you wish for things, I have to do them. Good or bad. Like Kavlin. I don't have a choice." He felt her guilt, and he pushed it a little. "When you make wishes like that, you are not treating me like a friend; you are treating me like a slave." And then he flooded her with guilt.

"Oh, DeSalvo! I am so sorry." She began to cry. She didn't know what to do, so she froze. In her mind, she was beating herself up. DeSalvo realized he pushed her too far.

He knelt and let her hug him. "It's going to be alright."
He began to lower his hold on her guilt slowly until she could
regain her faculties. "You didn't know."

"I wish I never made that wish." She said as huge tears
fell from both eyes.

"And so, you didn't."

"Oh wait! I did it again! I'm sorry." She put her hand
over her mouth.

"It's okay. Just try really hard to think before you
wish, okay?" She nodded, and he pried her off him. "It was
an accident, and I am not mad. Now, can you give me a
smile?" He released her sadness, and she smiled. "Are we still
best friends?"

Xoxann nodded and hugged him again. "Yes. The bestest
of friends."

"Then I will tell you the tale if you ask." He smiled at
her and began to walk again.

"Yes, please. I would like to hear the tale." They walked
through the dead city as he told her the tale, and the remnants
of anything that once lived there let them pass unnoticed.

"The Creator Being was actually one of two, both of
them were formless and perfect. They were alike in most ways,
but there was one significant difference that separated them.
One of them believed that anything they created was theirs to
control and destroy. They saw whatever they created as mere

constructs. It created and consumed worlds with no thought of or regard for these creations. Even if people lived in the worlds they made, they had no regard for them either. For this being, the people they created were nothing more than toys. Let's call him creator number two.

"The other saw it differently. The other, we'll call him creator number one, had been working to build a better being. With each new world it created, it took the best of everything learned from the previous and added it to their development. It would design them and watch them grow on their own. When he created a people that he believed were ready, he sent a messenger into their world that helped them evolve into something new." DeSalvo scoffed. "The Grey." They were getting close, and her last wish had worked well. DeSalvo had cast a version of the Hidden Spell, strong enough that it worked on the spirit world as well.

"Just as the first Creator Being marveled at what it had created, watching it evolve past its limitations, the second of the two found the world. Much to the dismay of the first. The second creator did what it always did and brought the whole darn thing crashing in on itself. That world's destruction was the catalyst for what the first creator did next. With only a handful of people from his special world who had ascended and were spared, he built a new world. When it was first created it was hidden away from the sight of the other creator and protected with barriers and magic. A promise was made by creator number one and his Grey Continuum. They would stay and protect the new world for all time and never let what happened here ever take place again. They would stay and be its guardians.

"It has been said that it is folly for man to play god. Well, the opposite is also true, and it was folly when this being tried to pretend it was a man. It decided to take a corporeal form so that it could experience things like wind in its hair and watching a sunset.

"It created a body by making a species, refining it over a couple of thousand years until it was happy with what it had evolved into. Then it became one. From then on in, he walked amongst his world as one of its own.

"He maintained his powers and used them to create a city. He created and instilled into the city the three Spheres of Reality and Magic. It was called the City of Dreams because your wildest dreams were real there, and your deepest wishes could be fulfilled. At first, he made no attempt to hide who he was, and because of this, people worshiped him, but even in a world where his people were happy, and they were fulfilled, he was not. He didn't want to lie to his creations about who he was, but he also didn't want to be worshiped like a god; he wanted to be seen more like a brother or a friend. So, in some ways, even though he was often surrounded by people who adored him, he was often alone.

"First, he reached into the Divine field and created the first of four gods. All Father was a reflection of him in many ways. He was a creator god, and from then on, he took credit for the creation of the world and its people. He would be the Word of God. The second was the Goddess Aware. Aware was the connection from the Divine to the corporeal, and through her, the Word of God could be heard. The third was Allegro. He was considered the God of Connection. His domain had to do with how and why the word connected to you and was often worshiped by storytellers and bards. All Father is the music. Aware is why you can hear it, and Allegro is why you dance.

"What about the fourth God?" Xoxann made a little hop over a crack in the walkway. She wasn't very good at just holding still, so she was keeping herself entertained by trying to avoid all the cracks as DeSalvo told her the story.

DeSalvo smirked with a snort. "The fourth is a multi-faced god that can be seen as many different people; it was given to the Grey."

"The Grey?" Xoxann asked with curiosity. "What do they do?"

"If the All-Father is the song, Aware is why you hear it, and Allegro is the reason you dance, then The Grey is the one who is singing the song. They are the makers of dreams." DeSalvo took another long look around. "So, with his Divine Quartette, he relinquished the role of worshiped god and hid away in the depths of his magical City of Dreams. After a few generations, people forgot he was real, and he slipped into legend and myth.

"He was still alone, so he made the city itself sentient. He spent years talking to it. After enough time, he began to call it... her, and after a while, she believed it. He called her Dreamer, and for a long while, neither of them noticed the passing of time.

"When he made her sentient, he created it much like a Jinn, with the ability to bring dreams and wishes to fruition, and the Jinn will say that the City of Dreams is their home. She spent decades creating the dreams and wishes of the people who lived there. Except for one, the one she wanted to help the most.

"One day, she asked the Creator if she could make his dream come true. His dream was to find someone to love. Dreamer was an amazing friend, and he cared for her, but she was a city that he had made sentient, and even though they were close, he didn't love her the way that he had seen the people of the city love one another. As he wished it, Dreamer used the creation power of his will to empower her ability to make his dreams come true.

"At the center of her being, a large crystal began to form, the size of your thigh from hip to knee; it had a light within it that slowly began to grow. After a short while, it became sentient. She had become a mother.

"The daughter was created overnight with all of the knowledge and skills of her mother, but she had another ability that her mother did not. She could create a body to inhabit for a short while. At first, it was only moments, but after practice, she could hold it for a few minutes. It was like flexing a muscle. The more she used it, the stronger it got. Once she could sustain a body, Dreamer thought it was time for the Creator and her daughter to meet, and when Venger met Dorn, it was love at first sight. There was a bond between them that neither of them could ignore."

"Do you mean the real Venger? The Venger I live in?" Xoxann was shocked at the idea. She had heard the tales and not just from other children. The adults had talked about

Venger being a city, but they also referred to it as Lady
Venger, who was once queen of the city.

"Same Venger."

"And Lady Venger?"

"Is just a construct the city makes so the city can be
a person."

"Because she is the daughter of the City of Dreams and
the love of the mythical Creator Being?"

"Yes."

She got so excited she almost vibrated. She hopped up
and down. She was singing a made-up song in her head about
how she lived in a magical city.

DeSalvo let her get her energy out. He couldn't help
but be amused by her dancing and singing, but as he smiled, his
old pain began to surface. Joy had been something to avoid.
It came with too many memories, so instead, he refocused and
continued with his story. "It had been long, a long time; the
Creator Being had decided that he had hidden long enough and
wanted to leave the bowels of the City of Dreams and show
Venger the world. Dreamer warned him that the world had
changed without him, and the dreams of the people had become
dark. The wishes that were being asked for were selfish and
filled with aggression. She had allowed it because The Creator
had wanted the world to make their own choices; if they were
going to return to the world, she would no longer be able to
protect them, and she wanted them both to be safe. When they

returned, they realized Dreamer had been right, and what he found was not the world he had left.

"What did he find DeSalvo?" They had made it to the castle. It was dark inside and hard for her to see. "Would it be okay to wish for some light?"

DeSalvo's plan had worked. She was now asking permission to make wishes. "Yes, you can, little one."

"I wish there was light." She paused for a moment and then added, "Please."

"As you wish, my dear." DeSalvo opened his hand, and as he did, light began to move through his arm and coalesce in his hand. Once he had an amount about the size of a good snowball, he threw it in the air, and it flew up about four feet above his head and started to glow as bright as a torch.

"What had happened in the city?" Xoxann asked as they began to climb the main staircase.

"His twin had found them. It was Venger's creation that had gotten its attention. It had seen what he had become, and it was disgusted. It hated Venger. It hated her for existing. It hated her because Dorn loved her, and it swore an oath that it would destroy her at all costs."

"Why did it hate Venger so much?" Xoxann asked as they made it through the stairs and down a hallway to a spiral staircase that led to one of the towers.

"They had been paired since the beginning of time, and Dorn had abandoned it. Hid from it and shut it out. Then, he had diminished himself to being a corporeal being and now was in love with this lesser being. You see, it loved him. In whatever way, something like that can love, and it was hurt. Its heart had been broken, and now, it was going to get back at the person who hurt it by hurting him. And how do you hurt a god?" Xoxann frowned and shrugged her shoulders. "By hurting the ones the god loves. So, Venger had to die."

They made it to the top of the tower. The walls and ceiling had been destroyed, and so as they came up the stairs, they stepped out to an open floor at the tallest tower of the castle. From here, she could see the entire city. There were scorch marks everywhere, and as Xoxann looked out, she could tell that the blast that destroyed the city happened from the center of the city outward.

Xoxann looked out in wonder and awe. "What happened here, DeSalvo?"

"This is where it all happened. This is where so much destruction happened. In the name of love. To enter this world, Dorn had created a body over time and became corporeal in a very natural way. Doing so causes no problems or rifts in this world. But the other Creator Being was not as patient, nor did it care what holes it ripped, in reality, to get here. On this very spot, it began to rip a hole in the world, and when that happens, time and space do really odd things. Which is why parts of this castle are warped and bent. When you add magic on top of it, you have an apocalyptic disaster on your hands."

Xoxann looked out over the remains of the City of Dreams and began to tear up at the destruction. "What happened, DeSalvo?"

"It was already too late. By the time they arrived here, Dorn's other half was ready to rip its way into this world in the form of a black Chaos Dragon, and it was burning everything in sight. The hole it created, in reality, was going to implode to close itself, and it was going to take everything in a five-mile radius with it. It planned to destroy everything, including itself and Dorn, forcing him back into his original state. Most of all, he wanted to destroy the thing that he loved so Dorn would have no reason to go back and would remember who he truly was.

"Dreamer couldn't bear to see her daughter lose everything, and whether or not Dreamer could admit it, she loved Dorn in her own way. In her final moments, she made a wish to save them both. She stopped time, and I don't mean she slowed it down to a crawl; she stopped it completely and solidified it into a gem, trapping the Chaos Dragon within it. Frozen in a single moment of time."

Xoxann looked away from the city and aimed her attention back at DeSalvo. "Is that why the city is still frozen in time?"

"Look how smart you are." DeSalvo forced a smile and gave her a nod. Yes, little one, and all that Dorn or Venger could do was watch from outside the city gates where Dreamer had teleported them for their own safety. They watched as everything alive in the city was sucked into the tear in reality as it imploded. The people, the grass, the animals, the trees.

All of it, even the buildings, were pulled into the singularity of time and space. Once everything was gone, the tear exploded with a ring of energy that blew the gates off the city and burned anything that was left save the foundations. Leaving the skeletal corpse of the City of Dreams.

"Dorn used his powers to protect them; after the blast, Dorn used them to return to the tower, and this is what they found." He pointed to a clear gemstone that was floating in the air, four feet off the ground.

"What is it, DeSalvo?" Xoxann walked over to the gem and looked at it closely but didn't touch it. "It's beautiful."

"That, little one, is the Stone of Time," DeSalvo said its name with a hint of reverence. "It is what we have come for." He smiled at the little girl. "You see? I told you this would be easy."

"What's it do?" she asked innocently.

"If it is used correctly, it can change time." His eyes were fixed on the stone as he rubbed his chin vigorously.

"What do you mean, it can change time?"

"I mean, little one, that when used correctly, it can make it so Kavlin was never wished away." He got on his knees so he was the same height as her. "This stone can help us both."

"How?"

"With it, I might be able to use it to stop Pax and maybe finally be free. Don't you want that?"

"I do. I don't want you to be a slave."

"Okay. Remember, if you wish it, it will come true." DeSalvo had brought her the entire way, and now it was time to spring the trap. "Do you wish to help me get that stone?"

"Yes. I wish it." DeSalvo moved through her and took control of her body, and with her hand, he reached up and took the stone. As soon as she had it in her hand, he let go of his direct possession of her and once again was seen as an outside being, hugging her and telling her how brave she was.

"That was scary!" Xoxann had not been ready for him to control her like that.

"I am so sorry I scared you. Once you made the wish, I thought you understood what was happening."

"What happened?" she was still scared, but DeSalvo was calming her from within her own mind.

"You helped me get the stone. Look in your hand. You got it!" He clapped his hands and pretended to be happy with joyous smiles.

"I did good?"

"You did great! I am so proud of you." He removed all of her fear, and he danced with her in celebration. That's when he saw it. There was a small hole in reality. A small hole that the stone had been holding together. Time began to move there, and DeSalvo watched as the hole began to expand and then retract again and again like it was breathing.

Something caught DeSalvo's attention; he moved closer and looked directly into the hole in reality. What he saw caught him by surprise. "Xoxann, quickly!"

Xoxann stopped dancing around the room and asked, "Yes?"

DeSalvo looked away from her out over the city at nothing in particular. He had seen past reality and knew that they were not really alone.

"Do you wish to stop all parties from seeing what we are doing, no matter where... or when they are?"

She shrugged. "Yes. I wish that."

DeSalvo smiled and held his gaze outward. He wiggled his finger in a patronizing farewell. "Bye."

17

LEAPING FROM THE FALLS

Fulcrum at first kept Gnomon back. He wanted her to be checked out by their healers just to make sure everything was okay. They examined her and were impressed by how well she had been healed. Brother Peace had been trained by Master Love, making him a powerful healer, and his powers had been amplified by the tool from the statue. It was capable of causing great harm, but Peace could also command it to create a ball of healing light capable of miraculous healing, so within seconds, Gnomon had been completely healed as if being launched from an erupting tree had never happened.

Once she had obtained her bow, her body had reverted to being just an elven girl, but she could feel the blessing within her and knew that if needed, she could call upon that form again. It was a part of who she was now, and it was the same for Hope. She would always have her gift and call upon it if needed. They had run together and were now connected in ways that transcended the physical and would be as long as they lived.

Fulcrum expressed that since Hope ran with his house, it would honor him to count her as a part of it but left the choice to her. She graciously agreed and thanked him. Hope told Gnomon that they were sisters now and said that she and her father would be honored guests if they ever wished to visit, leaving them with an open invitation. Hope excused herself to go and speak with Queen Adila.

Gnomon was sad that Hope and Oubliette would be leaving shortly. Hope had the Earth Blade and had to return to Venger to harmonize the seal once more, and Oubliette was about to leave with an elven guide who was going to lead them to the Cave of Unalloyed Truth, the home of the Oracles.

She wanted to say goodbye, and Gnomon could not wait another moment. She did not want to miss Hope before she left, so she told her father to stop his prattle and headed out to find her. When she did, the two queens were finishing a conversation that ended with smiles and hugs.

"I brought you something. I wanted to give you this to remember me by." Gnomon handed Hope her doll. "As of this morning, I am an adult and a hunter, so I wish to give you my doll because you were with me in the last moments of my childhood."

Hope took the doll and looked at her closely. It was a wooden doll that was articulated at the hips, shoulders, and head. The dress was made from a beautiful piece of green silk, and it wore green leather boots. "She's beautiful. What's her name?"

"Neldaria. It was my mother's name." Gnomon reached out and touched the doll's dress, bringing back fond memories of her mother.

"Wow. She sounds important." Hope hugged it close. "Are you sure you want to part with it?"

"It is important," said Gnomon with certainty. "That's why I want you to keep her."

Hope tapped her pin, and the doll disappeared. "Now, it will be with me forever." She then tapped it again, and she was wearing her hunting attire. She pulled a silver arrow from her quiver. "This arrow is enchanted and will never miss." Hope gave it to Gnomon. "A gift to the newest hunter of your clan."

Gnomon studied it closely. The arrowhead was made of celestium and was carved to look like a falcon in flight. She put it into her quiver that was slung across her back. "Thank you. I will treasure it for all my years." She smiled and said, for an elf, that is a long time."

They both laughed and hugged each other. Then Hope said that she had some final words for her Vengerian Guardians before they parted ways, so for now, it was fare well.

Hope then went back to their camp, where everyone else had already packed up, and policed the area, making sure that by the time she arrived, there was no sign that they had ever been there.

"Thank you. Everything looks wonderful." Hope brought them all in and made them give a group hug. While they were close, she spoke to them one last time. "I could not have asked for a better team of guardians to have been with me on this journey. You have done Venger proud, and you have kept to your word. I did not fail."

"The honor was ours, Your Majesty." It was Sir Adam who spoke, but everyone nodded and agreed. "I feel odd that we aren't accompanying you back to the castle."

Hope gave Sir Adam a sweet smile. "Do you want to accompany me back and then return once I am safe?"

"Jobs not done until you are home safe," added Travis. "It will bug him the rest of the trip if you don't."

"Good man." Hope was right next to Sir Adam in the huddle; she patted him on the back. "As my personal Vengerian Guardians, your work is not done. I am giving you leave, but I would like to think that if I called upon you again, you would heed my call."

"I would." Sir Adam said without hesitation.

"I would, too," said Brother Peace.

Travis looked to Becky, who nodded. "You can count on the both of us."

Dalen looked Hope in the eyes and nodded. "If you need me, I will answer your call."

She took a deep breath and let it out with a sigh. "In that case, I give you leave for now. Go find a way to save your friend and Venger as well." She paused for just a moment and then reached into a small pouch that was on her belt. "Mr. Pax, I have something that you will need."

"Absolutely. What is it?" Dalen asked.

"Before you are done, you will need these." She handed Dalen two more Vengerian Pins. "They are set to the harmony of our team."

Dalen looked at them for a moment. "What are they for?"

"Not what Dalen, but who."

Dalen smiled. "Who are they for?"

"The other two members of the team. You will know who they are for." She smiled and raised an eyebrow. "In time."

Queen Hope then took her Vengerians back to the elven queen. The gift that Hope had brought for her was a portable arch that, once activated, would create a portal leading directly into Venger, surpassing all security that kept individuals from being able to teleport directly into the city. These gates had been used as diplomatic gifts for generations and allowed trusted dignitaries to enter the city in the outer ring, where there was a facility with multiple gates being watched over by highly trusted personnel. A hub of portal gates allowing for safe arrival into the city. Giving the Elven Queen this gift was the final demonstration that Venger had come to trust their allies in the south and that they were considered worthy of that trust.

Once it was up and activated, they all said their goodbyes, and then Sir Adam and Hope walked through the gate to the other side. Upon arriving in Venger, their pins automatically reactivated their location ability; each touched their pins and bamphed away. A few moments later, Sir Adam bamphed back. He spoke to someone on the Venger side of the portal that nobody else could see and then walked back through to the eleven forest. Once he was across the threshold, the gate closed behind him and was collapsed back down, ready for travel. The elves were happy to be heading home to get some much-needed rest. It would be months before another Running of the Trees, continuing their tradition until the forest was whole again. Their queen had no intention of leaving the gate at this location, and so it was packed up and taken with them.

"You were right." Sir Adam said. "That would have bugged me."

Travis gave him an understanding nod. "I know you like I know myself, bro.

Sir Adam gave his brother a high five in concurrence. "So, what's next?"

Next was a trip into the deep woods with a guide. They traveled for two days, during which the guide would sometimes steer them around areas that he explained were sacred and sometimes would cut through an area so fast that it was hard to keep up with him. He explained that there were predators in the woods, and they considered this their territory. If a

predator found them, it would attack, and it would be shameful
to have to kill something to protect the party. Especially
when moving through its territory, where it would be acting on
instinct to protect itself. By the end of the journey, the team
had arrived at a river where the guide pointed out a cave that
lay along its bank.

"There lies the Cave of Unalloyed Truth. You will find
the oracles you seek inside." The guard gave them a small bow
and started to head back. "I wish you luck."

"Wait, hold on for a moment." Becky very rarely missed
hints that people dropped. "Why would we need luck."

The guide smiled and said, "The Oracles have a rule. You
are not allowed to cause any physical harm to anything in their
cave if you wish for them to help you. They do not take kindly
to those who inflict pain to achieve their goals."

"Thank you. Pro tip. No physically hurting anything in
the cave." Travis was writing in his book again. "Anything else
you can tell us?"

"Yes." said the guide. "It's not called the Cave of
Unalloyed Truth for nothing. The Oracles don't pull punches,
and they don't like secrets."

Travis was finishing writing in his book. "Doesn't like
secrets. Thank you."

The guide wished them luck again and then made his way
back to where they had come from.

Brother Peace touched his pin. ‹Going on quiet mode.›

Everyone agreed with this idea and activated their pins as well. Each of them also tapped their pins, and their clothes changed from travel gear to adventure gear. They were armed now, but they kept their weapons sheathed.

It was past midday when they arrived. They still had light, but within a few hours, dusk would be upon them. They still had to traverse some land to get to the cave, and they knew that if they were going to get out of the cave before it was dark, they had better get moving.

This section of the river was a cascading landscape. The river was moving from the mountains and flowing downhill to the southeast, which created numerous waterfalls and pools along the river's path. The cave itself was nestled into the rock along one of the pools. They were going to have to negotiate going about thirty feet down the rocks along a waterfall to reach the pool where the cave was near.

‹Okay. What's the plan to get down?› Travis was peering over the edge, looking for a safer way than scaling the rock face. "Because it looks like a long way down."

Both Peace and Dalen gave each other a look. Both of them had spent years staring over a cliff edge hundreds of feet high, and their teachers expected them to jump.

‹Would you like to offer the first suggestion, Brother Peace?› Dalen said with a bow and a gesture toward the edge.

‹I believe I can come up with something Brother Truth.›

replied Peace.

Both of them gave each other the bow from the temple, and together, they took a couple of steps back.

‹So...› Travis looked back at them. ‹Do you have a suggestion?›

‹Indeed, we do› said Peace with a mischievous grin and a glint in his eyes as he ran to the edge. Dalen followed right alongside him. Both of them launched off the edge in unison and flew through the air.

As they ran by, Becky thought ‹No, no, no, no.›, in time with their steps.

Travis cried out in their heads after them, ‹ That's a terrible suggestion!›

As they leaped, they knew they would be fine. Thirty feet was not enough distance to gain enough speed to be concerned about. Both of them had studied the waterfall at the Temple of Light and had learned that the water over thousands of years would have eroded the rock. There was a better-than-fair chance that the pool was deep enough to slow their fall before they hit bottom. If either did find themselves hurt, they would be right next to a healer able to fix them. In their minds, it was absolutely safe.

Dalen slowed time down to a crawl for both of them. He and Peace hung in the air, soaring like clouds. When Dalen had met him, things were much different. Ben and Toad were on opposite sides of everything. Ben had bullied him and teased him, but instead of hating him and wanting revenge, Dalen reached out to him at the moment it mattered, and now he had a brother.

They glanced at each other with a look on their faces that could not be described to someone who has not experienced leaping off a cliff. Flying through the air together, they were alive, and they shared the moment of truly living together as friends and brothers. Dalen took it in, slowing the frames of time even further, taking the time to really respect Peace and all that he had become.

Brother Peace soaked in the moment as well. His body was still in slow motion, hovering over the drop-off to the pool below, but his mind was moving at the same speed as Dalen's, and he had time to take in the view and know what it felt like to fly. ‹I could stay up here forever.›

Dalen grinned. Knowing what was to come. ‹I can stay up here, but you can't.›

Brother Peace didn't see it coming. ‹Why is that?›

Dalen let go of time, and he had enough time to sing, ‹because I have Silver Balls›, before gravity took Peace and Dalen waved bye, as he stayed floating in the air.

‹Oh, you little...› Peace's thoughts were interrupted as he hit the water.

Dalen was still enjoying the splash as Adam, who had changed out of his armor and into a swimsuit, landed on his back like a horse, sending them both plummeting toward the water. "Ye-Ha!" Hooted Adam as he gripped onto Dalen's waist with his knees and held on to the back of his collar with one hand, swinging his arm in a lassoing motion all the way down.

As Dalen resurfaced with Adam, Peace was cheering. "Ha-ha! You have avenged me, brother!" Sir Adam gave him a high-five.

‹Gentlemen.› Becky's tone was scolding in their minds. ‹Would you like to remember that we are in quiet mode, and you three are whooping and screaming all the way down?›

‹Sorry, Becky.› The three of them sent in unison.

‹Okay. Let's see you get down.› Sir Adam thought as he swam to the edge.

Dalen looked up from the water, and his mind flooded with a memory that hadn't happened yet. He didn't fight it; he just let it flow. Before, when he would have moments when he remembered the future, it was disorienting. Normally, it caused him to lose sight of the moment he was in, but this was different. Dalen was sure it had to do with the stone he removed being an artificial power, and now that his mother had helped him create a true Heartstone, things flowed easier.

He watched as Becky leaped out. She had her hood up, and both of her weapons in her hands, with the blades retracted, so just the hilts were in her hands. All at once, the blades stopped moving in midair, and she swung on them like a gymnast on a horizontal bar. At the apex of her swing, the hilts released, sending her forward and upward, feet first.

She used her momentum to complete a backflip just as gravity beat her momentum, and she was weightless. She was still head-first, but now she was face down, falling forward. She dropped several feet when her hilts caught the air again, which caused her to swing like a gymnast once more. She repeated the movements until she ended her swing at the bottom of the waterfall. Turned off her hilts and completed a final backflip onto the ground, landing on her feet.

It was amazing, but it hadn't happened yet. Dalen opened the Quantum field and allowed himself to be in two locations at the same time. He stood there next to Becky and Travis. ‹I know how you are going to get down.›

Becky yelped aloud.

Travis had a confused look on his face. ‹I watched you fall.› He looked down and saw Dalen swimming in the water and looking up at him. ‹Dear God. There are two of you now?›

Dalen smirked at Travis's comment. ‹No. Just one of me. Just in two places at the same time.›

‹Which one of you is real?› Becky asked and reached out to see if she could touch Dalen. When her fingers contacted his arm, she gasped and pulled back.

‹Both are real because there is only one, and that one is real. It's just that the one real thing is in two different locations at the moment.›

‹How can there be only one of you?› Travis asked. ‹I can see two of you from here.›

‹I am using magic to directly force the Quantum field to allow for two locations of probability instead of just one.›

‹ What's going on up there?› Sir Adams's thoughts were more mocking than concerned. He meant it light-heartedly. ‹Are you coming down, or do you need some help?›

Travis waved at his brother. ‹Yeah. Just... Getting ready.›

‹So, Becky. Remember how you used to take gymnastics?› Dalen began.

‹I remember that was a year ago and never to be talked about again after my whole team was disqualified because Jodi Blanchard didn't pass her drug test.›

‹You were good. You were really good, and you know it.›

‹Yeah. Okay. What are you getting at?›

Dalen took her right to the edge. ‹Imagine that there was a bunch of uneven and parallel bars all the way down, and I mean anywhere you wanted one. You just reached out, and it was there.›

Becky snorted. ‹I would kill it. If I could have them anywhere I wanted, I could get down this doing backflips the whole way.›

‹Bet you couldn't› Dalen thought, almost daring her to do it.

She put out her hand and cocked her head at him. ‹Bet
I could.›

Dalen took her hand and shook it. ‹You just made a bet
with a Jinn. That is a magically binding contract.›

‹You are a tricky little Jinn, aren't you?› Dalen could
see she was more impressed that he got her than anything else.
‹So, how do you intend to make that happen?›

‹I have no intention of doing anything other than
watching from the bottom. It's you who will do it.› He smiled
and tapped her weapons that were sheathed on her hip.

"You want me to what?" she said much more loudly than
she intended.

‹Your handles. You can make them stop in the air, right?›

She pulled one out. The blades were retracted on her
belt, but once she pulled it, the blade extended. Then she
squeezed the handle twice like two pulses, and the blade
retracted. She then put her thumb to a gem in the pummel and
let go. The hilt did not move from its position.

Dalen examined it through an object-identifying spell to
try to understand it, but even with all of his knowledge, he was
not able to grasp what the device was actually doing. ‹Must be
Gnome-make because it doesn't have any clear reading.›

She grabbed the handle again and thumbed the gem in
the pummel once more to make it release. ‹So, you want me to
just jump out and swing down?›

‹That was the bet you made. Wherever you reach out, you will have something to grab onto.›

Becky looked up from her weapons and made eye contact with Dalen. ‹I know that I have all of this power and skill in me; I just wish I knew what it was and how to access it.›

‹Granted.› Dalen smiled mischievously.

‹Wait, what?› Becky said. ‹I didn't mean...›

‹Oh, it's too late for that, my friend. You have to be careful what you wish for.›

‹All right. What do you have for me?›

The answers poured into his mind as if the universe were trying to answer her wish through him. It came in odd images that Dalen then had to explain.

‹Did you ever go to the Grand Canyon?›

‹Yeah. I went with my family four years ago, just before we moved to town.›

The image of her riding a burrow played over and over in his head. ‹Did you stay at the top?›

‹No.› she replied. ‹We rode burrows down to the bottom. It was a little scary. Some places are really close to the edge.›

Dalen's mind could see her father as if he were in front of him riding a burrow. He leaned back and turned around to say something, but Dalen couldn't make out what he was saying. ‹Did your dad say something to you about the burrows?›

Her eyes lit up. ‹Yes.› She closed her eyes and tried to remember. ‹I was scared to steer the burrow so close to the cliffs. I had never done it before. He was ahead of me, and he turned around on his burrow and told me not to try to steer the burrow. It had done it a hundred times and knew exactly what to do; I had to trust it and let go.›

‹Damn, D.› Travis patted Dalen on the back. ‹I don't know how you knew that story, but that was deep.›

Becky looked over the edge and then took four or five steps back. ‹I don't think I can do this.›

‹Then you can't.› Dalen said it very matter-of-factly, and it made Becky annoyed that he would just agree with her like that.

‹How dare you say that?›

‹Look.› Dalen said with a bow. ‹No offense. I know you can do it; I have already seen you do it, but as long as you keep telling yourself that you can't... Then you can't.›

‹Okay, I get that.› Becky smiled sheepishly. ‹Sorry. I just don't know if I can do it.›

Images of Becky filled Dalen's mind. Then he saw her step back and leave just the hooded shadow of Oubliette standing in her place. Through the shadows, Dalen could feel Oubliette smiling at him, and she gave him a little nod.

‹ That's my point. You don't have to. Let Oubliette do it. For her, this is a walk in the park.›

Becky smiled. ‹I get it. Becky has never done anything like this before, but Oubliette has done this hundreds of times. I just have to trust her and let go.› She got quiet for a moment, and Becky lost all expression as she pulled up her hood, and her face went black, hidden in the shadows of her garb.

‹I have to go now before I change my mind.› Oubliette whispered from the darkness. She made a full run toward the edge, and as she got there, she did not flinch.

‹Go get it!› Travis sent his thoughts from the sideline as she made her leap from the edge.

Dalen let go of the version of him that was still at the top and watched as his memory played out. When she landed, she didn't say a word; she just stood there for a moment. Her hood was still up, so no one could see her facial expressions.

Are you okay? Dalen's thoughts in her head snapped her out of her daze, and she flinched a little. He felt her confusion settle, and then, from deep within, she began to feel a jubilant sense of joy. It grew until it erupted into her body; she flipped back her hood and jumped up and down. Becky's thoughts were excited, and she almost squealed in their minds, ‹Oh my God! Oubliette is amazing!›

Dalen levitated himself out of the water and floated over to her. *I hope you remember this moment because that was all you.* Dalen was connected to all of them now, and he wanted them to understand this. *The first rule of magic is that you are only as powerful as you believe yourself to be.*

‹How very Master Truth of you.› Peace gave him a small bow.

‹Wait. You let me jump off of there thinking I was someone else?› Becky was getting mad.

Dalen pulled out his teacup and allowed it to fill. ‹ At that moment, you were someone who absolutely believed in what was about to happen. You believed in yourself and Oubliette. Now you are full of doubt again.› She turned to look away from him. He floated around to her other side and looked her in the eye. ‹And look at the results.› He took a sip of his tea. ‹I told you before you jumped. I knew you could do it because I had a memory of it happening before you jumped. I saw you do it. I had no doubt. I didn't let you jump, not knowing the outcome. But you had to believe in yourself. From one point of view, Oubliette is very real. She was real while you were choosing to be her.›

‹So, it was me who did that?› Becky's thoughts were unsure.

‹Yes! Yes. One hundred percent you... Being Oubliette. Or, more to the point, Oubliette is only real when you choose to be her.›

‹But isn't that just the powers from the statue, and not me?› Becky asked.

‹That power gives you a limit to how powerful you can be. But you still have to be it. It gave you the ability to survive and the strength to hold on. The ability to jump was you. How you chose to come down in backflips was you.› Becky looked back at him again. ‹You could have gone down foot by foot, going slowly around and around, or climbed down like a ladder. The strength and power came from all those people, but what you choose to do with it is all you.›

‹Okay. Actually, that makes me feel a lot better. I am glad to know it was me. It's important to me...› Becky seemed almost lost in her thought for a moment. ‹To know that it was me.›

‹Me too› said Peace and Travis almost at the same time. That's when everyone remembered that Travis was still up there.

‹It was amazing!› Sir Adam was being very genuine. ‹You were awesome! No! You were the bibitz! That may be the most bibitz thing I have ever seen, ever.›

Becky blushed and did a little curtsy. ‹Thank you, Sir Adam.›

‹Which leads me to my next question to my twin brother. How do you plan to get down?› Sir Adam's tone was no longer of mockery. Instead, he was excited and just wanted to see something else amazing.

‹Yeah! added Becky. ‹ Let's see you do it.›

Travis shook his head and rolled his eyes at everyone. He reached back and grabbed his bow with one hand, and drew an arrow with the other. Without so much as an explanation, he fired an arrow that whizzed through the air and planted itself just in front of Sir Adam's feet. As Adam instinctually backed up from having an arrow fired at him, the arrow vanished, and in its place stood Travis, who wiggled his eyebrows at Sir Adam and smirked at his twin. ‹Will that do?›

"Well, sure. If you wanted to do it the easy way." Adam laughed aloud. He couldn't help it, but he quickly clapped his hand over his mouth, remembering to be in quiet mode. ‹Sorry.›

Travis found an area that was not covered in river rocks and began to discern what tracks he could make out. ‹Looks like standard wildlife. Deer, Racoon, and.... Hello. What are you?› He was looking at an odd footprint in the dirt, and none of them could place it. Travis looked further in the direction the tracks were coming from and found another. ‹ It's a biped. You see how its pace is. Quadrupeds like cats and dogs have a distinctly different gate.›

‹Did you learn how to track from the statue?› asked Peace.

Travis looked up from the tracks for a moment. ‹Boy Scouts. Wilderness survival.› Then he went back to the footprints ‹As deep as the prints go, my guess is, they are about half our size.›

‹If you had to take a guess, what would it be?› asked Dalen.

‹I honestly don't know. I have no idea about the fauna here.› Travis started drawing the print in his book.

Adam looked at it closely. ‹Yeah, but with all of the adventure games you have played, you can make a guess.›

Travis, inspecting the tracks again, followed them right up to the cave. He huffed, and his posture slumped a little. ‹Goblins. If I had to guess, I would say Goblins.› He pointed to the cave. ‹And that's their lair.›

18

THE GOBLINS

The sunlight was pouring into the cave, giving enough light to see well into the first part of it, but the first thing that the team of adventurers noticed was the smell. It was a musky stench, and it burned their noses as they entered.

‹What is that awful smell?› Becky was glad that they could communicate through the pins. She had no intention of opening her mouth in that stench.

‹I know, right?› Sir Adam had been the first in the cave and was trying to ignore the odor long enough to get a good look in the shadows before his eyes began to water. ‹The smell is bibitz. A combination of poo and death.›

‹My guess is that you are exactly correct.› Travis was inspecting the tracks that he could make out in the sunlight. ‹My guess is that the smell is the pungent aroma of decomposition and dung. Dung usually only smells bad like this when it's the scat of a meat eater. It has something to do with how meat breaks down in the guts and a natural warning system for herbivores. Warning: predators are nearby.›

Becky had made it through her first trial, and she was not one for having to learn things twice. She pulled up her hood and was now intentionally being Oubliette. She moved out of the light and into the shadowy places, where she started moving along the walls. Her instincts served her well because as soon as she got into the darkness, her vision distance tripled. ‹With my hood up, I can see better in the dark. The darker it gets, the better I see.› Oubliette's voice spoke like whispers in their minds.

‹Excellent! I suggest you stay in the shadows and try to get a good read of this cave.› Travis looked over to where he believed she was. In the shadows, she had become undetectable. ‹Please keep us in line of sight. Come back, the first sign of...› he looked back down at the tracks. ‹Residents.›

‹On it.› and with that, any sense of Oubliette's location blended into the shadows. ‹I know my job. You don't have to tell me what to do like I never gamed before.›

‹Alright now, you two.› Dalen was trying to steer the conversation back to the task at hand. ‹What can you tell us about the tracks?›

Travis got up and started to move into the darkness. ‹It's like I said. We have multiple biped carnivorous predators that stand about three feet tall. Their tracks neither suggest reptile nor anything with a hoof.›

‹Dude.› Peace looked over the tracks again. ‹You got all that from this?›

Travis looked back at the tracks to check his work. ‹Yeah›

Peace hit him in the shoulder lightly. ‹Well done.›

Travis smiled and whispered, "Thanks."

‹Oubliette?› Dalen squinted into the darkness. ‹How many passages does this cave have?›

From somewhere in the shadows, Oubliette whispered into their minds. ‹One in the back. It's about thirty yards from where you are, at your two.›

Travis corrected his course by turning slightly to his right and started to head in the direction she suggested. ‹We are on our way to you.›

Peace brought forth his weapon and ignited the ball of light. It lit up the cave like a torch and allowed them to see how to navigate through it.

Dalen still had not set foot on the ground since he levitated out of the water. He found the feel of floating to be more natural now than walking. He knew he could force himself to the ground, but it would be something he would have to focus on, and his attention was needed in the here and now, focusing on the task at hand. While that was both logical and made sense, there was another reason he chose to hover instead of walk. It was, by far, the coolest thing ever. Dalen was free of the confines of gravity.

In truth, he thought that flight would have felt different. He expected to feel a sense of being held up in some way by a magic force. Some sort of lift that pushed him against the constant force of gravity. This felt nothing like that. It was more like he was slightly phased from the world. Meaning that he was physically there but didn't hold the properties of mass, which rendered him weightless, allowing him to literally neutralize gravity as part of the equation. It was an easier process than trying to lift all of his weight against a constant like gravity. He had never noticed it before, but gravity had always been pulling on him every moment of every day, and now that it wasn't present, the world felt different. Almost as if being weightless weren't real, and Dalen felt as if he were dreaming.

Because of his training with the mind sphere, he understood how to manipulate superposition, allowing him to be wherever he chose to be. This meant he could move in any way he desired with just a thought. He thought to flip upside down and walk along the ceiling. His body responded and reoriented itself, and from his perspective, he was now hovering slightly off the floor while watching his friends walk along the ceiling. He had been fine while flipping over but now felt a little queasy as he looked at everyone else.

Now, why is that? He thought to himself. He turned away from everyone, and once he did, he felt only the sense of being in a space covered in rock; there was no 'up' or 'down,' and there was nothing that was pulling on him to create down in his mind. He rolled, spun, and twisted about but felt fine. Once he turned toward his friends again, viewing them from an upside-down position, he felt the nausea return, and it only let up once he repositioned himself to match everyone else's direction.

It frustrated him that he was unable to manipulate his position the way he wanted to, but he took a moment to calm down and reminded himself that this was going to be a process. It was going to take practice and time. He remained in an upright position, the same as everyone else, and continued toward the back of the cave. There was real peril here, and as much as he wanted to pursue this new ability, he knew that there were more important things afoot; he set aside his frustrations and turned his attention to the current mission.

‹Where are you?› Travis asked as he reached the place where the entrance zone of the cave ended, and a small pathway led further into the cavern.

‹Peace's light was making it difficult for me to see, so I moved further down the corridor.› Oubliette's voice was still whispering in their mind. ‹Don't worry, I am not too far ahead. See?› A rock was lobbed from the darkness toward them. ‹Wait there for a moment, and let me look ahead.›

Dalen was straining his eyes against the darkness, so he chose to see with his mind's eye instead. He connected to the body sphere and activated the Element of Earth. He blinked a few times and then became able to see as if it were daylight in the cave. Peace's ball was still giving off a glow, and Dalen could tell where the light was and how far it went out, but it didn't really affect his sight because light affects the eyes, and that wasn't what he was using. He was perceiving everything in the cave by sensing it, tapping into a kind of blind perception.

He tried to make out color, but again, color was an aspect of
light. Dalen didn't see it, but he could feel it. He had stopped
using the signals from his eyes to paint a picture in his mind.
Instead, he was directly sensing the cave's presence; his mind
was accepting this and drawing in an image.

The room they were in was about ten feet high, oblong
in shape, and made of Granite. The area where everyone was
walking was smoother due to years and years of whoever was
living here using this as a passageway, wearing it down over
time. He could see Travis, Adam, and Peace standing at an
opening that led down a corridor.

He could see Oubliette down the corridor, but she
showed up in his vision like a ghost. She was swinging hand
over hand using her tools like monkey bars. She locked one into
place and, swung herself up a little higher and released. When
she reached the apex of her arch, she placed a handle under
her butt and activated it while putting the other out in front
of her and activating it to steady herself, leaving her sitting in
mid-air.

‹Peace. Put out your light. You guys got incoming.› She
whispered into their minds. ‹I count four. Goblin, by the look
of them.›

‹What do we do?› asked Sir Adam as he reached for
his sword.

‹Stay your weapon.› Peace said as he allowed the light
on his weapon to go out. ‹Remember what the guide said. We
can't cause any physical harm.›

‹Well then, what do you suggest?› responded Adam. ‹Oubliette. How much time do we have before they arrive?›

Oubliette's voice whispered in their minds. She was calm, but they could feel her urgency. ‹You boys got about twenty seconds. Be advised they are armed.›

‹We have to make a choice.› Adam, Becky, and Peace looked to Travis for an answer. ‹Top priority: we can't hurt them. So, don't attack. Is there a possibility that the oracles we seek have been taken by these goblins?›

‹Ten seconds›

‹Sure.› Peace agreed. ‹But there is just as much of a chance that the oracles we seek are goblins.›

Travis whispered, "Bibitz." ‹Didn't think of that.›

‹Five, four...›

‹I can make them not notice us.› Dalen had first been shown that spell the day he stole the Beads of Fire. It didn't cause someone to become invisible, but it created a sense of invisibility where people or creatures walking by simply refuse to notice you.

Travis excelled in moments where quick thinking was required against a ticking clock, and his mind was now running at peak efficiency. ‹No. Save that for a possible escape. Let's try talking first. Quick, everyone change to any outfit that is unarmed.› The three of them reached up and touched their pins.

Dalen still cast the Hidden Spell on himself, so as the four goblins approached, they only saw Travis, Sir Adam, and Brother Peace standing on their front porch. This alone made them very unpleased.

‹Tap the middle ring, then the center, and then slide to the outside ring.› whispered Oubliette, and Travis and Peace both did as she suggested.

‹What does that do?› asked Adam.

‹I swear, you boys just refuse to read the instructions. Telepathic translator.› Oubliette was in the dark and invisible, but the rest of the team could feel her disappointed look. Sir Adam reached up just in time to turn it on as the goblins came into view.

"Greetings, and a good afternoon to you." Travis was being as cordial as he could be, but goblins don't take well to trespassers.

"We don't take well to trespassers!"

There were four of them, each wearing only loin cloths that allowed for most of their bodies to be visible. They had dark blue skin on their arms and legs that faded to a smoke-colored blue-gray on their torso, with matching colorations in the palms of their hands and feet. The grayish blue hue moved from their chest upward through their neck and up into their faces as well as down their inner thighs to about their knees. Each one of them was covered with ritual scarring along their entire bodies, starting in their face and chest and then down their arms and legs. All three of them wore white war paint on their face and arms consisting of different sets of parallel lines; one of them had his entire face painted to look like a skull.

The one who talked had multiple feathers on his spear, where the others each had one. Travis completely ignored the goblins hostile tone and just smiled and pointed at his spear. "That is a beautiful spear. You must be very important to have such decoration."

"It is. I am a great warrior." The goblin growled. "Careful." He pounded his chest hard with a fist. "I will kill you, giant."

"No need for violence. We mean no harm or disrespect. We are here to see the oracles that live in this cave and have no quarrel with you and your tribe." Travis was doing his best to be respectful and not condescending.

"You speak our tongue and show respect. Maybe I won't kill you right away." The Goblin grinned or snarled, or perhaps both. "Your face makes words you do not say. What magic is this?"

Travis had hoped they wouldn't notice that the words they were speaking were in a different language than what the goblins were hearing. He looked at the other two, hoping one of them had a plan.

"We changed our tongues to honor you." Brother Peace gave them a respectful bow.

"Your respect and honor has bought you some more time in this world. I choose not to kill you for now." said the more decorated of the bunch.

"That would be our choice, too." Travis smiled.

The goblins reacted to him aggressively. They stepped back and took a defensive stance.

"I think you need to stop smiling, Travis." Peace said as calmly as he could. "I think that they are responding to you baring your teeth at them."

Travis closed his smile and lowered his head. Peace was right. Once Travis stopped baring his teeth and took a passive stance, the goblins relaxed a bit.

"I'm sorry," Travis said. "That was a nervous response, not an aggressive one."

It was obvious that the goblins were not used to being talked to like this from outsiders. They tried to speak quietly amongst themselves, but they could still be overheard.

"What do you think?"

"They are not warriors. They are talkers." said one of the goblins in the rear.

The other goblin in the back shook its head. "We should kill them."

"We should eat them." said the one in skull face.

The leader looked over at him and stuck out his tongue. Skull-face returned the gesture.

‹Eat us?› Sir Adam thought to his brother. ‹I am not going to stand by and let them eat us, no matter what the guide says.›

‹Say the word, and I will handle these guys.› Dalen started to prepare a spell that would hold the goblins in place but not directly hurt them.

‹Hang on. They misunderstood my smile. I think that is what we are doing, too.› Travis stuck out his tongue as well.

The leader of the goblins saw Travis and put his tongue back in his mouth.

Travis nodded. "Funny joke." And then he put his tongue back out.

They just stared at him for a moment, and just before Travis was about to give up, the leader said, "Yes. Funny joke. It is funny because it is true. Scrape is a Blood-Spear. He would eat you." All four of them stuck out their tongue.

‹They are going to eat us.› Sir Adam began to clench his fist and then opened his hand and stretched his fingers. He was warming his up hand for combat.

‹Before you draw, try it my way. Both of you stick out your tongues.› Travis nodded at both Sir Adam and Peace, who stuck out their tongues as well.

The goblins all stuck out their tongues and pointed back and forth at Travis, Adam, and Peace. The boys mimicked their motions, and it worked. All of the goblins stopped carrying their spears-like weapons and stood them up, holding them one-handed with the spearheads pointing upward.

‹It's their laughter.› Dalen let out the breath he had been holding in relief. ‹Well done, Travis.›

‹Rule Number Thirteen. Learn local customs. It may save your life.› Travis shot his brother a look, and Sir Adam did his best not to laugh.

‹This is why I love you.› Oubliette's whisper was only sent to Travis.

The Leader of the goblin quartet raised his hands, and the other goblins straightened up and put their tongues away. "Alright. I am Stone Jaw. We will take you to see our leader. They will decide if you can see the Oracles. If you wish to see the Oracles, you will relinquish your weapons."

"We are unarmed." Travis raised up his arms and slowly turned around to show the goblins he had no weapons. "We came for the Oracles help, not to slay them."

‹I have my concerns, but I trust you, brother, and so far, you have been right.› Sir Adam pulled a dagger from his belt. "Here, I have this right now."

‹What are you doing?› asked Travis.

‹They were never going to believe we made it all the way

out here with no weapons.› Adam thought as he handed over the dagger.

‹I'm not worried; neither should any of you be.› Peace let the goblins frisk him. ‹Don't forget we have Brother Truth.›

‹The truth will set you free.› Everyone had to fight back, not snickering, as the goblins began to lead them further into the depths of the cave.

‹And the shadows are on your side as well.› whispered Oubliette.

‹And this is why I love you.› said Travis to her mind alone.

Dalen was covered in the spell, so as long as he didn't touch anyone, he was unnoticed. He continued to float, so there were no extra footprints. He stayed in contact with Oubliette, who followed close behind. The more she used her tools, the more she was at home in the air, but no matter her skill, it was tiresome, and she wanted to save her strength, not knowing what was to come. She made the choice and dropped down to the ground to give her arms a rest and quietly just slinked along in the shadows.

The goblins took them deeper into the cave, but after a time, the passage opened up into a vast void within the rock.

‹Hey, Dalen?› whispered Oubliette into his mind.

‹Yes?›

‹Do you see what I see?›

‹Big giant cave with a goblin city carved out of it?›

‹Yeah.› she whispered telepathically. ‹Then it's not just me.› Once she was in the open part of the cave, she turned and ran to the cave wall. She made it up the wall about three steps before she lost momentum. Just as her body became weightless, she jumped outward off of the wall. She reached out with both hands and locked her handles in place. She used her momentum to swing as high as she could. She gained more momentum on the backswing, and when she swung forward again, she released her handles at the right moment to propel her in an upward direction. She did this a few times and ended up about twenty feet in the air. She stayed with them at that height while Dalen began to fly around the area. He activated the Eye of the Beholder on his pin so each of them could see what he saw if they chose to.

Dalen flew past the gate and into the main part of the city. As Dalen looked about the place, he noticed that the goblins seemed very primitive. Too primitive to have built the carved stone city they were living in. Dalen guessed that this was once an abandoned city belonging to someone else, and the goblins had claimed it. Just past the front gate, there was a large courtyard where it seemed most of the goblins were. This looked more like a goblin hold than a city. There were younger goblins, but Dalen didn't see any infants. There were some elder goblins that were teaching young ones how to hold a spear; others were teaching how to make them. Judging by what he saw, he believed that most of the goblins here were warriors. They looked strong for goblins, and almost all wore the war paint, and every one of them, young and old, had different ritual scarring.

As the guys were brought in, their presence created a great stir. Many warriors wanted to kill them instantly, but the head of the quartet guarded them and demanded they stepped back. He declare that they were his prisoners, and it would be up to him to kill them.

"Why haven't you killed them already?" one of the warriors demanded to know. His face had been painted to look like a skull as well.

"They are not combatants. They are unarmed." Stone Jaw said.

"Then it should have been easy to kill them!" demanded the skull faced warrior, prompting many of the goblins to shout blood-curdling war cries.

"That is Knife-Breaker." Stone Jaw pointed out. "He is the head of the Blood-Spears. He would eat you, too." The four goblins that brought them down looked at each other and stuck their tongues out for a moment, nodding at one another. "He is the leader of all the warriors. You should be glad that your fate is not up to him." Then Stone Jaw spoke loud enough to be heard over the whooping. "They have come to see the Oracles!"

The town square grew quiet.

‹I am not sure if that is a good thing or a bad thing.› Oubliette whispered.

Kinfe-Breaker stepped forward. He, too, had many ritual scarifications. "No one gets to see the Oracles. Kill them

now." He leaned in at Travis and smelled him deeply. "They are
stinking up our home."

Peace gave a small bow and said, "Hello. I am
Brother Peace."

Knife-Breaker hissed at him. "If you speak to me again, I
will kill you where you stand."

"Perhaps, but that is for me to decide and not you
Knife-Breaker." As soon as the voice spoke out, the goblins
shaped up like a bunch of children whose parent just walked in
the room. She was an elder goblin who wore a bone headdress
woven into her grey hair. "Stone Jaw. You have captured three.
For this, you shall be rewarded. A line for each one captured.
How do you wish to delegate them?"

Stone Jaw bowed to her and then responded. "My queen.
I wish to delegate them to each of the goblins who were serving
under me. One each."

The Goblin Queen considered his suggestion and then
gave him a questioning eye. "No honor for yourself?"

Stone Jaw nodded and gestured to his team. "I would
not have been able to capture them alone. If it weren't for my
squadron, there would be no honor to have, My Queen."

"Then let it be done." As she turned her attention to
the guys, the three goblins lined up one by one and had their
arms cut horizontally above the elbow with a red-hot knife
that had been kept in a nearby fire. They didn't make a sound
while being cut, and once they were, they then stood in front of

Stone Jaw and slapped their wound.

"Anyone who chooses not to take power is weak," Knife-Breaker said to Stone Jaw under his breath.

‹Alright.› asked Sir Adam. ‹Who's done with pint-sized Skeletor over here?›

‹Me› whispered Oubliette

‹Yup› Brother Peace nodded.

‹Pint-size Skeletor!› Travis snorted.

‹Remember, we can't physically harm them. Stand down.› Dalen did prepare his holding spell, just in case.

The Goblin Queen approached the guys and then asked something that they weren't ready for. "Where are the other two?" Travis started to ask what she meant, but she shushed him and said, "The Oracles have told me. Five will come. One hidden in shadow, the other hidden in plain sight. Before you try to lie to me, know that the Oracles are never wrong, so there are two more of you hidden."

"There are." Brother Peace said. "There is no point in saying anything different. Yes. They are hiding. We have walked into a very dangerous situation, and it would have been foolish for them not to, but as you can see, no one is attacking. They are hiding to protect, not attack. We have no intent to harm anyone."

"This pleases the Oracles, but it does not please me." She tilted her head farther up than needed so she could still feel like she was looking down on them. "You have snuck individuals into my home. People I cannot see, who are no doubt armed and a threat."

"They have lied to us, and I demand they pay with blood." Yelled Knife-Breaker, which was followed by screams and whoops from the goblins.

"We meant no disrespect." Brother Peace offered.

"Yet, Knife Breaker feels disrespected." added the queen.

"Yes!" Cried Knife Breaker. "I have been disrespected! My honor demands we fight."

The queen rolled her eyes at him, and in that moment, Dalen connected to her through the Natural Element and listened to her surface thoughts. ‹Guy's, we have an opportunity, but I don't have a plan. The Queen is fed up with Knife-Breaker. She also believes he has grown too bloodthirsty and is becoming afraid of him. She is going to push for us to fight him because she is hoping that we will kill him so she can put Stone Jaw in power. She will help us get to the Oracles if we can remove him from power.›

‹How are we supposed to do that without harming them?› Sir Adam asked. He was beginning to warm up his hand again.

‹There has to be a way to defeat him without harming him.› whispered Oubliette. ‹A way to make him lose honor?›

‹Lose honor. That's it.› Peace grinned mischievously. ‹Thank you, Oubliette, there are times I feel your insight in supernatural.› "Very well. I shall meet his demand." Peace stepped toward Knife-Breaker: "If your honor is so weak and fragile that you must fight me to prove how strong you are, I will help you in that, but you should ask yourself, who are you trying to convince, and why do they need convincing?"

Knife-Breaker lost all sense of decorum and screamed at Peace. "I... Will... Destroy you!"

Peace openly mocked him with imitations of his scream and then laughed at him and told him he was very adorable.

‹What are you doing? He is going to attack you any second.› asked Travis.

‹I am using the same kind of diplomacy on him that Dalen used on me that day we almost fought in school. But backward.› Peace sounded like he had a plan, so everyone just relaxed a little and waited to see how this played out.

‹You do realize that you aren't allowed to fight back?› whispered Oubliette.

‹You are just going to have to have faith in me. I have a plan.› Brother Peace turned to the Queen, and with all the manners and grace of a devoted Brother of the Temple of Light, he gave the Queen a bow and said, "With your permission, of course."

The Goblin Queen studied his face and considered her options carefully before she agreed. Peace was taken out into the middle of the courtyard. There, the goblins encircled the area. They all started chanting Knife-Breaker's name.

Dalen reached out with his mind and tried to contact the queen. She sensed it and allowed the connection to happen. *I am the one who is hidden in plain sight.* The Queen nodded. *Once my friend removes your problem, you will take us to the Oracles?*

"Agreed." said the Queen.

‹What do you want us to do?› asked Travis.

‹Nothing until I fail. I have no intention to fail, but if this goes sideways and things go bad, then jump in.› Brother Peace was taking a few shadow punches to warm up. ‹I am going to need to focus, so I am going to turn my pin off. Don't worry. I have a plan.› Peace reached up and, turned off the link to his friends and began to change his breathing.

Dalen's eyes were still seeing the world through the eyes of magic. He watched as Brother Peace's mind and body stilled, and both spheres harmonized with each other. He became very still, and his breathing became almost stopped. Dalen watched as Peace's Ki began to charge, and from Dalen's point of view, he began to glow.

The Queen commanded that the fight would go on until one was defeated, at which point the winner could choose the fate of the loser, and if Peace won, they would be taken to the Oracles. Then she commanded the fight to begin.

Our heroes stood there and watched one of their own up against the leader of the warriors, a Blood Spear. Their emotions were a tangle of fear and respect, but more than anything, they wanted to know what Peace was going to do to stop this little monster who wanted to kill him and eat him without physically harming him.

Knife-Breaker was still furious and swore he would kill Peace in three hits.

"I accept your offer." Peace spoke loud enough that the crowd could hear him.

"What?" Knife-Breaker snarled at Peace.

"I will give you three hits to defeat me, but after that, I will defeat you. Agreed?"

"You cannot defeat me!" Knife-Breaker screamed, and the crowd roared with him.

"Then we are agreed?" Peace was calm and still hadn't moved. His eyes were not looking at the goblin directly. They stayed locked in one place even though the thing he was watching was pacing side to side to work up the crowd.

"We are..." Knife Breaker said slowly as he started to move into range. "Agreed!" He sprang into the air and spun, coming down with a slashing motion towards Brother Peace.

Peace took two quick steps forward. He didn't even try to block the incoming blow because he cleared enough distance between them with his movement; the spearhead was behind him, and Peace just let the shaft of the spear hit him in the arm. "That's one."

Knife-Breaker screamed again and tried backing up to get range, but Peace just moved with him, so he took another large step back and swung his spear around behind him, trying to attack from the other side with a long sweeping motion. Peace leaped forward and got behind the spearhead once more. Peace again didn't bother to block him, and when the spear shaft hit him in the other arm, he just smiled, knowing it would be taken aggressively, and said, "That's two. You better be careful. You are going to have to drop me in one hit."

Knife-Breaker was furious, but he was also a skilled fighter. He pushed at Peace, and as Peace took a step back, he did as well, putting himself in a better position to use his spear. Instead of slashes, he switched to thrusts. He came at Peace with a barrage of quick, fast stabs aimed at his face and torso.

The goblin did have skills, but there were things that he did not know. He did not know that Peace was Brother Peace of the Temple of Light. He didn't know that he had trained relentlessly for three years. He didn't know that not only was he trained in the body sphere, but he had been trained in the mind sphere and had already harmonized them together as one. In that state, he had the ability known as 'Moving Faster than Thought." An ability that allowed him to slow down his perception of time as his mind took in more frames per second. He didn't know that Peace was watching the stabbing strikes in slow-motion and had time to consider whether to block or dodge and had the skill to do either with perfect timing.

Peace sidestepped the first two, and as the third came at his face, he turned sideways and bent backward at the waist. As the fourth came in, he stood back up and stepped forward, allowing him to dodge the strike completely. The fifth stab came lower. Peace raised his leg to dodge that strike but then stomped back down on the spear, driving it into the ground.

The crowd began to quiet its roar. They stared as the leader of their warriors continued to hit nothing but air.

Another flurry of thrusts came at Peace, but he continued to dodge and move out of the way. On the final thrust, Brother Peace sidestepped the spear and caught it below the spearhead. Knife-Breaker tried to pull his spear free of Peace's grip, but the monk was twice his size and had no intention of letting go just yet.

"You should quit now. Do you yield?" Peace maintained his grip on the spear as Knife-Breaker tried twice more to free it. "Do you yield?"

"I yield..." Knife-Breaker said, and Peace let go of his spear. "...to no one!" and stabbed Peace in his side near his hip.

Peace winced in pain and grabbed the spear again. "That was three." Peace pulled the spear out of his side, and then, with the other hand, he palm-struck the spear just below where he was holding it and snapped it in two. Knife-Breaker swung the shaft at him like it was a club, but Peace punched the spear in mid-swing and snapped what was left in half again.

Knife-Breaker flipped the broken shaft around so he was holding it in a stabbing position and leaped into the air toward Peace.

Brother Peace dropped the spearhead that he was still holding, and with his other hand, he caught Knife-Breaker in mid-air. With his other hand, he reached out, and his weapon appeared, ready to do his bidding. He ignited it, and the light began to grow into a pure white ball.

Frantically, his team was trying to reach him on his pin, but he had turned it off.

Knife-Breaker plunged the broken shaft into Brother Peace's arm, and he gritted his teeth and screamed through them.

Peace charged his ball with all he had and, with one movement, engulfed the goblin in its light. The crowd of goblins howled in panic and shock. Peace dropped the Knife-Breaker unceremoniously. "There." He said as he backed up and grabbed the wound on his side. "That should do it."

Knife-Breaker got back up. He was not harmed in any way. He screamed that he was still going to kill Peace, but no response came from the crowd. They all just stood there and stared at Knife-Breaker in disbelief.

He tried to rile them up, but they just stood there staring. He called for the Blood Spears, but no answer came. He called out for them a second time, but all of the goblins who had been cheering him on were silent, and slowly, they all turned their backs to him with looks of pity on their faces.

"What did you do to me?" demanded Knife-Breaker.

"I healed you."

Knife-Breaker looked down at his arms and his chest. Brother Peace had used his tool's healing light and removed all of his scars. He stared at his bare skin in horror. "What have you done?"

"I took all your honor from you. Now you are nobody." Peace said with certainty. Knife-Breaker fell to his knees and began to feel his face for all of the honor scars that were no longer there. "Now, as dictated by the queen, I choose your fate. You are not allowed to re-scar your old victories. They belong to me now. You must start over from the beginning." He leaned into Knife-Breaker and said, "This is how I defeat you."

Before he could attack, Stone Jaw and the goblins under his command detained him. "Just kill me." Knife-Breaker pleaded.

Brother Peace raised his voice so all could hear. "You wanted to eat me and thought we should be killed." Peace looked him right in the eye and said, "No."

"Please." The goblin pleaded again.

"This is what you deserve. Now go. Find your redemption." Peace said and began to walk out of the circle.

The Goblin Queen announced that Peace had defeated Knife-Breaker and that his judgment stood. Then she announced that Stone Jaw would take his place. Many of the goblins cheered. She commanded that he get everyone back to what they were doing because she had a promise to keep, and she was to lead them to the Oracles.

She led them deeper into the city. As they traveled through, they realized that most of the city was abandoned and unused.

"Why don't your people live in the rest of the city?" asked Travis.

"When it was given to us by the Oracles, we had no need for all of this. As our people grow, we will expand into it, and besides..." she said with a snarl on her lip, "...it still smells of humans."

They traveled to the far side of the carved-out city to another cave entrance and then across a long stone bridge that crossed a ravine with a depth much farther than Dalen wanted to fly. He traveled down until he could barely see the team but had not reached the bottom, so he returned to the top. When they got to the other side, the Goblin Queen stopped them and asked, "Could the other two now make themselves known?"

Oubliette stepped out of the darkness, and Becky pulled back the hood to reveal her face while Dalen removed the spell that hid him.

The queen stared at Dalen. "What are you?"

Dalen mused at the question and answered, "Friendly."

The Queen stared at him, trying to assess his answer.

Dalen's stones glowed brightly, and he could see by her
expression that she had never been in the presence of a Jinn
before. She could tell that he was no one to be trifled with.
"I am glad you simply came for the Oracles. I can imagine what
might have happened to my people if you were not so friendly."

"It's not in our nature." Sir Adam offered to the
conversation as he tapped his Vengerian pin, and his armor and
sword reappeared.

The others switched back to their adventuring gear
as well, and the Goblin Queen watched unblinking in awe.
"Are you gods?"

It was Dalen who answered. "Not that we are aware of.
We are just people trying to save our friend."

"He was cursed by a genie, and we seek the oracles to
find a way to free him." Travis gave the Goblin Queen a small
bow. "We come from a city called Venger, not too far to the
North. Perhaps we may cross paths again one day, but for now,
we have to make our leave."

The Queen gestured down the corridor. "They are at the
far end, waiting for you."

19

THE ORACLES

The corridor was about twenty feet long and opened up to a veranda overlooking the forest. Fluttering about were two Pixies.

The one that was further back had long black hair with streaks of red. She wore black boots and pants that had a strip of fire embroidered on them. The one closer had short blond hair. She wore short pants that went to her knee and a top that had thin straps at the shoulders. It was hard to say what color her clothes were because they continuously changed as she moved about, going through the entire spectrum in an oscillating pattern resembling tie-die.

The blond one flew up to them, and with a jokingly grumpy face, she put her hands on her hips and said, "Oh sure, just take all my fun away."

"Don't mind her," said the other, who was fluttering in the air about head height. "That's her way of saying, well done in handling the goblins. No one has ever thought to heal them of their scars, thus removing all honor and status. Impressive. We are the Oracles that you have come to see."

"They cheated!" The blond pixie folded her arms and gave them all an over-exaggerated harrumph.

The other one shook her head at them and mouthed the words without making a sound, "No, you didn't."

The blond pixie's back was turned, yet she responded as if she knew what the other was doing. "They did, too!"

The dark-haired pixie was still trying to keep them at ease, letting them know that her partner was, overall, just playing. "You're fine."

The other one pouted for a good twenty seconds more then sighed. "Fine." She threw both of her hands in the air. She fluttered there for a moment, scowling at them once more before giving in. "It was beyond brilliant, and I am only mad because I didn't see it coming. When you are an Oracle, that's a hard thing to take."

"So, let's get the obvious out of the way." The darker one fluttered over to the blond one, who was now standing at a nearby table. She gestured for them to sit down. "We are the Oracles that you have been looking for and we know why you are here."

"You do?" asked Travis.

The flickering outfit of the blond pixie changed color with her mood. It shifted only slightly and was now producing beautiful blues and purples as she put her hands on her hips. "We wouldn't be much of Oracles if we didn't."

The darker of the two leaned over and nudged the other with her shoulder. This one is Cloud Song. You can call me Dew Dust."

"It's nice to meet you." Dalen gave the pixies a small, respectful bow. "I am Dalen Pax."

Dew Dust nodded, "We know who you are, Dalen Pax."

"I have bad news for you." Cloud Song didn't really look like she had bad news. In all actuality, she seemed amused. "We will not be answering your questions at this time."

"Did we do something wrong?" asked Becky.

"Not specifically, dear." Dew Dust said with great compassion.

"Yeah," added Cloud Song. She looked right at Travis. "But why should we share our secrets with you if you are already keeping secrets from each other? Then she shifted her gaze to each of them. "Even if you haven't done it on purpose, we will not help you until each of you is ready to stop hiding from one another because that is not what you need right now."

"Before your instincts try to fight this, please consider the truth of it," added Dew Dust.

"Yeah? What's that?" asked Travis. It was obvious that he was getting frustrated with them and their lack of willingness to help.

Cloud Song yelled at him as if she were angry with him. As she scolded Travis, her clothes turned to reds and oranges, giving her a more fiery look. "Because we know what you know, and more than that, we have seen past what you know. We have looked at this from many angles! We have considered the pros and cons, and after knowing... Everything!" She took a breath and calmed down; with it, her top began to demonstrate cooler colors like emerald and sapphire. "We decided this was the only way to truly help you."

Dew Dust shrugged and nodded. "We aren't trying to hurt you or break you. We want to save you. We believe in your cause, and we want you to succeed, but this success will only transpire from one outcome. You have come to us for answers. Direction. You have come here to learn what must be done. We are answering you. The foe you face will use your secrets to try to turn you against each other." Her voice was kind and soft. "It is better to face it now, on your own terms, here, where you are safe and have time to work through them together."

Now Cloud Song's tone was compassionate too. "We also know that you wouldn't have shared your secrets otherwise. So, we have decided to hold the answers you want for ransom. Until you do what we tell you." She laughed, "I'm kidding. Well, no. I'm not, but I am. How did you put it, Dew?"

"Once they were ready to face their future together in the light of truth, we would reward them with the knowledge they need to save the entire universe from plunging into eternal darkness."

Cloud Song pointed at Dew Dust. "What she said."

"I am willing." Sir Adam had his finger held up. "Roll initiative."

‹Wait.› urged Travis. ‹We haven't even talked about whether or not we are going to do this.›

Sir Adam looked at his brother. "What's there to talk about? They want us to stop keeping secrets from our own team. I don't care where you are on your list. Rule Two." Adam grabbed Travis with both hands on his shoulders and looked him dead in his eyes. "Don't keep secrets from your team." Adam didn't let go. He just continued to look into his brother's heart. "What are you hiding, Travis?"

"Before you answer that, Travis, I want everyone in the room to remember something." Cloud Song could stand in the palm of your hand, but her voice suggested the magnitude of the situation. "Each one of you has a secret, so before any one of you gets too big for your britches and starts judgmentally asking why whoever kept their secret kept it, I want you to remember what this is about. It is not about getting upset that someone kept a secret. It is about understanding."

"It is about forgiveness." Dew and Cloud leaned in and hugged each other.

Cloud whispered something in Dew Dust's ear. She smiled and said, "I know."

"Okay. Travis, why don't we handle the big one first."
Dew turned toward Becky and Adam. "He has been trying to
hold the weight of this because he loves you. It may have been
a mistake, but he did it because he truly cares about saving
you both pain."

"What are they talking about Travis?" Becky was
openly frightened.

Travis was visibly nervous. "You know how when we got
our items from the statues, and each of us got a moment where
we understood what everyone actually gifted to us and why?
You know, all the wishes and prayers?"

"Yes. Most of the people who went to Oubliette's
statue were either thieves or acrobats." She stopped and
thought about it for a second. "Oh, I get why now." Then she
returned to the question that Travis asked. "They went to
Oubliette's statue because she was the one who was most like
a skill master, thief, or acrobat. That's why they chose my
statue and why Brother Peace had mostly monks and healers."

Adam had a look of concern on his face. "Yeah, and
most that went to mine were knights and paladins because they
connected me to what mattered to them." Adam's concern was
growing. "Why did they go to yours?"

Travis smiled and opened his mouth to talk, but on his
first attempt, nothing happened. He decided to come at the
question from another angle, and that at least got his mouth
working. "Many of the people who went to my statue were
archers in some form or another. But the royal family has kept
a secret for years about me and who I am." It was the first

time he was going to admit it aloud, and his knees betrayed him. As he began to fall, Dalen moved a chair underneath him, and Travis sat down hard on it. Tears were in his eyes, and he started to pale out.

Adam dropped to one knee and started rubbing Travis's back. "Stay with me, Travis."

"It's me." He said practically under his breath.

"What?" asked Becky. "I didn't hear you."

It had been five days since Travis had found out the truth at his statue, and even though it had been less than a week, it seemed like years for him. He had tried so hard to avoid it and pretend like it wasn't there, but now, it all came at him at once, and he began to cry. "It's me." This time, it was loud enough for everyone to hear. "I am the one who sacrifices everything. I'm the one that stops the Time Mage." Sadness turned to anger. "Me! I'm the one..." and just as quickly as the anger rose, it faded, turning into despair. "... who gets wiped from time. Like I never existed."

Adam looked into his brother's eyes, trying to read him as he had done since they were born, but now, at this moment, Adam only read sadness. "Are you sure?"

Travis nodded, hung his head, and let the tears fall from his soul.

"No. That's impossible." Becky backed away from him. "It's untrue." Becky's mind tried to protect itself from the pain, so it actively went into denial.

"Becky, what I got from the bow was king after king and queen after queen, coming to my statue to give thanks for my sacrifice and saving the world. It's also what Venger said to me when we met!" He was stressed, and he didn't mean for it to come out as yelling, but it did.

This gave Becky something to attack. "You don't know what that means!" She was now yelling, too. "That could mean a lot of things. You don't know!"

"No! You don't know. I am the one who experienced it!" Travis was standing again.

Peace just watched. He knew they had to get this out. If things turned bad he would get involved, but he knew that if they were going to be ok with this, they were going to have to be honest about how they felt, and they would have to feel it with each other. In his eyes, making them calm down would have been a disservice to them both.

Becky was dedicated to proving him wrong. "Then tell me this." She crossed her arms and cocked one hip. "If you do what you say you do..." She made it that far into the question calmly but then erupted into screaming, "Then how does anyone know you exist and make statues of you to be prayed at!? How does ANYONE know to thank you for anything!?"

Travis stalled for a moment. That was a good question that he had not thought of, and in the middle of the fight, he understood what Cloud had meant about missing something.

"Ha!" With her argument holding for a moment, her denial retreated, and victory took its place. She stopped yelling but was still loud. "You see. You have nothing to worry about. If you got wiped from history and time, they couldn't remember you, thank you, or make statues of you. That statue had your name on it. None of that is possible if you are wiped from time." Feeling that she had won this argument, she switched gears and tried to comfort Travis, so she stepped close and hugged him.

Travis didn't hug her back. Not because he didn't want to but because his mind was still trying to understand. "But..."

Becky pulled back and kissed him to shut him up. "But nothing. This is checkmate."

"But they all said I sacrificed everything." Travis was so sure, and now he didn't know.

"Maybe you have to not only give up your power to Christophe, but you also have to give him your bow, leaving you with nothing." Becky saw he didn't like that answer. "Okay, maybe there is some crazy event, and you go through great suffering or almost get killed to save everyone, and then Dalen and Peace have to heal you." She turned to Dalen. You can heal him up to death, right?"

"With Peace's help, I think that I could even bring him back to life if we are quick. As long as the soul still clings to the body, the same way you can perform C.P.R. on someone after they drown, but I mean, we would have to be right there."

"See. Maybe it's as simple as you just sacrificing your life, which is amazing, and then we bring you back to life, and everything is fine." She turned to everyone else,

"Help me out here."

"Maybe the only way to get back to our own time will be to have one person stay behind. You volunteer and sacrifice everything to get us home." Dalen said with a whimsical tone. "Or... Or... Perhaps Travis is right, but with the combined strength and love of this group, we find a way to remember you, and then we find a way to save you so you won't be lost forever." He gave Travis a nod, and Travis was reminded of the promise that Dalen had given him. "Or maybe something completely different."

Brother Peace added to Dalen's thought, "The most dangerous part of a prophecy is how easily they can be misunderstood."

"Ain't that the truth." The Oracles said in unison.

"You see?" Becky's tone became soft. She wanted him to hear her. "Is it possible? Even a little possible that any one of those answers could be true? Especially since it seems that the world still remembers you."

Travis's mind was trying to consider the possibilities. Because of what Venger had said and what Dorn had said to him when they met. He wholeheartedly believed he knew his fate. Because of all the royal family members who continued to pay him homage, he had been so sure that he was going to be wiped out of time, but Becky's point had created doubt. Brother Peace also had made a good point. If that were the case, there were possible other explanations for what had been meant. "You're right. There are other answers. Maybe it turns out okay, maybe I do die, and that's why they say what they do because I am the only one who dies saving Venger."

"Well, let's stay away from you just dying," Becky said.

"Yeah." He was listening, but his mind was busy. "Look, I don't want to die, but Just dying is so much better than being erased from time."

Becky was not ready to look at that either. "Travis!" She waited for him to make eye contact. "The goal isn't to become a martyr. Let's aim at surviving this." Travis nodded and hugged her back.

Then she punched him in the chest. "You weren't going to tell me?" The crisis was over, and now all that energy had to go somewhere. "You were going to let this relationship build and never tell me you were going to just disappear?"

"Whoa there." Travis was now on the defensive. "That's not what I meant to do?"

"Really?" Her anger was building. "You were just going to let me love you. Fall for you more and more, and then just leave me? You Ass...Hole!"

"That is not what I planned." Travis looked around at everyone and then refocused on Becky. "I thought I was going to die; I thought I should be brave and live while I could. I love you and want to have this relationship with you, but I didn't want every minute of it to be filled with the pain of knowing it would be over soon. Same with Adam." He turned to his brother. "You were so happy; this was the adventure you've always wanted. How could I stain it by letting you know that the adventure you've always wanted was going to be the reason I stopped existing? I couldn't do that?"

Adam took a breath and asked, "Yeah, but what happens when you do die and you do leave us?"

"Yeah!" Becky yelled. "Have me love you and then just leave. Then what?"

"Then nothing!" Travis yelled, with tears in his eyes. "Then I never existed in the first place, and neither of you are the wiser that you lost anything. Doing this my way, you never would have gotten hurt. You would be happy until the moment I was gone, and then you would still be happy because none of you would remember me. I wouldn't even be a memory. I would be nothing!"

Dalen decided he had to do something. He opened up the Spheres of Reality and linked Travis, Sir Adam, and Becky together. At that moment, each of them didn't just hear each other's thoughts; they thought them as if they were their own. They were one being tied together by three minds that thought in perfect harmony.

All three of them stood there in perfect telepathy, to the point that there were no words to send. It was a connection much deeper than I thought. It was a connection of heart. After a few minutes, they reached up and held each other in a group hug. Then hands reached out, and Peace and Dalen were pulled in, and as they were, they were added to the collective.

The team harmonized with each other, and their collective strength became each of their own. Brother Peace stepped back and extended his right hand out. His fingers open with his palm to the side. One by one, the team stood back and matched his movement with each of their fingers touching each other. They closed their fingers together into a spiral. The oracles leaned their heads together and held each other as they watched the beauty of it all from the eyes of the universe.

"Okay." Sir Adam took a breath. "I'll go next."

"What secret are you keeping, Adam?" Travis asked.

Sir Adam thought for a moment and then slowly nodded when he was sure it was his truth. "After everything is over, I have no intention of going back home."

"What do you mean, Adam?" asked Travis.

"I mean, I will never live in my birth home again. I have thought about this a lot, and this is where I belong. I have no intention of going back permanently."

The connection was still strong, and all of them understood. Dalen said, "As long as I am around, I will be more than happy to move any of you back and forth so you can go back home and live your lives where we came from. Sir Adam, if you want to move here permanently, I'll back that completely, but if you ever wish to, I don't know, visit the folks for the holidays and then come back, I can do that."

"Thank you," said Sir Adam as he wiped a tear. I would wish that very much." He sniffed hard. "I made a vow to protect Hope, and I want to go back to Venger and continue with that vow once we are all done."

"I can respect that, and I think Mom and Dad would respect that too." Travis gave his brother a nod, and Adam nodded back.

Peace closed his eyes and let all of his doubts and fears fall out of his mind and out of his mouth. "We are moving closer and closer to this inevitable outcome. Somewhere during this, I am supposed to become this amazingly wise person whose wisdom becomes the foundation of Vengerian philosophy. And although I have been trained for the last three years to let go of doubt, I am terrified about what needs to be done to become this person."

"Which part scares you, Brother?" Dalen could feel his fear and conflict, but he knew that Peace had to face them.

"I didn't spend my three years at the Temple of Light trying to get through the nightmare of those nine days stuck in a time loop. I mean, yeah, that took a while to get over, and it was years before the nightmares stopped, but what took me years to find is who I have become. I had to fight so hard to let go of so many aspects of who I had programmed myself to be. This stupid image of myself was spoon-fed to me by society. I was cruel and violent, and I was rewarded for it by my peers. I was loved for who I was, and someone like Dalen, who was decent and not full of himself, was attacked and picked on. It took me that whole time to figure out who I am, for me, with no one else's expectations put upon me. I needed to be the person I wanted to be, even when I was alone. Then I had to learn how to be that person around other people." He laughed. "Three years, and once I find myself, I find out that the expectations on me are huge. An entire culture is counting on me to know the right thing to say when it matters, and it terrifies me." He breathed a huge sigh of relief. "Oh damn! It feels good to get that off my chest." He gave a high-pitched whoop.

"Brother Peace." Travis was smiling. "I get the weight of trying to live up to what we know the world expects from us." Everyone nodded at that. "But remember, it was you who figured out how to beat your enemy by healing them. You are one of the wisest people I have ever met."

"That is a big compliment coming from Travis." Sir Adam squeezed the spiral just a little harder.

"I believe in you, Brother." Dalen meant it. They may have had a rocky start, but Brother Peace had proven to be a true and real friend.

"Thank you," added Peace. He could feel how much it meant to Dalen to be able to say it, and the others nodded in agreement.

"That brings me to mine." Becky looked sheepishly at everyone. "I think I know what Peace means about being the real him."

"Yeah?" asked Brother Peace.

"Yeah." She blushed a little. "For years, I have fought to be myself. You all know that. It's why I was never popular, but no matter how hard I tried, and even when I was with you guys, there was a part of me that I always hid."

"That's true for everyone, sweety." Travis was next to her in the circle. He put his hand on her shoulder. "That's a part of being human. I mean, I hope you are you when it's just you and me."

She shrugged. "You know the real me more than anyone else, but there has always been a little bit of myself I still hide away..." She paused and looked at everyone. "Until today."

"Until today?" asked Adam.

"When I pull up my hood and slip into the darkness, there is a part of me that comes to life, and it's not just the magic." Becky took a deep breath, and Oubliette let it out. She continued, but now she only whispered. "It's something that has always been in me, but when I am Oubliette, the part of me that has been asleep my whole life wakes up, and I never want her to sleep again."

Dalen and Peace looked at each other. "Did you see that?" asked Peace.

"That's what I was about to ask you," replied Dalen, and then both of them smiled.

"What?" asked Travis.

Brother Peace confirmed with Dalen through a glance, and Dalen nodded in acknowledgment. "One of the techniques that we were both taught at the Temple of Light was creating something called a Tin Soldier."

"What's a Tin Soldier?" asked Adam.

Dalen reharmonized the spheres so that the team would get flashes of both of their memories, as he explained. "While training, we had to learn to be one with ourselves and one with the actions that we were doing. This ability has been an integral part of our training from the beginning. Using the tin soldier as a method of harmonizing yourself to that version of you."

"So, it's like creating a character?" asked Travis.

"Yes," explained Peace. "As long as the character you create is truth."

"What do you mean?" whispered Oubliette. She was listening closely and beginning to relax.

"Okay." Peace took a moment to figure out how to explain it. "You said that Travis knows you better than any of us. Does that suggest that you are lying to us about who you are?"

"No...but" She was going to continue, but Peace cut her off.

"When you are just with your family for the holidays, and you are talking to Grandma, are you being the same person with her as you are when you are hanging with us?"

"Yes, but no," she whispered.

"In either case, are you lying about who you are?" asked Peace.

"No. It's always me, just different aspects of me." Becky was starting to sound like herself again.

"Correct." Peace smiled. "Granddaughter, daughter, friend, girlfriend. Each one demonstrates a different aspect of yourself, and each one of them is a different person, but all of them are you."

Becky began to feel like herself to everyone who was connected to her, and she spoke aloud once more. "Okay, I can follow that."

"If you think about it, often you switch subconsciously depending on the environment, right?" asked Dalen. Becky nodded. "A tin soldier is when you create an aspect on purpose that you can activate willingly although still completely you. No lies or stories, but a real version of yourself that is empowered to do all the things that other parts of yourself tell you that you can't do."

Peace picked it up from there. "Right. The training is built so that you can let go of the persona that you wear as a mask to the world on a day-to-day basis. Once you can free yourself of the false image that you keep telling yourself you can and can't be and become a raw, real form that is not held back by doubt and fear, you can create tin soldiers. We think you figured out how to do it naturally. We have watched many monks switch between themselves and their Tin Soldier, and I swear you just did it."

"So, I am not insane?" Becky said aloud.

"Insanely brilliant, maybe, but that's all." Peace smiled

at her. She took a deep sigh of relief. "I say be it. Be it all the time."

"Maybe that's what you need." Becky's eyes were moist and glistened in the light. "Make the tin soldier called Master Peace."

Peace smiled for a moment; he thought about it and then laughed. "I think you're right. I'll make you a deal. You be the real you, and I will be the real me."

Becky smiled and winked at him, accidentally releasing a tear. "Deal!"

"I first had to build three, and the fourth is the one you see now," added Dalen. Flashes of Brother Truth and Father Light appeared in their mind. It was his turn, and he had more than one to give.

"The night before Hope ran with the trees, I heard a voice that was calling me in the forest. When I went to find out who was calling me, I think I found my real mother." This brought questions to the lips of everyone, but they held their questions and let him continue. "As a Jinn, the stone from the statue was poisoning me."

"How was it poisoning you?" asked Peace.

"All of my true abilities are based off of my belief and faith in myself and my power." Dalen scoffed and rolled his eyes. "Rule one." He found it amusing how often that was the answer. "With the stone from the statue, I started to cast disbelief in myself. I got to a point where I didn't know if I could still be me without it. Your gifts empower, and for the better, but mine empowered me to doubt and fail, so I had to remove it."

"You relinquished your power?" asked Sir Adam, impressed.

"I did. It was hard to do, but in the end, I am built to do hard things." Dalen shrugged.

"Okay, but you're a Jinn again. What happened there?" asked Travis.

"My mother. I told you she was there. She gave me my heart of stone."

"Heart of stone?" asked Becky. "It sounds cold and hard."

"No. More like a brilliant emerald, it is a stone made of pure love." Dalen cast a quick illusionary spell so they could see what was happening, and then he ignited the fourth sphere of reality within himself. The gem that was over his heart began to glow. As it did, the true Heartstone of Power appeared above their hands, which were still formed as a single spiral galaxy. It radiated a beautiful green light, and since they were all connected, Dalen allowed them to feel it through him. It touched their hearts and souls, and the binding that held them together grew stronger. "Behold, my friends. The Heart of Stone."

Time held still, and each of them found themselves connected to the greatest version of themselves; they stood in the glory of it with no masks. Together. As one. "My mother took a piece of her own Heartstone and gave it to me to create my own. I am now a Jinn because I am a Jinn, not because someone else decided I was. I have been Brother Truth. I have been Father Light. I have been the Reality Bender, but now there is only me. Dalen Pax... The Jinn."

"That explains why you don't look sick anymore and why your stones turned silvery," added Travis.

"What did Master Ki think of all of this?" whispered Oubliette.

"That's the thing. I have often been connected to them, even when they were not physically there, but I have not heard from them since that night," admitted Dalen.

"You haven't heard from Ki since the trees?" asked Travis, a little surprised. "I thought that he was going to stay in contact with you during the journey."

"He hasn't been in contact since Venger; for a while, I was in contact with Master Truth, but he went silent that night. My Mother said I no longer needed those images to complete what I was doing," mentioned Dalen. "I thought that she just meant while I was creating my own Heartstone, but I haven't heard from them since."

"Why didn't you... Oh yeah, right. Okay. Fair." Travis had remembered what the pixies had said.

"Do you know where they went or when they are coming back?" asked Becky.

Dew Dust cleared her throat, and everyone looked over. As they did, the connection broke, and they all let go. Reality came slamming back, and they remembered that there was more going on.

"The question of where Master Ki and Master Truth went will be answered at the Fountain of Truth. Dew Dust shrugged, "I am sorry, friend, but it is destiny that decides when that secret is given, and it is not our secret to share. You will see them both again."

"It is when you will see your fiery friend as well," added Cloud Song. "After that..." She threw her head back and cackled. "They will be with you forever... ever...ever..." She pretended to be her own echo for a moment and slowly faded her voice as she said it again and again until she was too quiet to hear. Then she looked around at everyone. "What?" she cocked her head to one side. "Too dramatic?"

Dew Dust made a gesture of nearly squishing her index finger and thumb together and held it toward Cloud, "Yeah, A little bit." She turned back toward Dalen. "But she is right. There is something you must do before you get to learn that secret. I'm sorry. I hate telling people that."

"I have good news, though!" Cloud Song said triumphantly. "Now that you have told your secrets and faced most of your fears. You are closer than you were, and you are ready to face what awaits you. The Cave of Fears."

Dalen's mind flashed to the dinner at Dorn's. He remembered he had a vision that there was a cave. A cave filled with fear.

"That would be the one." Dew Dust blurted out as Dalen thought of it. He looked at her like he was going to ask how she knew what he was remembering, but before he could, Dew Dust pointed at her and Cloud and said, "Oracles."

Cloud Song continued. "The Pillar of Time is nestled inside a mountain that the Red Dragons use as their breeding grounds."

Travis and Adam said slowly and in unison, "The Red Dragon breeding grounds?"

"Yes," replied Cloud. "There will be many of them."

Dew Dust focused her attention on Dalen and said, "Your... old friend, DeSalvo, found a path along the outside of the mountain to the southwest. It's a long corridor of rock, a tunnel, really, but on the far side of it, there is a stairway that will lead you directly to the Pillar of Time. DeSalvo is a master of anger, guilt, fear, and secrets. He uses them as tools to get what he wants."

Cloud Song chimed in with, "Yeah, he got some poor fool to make a wish, and now that cave is filled with your fears and secrets. Whatever they may be."

"That's why you made us let go of our secrets and the fears we had with each other." Peace began to laugh. "That way, it can't be used against us in the cave."

"Exactly," said Dew Dust.

"Like I said," added Cloud Song. "It was the only way

we could really help."

"On the table here, there is a map case. Inside, you will find precise directions to get you there without problems. Dalen, this is going to hinge on you and your ability to learn a new Jinn power on the run. Deviate from the directions at your own peril."

"Is there anything else?" asked Dalen.

"Of course," said Cloud and Dew together. "What kind of Oracles would we be if we left you with that?" They took turns starting with Dew Dust.

"Oubliette, just because you thrive in darkness doesn't mean that you have to be it. A torch is most useful when it is in the dark."

"Peace. If you follow your own teachings, then you are as powerful as you choose to be. Choose to be a Master Peace."

"Sir Adam. You take only what you bring with you. Pack wisely. Your armor is strong, but there is something else you have that will protect you even better."

"Travis. We will not tell you what we have seen on the day in question. Some good points were made, and the point that there is a statue of you leaves questions about your logic. No person should know their fate, and now, neither do you. We free you of such burdens. So, live now while you can because nothing is promised."

"Dalen. I know the story of who you are. I have seen the past and the future of it. Perhaps in another life, it went differently. Perhaps in another life, it all went wrong, but Dalen, know this." Dew Dust failed to fight back tears as she spoke. "This is the best version of you I have ever seen, and I am so very proud of you."

Cloud Song had tears in her eyes as well and nodded. "We all are."

It was time. Everyone got ready, but it was explained to them that if they showed up as a group, they would be seen immediately. Dalen was going to have to do the first part by himself. One person would be harder to pinpoint, plus the spell, if Dalen could learn it on the run, would allow him to go unnoticed. He would be able to cross through the Dragon lands and make it to a large dead tree. Dalen's memory of the tree filled with sadness flashed in his mind. That will be the landmark where the opening of the cave will be.

"Slow time down the moment you arrive. You will need every moment you have. Once the Dragons know you are there, you will not last long. Remember, they are guarding their breeding grounds." Dew Dust honestly looked concerned. There are a hundred ways this goes bad and very few that this goes right, and all of it will depend on whether or not you can listen to your heart."

Cloud Song rolled her eyes and said, "That was a little on the nose. Don't you think?"

Dew Dust shrugged and said, "What do you expect from an Oracle of the Cave of Unalloyed Truth?"

Cloud Song put her arms around Dew Dust and kissed her. "There are moments when I remember why I decided to be your partner."

Dew Dust looked at her with false shock and said, "Only moments?"

Cloud Song pushed her away playfully and said, "Oh, you." Then she turned her attention back to Dalen. "Yes. Listen to your heart. It is important that you do that." She shrugged dramatically. "Who knows where that will take you."

"Umm, we do," said Dew, but she was shushed by Cloud Song. "Oh right..." Dew waved her hands in the air like she was casting a spell and spoke in an exaggerated tone. "Who knows where that will lead."

"Okay. Point taken, listen to my heart, got it." Dalen took the case and checked the spell and instructions inside. He read them and understood what he had to do. "Alright. I'm leaving." He laughed. "Wish me luck."

One by one, the team sincerely and enthusiastically wished him good luck. They were going to stand ready and wait for his signal; right now, everything rode on Dalen's shoulders.

20

THE TRUTH
ABOUT DALEN

The directions were clear. Dalen was to make most of the journey alone. He was to use his magic to teleport to the Tree of Travel that stood at the edge of the valley near Venger. Once he was there, he was to connect directly to the tree.

While he was connected to it, he was supposed to open the mind sphere and observe each of the locations it was in. One of the locations was near a volcano with dragons. That was the one where he needed to be. If he did it correctly, he would then be at the travel tree that was closest to the Pillar of Time.

The next step was to learn a new ability from the chart that he had been given. He had never seen anything quite like it, even in his twenty years at the Temple of All Faith. It was built in the style of magic that he was familiar with, using the Elements of Reality, which meant he could follow it, and Dalen knew instinctively that it was jinn magic.

It wasn't a spell in the traditional sense, where it was a bit of magic that would create an effect, lasting for a particular amount of time and then dissipating. This was an explanation of how to move his body in conjunction with the soul sphere and to be able to control that state with the mind. This is how he was going to get to the passageway without being seen by the dragons.

Dragons have amazing eyesight. They can see a field mouse four miles away as it hides in grass two feet high, and if it were just their sight, that was the concern, he could just use the Hidden Spell. But dragons have more than just sight; some stories of dragons suggest that they are merely winged lizards. Nothing could be further from the truth.

Dragons are an extremely intelligent race. Their origins are the stuff of legends and myths. Created by the All-Father after the fall of Dreamers as guardians of this realm, he empowered them to be brilliant and magical right down to their very bones. There is not a piece of a dragon that can't be used in some form or another for alchemy or spells. The All Father also granted them great strength and size. It was a dragon that almost destroyed the world, and now it would be dragons who guard it.

Being made of magic, even as hatchlings, dragons have magical abilities and a natural resistance to spells. By the time they have aged to young adults, they are as powerful as most practicing wizards or witches, and by the time they make their way to the breeding grounds in the Draconic Mountain, they have magical knowledge and abilities that surpass most other creatures in the world. They are immune to most magic that can be wielded and highly perceptive. There was more than a small chance that even if they could not sense Dalen with the Hidden Spell, they would be aware of the magic being used and curious enough to investigate.

The moment that Dalen appeared at the tree, he slowed down time to almost nothing. He was going to need as much time as he could get, and he needed it the second he arrived. As time slowed down, giant pillars of fire launched into the night sky. As the pillars of fire reached upward into the heavens, silhouettes of dragons could be seen against them as they slowed to the speed of a flower blooming.

Dalen opened up the scroll and began to study it. The scrolls chart was easy enough to follow, but the language everything was written in was not one that Dalen was familiar with, so he cast a spell to allow himself to read it, and as he did, he understood that it was written in the language of the Jinn. His mind opened up, and the entire knowledge of the language was passed to him. It came to him quickly, and he felt as if it were more like remembering the language than learning it. The title of the scroll was, 'Letting Go of Reality.' What it was asking for was physically impossible, which was the point.

Dalen read the instructions of what to do, but it was backward to everything he understood. Usually, when he cast his magic, he used the method that he learned at the Temple of All Faith. There was a continuous light from the divine source that shined down on a magic circle. Stepping into the light, it would pass through him like a lens, and his intent would bend the light like a prism, creating whatever casting circle was required onto the ground. It's how he always had done it. The Divine (Soul) would pass through his intent (Mind) to create a physical outcome (Body). Soul through Mind to enact Body, and now this scroll was telling him something completely different.

The Spheres of Reality are the Body, Mind, and Soul. Once they are harmonized together, it creates the Reality Sphere. Jinn Magic worked on this fourth sphere. Moving within one sphere affects all three in conjunction with one other. Because, like the Tree of Travel, there really is only one.

Dalen glanced back to the pillars of fire that were still hanging in the air, and he saw the dragons flying about in the distance. From the point of view of the dragons, he had been there less than a second, and even with their heightened perceptions, they had not noticed him yet. Dalen's eyes moved down the scroll to something he had never seen before. 'How to invoke the Inverted Reality Field.' The spell was intricate and suggested that everything that Dalen had learned about the Reality Sphere up until then was basic and only considered 'Step one' in his learning.

It indicated that what he knew so far was only the positively charged version of the Reality Field. But there was a way to invert it. A way to realign the spheres so that the charge was negative. Not to confuse positive and negative with good and bad. One-half of a magnet is not evil.

The positively charged Sphere of Reality has to do with intent and willpower moving outward, pushing out from the center. It's how wishes are granted. The spellcaster brings the power from the Divine field in and then expels it outward to manifest the spell. The negative field is about the creation of perception within.

Jinn were divine beings by nature. Neutral angels to explain it quickly, but it doesn't quite give the correct image. In the world of divine beings, there were good ones, such as angels. Some beings were considered evil, such as Demons for example. The jinn were neither of those. Neutral in all respects, free to choose, and not tethered to a demanded role or responsibility, but still divine beings.

The scroll revealed that instead of pulling from the infinite divine field, the jinn were supposed to call upon themselves to seek inward for the divinity within themselves. Then, they were to use that divinity to empower the Inverted Reality Field, activating their ability to become incorporeal. The state that most jinn he had met were in, except for his mother, who needed to be there physically. It was only after understanding what was needed that Dalen understood what the scroll meant by letting go of reality.

There was going to be real danger for him. To achieve an inverted field, Dalen was going to have to perform something he never had done before, and worse than that, in trying to do it, he would have to give the ability his full concentration. Which meant as soon as he tried to create it, he would lose his concentration on time. If he weren't successful on his first attempt, he would assuredly be seen.

What the scroll instructed him to do was to pull from the Divine field and harness it into Arcane energy; he then would pass that energy through his perception, taking with it the idea of becoming incorporeal. Once the energy was harmonized with the frequency of his intent, he would use his ki to channel it through him and into the ground. Much like how a child would pluck a dandelion, hold it close to their body, make a wish with all their heart and imagination, and blow it into the wind. This is where the symbols on the floor would normally appear if he were casting a spell, but the scroll explained that to activate this ability, instead of empowering a spell, Dalen would be using that energy to ground and harmonize himself with the world, allowing the energy to sink into the corporeal world and ripple out in every direction. This was a skill he had mastered during his time in the Temple of Light, and Dalen was sure that he could combine all three spheres to this point, but after that, Dalen was walking into unknown territory.

As the magic rippled outward, time would start moving at normal rates, and Dalen would have to act fast. First, he would have to stop the motion of the flow expanding outward and force it to return inward. This was going to create a magical charge twice the size of what he had put out, and there was no question that, at that moment, he would be detected by any of the dragon guardians that protected the breeding grounds.

When the magic flowed outward, it would expand and then dissipate the further it went out from the center point. As it retracted, it would intensify and build a charge as it pulled back against its original flow. The way that stirring two opposing whirlpools in a teacup creates a pull of intense energy. Once the inverted magic came back to center point, instead of sending the energy out to the Divine Field, he was to take all the energy into himself through the solar plexus Chakra stone that was connected to the Divine element. As it passed through, he was to channel all of it into his Heartstone. If he did it correctly, he would awaken his divine form and be able to become incorporeal.

Master Ki. I could really use you right about now. Dalen strained to hear anything, but no response came. *When I chose to stand on my own two feet, I did not realize that meant that I would lose you and your council.*

Dalen looked out at the mountain and watched as the pillar of fire reached its apex. In the light of it, he saw the dragons, and he knew that they would be his demise if he wasn't able to complete the Inverted Field.

The fire reminded him of the jinn whom he first met and who had taught him Jinn Magic. *You never taught me this! How am I supposed to do this alone?*

Dalen's heartstone began to glow, and he heard the voice of the Earth Jinn in his mind. *Who are you talking to, son? I thought you understood.*

I am just looking for guidance. I have never had to do this before, and when I have done this, it was in very controlled situations. I need Master Ki or somebody to explain to me what I am supposed to do because I don't know if I can do this alone.

Dalen could see her now, but he knew that she was not really there. *What do you mean? You have always done it alone.* Before Dalen could respond, she said, *Split yourself and be where I am. Follow our connection using the heartstone within you.*

As Dalen had done a few times before, he opened the mind field and convinced the world that he was in two different locations at once. He was still standing there, at the foot of the volcano, almost frozen in time, yet he also stood in front of his mother. Rather than thinking of a place, he thought of her, and the connection between their Heartstones led him directly to her.

She met him with a warm embrace. "Well done, Dalen. It is good to see you."

When she let him go, he began to look around to see where he was. It was rather dark, but Dalen could see that they were in a manmade room. It was symmetric, and the floor and walls came together at right angles, but it still had the feel of a cave. The air was moist and heavy as he breathed. The only light source was another room nearby, and its light was reflecting off of water. Waves of blueish light refracted in water patterns on the ceiling and walls.

"You make my heart go..." and with a high-pitched voice, she yelled, "Bing!" and it echoed through the chamber with a strong resonance.

Dalen was confused. "What?"

"BIING!" she laughed. "But this time, it is not a bing of despair. It is a bing of joy and pride."

All of a sudden, it came flooding back to him. It was a joke that Ms. Warren had made while giving him a lecture about scaring her the night he had found Mathias and spoken to him. The microwave had gone off, and she said it was the sound of her heart going 'bing.' "How do you know that?"

"I was there." She looked Dalen right in the eyes and made sure he was paying attention. "As soon as we found out which world you and your brother went to, I came to find you and bring you home. I was sent back in time as a human so that I would be in the right place at the right time to find you both."

"You were Ms. Warren all along?"

His mother's face was a mix of love and amusement. "Yes, and you are grounded for sneaking out and robbing that museum."

Dalen had barely begun to understand what she had said, and being grounded derailed his entire thought. "Wait, what?"

"I mean... I can't believe you would do that and just not even come home. Your brother covered for you well, but now that you know the truth about me, I imagine you know I could tell."

They both laughed and this time, it was Dalen who hugged her.

"Thank you. Mom." He held her close, and through the connection of their Heartstones, they once again could deeply feel how important this was to each of them.

She almost cried but just nodded and patted him on the shoulder. "We were meant to return once the year was over, and I could take you both without anyone being suspicious. Then you were both going to be told everything, but DeSalvo had other plans. Dalen, do you know the difference between you and DeSalvo?"

"I am a jinn, and he is a genie," Dalen responded, not sure where this line of questioning was going.

"Yes. But he once was a jinn, as were all genies. The difference I speak of is that DeSalvo would have never let go of the stone. He is so afraid he's not enough; he wouldn't believe that he could be powerful without the power the stone wields, so he would probably never set it down. Even if doing so meant his freedom. The real power he hunts is the power you have already demonstrated. Your free will. Your ability to take the impossible steps."

"Yes, but I was trained to do those things." Dalen felt like he was disappointing her. "I'm sorry. I know that when you gave me a piece of your Heartstone, that meant that I had to believe in myself, and I did. I merged all three spheres and became one with myself. Even then, you were with me, and now I have to take another step, but no one will be there in case I fail."

She folded her arms and gave him a look that made him question his answer. "And now you think you are alone?"

"No." Dalen shrugged and made a gesture toward her. "You are here. Is that why you brought me to wherever this is? It's because you are going to teach me how to ignite the Inverted Reality Sphere?"

"I am afraid not." She smiled softly and stroked his hair. "I am here to help you through the last lesson you will ever need from those who trained you."

"I don't understand," Dalen said quietly.

"Just as Spring becomes Summer. Summer must also become Autumn. It is the way of things. Young birds leave the nest once they learn to fly." She laughed. "Sometimes they learn to fly on the way down once they are kicked out." She started walking toward the source of light and water. "I know it seems harsh, but living is not for the meek; they can do no more than merely exist." She stopped and studied Dalen. "To be a jinn is to be alive." She turned back and continued into the next room. "In this same way, it is time for you to leave the protection of your illusions. That nest no longer serves you. It now only stands as a reason to tell yourself you can't do it alone." She scoffed. "I'm here to push you out of the nest. I believe you are ready to fly. I guess we will find out together on the way down."

Dalen entered the room with his mother and saw what was casting the light. A giant crystal hung in the air, weightless. It gave off a beautiful blue light and filled the space with warmth; it was bright enough to see that there was another exit on the far side. Directly under the crystal was a pool of water that cast the light outward, creating beautiful ripples of light on the walls around it. In the center of the pool was a stone that held five blades.

Dalen blinked his eyes a couple of times to make sure he saw what he thought he saw. He had been here once before. "This is the Heart of Venger."

"It is. Those are the four Elemental Blades and the visage of the blade known as Dorn's Promise. It's a weapon beyond this world and is only created when the elemental blades form the Horn of the Unicorn and the Eye of the Dragon; only when all four blades are present will Dorn's Promise appear."

Dalen turned to her and asked, "Why are we here?"

"The pool around the blades is a natural residue from the crystal. It is the essence of the jinn, and with it, one has the ability to see through all illusions, do you know what they call it?"

Dalen knew the answer as she spoke the words. He was here. He had made it. "The Fountain of Truth."

"Indeed, it is." She put her hand against Dalen's lower back and pushed him towards it. "You need to know the truth."

Dalen started to walk toward the Fountain of Truth but then turned back and asked, "What am I supposed to ask?"

She cocked her head and smiled sarcastically. "How do you expect to understand the answer if you can't even think of the question? Make wise choices. You only get to ask it one question right now."

Dalen looked over at her with an unsure look. "Right now?"

His mother nodded. "If everyone does their part and nothing else gets changed, you will be here once more after you and your friends save the world. It is then you will ask the question that matters most, and in the end, it will be the most important question you will ever ask in your lifetime."

"Yeah? And what question is that?" barked Dalen.

She scoffed. "Well, if you are going to go about it like that, then I am going to make this short and sweet." She walked up right behind him as if she were going to leave and kissed the back of his head. "I believe in you."

Dalen panicked. "I'm sorry. I didn't mean to make you mad. Don't leave me to do this alone."

She took him by the shoulders and gently turned him around. "What kind of divine being would I be if I lost my cool over you merely being afraid and taking it out on me?" She scrunched up her mouth and looked up and to the left like she was thinking about something. "What kind of mother would I be, for that matter, too." She kissed him right on the forehead. "I lost you for years. I'll never leave you like that."

Something happened in Dalen that he wasn't expecting. Some part of his soul that was still a seventeen-year-old foster kid who never knew his real parents and never knew if they truly cared about him needed to hear that. Years of walls built to hold him up splintered, and a rush of emotion that he had long since forgotten came to the surface.

Dalen's mother caught him as he slumped to the floor, and they sat in the light of the Heart of Venger while she let him cry, stroking his hair as he wept in her lap. Her heart and his were connected, and she felt the years of pain and a sense of abandonment wash over them. "Don't fight it, Dalen. I'm here."

Within the center of his heart, he could feel her with him, as memories of being alone in dark places and sounds of anger filled his mind from an early past he could not quite remember. More intense emotions flooded in as he remembered always being an outcast, different than others. Echoes of voices from his life, telling him he was weird or different, reverberated through his thoughts.

Dalen's mother held him and tried to hold back her own emotions as she felt her child's pain firsthand. "Being alone was the fire that burned you, but it was also the fire that forged you. You only had you, so you saved yourself."

Dalen felt defeated. "I don't understand!" It was in that moment of declaring his truth that he made his choice, and Dalen Pax knew what he needed to ask.

The Fire Jinn's words kept echoing in his head. It was the question she told him to ask at the statue. The same question that he asked when he found the Heart of Stone, and now, the question was the only thing on his mind. He got up and started walking toward the Fountain of Truth. His mother could feel his resolve, and she knew in her heart he was ready to fly.

Dalen reached into his garb and removed his cup. He was going to miss his mint tea, but that enchantment could always be restored at Dorn's. He dipped it into the pool and then raised it to the Heart of Venger, then to the Elemental Blades. He then turned to his mother and gave her a bow of respect.

Tears poured from his eyes, and he had no idea if he was right, but he was ready.

"I was trained by three different jinn. One taught me to move. One taught me to think, and one taught me how to connect to all of it. I was told by many that this is where I would see them again. Yet here I stand alone." He turned back around and raised his cup to the fountain. "Why? Why was I trained by these jinn, and where are they now?" Dalen poured the liquid into his mouth. As he swallowed it, he could tell that it was much thicker than water, and it ran down his throat as if he had taken a shot of maple syrup.

Dalen had no recognition of the room he had been in or the events that were taking place elsewhere. All he could see were the flashes of his life that the Fountain of Truth decided to show him.

He was in the lower part of the museum right after he had first activated the Beads of Fire, and the jinn appeared. She looked at him and said, "Dalen, I am going to need you to focus on this moment, and yes, if you tried to run, I would be there." Her voice was soothing, but the idea that the jinn could read his mind terrified him. The Jinn glided right next to him and began to stroke his hair. "You see, I am not here physically. The Beads of Fire are allowing your mind to make a connection to me, and as long as you wear them, I am also connected to you..."

Dalen realized that the Fountain of Truth was delving into his mind and using his own memories to answer his question. The scene fazed and went blurry, and when it refocused, the Fire Jinn was standing directly in front of Dalen.

She looked him in the eye and said, "My friend, I am not a corporeal being. I do not have a physical form. What you are seeing is the closest thing your mind can perceive to what is truly happening. The picture of what you see is an image being drawn into your mind one frame at a time." She raised a sarcastic eyebrow. "Now pay attention because this is where it gets fun. Being an incorporeal being, I do not actually have a form. If I did, I would imagine it to be close to a maelstrom of light and smoke that can shift from being smaller than an insect to larger than your sun." Dalen's mind flashed for only a moment to the storms within Master Truth's stones. "Your mind can't perceive that I'm talking to you in this room, so it has to create from its own imagery, much like when you dream. Which brings me back to my point. This is not what I am. This is what you imagine me to be."

The memory that the Fountain of Truth was using changed again, and Dalen was standing in his training circle. It was the first day of his training. The Fire Jinn was standing by, but she just stood there waiting for him.

"You aren't actually here." Dalen's words echoed in his mind.

"So?" The fire Jinn asked simply.

"So, I am the only one actually here."

The Jinn smiled. "You're two for two."

"Since I am the only thing that may very well be real here, it is going to have to be me that makes the choices." Dalen didn't really believe it until he heard himself say it aloud. "I have to teach myself how to do magic. You are only here to help me when I have questions."

She nodded. "That is correct."

"Is this how you learned it?"

"This is how it is learned."

The memory changed again, and he was at the Temple of Light. It was his first day, and he had been sent into a training room to be trained by Master Ki. When he first arrived there, he didn't see Master Ki, so he walked around the room for a bit until he began to pay closer attention to his environment and started to look inward toward the center of the room. His eyes caught a glint of something that was lying on the grass mat. When Dalen walked over to it, he noticed that there was a set of prayer beads that were almost identical to the Beads of Fire, with the exception that they looked as if they were made of drops of water. Dalen knelt on the grass mat facing another larger mat and wrapped the Beads around his wrist. When the jinn rose from the basin and formed in the shape of a humanoid with no distinguishing features, it spoke, "You passed your test."

The world flashed, and Dalen was aware of his surroundings once more. "Yes," Dalen called out. "I know that they were incorporeal, so they weren't actually there."

"Yes, but were we?" Dalen turned around just in time to have the Fire Jinn scoop him up in her arms and twirl him around two or three times.

After she set him down, he looked around and saw that not only was she there, but Master Ki and Master Truth were there as well. Dalen smiled and gave them collectively a bow. "It is good to see all of you."

"It's good to be seen," said Master Ki.

"Where did you go?" Dalen asked them. "After I got the Heartstone, you vanished."

"Going somewhere suggests a physical form. Are you suggesting he went somewhere?" asked Master Truth.

"That's not what I meant, Master Truth." Dalen felt a little ganged up on. "I just meant you were no longer perceived, and I wish to understand why."

"This is a big one." said the Fire Jinn. "You know how whenever there are moments where everything you know gets tossed out, and you now have to start fresh with a new truth, I show up?"

"Yeah," Dalen answered cautiously.

"Yeah." She gave a friendly grin and waved. "Hi."

"You know how when you needed to be able to understand those truths, you and I would sit and talk," said Master Truth.

"Remember when I would then show you how to act upon those truths?" asked Ki.

"Yes."

The Fire Jinn shrugged. "Your mom was right. The fires that burned you were also the fires that forged you. You only had you, so you saved yourself. Dalen, in all of those moments, you were alone."

The world flashed, and he was standing in the courtyard of the Temple of Light on the last day of his training. Master Ki had created four Elementals for Dalen to face and learn to overcome. The Elementals were in the shape of Dalen's understanding of each Natural Element. Earth, Fire, Water, and Air. They took the shape of Master Ki, Ms. Warren, Master Truth, and the Fire Jinn. He had tried to just survive the attack at first, but he got in a few good hits before the four of them had beaten him to the ground. That's when he heard the voice whisper to him, "Dalen, you are alone in the courtyard."

After that, the combatants no longer looked like the jinn; they looked like him. Dalen won that fight because, at that moment, Dalen came to understand that each of the elementals were just aspects of himself. His eyes shot to Dorn's Promise. The blade that only exists when the other four elements are in harmony.

Dalen turned his gaze back to the three jinn. "Dalen." Master Ki said as he held up his cup in toast. "We... I have been with you since the beginning of all of this. "Body..."

Master Truth raised his cup and said, "Mind..."

The Fire Jinn held up her cup and said, "And Soul."

Together, they took a sip in single harmony, and Dalen realized that they all had the same kind of cup. His mind flashed to moments at Dorn's, sitting at one of the booths talking to the Fire Jinn. He had just glanced away for a moment, and when he looked back, she had a small cup with her that continued to fill on its own as she took small sips from it while they talked. Then it flashed to Master Ki training him in the courtyard and how he would pull a cup from seemingly nowhere and take small sips off it while he taught. The memory melted, giving way to another, and Dalen found himself having tea with Master Truth. Every morning, he would bring an extra cup for Master Truth while they talked in the morning. He remembered that although he never took the corporeal cup, he always had one as they sipped tea together and talked.

When he was training at the Temple of Light, the Fire Jinn was gone. Dalen thought that he no longer had the Beads of Fire, but they appeared on his wrist when he made the Leap of Faith, and later, at the Temple of All Faith, she claimed that she had never left him. While he was at the Temple of Light, he spent his mornings talking with Master Truth about truths and philosophies and then the rest of the day with Master Ki to work his body, but they were never at the same place at the same time.

It was so obvious to him now that he knew what to look for. It was the same. Always had been. "The three of you are one Jinn. None of those images were really you; they were always just images of what I needed to understand at the time. The elemental nature of the change I was going through. Fire when it was big and life-altering. Air, every time I needed to comprehend a new understanding and embrace it as truth. Water, throughout this journey, helps me remember that even though I have changed my form, the essence of who I am is still me. I was looking at each of you through me. Even my mother I see as Ms. Warren because Earth is connected to Mother, and Warren is the only person I can picture in that role.”

“Warren was a wish made by your mother. It was the closest thing to being there herself that she could do. Once they figured out where you and your brother had gone, she wished for a human version of herself to be sent to that world to find you. She believed she would have a better chance of finding you because she was your mother.” Master Truth explained. “She does not look like Warren. Warren looks like her. But as for the rest, I am proud of your grasp of why you have perceived us as three different beings, and each of us an Element of Change.

Dalen folded his fingers and put them on the back of his head. “I wish to see you for who you really are. I want to meet the jinn who has been my best friend: Mind, Body, and Soul.”

“As you wish.” said the fire jinn. “But remember, you asked for it.”

Dalen’s eyes began to burn as if something was being washed away from them with magic fire. The three of them moved together and formed a single being. There was so much light coming off him that Dalen couldn’t see who it was. He squinted and tried to block the glare with his hand.

“Still refuse to see me?” It was the same voice from the courtyard at the Temple of Light. “Perhaps there is another truth you’re having trouble looking at. Perhaps you need another drink.”

Dalen looked down at his cup, and flashes of gaming with his friends in the world where he came from moved through his eyes, while others drank soda or coffee, he always sat there sipping tea. His memories flashed to the courtyard, where he had tea each morning. He watched himself talk aloud to the morning and sip tea by himself. Even as he spoke with Gnomon and taught her, he took small sips of his tea.

"Dalen." The voice said. "You are alone even now."

Dalen remembered speaking with Master Truth at the beginning of this quest. Master Truth said, "I see a moment in time. It is a beautiful moment when everything comes full circle, and you come to know who you truly are. That moment will help define you for the rest of your days."

"This is it. This is that moment!" Dalen shouted aloud in shock. It's me!" He looked at the cup. He quickly put his hand over it and turned it over. Then, hurriedly put it away. "It's me." He looked back at the other person in the room and looked himself in the eyes in disbelief. "Is it really...?"

"You?" The other version of Dalen asked rhetorically. "Indeed. May I introduce myself properly after all this time? I am Dalen Pax. Master of Time."

"How is this even possible?"

"The Beads of Fire." He answered simply like his answer was supposed to answer all of Dalen's questions. "What they did was raise your perception high enough to hear the jinn within you. They are a part of what it means for us to be a jinn and only would have ever worked for us and us alone. It would have done nothing for Adam or Becky." The new version of Dalen sat there patiently waiting for Dalen to grasp what was being told to him, and the moment he thought he comprehended, The Master of Time continued. "So, when they were activated, you were put in contact with your own soul."

"My soul?" Dalen was barely hanging on to reality.

"Yeah, but your mind had no idea how to perceive it, so it created something you could understand. It was a life-altering moment, so as the name suggests, the beads changed your perception through the element of fire, so you saw a Fire Jinn."

"Why is my soul a girl?"

"Fire is often connected to the feminine, and also..." He laughed at the memory. "You were a seventeen-year-old, straight male. Of course, you envisioned a hot girl, and to be fair, you were told a few times that she wasn't a girl."

"She said she didn't have gender."

"Your soul does not."

"What about Ki and Truth?

What about them? he asked.

"Was any of it real?" Dalen began to feel loss as if they had died. "They were my friends."

The other Dalen took a deep breath in and let it out from his nose. "They are my friends too. They have been a part of who I am for a long time now. A long time. The same way that they are a part of you."

"So, I can see them again?"

"You are them, and they are you. The three of them are your Tin Soldiers."

"Yeah?"

"Yeah!" The newer Dalen shared a memory from his past, and at the same time, Dalen felt he received a download of the future. At one point in Dalen's existence, he goes back to the beginning of this world, and he creates the Temple of Light. and on that day, the very first day of time, he takes the rank of Grand Master and begins to prepare the temple to one day become the place of learning and enlightenment that it becomes. "The same way we are Brother Truth and Father Light, and the Reality Bender... We are also Master Ki, Master Truth, and the Fire Jinn."

"You still call her that?" Dalen asked.

"No, but I I'm not going to spoil everything."

He gave a nudge into Dalen's shoulder. "Speaking of spoilers, I am going to help you with the Inverted Sphere, but first, I want to do something before this vision ends, and you will be back with Mother.

He bent down and looked at eye level to the pin I gave Dalen to wear. "Hello, Will. Much Love. At one point in everyone's life, there are certain things that they wish they could go back and tell the younger version of themself. This... This right here... Is my one real chance. It's personal. It's private, and I am sure you understand." He waved goodbye to the pin. He took a deep breath in and warped time in a way where I was unable to see or hear what was said in those precious few moments. It is a secret kept in time.

Well played, brother.

The fountain finally released Dalen from his vision, and Dalen found himself still staring at the fountain. He turned to his mother with tears in his eyes. "Mother, I know."

"Then fly, my son. Fly from the protection of the nest and spread your wings." She gave him a hug and kissed him on the forehead. "Now go forth from here, and remember," She touched her Heartstone, and Dalen's responded. "You will never be alone again."

Dalen gave his mother a cognizant look of understanding. "As you wish." He closed his eyes and released his hold on the quantum space that was allowing him to split himself into two places at once. His entire being reconnected to the physical location he was still experiencing as fire bloomed from the volcano.

21

TRYING TO NOT
BE REAL

"Are you ready for this?" asked the Fire Jinn

Dalen looked away from the volcano and focused on the trio of jinn who were with him in his moments of triumph or defeat, and Dalen knew that they would be with him for every step of this journey. He only needed to look inward. "Mind, Body, and Soul."

"Do not doubt yourself. Choose the flow and then relent to the current." Encouraged Master Ki.

Master Truth gave Dalen a bow that was normally reserved for masters. "The only challenge left is yourself."

"If I had a gold coin for every time that was true."
All three of the jinn laughed at Dalen's joke. Some more than
others. "I'm ready."

In unison, the three greatest teachers in Dalen's life
gave him a nod. Took a sip from their cups and tauntingly
commanded, "Show me."

Time was moving at a normal speed, and Dalen could
now feel the heat from the volcano. "Why couldn't I feel the
heat before?"

"What heat?" asked the Fire Jinn.

"The heat from the volcano," Dalen explained. "When I
first arrived, I didn't notice it."

"I hadn't noticed." The Fire Jinn, in classic form, gave
him a devilish grin and raised one eyebrow.

Dalen stopped long enough to give the Fire Jinn a double
take. "You got jokes?"

"Did you catch the one where I am a figment of your
imagination, so I am not really here and can't actually feel the
heat, or did you get the joke about how I am made of fire?"
She flared up a bit to highlight the joke.

"Both. You're hilarious." His breathing was short, and he
had to catch his breath. The air was so hot it made it difficult
to breathe. He could feel the heat coming from the ground, and
he knew that the soles of his boots were beginning to melt.
"Well, the part of you that is me is roasting alive."

"You didn't notice it before because you weren't here long enough to heat up. Now that time is moving normally, you are slowly cooking. I suggest you hurry up and go incorporeal before you die." She was slowly floating around him in a big circle like she used to. "Would a big giant death clock help?"

Dalen looked at her like she was insane. "No." Dalen shook his head and laughed. "Why would you ask such a thing?"

She pointed out toward the volcano. A dragon had spotted him and had started a trajectory to intercept.

That all too familiar feeling of abject fear grabbed Dalen by the spine. His limbs locked up, and he could do nothing but stare at his impending doom. "Bibitz!"

Master Ki took Dalen's face in both hands and made Dalen look at him. "Marvel at it from the other side. Act now or die."

Dalen took a quick breath in. He pictured himself awakening his divinity. He allowed that image to be the filter of his perception. He grounded himself, directly connecting to the world. The idea was that once he inverted the field, this grounding, this connection to the earth, should help him break free from this reality. As he permeated the ground with his essence and focused, the ground shifted, and seven colored stones of power erupted from it, creating the elements of his casting circle.

"You're doing great." The Fire Jinn wasn't watching him. She had her eyes on the dragon.

Dalen reached out and connected to the Divine Elemental field that was present all around him and pulled it in close. As he did, he focused the divine energy with his ki and moved it through the field of his intent. Once it passed through his vision of what was to be, Dalen channeled all of it using his ki, and with a single strike into the ground, he sent it out. The center stone lit up, and then the six elemental stones, and as they activated, a blast of magic energy rippled out in a circle that expanded into the horizon like a white ring of light.

"Pretty!" squealed the Fire Jinn.

"Yes," said Master Ki. "Do it again. This time, draw the energy back to you."

Dalen looked over at the dragon to see how close it had gotten. It had cleared a third of the distance. It roared with fury as it pulled in its wings to gain speed.

"Tell me, Dalen." Master Truth's words were calm. "Does the dragon have anything to do with what you are trying to do?"

Dalen turned his focus to Master Truth. "If I don't get this in time, it's going to kill me."

Master Truth took a sip from his cup and said, "Then it only has to do with your failure. You need to stop worrying about what happens if you fail and pay attention to the actual thing you are doing, which is succeeding. Stop... focusing... on the dragon."

Dalen listened and wiped the dragon and all of the

terrible things that would happen if he failed from his mind. He grounded himself again and then reconnected to the Divine Element. He sent it through his thoughts and then into the ground. It lit up the stones and rippled out like a ring of light.

"Stay connected to it," shouted Master Ki, and Dalen held his connection. He could feel it as it expanded across the landscape. Dalen quickly thought to himself that doing this alone could be a useful tool to search a large area because he was grounded; he was connected to everything the ring of light touched. "Yes." Master Ki interrupted. "It works well but give that thought its respect at a different time. Stay focused. Now, draw the energy back to you."

Dalen did as Master Ki commanded, but when the energy returned to him, it channeled right through him and went back to the source.

"Damn it!" Dalen screamed.

Master Truth was still as calm as ever. "You can sit and be mad about it, or you can survive; there is not time to do both."

Dalen could hear the dragon's wings as they cut through the air. He could hear its roar and feel its presence.

The three of them looked at Dalen and exclaimed in unison, "Do it now!"

Dalen's focus shifted, and he became one with what he was doing. The energy reached out for him in anticipation of his moves. His mind was clear, and he knew what he had to do.

The ripple he sent out was perfect, and in his mind, he agreed with the Fire Jinn. It was beautiful. He flipped his polarity and pulled it back to him; it obeyed with great swiftness. The outer stones of the casting circle ignited, sending a wave of energy that sparked the one in the center that Dalen was standing on. This time, as the magic moved through him, he opened up his chakra point that was connected to the Divine Element and channeled all of the energy through it and into his Heartstone.

The dragon snapped his jaws shut around Dalen, and he flew right through him. Dalen let out a scream as he squatted down and cowered as the entire dragon passed through him.

"Yes!" Dalen screamed as it dawned on him that he didn't die and threw both fists into the air.

The Dragon pulled up quickly and circled around. Dalen could see the energy of its soul illuminating through its body. It was by far one of the most beautiful and impressive things he had ever experienced in his life. A dragon may be terrifying, but its soul was a brilliant construct of light that flew in the air, and it reminded Dalen of an angel. It landed in front of the Tree of Travel and spoke directly at it, thinking that whoever had been there used it to escape.

Dalen was no longer in any danger, but the sheer size of this gargantuan being still caused him reason to back away from it. Its head was the size of a full-grown mammoth, and its voice shook the ground as he spoke. "That's right. Run, little one." Its voice was low and rolled like thunder. It snapped its teeth directly in front of the tree. "You are not welcome here, and if you come again, I will kill you."

It stood there for a moment, waiting to see if someone was going to return. Its energy was bright red, but as it sat there, it calmed and started to become orange. The entire time, Dalen was just a few feet away, and the dragon made no indication that it was aware of Dalen's presence.

Dalen slowly looked around. Instead of finding his friends, the jinn had once again all formed into a single being that would be future Dalen. "Thank you for all that you have taught me."

"I had a brilliant student." They both laughed at the fourth-dimension humor of it. "Remember what I told you, and remember, the masters are never gone. They live within you."

"I won't forget, and I'll keep my promise and do it the way you suggested."

"I know it sounds crazy to go that way, but... here I am. Proof that it works."

"Wait!" Dalen called out before the other vanished. "What is the question that I need to ask the next time I get to the Fountain? What is the one question that will shape my life and be the most important question I will ever ask?"

"Do you think I would really tell you that?"

"No."

"Well, you are wrong." He laughed. "When you get there, you will only be allowed one question, like last time. Ask how to save David."

"That question changes my life?"

"No." He waved and started to fade out of time. "The answer does."

Dalen waved back. "Some other time."

. . .

It was time for Dalen to stand on his own. He found himself alone at the foot of the volcano. He was incorporeal now, and the heat no longer bothered him. He also realized he was no longer breathing, but he could if he chose to. He looked at his hands and stretched his fingers. It was different in hundreds of little ways that were hard to describe, such as there was no actual physical sensation of touch, yet he could feel things and a sense of being detached. Dalen thought that it felt like he was dreaming.

Dalen was on the Eastern side of the volcano. Since the passage was on the southwest, he decided to travel around it in a clockwise direction. Propelling himself while corporeal had to do with moving himself, a physical self, through a three-dimensional space. However, in this state, it was a different beast altogether. Moving now had to do with propelling himself to where he envisioned himself to be. He would look to a particular location and choose to be there. When he did that, he instantly appeared there. He tested this three or four times but decided that it was too jarring and disorienting, and he wanted to find a better way to go about it.

He began slowly. He floated around in a small circle. He kept his sight on one location but used his memory of movement and flight that he had learned since he created his Heartstone. His mind quickly adapted after a couple of failures, and eventually, he figured out how to move. It almost seemed to be the reverse of what was normal. Normally, he would move, and then his senses would acknowledge it. He would walk or run to a certain location, and his body would accept the new space. Now, he had to move his perspective first; then, the movement would catch up. He would think of himself at a location, and his incorporeal form would move him to match this new perception.

Once he was able to maneuver around, he began to move in the direction he needed to go. At first, as he began to move forward, he looked too far forward to see what was coming; this caused him to instantly jump to that location, which always ended with him at a dead standstill. He would look around to reorient himself, but that failed miserably because every time he looked in any direction, he would instantly be at that location. A few times, he ended up too close to the volcano and found himself wading in lava and being very thankful that he had nobody to burn.

Once, while he was trying to stop bouncing around everywhere, he just looked straight up into the sky and found himself hovering over the entire volcano and in the direct flight path of a dragon. He balled himself up and braced for an impact that didn't come, but Dalen was given the complete tour of the inside of a dragon as it flew through him for the second time that day.

"I have got to stop doing that." He shook off the ickiness of the whole ordeal and decided to make a quick return to the ground.

He began again. Slowly, at first. About the speed of a walk. Once he was able to maintain that, he moved it up to about a run. After his last few attempts, he figured out that it had to do with the mind sphere because he no longer had a body to speak of on the physical plane. Dalen was going to have to rely on the Imagination Element. The power of his observer. He could observe the environment around him, but once he specifically looked at something directly and his focus was given to that location, his mind would center on it. He had to remind himself that he actually wasn't there. He was just moving his conscious around.

Dalen began to pick up speed, and he reached a place where a small event horizon formed. Once anyone is moving fast enough, there is a difference between where the ground appears to be moving and the space where the ground appears to be static. There is an edge line where these two spaces, the static and the moving, meet. Dalen concentrated on that exact spot. As he did, he realized that he could move that horizon line to regulate his speed. He used the connection to the mind sphere to manipulate where the horizon line was at any given time. If he moved the line farther, the faster he would go. Closer, and he would slow down. and if he just observed the ground beneath him, he would stop, hovering slightly above the ground.

He laughed and threw his fists in the air victoriously. "Okay, Dalen. Let's try this again." He looked right at the ground below him and then pushed the horizon line forward and took off.

He let out a scream of joy and leaned into the ride. He didn't know how fast he was going, but he knew it was faster than he had ever gone before. The terrain flew past him, and it almost seemed to him that the volcano that stayed to his right side was slowly revolving.

He had just about mastered his movement when he came upon a dead tree. The directions said that he was to stop there. The oracles had given Dalen a magical rod that was to be planted into the ground once Dalen arrived at this landmark. It was a teleportation anchor in the corporeal world, and once activated, Dalen's friends would be able to join him at that location. A special casting circle had been prepared for them back at the cave by the Oracles so they could bamph to him from such a far distance safely.

As Dalen approached the tree, he began to feel a sadness creep into his heart. Once he stopped moving toward it, his suspicions were confirmed, examining the tree through a magic vision, he could see that a great sadness had been imbued into the tree.

Returning to the physical world was easier than he thought. The hard part had been learning to invert the field. To get back to his former self, all Dalen needed to do was reignite the standard Reality Field within himself, and his body became corporeal.

The moment he became corporeal and was standing in front of the tree, he recognized that exact instance as the memory he saw at Dorn's. He had found The Tree of Sadness. He had almost forgotten about the image until he was standing in front of it. The sadness throbbed from it in waves, and Dalen had to focus to be able to think through the pain that was tearing his heart apart. He was surprised that the Oracles would tell him to summon his friends here. On the other hand, any closer to the Pillar of Time and they would face protection put in place to guarantee that no one could just bamph to it. This tree was the marker for as close as you could teleport in, so Dalen found his balance, drove the rod into the ground, and reactivated his pin.

22

THE TREE OF SADNESS

‹There you are.› Becky's voice was filled with concern. ‹That took a lot longer than you thought.›

Dalen refocused his spheres and was able to ward off the effects of the Tree of Sadness enough to function, but he had to be diligent. The sadness of this tree was ever trying to penetrate his soul. ‹ It's much harder than I thought. Got some help from some old friends.›

‹You found Master Ki?› asked Peace.

‹Yes. I found all of them.› His heart began to burst. He missed the Fire Jinn so very much. ‹Damn tree.› he recentered himself again. ‹ That's a story for when I can think about it without succumbing to this accursed weeping willow. Listen, coming here, you're coming in hot; the Tree of Sadness is no joke. Prepare yourself.›

‹Acknowledged.› Travis's thoughts were coming through, and Dalen could tell he was already trying to prepare his mind.

Adam bamphed in. As he appeared, he clutched at his heart for a moment. "Damn." He dropped to one knee. He began to cry. It wasn't some sappy blubbering, nor did he merely weep. He just knelt there, and tears fell like rain.

Becky bamphed in next, followed by Travis. It seemed to hit Travis harder than Becky as they clung to each other.

"I don't like this place. It feels like death." Travis said. His voice was weak and almost a whisper.

Becky was maintaining, but those words broke her heart, and she began to cry into Travis's shoulder.

It did feel like death. This tree was not just filled with sadness but a sadness that came from deep loss. This tree had been cursed somewhere in time with such a powerful sense of pain and loss that it echoed through time and space itself. It's said that the pain and sadness actually came from another timeline, one that had been destroyed because of this great loss. The sorrow was so powerful that even when new timelines were created and the world rewrote itself, the pain remained.

Peace arrived and surveyed the situation. All of them were locked in the grips of the tree. He could feel the sadness, but he had gone through his 'Dark Night of the Soul.' Sadness, despair, and loss were old friends of his.

Brother Peace went over to Adam. He got down on one knee so he could look him in the eye. He slowly reached over, and with two fingers under his chin, he lifted Adams's head. "Sir Adam?" Adam looked up and met Peace's eyes. "These... These are the moments you live for. I am going to need you to stand up now... Sir Adam." Brother Peace watched as Adam picked up the mantle, and Sir Adam of Venger rose to his feet. Peace swatted him on the arm. "Good man."

Sir Adam nodded and said, "Thank you."

Brother Peace looked over to Dalen. He was staring at the tree and whispering something to himself. He moved closer and listened.

"It's my fault," he said. "I brought them here. It's all my fault."

Brother Peace took Dalen by the shoulders and turned him away from the tree. Dalen blinked a couple of times and then looked at Brother Peace. "It is not whether or not you fall." It was a teaching from the Temple of Light that they both knew. Peace got through, and he and Dalen spoke the other half of the lesson together. "It is whether or not you get back up."

Dalen took a deep breath and nodded. "Thank you, Peace. I needed that."

"It's what we do." Peace smiled and gave Dalen a bow. Then he moved to Travis and Becky. "Travis. I can feel the sadness and the loss, too, but do you know what?" Travis looked up at Peace. Peace smiled at him and put one hand on his shoulder. "Nothing is permanent. Everything is here for only a short while. That is what makes it precious. That's what gives it worth. Do not focus on the loss; focus on the worth. Live every moment like it matters because tomorrow is not promised."

"Travis's eye welled up, but he nodded and began to try
to pull himself out of the dark cave he had allowed himself to
wander into.

Peace switched hands and touched Becky's shoulder. She
looked up with tears in her eyes. "You are standing in front of a
cursed tree that is affecting you emotionally; what do you do?"

"I don't know?" her brains were pudding. The sorrow and pain
were a lot, but then to see Travis cry had been too much. They had
been feeding off each other, and Becky went deep down.

"Everyone tells me that you are the one to go to when there
is a puzzle to be solved." She tried to look away, but very gently,
he turned her head back to face him. "Don't run from this. Stay
with me. What do you do?"

"I don't know!" She screamed at him. She let go of Travis
and faced off against Peace. "Look! Right now, I am in no shape to
answer any kind of puzzle. I am so broken right now; my whole world
is darkness!"

Peace didn't flinch. He remembered living that over and over
again. Master Love had been working with him on his healing, but
when they got close to something that was still raw, he would lash
out and scream at her, but she understood, just like he understood
now. It was during that time his teacher taught him about making
a Tin Soldier. Something that was still him, but stronger and able
to withstand the pain and sadness that he could not, so he could
have a clear head so that he could solve his puzzle... himself. That's
when he started being Brother Peace.

"Do you know who has no pain to draw from and is amazing in the darkness?" Becky said, and he watched her get her hood ready to pull up.

Brother Peace took a step back, looked her in the eyes, and said with compassion, "You are right, but you can't just hide in the darkness. You are strong enough to face this without her. You, Becky. Even before all of this, you were the only one to be able to see me. I believe in you."

Becky nodded. She took a deep breath in and then gave a dirty look to the tree. "Remove the curse."

"What?" asked Brother Peace.

"I'm standing next to a cursed tree that is affecting all of us emotionally to the point we cannot function." She had to catch her breath. The sadness was unbearable, but she fought through it. "Remove the curse."

Peace nodded. "Excellent! How do we do that?"

Defiance shot across Becky's face. She swung around away from Peace and stared down the tree. She got real calm and smiled. She didn't lift her hood, but she tapped her pin, and Oubliette's voice whispered in Brother Peace's mind. ‹Heal the tree.›

The ball of light was in Brother Peace's hand before he turned, and it was growing in size as he approached the tree. The one thing he was not counting on was that the effects grew worse the closer to the tree he went. He got within ten feet of it when he stopped. Pain that he had not felt for almost three years crept up on him slowly.

When Ben first arrived at the Temple of Light, he had been broken by nine days of hell. He had been hurting for some time before that but believing he not only had killed Dalen with three of his friends, but also having to relive the next day over and over had become torture. Believing the entire time that he would never escape.

He began to relive those memories; he was unaware that the guilt and the sadness emanating from the tree had gotten to him. Memories of the beating that he gave Dalen played and replayed in his mind. Standing at the foot of the Tree of Sadness, Ben stood once more in the grips of what he had done. The light went out, and Ben just stood there, staring at the tree, with The Greatest Hits of his guilt playing over and over again, wreaking havoc in his mind and heart.

Then Ben heard Dalen's voice over the storm of sadness. "It is not whether or not you fall, Brother."

Ben forced his mind to remember his teachings. He forced his mind to remember what Master Love and told him. What was it? What had she said? It isn't whether or not you fall...

"It is whether or not you get back up!" Ben yelled at the top of his lungs, and Brother Peace took a step forward.

This is it, he told himself. This was the moment he had to make a choice about who he was and what he could do.

His light reignited, and Brother Peace took another step toward the tree.

It was almost unbearable as the pain and suffering from the

tree saturated him. He felt the pain and loss of friends who were beloved. He felt the hopelessness that came with knowing they all died because of him. He had failed them. He had led them here, and now all of them lay dead at his feet. All at once, it came to him. This was not his pain. This was not his sadness.

Brother Peace charged his Ki, and with a loud scream from the center of his being, the ball ignited into a white flame with blue tips, and Brother Peace took one more step toward the tree.

He was there, but the pain and sadness were overwhelming. He kept trying to focus on his training. The training that helped him find peace, but his memory kept fading in and out to this broken memory that was not his own, of killing everyone he knew and the absolute hopelessness that came with it. It forced him to remember his own pain about living forever in a loop, believing he had killed Dalen.

He had found peace with it. He had earned his name, but this magic was pushing him far beyond his resolve. It was using his memories of sadness against him, actively amplifying them supernaturally far beyond any truth, forcing him to have to find a new peace within himself, to be able to do what needed to be done.

He focused on his moment, the moment he had killed Dalen, and it echoed back into the tree. Whoever's pain he was feeling had been tricked into killing someone as well. He could feel the regret. He could feel the sense of betrayal. It wasn't his fault.

"It wasn't your fault." Master Love told him one day. "You were under a spell and forced into your action. If you had a choice, is it what you would have done?"

"No," said Ben. "I would have never taken it that far, but I was out of control."

"If it wasn't your fault, and you were tricked, then you need to find forgiveness."

"Dalen forgave me before I came here. It didn't help."

"The person who needs to forgive you now is you."

"How do I do that?"

"Let go of the pain and guilt that does not belong to you."

That was the moment that Ben began to find Peace.

Now, Brother Peace had to take his final step and truly let go of all of it and genuinely find peace within his heart and soul.

Dalen had been watching, and he could see something growing in Brother Peace. He watched as Brother Peace looked at the tree and said, "I don't know what you think you have done, but it wasn't your fault." Brother Peace took a deep breath. "I free you of this prison of pain and suffering." Brother Peace brought the ball of light up, and he placed it against his forehead. "You are forgiven." Master Peace took one more step forward and touched the tree with his light.

The light expanded, and Peace and the tree were engulfed in a light too bright to look at. Dalen looked at them with his third eye. Peace was holding the orb against the tree. He, the orb, and the tree were pulsating with golden light in ripples that flowed from them and pulsed out into every corner of existence.

It was over. Sir Adam's heart released, as did Travis's, Dalen's, and Oubliette's. Each of them breathed a sigh of relief and release.

Master Peace stood staring at the tree. He was out of breath, but he was catching it quickly. He reached out and touched the tree as a tear of true peace from within his heart welled up and rolled down the side of his cheek.

One by one, they joined him in a group hug.

"That was the Bibitz." Sir Adam said, and it made them all laugh. They needed it; all of them released in an explosion of laughter, and for the first time, the Tree of Peace and Forgiveness bloomed, and a shower of white flower petals fell all around them.

23

THE CAVE OF FEAR

With the amount of light that was expelled from the tree and the amount of magic that had been moved, Dalen was sure that the dragons would be coming to investigate immediately. "I wish we had more time to celebrate and Peace; congratulations, but we have to move. The instructions said the cave is nearby, and we have to find it before the dragons find us."

Dalen found it quickly, but when he called everyone to him, none of them could see it.

"Dalen, I believe you." Master Peace stared at the opening. "All I see is a rockface." He looked and squinted his eyes. "What do you see?"

"I see an opening to a cave. Ten feet across by eleven high." Dalen put two and two together and understood that there must be an illusion there. Being a Jinn, Dalen was somehow immune to it and could see right past it.

Master Peace must have come to the same conclusion because he just shrugged his shoulders and said, "Oh. Well, there you go." and walked forward at a normal speed.

Dalen watched Master Peace walk into the cave with no problem. Sir Adam, Travis, and Oubliette flinched as they watched their friend walk headlong into and through a rock wall. On the other side, Peace had turned to look back at what he just walked through.

"It's only an illusion looking in. I can see the four of you as if there was nothing there." He reached out his hand, trying to feel for anything.

"That is so creepy." Travis looked almost disgusted. From his point of view, fingertips were defusing out of the rock face; then, he visibly flinched as Master Peace's head popped out of the stone.

"Are you guys coming or what?" Peace stepped all the way out and turned sideways. As he looked out toward the volcano, his eyes widened, and his nostrils began to flare. "There is a dragon incoming. We have got to move Vengerians." Then he leaped with enough force sideways to completely disappear back into the stone face.

A roar echoed through the mountains; seconds later came another, and that one sounded closer. The dragon was close and closing in. Travis and Oubliette took that as an exit cue and walked through the illusion.

Dalen got in but noticed that Sir Adam didn't move. "What are you doing, man? A dragon is coming."

Sir Adam waved him off. "I want to see it."

"You want to see it?" Travis asked. "My god, man! The moments you live for, one day will be the moment you die for."

Sir Adam shot a look back toward Travis that he had never seen from him before. It was powerful, and the words he said he meant like nothing that Travis had ever spoken in his entire life. "There is no better way to die than in the act of living." He looked back up into the sky for a few more seconds, and then he took a quick step back as a shadow flew overhead, and another roar, like screeching thunder, shook the ground. "See. There I saw it." Adam stepped quickly through the illusion. "Okay. Yeah. Wow. That was a lot bigger than I had expected." Everyone could tell that Sir Adam had gotten closer than he had intended. He looked around at everyone and scoffed. "What? I am also not a fool."

The brothers laughed and then turned to look down the hallway. They all peered and stared into the inky black, nothing that was the cave of fears. They glanced at each other and took a deep breath.

"Remember, the instructions suggested that we have to keep moving forward. No matter what happens, the exit is directly in front of us." Travis was doing his best to sound confident and was doing a fairly good job.

They braced themselves for whatever was going to happen next and took a deep breath. "Strait forward," said

Sir Adam, and side by side, they stepped into the blackness. It was tangible, and they pushed through it like a thick black fog. Within three steps, they could see nothing. Nothing at all. They reached out for each other as if they were blind, calling out to each other.

Dalen watched while the team reached out into nothing. He looked around and saw that about sixty yards ahead was an opening, and Dalen could see light on the other side. Dalen guessed that, like the entrance, there were illusions at work that Dalen was oblivious to.

As the light poured in from the other side. It filled the natural hallway. Dalen could see the corpses of hundreds of people who had tried to reach the Pillar of Time but never made it through the Cave of Fear alive.

Dalen slowed down time until things moved at the speed of grass growing. It gave him the time he needed to try and figure out what happened to them. In the hopes that if he could figure out what killed these people, he could save his friends.

Dalen knelt and looked at one of the people who had met their fate in the cave. Whoever the man was, he had died some time ago, but it seemed his skin showed evidence of multiple deep cuts in his chest.

Dalen pulled out his teacup and activated it. He knelt there talking to himself, pondering different ideas about what could have taken place to have him end up with those wounds. "It could be a bunch of different things I guess. In the end, there is no way to be sure." He looked at a deep cut that went right through his chest. "This is probably how he died, but I have no idea why. How and why did you die?" Dalen took a sip from his cup, and as the thick liquid touched his lips, he remembered that his cup no longer had tea in it.

Truth, like magic, has a price. For most, the price of truth is simply a bell that can't be un-rung. For those who drink from the Fountain of Truth, the price is often accepting a world that has now been changed; for someone who steals the truth and drinks the water from the Fountain of Truth away from its source, there is another price to pay.

Dalen's eyes rolled back in his head as his muscles locked up and his body began to seize. It hurt, and it burned as the liquid from the Fountain of Truth took its toll on Dalen, who was drinking away from the source. He lost all control of time, and Dalen could hear the team calling out for one another as flashes of images passed through his head.

Travis reached out and grabbed Oubliette. She let out an audible scream that surprised Travis, and he let go, but Oubliette responded as if he had not. "Get it off me," she whispered and fell to the ground, slapping at whatever she saw; whatever it was, it was moving up her arm.

Becky was breathing too hard, and she couldn't see the thing that was crawling on her, so she pulled back her hood to see it. As she did, she wished she hadn't. The spider was the size of Travis's hand. It had black beady eyes set into a brilliant red body with long hairy legs that were propelling it toward her face. She panicked and screamed, "Spider!"

She fell to the floor, and Travis stumbled blindly at her, trying to find her by following the sounds of her screams. He found her, but she couldn't see him, and every time he touched her, she reacted as if another spider had crawled on her. She stared in fear at nothing except the monsters in her mind as she drew and extended her blades.

Dalen lay six feet away and could do nothing about Becky's screams while flashes of how the people in this cave died raced through his head. It was brilliant and horrific. The images projected by the cave created fear within people. It had played them against each other. No longer able to distinguish friend from foe, they would kill each other while they thought they were vanquishing their fears.

Travis couldn't find Becky; he felt along the ground blindly in the darkness, but her voice was getting further and further away. He had lost her. After everything, he had thought it was him that was going to die, and now, just after he had hope for the first time since this began, he had lost her. He touched something moving on the floor. She had screamed spiders; perhaps they had come back and now were after him. Travis backed up and pulled his bow.

Sir Adam was walking in a straight line. He heard the screams but didn't know if he could trust them. Their Vengerian pins wouldn't work so close to the Pillar of Time, which is why Dalen had everyone show up at the tree. He couldn't bamph to her to help; he didn't even know if the sounds he was hearing were really Becky or just the cave messing with him. They had agreed. No matter what, keep moving forward, and that was exactly what he was doing. His heart screamed at him to turn around and check on his friends. "How could you just abandon them?" it cried out to him in the darkness. "Your friends are dying, and you are going to sacrifice them all to save yourself. You are... no hero."

Master Peace was walking down the sidewalk of the city where he grew up. It was barely dusk, and all of the light had come on. He had missed these streets and shops while he had been at the Temple of Light. He breathed in deep, and it was just like he remembered. He knew right where he was. The next intersection was right next to the theater. It was right where...

His thoughts trailed off because he knew right where he was. This was the location where, when he was younger, he and three of his friends attacked and almost killed Dalen. As he remembered, he saw in front of him a young man by the name of Ben cross the street with his friends and begin to harass a street magician who was harmlessly doing magic tricks on the corner.

Master Peace continued to walk but watched the worst moment in his life play out in front of him. An image of Dalen stepped in to save the magician, and then the four of them turned on him. Then it got violent. They were filled with rage, and Master Peace remembered how bad it was going to be.

"You could do something about this." The voice felt like it came from within, but it hadn't, and when he listened closely, he could tell that the voice was not his own. "You could stop this from happening right now. You have wished you could many times. Here is your chance. If you act now, you can save Dalen, and more importantly, you can save yourself from the guilt and pain you suffered. If you do nothing, you will have to witness the entire event again, knowing you could have done something this time but chose to do nothing."

Master Peace smiled and shook his head. "Well done, but I am not impressed. Nice touch by trying to offer me the guilt of not saving him this time, but you have miscalculated. You play on memories of pain, but this moment is the beginning, and often the beginning is painful. It's what gets us to begin in the first place."

The image of Ben that had appeared had eyes that flashed with delight as he and his goons began to viciously beat and torture Dalen. "This is who you are", it snarled.

"That was never who I was." Master Peace placed his hands together in front of his heart and bowed as he continued to walk. "I have moved through pain and time to arrive at this moment, and in this moment, I am not that pain. I have become Master Peace, and this memory can no longer hurt me." The image faded into the inky blackness. "You are going to have to do better than that." From the blackness, a troll came into view, walking right alongside him. "There you go. That's terrifying."

Dalen's body finally let go. His head was throbbing, and he could barely move. Every muscle in his body was now cramping or burning from the tears they had taken while he convulsed. The fluid had given him his vision, but it was in his system now and coursing through his veins like fire. Dalen didn't have the energy to scream; he just lay there and burned.

The spider was in the darkness, but Travis could see it moving. It wriggled and flailed about. This monster was not going to get him like it got Becky.

Becky had problems of her own. A giant demonic frog had crawled from the darkness. Its tongue shot out and found its mark. As it pulled its tongue off her, she could see it had ensnared many spiders that were on her. She almost thanked it, but then it looked at her like she was its next meal and began to give a guttural croaking noise.

Sir Adam looked to his right and saw a monster come out of the darkness near him. It was all black and moved with the misty darkness of the cave, making it hard to see in any type of detail, but it was moving alongside him weaving in and out of sight. Its eyes shined in the darkness a deep red, and when it smiled at him, its teeth were broken and jagged. From deep in the darkness behind it, Sir Adam could hear the sound of hundreds of bees.

Dalen could see them but was in too much pain to speak. He couldn't focus enough to send a message telepathically, and there was a good chance that if he could, he would just send them his pain. He had poisoned himself. He knew it. He was dying, so all he could do was watch as Master Peace and Sir Adam, who were almost to the exit, began to stare at each other like they were preparing for battle. Sir Adam had warmed up his hand and was ready to pull his sword.

He had to do something, or he was going to end up like all of the other dead people here, and so were his friends. He rolled onto his back and looked up at the ceiling. He tried to reach out to the Divine field, but he was in too much pain and could not focus on healing himself.

Travis pulled an arrow from his quiver and fired it at the spider, and he would have hit it too, except after he fired it, the monster leaped to the left and out of the arrow's way. Travis was not going to lose sight of the monster that killed Becky, so he tracked it as it moved.

The frog demon peered into Becky's soul, and she wanted to hide. She pulled up her hood and tried to vanish into the darkness, but the demonic frog could still see her somehow, and it spit one of the spiders it had in its mouth at her.

Oubliette leaped to her right and landed with a body roll to keep herself low. It watched her as she moved, so she got her feet underneath her and prepared to launch herself at the demon on his next attack.

Dalen closed his eyes and fought through the pain as he grounded himself. His breathing was fading, but with what he could manage, he took a breath in and reached out to the Divine field. "All I'm asking for," he whispered, "is to help me save them."

The divine field relented, and Dalen could feel enough energy touch him to be able to take one action. He had no strength to hold it, so he let it move through him into the floor of the cave. "You can do this. You have to do this." He told himself. "Alright, Dalen Pax." His body began to convulse again and started to shut down. "Live or die."

With everything he had and a little he didn't, he pulled the magic back to him and went incorporeal. His pain started to subside, and his mind started to clear. He had made it, but was it in time?

Travis fired at Oubliette; she leaped over his shot and used the handles of her blades to swing her up higher. Her feet hit the ceiling, and she disconnected the handles as she changed her trajectory. Leaping from the ceiling, she launched herself at Travis with her blades pointed toward her intended target.

The monster you are fighting is each other. Dalen wasn't using the pins. He was just using his own connection to them, and he came in clearly without confusion of his meaning.

Sir Adam looked at the thing in the blackness. His hand was ready to draw his weapon. He could feel it want to.

Sir Adam. I'm telling you that's Master Peace.

Sir Adam had to make a choice. This could be a trap. Maybe this voice was trying to get him to lower his defenses. On the other hand, the monster had not attacked.

Master Peace had the same questions. Was it possible that the voice he now heard in his mind was Dalen and not some other trick? Was it possible this monster was Sir Adam?

Oubliette was in mid-air as the message came through, with both blades poised to be plunged into the demonic frog. She fell slowly in her mind, trying to decide what she was going to do, but even as slow as it was, there was no time to have a debate.

She put away her blades, and as Becky landed in front of the frog, she pulled back her hood and kissed him.

Master Peace ignited his ball and held it up to the troll. By its light, he could see through the illusion and saw Sir Adam.

Sir Adam smiled and said, "Hi, Peace. It's good to see you."

Master Peace focused his ki and channeled it into his dragon claw. The ball at the end of it grew brighter, and the light it was casting felt warm and safe. Keeping both of them in the light, they chose to go back for the others. Dalen directed them through the darkness. Faces of monsters pushed out of the darkness but shrank from the light as they moved. When they found Travis and Becky, she was still kissing him.

The light got her attention, and when she looked at who she was kissing, she saw Travis. "You turned into a prince." She smiled and kissed him again.

Sir Adam cleared his throat to make them stop. They did, and when they both looked at him, he said, "As Travis's brother, I would like to point out that this is the scariest thing I have seen in this cave."

Laughter ensued.

They huddled together and stayed within Master Peace's light as Dalen gave them directions and slowly moved them out of the cave.

Dalen could focus again, and while he led them out of the cave, he began to heal himself. By the time he could get them out, he was well enough to return to his corporeal state.

He was still in pain and poisoned, but Master Peace healed him completely once his body had returned to its full physical form.

The room they were in was a naturally formed cave that was heated by magma flow that moved slowly through the room, creating a moat between them and the other half of the room. The channel the magma was flowing through was twenty feet across, but the flow was low, so the magma itself was about eight feet lower than the edge. The room itself had many stalactites and stalagmites, and there were a couple of places where the two had come together to create pillars that were made of lava rock and obsidian. One of them was glowing and was the main source of the light in the room.

A pillar of light radiating magic in all directions. The Pillar of Time.

"There it is. All of us have to get to the other side." Dalen knocked on Sir Adams's armor. "You don't want to cook like a baked potato, so I don't suggest a swim. If you wish, I'll take you across. Sir Adam thanked him, and Peace requested a ride as well.

"It's going to be hot." Becky said, "If we just go over it quickly, we should be fine." Oubliette pulled up her hood, took a couple of running steps, and leaped out over the channel. She pulled out her handles and locked them into place. She swung only once and launched herself to the other side. When she landed, Becky pulled back her hood. "That was a lot hotter than I guessed. Peace, I think I am going to need you to heal me when you get across."

Travis pulled an arrow from his quiver. He fired it about three feet from Becky. As it stuck into the ground, it was gone, and Travis was standing where it had been. Dalen took Sir Adam and Master Peace by the hands and opened up the Quantum field. He moved them into superposition, and when he brought them back, they were on the other side. Becky had taken some heat damage from her maneuver, but it was well within the healing power of Master Peace.

Dalen heard his name called. He turned around to see DeSalvo standing at the entrance of the cave.

"DeSalvo." He said to warn everyone. "What do you want?"

"Where," asked Sir Adam.

At the entrance. Dalen sent telepathically. "What do you want?"

They looked but couldn't see anything.

Dalen could feel their confusion. *Are any of you still wearing the rings I gave you at the Temple of Light?*

"No," said Becky. "Once you explained that Master Ki was no longer talking to you, we decided to take them off."

That would explain why you couldn't see through the illusions in the cave. Dalen shook his head. *You might want to see this.*

Each of them put on their rings, and once they did, they could see DeSalvo as well. He was just standing on the other side, smiling at them. They had never seen him before and were not expecting to see the frail-looking old man dressed in black. His eyes had sunken in, and his face had been warped and deformed with darkness and pain. The only thing that had any color was the banner he wore over his left shoulder that hung to his knee in the front and back and looked like there was a rippling fire that ran the entire length.

"I said, what do you want," repeated Dalen.

"Dalen Pax," DeSalvo said acidly like he hated the words. "If you are listening to this and can see me, that means you have made your way to the Pillar of Time. Good." His smile was dark and twisted. "I am going to destroy everything that you have come to know and love in this world. Starting with Venger. The Time Mage and I are going to finish my master's work and destroy it all. If you want to stop me, it is very simple. I will accept two alternatives. The first is that you return what you have stolen. Return to me the Beads of Fire, and I will spare this world." Then his eyes grew cold, and they blackened and became like onyx. "If you cannot retrieve them, I will accept your Heartstone. There will be no negotiations." Then, the illusion faded away.

"DeSalvo is behind the Time Mage. That's like, really bad. Right?" asked Travis.

"More like really, really bad," answered Dalen. It was clear now what DeSalvo was up to. He was going to get his power back at all costs, and he was going to threaten the whole world to do it. If there was any question before, there was no question now. They had to go back and save Venger and save the world.

One by one, they touched the Pillar of Time. Once they did, it disjointed them from time, and they could move to any place at any time. They also had the ability to change one moment in time, but they all knew the cost and refused the temptation.

Dalen was the last to go, but when he touched it, there was a moment where time folded in on itself, and he could feel an echo of himself that had been imprinted on the Pillar of Time. He remembered that in another life, he had been here before and destroyed his entire timeline for the opportunity to change one thing. He could feel the absolute desperation that the echo had, as if the two versions of himself were connected. With all his light, he gave himself strength and love and wished himself well.

Before he had left the Oracles. They had explained to them what they needed to picture once they got to the Pillar of Time. He thought about the image they had all agreed upon. A moment in time before the dragon arrived with enough time to do something about it. He closed his eyes and envisioned it, and like that, he was gone.

Acknowledgments

Jason DeBruhl

Thank you for your knowledge, time and skill.
You have my respect and trust.

Rhiannon Simon

None of this would have happened if it weren't for you.
You are my rock.

Ben Watson

You pushed me to grow in ways you could have never imagined.
May your life be a masterpiece.

Tannya Derby

Thank you for all that you have done to help me
learn my way and find my place.

Christian Francis

Thank you for being the voice of reason when I needed it
the most. You were right, and you have my respect.

DALEN PAX AND HIS FRIENDS WILL RETURN,

IN

DALEN PAX AND THE FOUNTAIN OF TRUTH

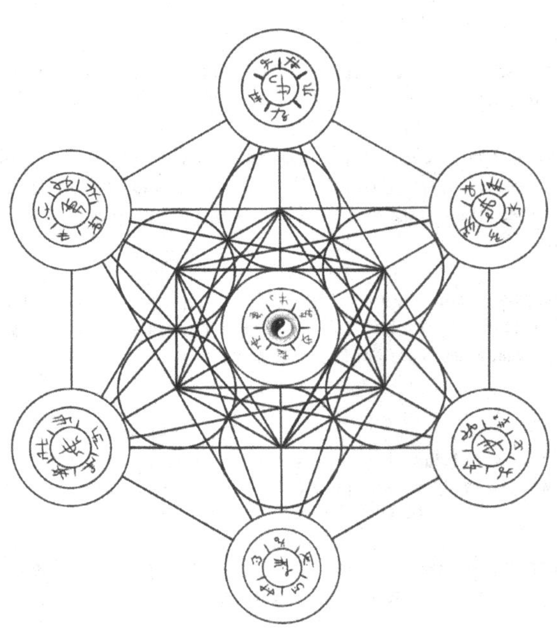

What is Dyslexie Font?

Each letter is given its own identity making it easier for people with dyslexia
to be more successful at reading.

The Dyslexie font:
1 Makes letters easier to distinguish
2 Offers more ease, regularity and joy in reading
3 Enables you to read with less effort
4 Gives your self-esteem a boost
5 Can be used anywhere, anytime and on (almost) every device
6 Does not require additional software or programs
7 Offers the simplest and most effective reading support

The Dyslexie font is specially designed for people with dyslexia, in order
to make reading easier - and more fun. During the design process, all
basic typography rules and standards were ignored. Readability and
specific characteristics of dyslexia are used as guidelines for the design.

Graphic designer Christian Boer created a dyslexic-friendly font to make reading easier for people
with dyslexia, like himself.

*"Traditional fonts are designed solely from an aesthetic point of view," Boer writes on his website,
"which means they often have characteristics that make characters difficult to recognize for people
with dyslexia. Oftentimes, the letters of a word are confused, turned around or jumbled up because
they look too similar."*

Designed to make reading clearer and more enjoyable for people with dyslexia, Dyslexie uses heavy
base lines, alternating stick and tail lengths, larger openings, and semicursive slants to ensure that
each character has a unique and more easily recognizable form.

Our books are not just for children to enjoy, they are also for adults
who have dyslexia who want the experience of reading
to the children in their lives.

Learn more and get the font for your digital devices at
www.dyslexiefont.com

www.ingramcontent.com/pod-product-compliance
Lightning Source LLC
Chambersburg PA
CBHW010512100726
47903CB00009B/2710